About the Author

Robert Appleton started work as a fifteen year old apprentice electrician. In his mid-twenties he qualified as a secondary Design and Technology teacher with a B.Ed. Honours degree. He eventually ended his thirty year career after teaching in four diverse comprehensive schools.

He now enjoys the benefits of retirement and can dedicate more time to reading, walking, cycling watching sport and his favourite pastime; caravanning.

He is married to Thelma and they have two adult children.

This is his second book which incorporates some of the principle police officers from his first crime novel, 'Contrived Fate'.

Dedications

To John and Elizabeth Appleton

Robert Appleton

CRUEL DECEIT

Copyright © Robert Appleton

The right of Robert Appleton to be identified as author of this work has been asserted by him in accordance with section 77 and 78 of the Copyright, Designs and Patents Act 1988.

All rights reserved. No part of this publication may be reproduced, stored in a retrieval system, or transmitted in any form or by any means, electronic, mechanical, photocopying, recording, or otherwise, without the prior permission of the publishers.

Any person who commits any unauthorized act in relation to this publication may be liable to criminal prosecution and civil claims for damages.

A CIP catalogue record for this title is available from the British Library.

'Cruel Deceit' is a fictional story and cannot be attributed to individuals.

ISBN 978 178455 002 8

www.austinmacauley.com

First Published (2014)
Austin Macauley Publishers Ltd.
25 Canada Square
Canary Wharf
London
E14 5LB

Printed and bound in Great Britain

Acknowledgements

Thanks to members of my family and friends who kindly proof read my story and for their encouraging comments and suggestions.

Chapter One

'I can't believe I allowed myself to get roped into this. I hate running and I feel like shit,' groaned Max Cooper. He involuntarily belched to release the build-up of pressure from his stomach. A stream of yellow bile bolted up his gullet to hit the back of his throat to mark its presence with a foul taste married with a nasty burning sensation.

'Oh just shut up Cooper, get on with it you snivelling wimp, we've only just started, for Christ's sake,' scolded Cora Grey.

Both of the young detective sergeants were taking part in a Sunday 10k circular fun run in aid of the charity, "Dreams Come True" based in Bladdington town. The wife of a retiring CID officer had asked her husband to put a sponsorship notice up in the police station appealing for runners. Grey had coerced Cooper into taking part in spite of his strong pleas he was not fit enough to run the distance but her skills of persuasion convinced him with a little training during the evenings he will be able to cope with what Cooper viewed to be an incredible distance to have to run, when he had often been heard to argue, it surely must be much easier to walk.

The date of the run soon arrived with Cooper neglecting to top up on his low level of fitness by finding a lame excuse to call off on the nights Grey had organised for them to train together.

Around about the 2k stage were heard the moans from Cooper complaining he badly needed to stop.

'What's up with you? We've only just started. If you'd done the training you wouldn't be whining now,' Grey hissed, annoyed she'd been put out of her stride.

She slowed to observe the pitiful Cooper, who was bedecked in his Dad's 1970s high thigh cut red nylon shorts together with a stupid pink tee shirt emblazoned with the words: "Don't mess with the Hoff", perform a sharp exit off the route to make a detour around the back of a table laden with 300 ml plastic water bottles.

Grey had chosen to be suitably attired in tight black lycra cycling shorts which finished just above the knee. The elasticated material showed up the hard feminine mounds and contours of her lower torso to erotic effect. The white short top she was wearing was manufactured from the same hugging material caressing snugly around her small but well defined breasts. The teasing glimpse of exposed taut stomach muscles exposed between her shorts and top, added to her visual appeal; especially to the delight of those vocal males purposely watching the race to catch sight of young athletic female forms.

Grey observed her co-runner looking around in a confused manner leaving her to wonder what the heck was the matter with him. She then saw him lean forward into a waist height black bin used specifically to collect empty water bottles for future recycling, and proceeded to let out a dramatic gargled retching sound followed by a long gush of thick dark yellow vomit which covered the immediate top layer of waste plastic bottles. He remained there motionless with his head trembling and tilted forward in anticipation of the next retching episode with both hands gripped either side of the bin's greasy rim to steady himself.

'Hey, what the bloody hell are you doing? You dirty sod. Somebody has got to sort those bottles when you have finished,' bawled an angry middle aged male volunteer charged with manning the station.

'Sorry, sorry mate. I just couldn't hold it back any more,' pleaded Cooper looking bashfully in the direction of the attendant through watery bloodshot eyes.

Grey, whilst watching the embarrassing spectacle unfold in front of her, kept warm by jogging on the spot and then later to roll her eyes when the volunteer attendant glanced at her in a shared non-verbal sign of disgust.

Noting these gestures, Cooper felt he needed to provide a logical reasoned excuse for his current state.

'Someone must have put something in that last pint I had, the swine. I was all right up to then.'

'Oh I see, so it was nothing to do with the eight pints before that one then? And don't let's forget the "Eat till you burst" Indian we had at Alibabas after you had that alleged doctored pint.' Grey sharply pointed out to her ailing green looking companion.

Without bothering to reply to her analysis of his desperate predicament, Cooper turned to hurriedly call over the distinctly unhappy attendant.

'I badly need to get to a bog, where's the nearest toilet mate?' he whispered.

'You're not thinking of doing it in my bin are you?' the man replied in alarm.

'I may have to if you don't stop dithering, just tell me quick,' pleaded Cooper frantically.

'There is a blue port-a-loo about hundred yards or so further on, but don't be surprised if there is a queue,' he replied with a grin.

Before Cooper could open his mouth Grey had roughly grabbed him by the arm and started to drag her pitiful friend in the direction of his hoped for salvation.

'You're a damn disgrace and if you empty your bowels before we get there, I'll stand over you until you have cleared every bit of the mess up, understand Cooper?'

During the short tirade Cooper gulped at the water bottle he'd taken from the table desperate to quell the effects of dehydration and to remove the remains of the bile vomit clinging on to the back of his throat.

Grey unsympathetically hauled him along the 10k route till eventually catching sight of the blue cubicle sited on the pavement up against a brick wall. Getting closer, she was pleased to notice that a queue had not been formed by similar distressed runners to her colleague. Just a few strides away from the tardis size toilet, Cooper warned Grey that his next fart may signal an involuntary evacuation of his innards. Reading the intentions of the runner directly in front of her, she recognised he too appeared to have a similar need for the toilets facilities but she was determined to get in there first. She released her tight grip from Cooper's thin arm to dart in front of the forward runner and to then grab hold of the lavatory handle.

'Sorry, sir,' she said to the frowning red, sweaty, competitor. Grey opened the door wide to usher Cooper forward and to then push him roughly into the space he'd been so desperate for.

'And don't be long,' she commanded facing the closed plastic door. Amidst the animal like groans emanating from the engaged port-a-loo alongside the dirty looks thrown in her direction by the cheated runner, Grey took up her running on the spot routine in readiness for Cooper's further participation in the run.

Taking part in the run was "Dreams Come True" charity fund raiser and organiser, Sally McCoy. At the ripe age of sixty-one, she had retained a slim smart physique; this was likely due to her thirty-four year career as a PE teacher together with careful attention to her diet and regular physical activities such as walking, cycling and participation in marathons and shorter distances. Her slightly diminutive presence wasn't being missed by many of the cheering onlookers who were giving her encouraging support for all of the great work she did for the local charity.

Present amongst the supporters, was photographer and senior reporter Eric Carter, employed by the *Bladdington Bugle*, who had been secretly told that this was to be Sally's final 10k run.

The reason given for this surprise decision was she wanted to spend more time with her husband since he'd decided both to accept redundancy terms and an excellent retirement package from the police force. Sally did, however, add that she would continue to manage the charity shop, which she had done for the previous six years, until a suitable replacement was found.

Sadly, the actual truth behind her decision was rather different. She had noticed over the past year that she was very gradually succumbing to the classic signs of dementia – a dreadful affliction both her mother and grandmother had fallen to in their late fifties / early sixties. Even though Sally had always been more than a little worried a similar fate awaited her, she was determined to swat away dementia's fingers by upping her levels of physical fitness and mental agility. Her efforts, alas, only cemented the stark realisation that no matter what she did it was not going to stop what had been irreversibly programmed into her genes.

Sally became increasingly distressed and frustrated when she failed to fully remember how to use the shop till. There were times too when she was quite unable to bring to mind the names of regular customers. Occasionally, days of the week would be completely forgotten and she'd have to make an excuse to slip out from the shop to go into the newsagents next door to check against a daily paper.

Ironically, some days were lucid and so clear which only deceived her into believing maybe she was mistaken about her own mental diagnosis. But the put down was always just lurking around the corner, with the symptoms re-surfacing without any prior warning of their unwelcome arrival.

This situation made her feel increasingly desperate, lonely and inexplicably ashamed. Sally wasn't yet ready at this stage of her condition to make a visit to her doctor only to be prescribed with all manner of mind altering pills and their undisclosed side effects, neither was she prepared to let her husband in on her personal battle, just yet.

Bruce McCoy, Sally's husband, on the other hand had a long history of not looking after both his mental and physical well-being. He was a career police officer and rose quickly from uniform into CID where he eventually achieved the position of detective inspector.

At the age of sixty, he had already gone beyond his expected years and having been forced to take redundancy, which proved to be a bitter blow to his ego.

He had increasingly taken to coping with the unrelenting pressures of the job by upping his intake of spirits, mainly whisky and brandy. He eventually followed the habit of many career alcoholics by foregoing nourishing meals, preferring instead to imbibe on large shots of spirits.

The near perfect white, strangely translucent skin appeared to be stretched like a rubber mask over his bony facial features. The only imperfection of note was something he nowadays rarely noticed himself when he looked in the mirror, but others seemed compelled to ask about or comment on.

A vertical neat narrow white scar ran down from the right of his high forehead to then pass over his eye socket and begin again, ending just below the protruding mound made by the cheek bone. A proud full mop of sandy coloured hair served to make his appearance even pastier and distinctively unhealthy.

Maintaining a slender five foot nine frame, which was usually draped in a casual suit looking to be one size too big for him, McCoy cut a figure many initially took no real notice of. However, unbeknown to those who did not yet know him, was hidden a character of tungsten steel ideally complimented by a sharp and agile mind programmed to outwit the most determined of criminals.

Having been free of alcohol during a lengthy spell in hospital for a jaundice liver condition fortunately made for a good rehabilitation. However, this had not saved Bruce McCoy from receiving a serious warning by the renal doctor he may not be so lucky if he ends up in the same trouble again.

Coming up to the 8k stage, Sally's petite features were covered with beads of light sweat cooling her body. Unexpectedly, a male runner jogged close up to her side, too close in fact for her liking, leaving her to sense that her personal space had been intruded upon. At first the man said nothing which was probably due to him struggling to catch his breath. His strained gasping gave a few precious moments for her defensive mechanisms to assess the potential threats of the uninvited interloper.

The male looked to be in his mid to late thirties, around six foot tall, tanned, slim to medium build and had well-formed biceps and upper torso which persuaded her to believe he worked out, probably at an expensive members' only gym. The myriad of tattoos etched into the skin of both arms were of a style she'd seen on other similar attention seeking, weak minded males. His infatuation with the art of the tattooist continued on the side of each of his poorly defined calf muscles which were inked in the style, what seemed to her to be, of a stack of kiddie's alphabet bricks. She noted from his low market running shoes that he did not take this sort of exercise seriously. Overall, Sally hoped he would soon move off to partner up with someone more akin to himself.

She became distracted from giving a vocal well-wisher in the crowd a wave on hearing the sound by the voice of the tattooed male jogging by her side.

'Hi, I believe you are the famous Sally McCoy,' the man said cheerfully while making uncomfortable eye contact with his co-runner.

His piercing look inexplicably sent a cold shiver running down her spine. Pulling her mind back into focus, she formed a weak smile before replying to the unnerving stranger.

'I can assure you, young man, I am not famous. I'm just doing what many others have chosen to do today. Are you enjoying the run?' she enquired trying to be outwardly friendly.

He seemed not to want to provide a response to the innocent question, while being more intent on introducing himself.

'My name is Barry Sproston; you would have heard of my family or at least know about my son, Wilson.'

Sally's mind suddenly fell into confusion. The man appeared to be so confident she must know of him or his son. Inside she scolded herself for becoming so forgetful again. Not wanting to be seen ignorant of the man's identity, she quickly summoned up a reply.

'Yes, yes your name definitely rings a bell. With all the excitement of today, it has simply slipped my mind. Please forgive me, but do you mind just reminding me again where I know you from?' she asked.

'Yes, my son is currently being treated for acute leukaemia at a specialist childrens' hospital in Florida, America. It's his last chance of a cure, the oncologist at Bladdington hospital had previously told me and my wife, Debbie, there is no hope for our son, Wilson.' Sproston appeared to have dried up at that point.

While maintaining a steady jog, Sally looked on to observe the man experiencing some difficulty in recomposing himself before he was able to continue.

'We are truly grateful for the help given by the "Dreams Come True" charity who are paying for our accommodation while we are tending to Wilson. Luckily, I took out a health insurance policy a few years back and this will cover the cost of his treatment. I just hope we will have enough.'

Sally was having internal mind wars desperately trying to connect the wiring in her misfiring brain to recall any of the details relating to what this stranger was so convincingly talking about.

'Shouldn't you be with your son and wife now?' she then enquired.

His reply was seamless.

'I've had to come back for a couple of days to see to some important business and I saw the announcement in the *Bladdington Bugle* about this 10k run today. So I thought why not participate and give a bit back to support the marvellous work of the charity supporting us in America. And, just as importantly, it gives me the opportunity to meet you in person to express my personal thanks.' His voice again appeared to crack.

A bustling finishing line appeared fifty metres or so ahead of the two runners. The easily recognisable figure of a photographer was busily aiming a camera to capture the glorious moment each competitor crossed a temporary white line chalked across the road. Joining him was a small band of enthusiastic volunteers who were excitedly hanging plastic gold medals around the necks of each of the finishing competitors.

As they approached the finishing line Sally turned to her co-runner to say, 'Please keep me informed about your son, Wilson. I would be interested to know how he progresses.'

'That may be difficult, I fly back to Florida tomorrow,' he replied forlornly.

'That's not a problem, you can get me on *Face2Face*, I assume you have an account?'

'Yes, yes, that would be great. I'll be able to send you pictures of Wilson and my lovely wife, Debbie and of course keep you informed on his progress,' he happily replied.

With five metres to go before they reached the finish line, Sproston grabbed hold of Sally's small hand to hold it aloft in a victory salute to the applause of a noisy crowd as they both finally crossed the line to complete the 10k run. Two individual plastic gold coloured medals attached to scarlet ribbons were thrust over each of their heads followed by lots of hearty handshakes, back slapping and words of praise.

Eric Carter then prised the pair from the small assembled crowd of well-wishers being eager to take a snapshot of them both together. Sproston appeared at first not to be keen to have his photograph taken and suggested that it should be Sally by herself while explaining it's her day and after all, she is the one who is responsible for making it all possible.

'Now don't be silly you must stand beside me,' Sally commanded flushed from the furore she received at the finishing line.

Sproston was carefully positioned alongside Sally McCoy, Carter then clicked away three times to ensure he'd get a great photograph of the victorious pair which was to appear on the inside pages of the next issue of the *Bugle*.

Once business of the picture taking was done, Carter took his note pad out and started to scribble replies Sally gave to some simple questions about her thoughts on the success of the run and how the money raised will benefit the children.

When she was about to respond to his question on how the money raised would be used, she turned to face Barry Sproston with a mind for him to assist her in giving a first-hand account of how important this fund raising is to both child and parent. But when she glanced around she found he was no longer there. She looked to Carter to ask if he'd seen him leave.

'Yes I did Sally, soon as I started to interview you he looked to be itching to get away. I watched him pushing his way through the crowds.'

'How strange, he told me his name was Barry Sproston. His son, Wilson, is in a specialist childrens' hospital in America receiving treatment for leukaemia. He said the doctors weren't able do anything for him at Bladdington hospital and his only option was abroad. Our charity is helping out with accommodation fees whilst they are over there,' Sally explained.

'Yes, I remember reading about it in the *Moulton Sentinel*. There was a photograph of the boy, who looked dreadful, poor soul, with mum and dad sitting alongside on the hospital bed. It struck me what an awful situation to be in as a parent. Not to mention the child's sad predicament.'

'Mr Sproston probably needed to rush off to get the plane back to America. I told him that he can let me know how things are progressing through *Face2Face*.'

'At least, I would have thought he'd spare the time to say goodbye to you,' said Carter.

'He's simply got too much on his mind,' replied Sally.

They gave each other a warm friendly hug before separating to attend to their own personal demands the day was still yet to bring.

Carter watched her approach a group of supporters to then become surrounded like she was some Queen Bee. While he was looking on this happy scene, he attempted to relate the facial features of the person Sally had said to be Barry Sproston to those of the man he'd previously seen in the photograph sitting alongside a sad looking young boy in a hospital bed. He decided he would satisfy his unexplained curiosity when he got back into the office on Monday. This was something he would forget to do.

Eventually Cooper and Grey crossed the finishing line and like the rest of the competitors, they each received a plastic gold medal and victory photograph taken by the local press photographer they were both familiar with.

'Should I email you a copy through to the station, Miss Grey?' offered Carter while struggling to hold back his mirth on seeing the distressed state of her running partner. Cooper then suddenly became alert to the photographer's suggestion.

'No you bloody won't, they'll take the piss out of me for ages if they see it, especially now Starr is back,' begged Cooper. He didn't know it yet, but his desperate pleas had fallen on deaf ears.

'Yes that would be great, I'll pin it up for all to view on the main notice board. It will bring back many fond memories when we look back in future years, won't it Max?'

'The way I feel now I don't give a toss. Just take me home Cora, I think I am about to die.'

Carter laughed to himself as he watched the comical spectacle of the two reeling figures heading in the direction of a municipal car park to collect Grey's car and then on to Cooper's apartment to drop off the exhausted invalid.

Chapter Two

A few weeks before the 10k charity run Eric Carter had been invited to attend a function organised by the Police Federation to report on a prestigious bravery award to be presented to DCI Dick Starr for his unstinting work and courage in apprehending a hardened killer who had slain four members of the Bladdington public and four police officers. The event was to be held at the Old Quarry golf club with local and national dignitaries in attendance to suitably acknowledge the detective inspector's heroic deeds.

The County Chief Constable was to be present amongst other high ranking officers swelling the attendance. The CCC also recognised the event would be a perfect occasion for the county to properly acknowledge the long distinguished service of a certain retiring DI.

Six months had gone by since the funeral of teenagers and lovers, Esme Fellows and Ben Wilkes. During those long months away from police duties, Starr was able to reflect deeply on the antecedents of the most terrible case Bladdington police have ever had to deal with. On the surface, the bullet injuries received from the gun of Allessandro Placino, had healed quite well. However, damage done to the calf muscle tissue required Starr to embark on an intensive programme of painful physiotherapy. He was not prepared to have to move about for the rest of his life with a pronounced gait and moreover wanted to fully dispense with the idea of having always to walk with the aid of a stick. Starr would reflect with a guilty conscience about the constant griping and complaining he'd subjected the physio staff to during his rehabilitation. Without such medical dedication he understood he may have ended up in a wheel chair. To Starr's great surprise, those in higher authority had not chosen to take this opportunity to put another creaking dinosaur out to grass by offering a generous redundancy package together with a golden pension, such as that accepted by DI Bruce McCoy. Even though Starr was of a similar age to his contemporary, he had a sneaky feeling that the county did not want to retire him off just yet as there was still some kudos to be wrung out of the epic story of how the brave forces of Bladdington nick had apprehended and then slain a notorious killer. Starr sensed his destiny was to be paraded around the county events like some bloody battalion goat mascot.

'Well if they think that will happen they are in for a big disappointment!' were his feelings on the matter.

During the Bravery Awards Ceremony a succession of high ranking speakers appeared at the lectern to read from pre-prepared notes, long winded speeches extolling police heroism and commitment to duty. Eventually, Starr was called upon to receive his worthy award to the rapturous applause of the invited audience. Before handing over the bespoke cut glass award, the CCC graphically described the first deadly scenes to be acted out in the dark of

Redgate Way. He expertly kept the audience gripped by moving the epic tale to the stage, where it fell on the shoulders of one of their own intrepid and fearless officers to take on a psychopathic mass murderer and to then emerge victorious against incredible odds.

With no more ado, the presentation of the bravery award immediately followed.

A range of expensive cameras briefly created a kaleidoscope of bright flashes to record the deserving hero receiving his award.

Starr was reluctant to make a speech but he recognised this to be an important showcase that can demonstrate to an often doubting public some of the dirty work the police have to deal with.

The CCC stood aside to allow Starr to position himself at the lectern. Without the aid of notes, he started first to express his heartfelt sympathy for those who had lost their lives at the hands of the Italian assassin. He followed by praising all of the team who worked so hard behind the scenes, especially his two young DSs Cooper and Grey and the invaluable support from Mansefield police for allowing a temporary secondment of DI Bob Stableford. The nurses and doctors at Bladdington hospital received his sincere gratitude for not only saving his life but making it possible for him to walk again unhindered.

Before he went on to deliver the last part of his speech, Starr paused to look around the array of smiling faces beaming up at him. Out of nowhere a lump formed in his throat, this was a sign for him to get on with what he had to say before he turned into an emotional wreck.

'The police do not always get things right first time, we all know that. Maybe it's through no direct fault of their own at times, or circumstances contrive to throw you into the wrong direction. But no matter what,' Starr stressed passionately, 'it's our absolute duty to make certain any conviction is based on rock solid grounds. If you cannot do this, then you must turn over every possible stone until you can. I have to live with my mistake; please do not let the same happen to you.'

Some in the audience were aware of the bungling by the DNA forensics that marred the initial investigation of the Esme Fellows murder case. These individuals were able to relate to Starr's expressed sentiments.

Seated and smartly attired at one of the white linen covered tables, were Cooper, Grey, Stableford and PC Stephen Dale, in unison they all stood and again started to applaud the legendary self-deprecating figure clumsily holding on to his heavy trophy. Within moments the rest similarly followed suit to raise the roof in rapturous applause in a moving show of appreciation and respect for one of their own.

With the main presentation being over, Starr was quietly ushered away to an annexe room which had been previously set up by Carter to take additional photographs of the gallant hero standing alongside Bladdington's Chief Superintendent Richard Palfreyman. The retiring Bruce McCoy, who was to also receive a distinguished service medal, was positioned to have his picture taken with the CCC for posterity. Some of the images recorded during the evening of celebration were to form part of a four page special feature to acknowledge the work of the county's police men and women which was to appear in the *Bladdington Bugle* and its sister paper, the *Moulton Sentinel*.

With the private shoot out of the way, the participants drifted off into the packed bar areas to mingle with others of their own status or rank. The room was full of laughing and loud conversation with many old friends reacquainting themselves avidly reminiscing life's past adventures. After an hour or so, those who had little connection to the county in which Bladdington was situated, were seen to be the first to drift off followed by others who also made their apologies to depart to see to other pressing matters.

Time passed quickly and soon the event was into late evening to eventually leave only Starr, McCoy and Stableford sitting facing each other around one of the circular topped tables cluttered with plates containing food remnants from the buffet mingled amongst half full and empty wine and beer glasses.

The trio had enjoyed each other's company along with that of some of their other colleagues who had added to the banter around the table at different times during the evening. Now in the quiet of the near empty room a more pertinent conversation struck up between the "long in the tooth" threesome.

'How do you feel about being back, Dick?' enquired McCoy with a whisky in hand with more than a hint of a slur in his voice.

Starr first placed his half-drunk pint glass of bitter onto the table cloth then folded his arms in an outward show of contemplation.

Having given some time to mull over his response he replied, 'To tell you the truth Bruce, I'm not really sure. Having those six months off work gave me plenty of time to think over my situation. I have known nothing but the police and to be honest, it has been my life. But, I also have to mention the sacrifices I have had to make to do the job the way I wanted it to be done, have on reflection, been too great. Just look at you two, you are both married, have lovely wives and I go home to nobody. It's my fault of course, I've had relationships but I always allowed police work to take priority. What woman is going to stand for that?' he asked while the two listeners peered into their individual glasses lost in contemplation thinking how their own spouses had had to put up with being the partner of a selfish police officer.

'So to answer your question Bruce, I suppose I don't mind too much about being back. Nobody is there for me when I wake up in the morning and the same when I get home in the evenings. I have to accept Bladdington nick is my home and family for now, at any rate.'

He then asked McCoy a question.

'You must be pleased Bruce, I bet they have given you an eye watering redundancy package and no doubt looked after your pension as well? You and Sally will be able to make up for the time you have lost together over the years.'

Stableford then followed by saying, 'Yes Bruce, it must feel great to have all that time in front of you, think of all the things you are now able to do, the walks, lie-ins, holidays abroad. And let's face it, I don't think generous redundancy packages are going to be around much longer with this shower in government. I say you are one lucky sod, take it and run!'

McCoy took his crystal glass and tipped the remains of the whisky down the back of his throat then clumsily placed the empty glass back on to the table. He lent back into the upholstered seat looking as if he had become lost in another world.

Bob Stableford broke the man's mesmerised state by enquiring if he would like another drink but his offer was turned down by a casual wave of his hand.

'Why have they forced redundancy on me? I wasn't ready to leave the police yet. The top brass said I wasn't up to the job anymore. I know my mind is not as sharp as it used to be and my memory is poor at times; don't try and tell me that isn't the same for most of us at our age.'

He pitifully pleaded to his dear friends after moving on from his contemplative mood.

'I was doing a bloody good job. I know I had that little problem when I went into hospital, but that is all under control now,' he continued to say whilst the two listeners subconsciously calculated the number of whiskies their supposedly alcohol abstinent friend had downed during the evening.

'Why didn't they ask you to go Dick? They all knew what a balls up you made at the beginning of the Esme Fellows case. How can they forget that? But now you are a fucking hero and I'm out on my arse. They should have got rid of you Dick, or maybe even you Bob, for Christ sake, we are all near the same age. Why me?'

Bruce McCoy lent his head forward causing his fringe to drop from its normal combed style to inadvertently disguise the tears rolling down his sallow cheeks.

Starr and Stableford carefully threw each other a look to telepathically agree it was the drink that had taken control over his tongue.

Stableford then pulled up his jacket sleeve to check his watch, he saw the time was close to one o'clock and the taxis would be arriving to collect them in a few moments.

'Right,' said Stableford, 'I'll just go and see if the taxis have arrived.'

After dragging the seat from under the table, and due to him also being a bit tipsy, Stableford staggered on his feet for a fleeting moment before carefully negotiating a path around the other glass strewn tables to get to the main reception area.

This left Starr and McCoy sitting alone at the table. To break the silence Starr said he was going for a slash before taking the taxi ride home, McCoy agreed to join him.

While both men were relieving themselves at the urinals, McCoy, having now come down from his previous high emotional state, found it necessary to give some form of explanation for his inappropriate behaviour.

'I am really sorry for what I said Dick. You are a fantastic copper, an incredible friend and you thoroughly deserve the award you received tonight, and most of all I'm really proud of you.' He fell silent while focusing his stream of urine on a cigarette butt causing it to spin round and round in the drain hole. 'I know why they have got rid of me; it's the fuckin' drink,' he slurred. 'I'm not kidding myself, I know it's getting worse. I've even been hauled in front of the fuckin' Chief Super, that lazy twat. He had the temerity to mention the drink and in the same sentence, mentioned my performance had slipped. Can you believe it Dick?'

While McCoy was struggling to pull his zip up Starr replied, 'I am not offended Bruce, you are probably right. I have been coasting for years and it is only because I have suddenly become the County's latest hero they haven't rushed to get rid of me. But mark my words, they will get their own road eventually with all the cuts still going on. I don't think the deals that are on the table this time, will be around for much longer,' said Starr while giving his hands a cursory rinse under the cold water tap.

'Well how much do you think the fools paid me to go?' gleefully asked McCoy.

'I have no idea. That is personal to you and Sally.'

'I will tell you Dick, but don't let anybody else know.'

Starr remained silent while looking at McCoy.

'I got £40,000 redundancy and £62,000 pension lump sum. They'll take tax out of the redundancy payment but even so, that's some dosh isn't it, Dick?' McCoy asked, in a manner designed to make his friend jealous of his exceptional pay off.

Starr, in response, just gave a long low whistle.

'I'll let Sally think about how we should invest the money; she has always looked after our finances. You know Dick, I might even treat myself to a new car, not too flash mind, but something that might turn the occasional head,' McCoy excitedly rambled on.

'Hurry up in there, the taxis are here.' Stableford's muffled voice suddenly called from the other side of the toilet door.

Starr followed McCoy to exit the gents, and then stagger a little around the tables before meeting Stableford in the main reception area.

When the silence of the Old Quarry golf club replaced the sound of the departing taxis, a toilet cubicle slide bolt was heard being pulled back from the inside lavatory door in the gents. Out stepped a man in his late fifties, who was the golf club's general dogsbody, Jimmy Melia, who'd heard every word of the two detectives' conversation.

Chapter Three

When he was aged twenty-four, Jimmy Melia was abruptly thrust into a world he was not prepared for. At that stage in his life his strong lithe physique, raven black swept back hair, which was probably a throwback to his mother's gypsy origins, and his "bad boy image" proved an irresistible combination to a certain type of female. It wasn't often he'd be seen with the same woman on his arm more than twice.

When reluctantly distracted from socialising, he worked for his father, Jimmy Melia senior, who proudly owned an established grounds maintenance business. Having only started in a small way by mowing pensioners' lawns and tending to their gardens, eventually Jimmy senior's widespread reputation together with making a brave investment in larger machinery, enabled him to bid and win contracts to maintain school grounds, highway grassed areas and golf courses throughout the County and beyond. Great pride was taken in the condition of his vans and machines and the state of their livery. He similarly insisted on high personal standards by enforcing a strict no smoking rule and the compulsory wearing of a smart work uniform.

One major clincher for him winning so many contracts was his reputation for being such a stickler when it came to implementing and the enforcing health and safety rules in his company's work practices. Likewise, Local authorities felt secure it was highly unlikely their legal services would have the need to become embroiled in costly long drawn out litigation when signing a contract over to Jimmy senior.

This did not come without a financial cost, as the business expanded. Jimmy senior was forced to employ other workers, with part of the reason due to his one and only son being often unreliable and on the days when he did turn in, was invariably incapable of doing much work due to the excesses of his previous night's antics.

Early one Monday morning Jimmy Melia junior was rudely awoken from an alcohol induced slumber by the sound of his mother's screams. Throwing the bedsheets aside, he stumbled to find his way to his parent's bedroom. There he was to find his mother propped up against the landing door leading to the bedroom trembling with her hands moving haphazardly around her tear streaked face.

'What's the matter, Mum?' Jimmy anxiously called before reaching to put his hand on her shoulder.

'It's your dad, Jimmy, I think he is dead, I can't wake him up.' she cried.

'He can't be, you must be wrong, let me in, I want to see him,' he desperately replied.

'No son, go and call an ambulance, quick!' She said while blocking his way in to the room.

At first, his mind became confused by not knowing what to do. He badly needed to see for himself if it was true his dad was dead or not, but this would waste precious time in getting the ambulance. It would be the intervention of his mother's prompting that sent him bounding downstairs, while wearing just underpants and socks, to reach the telephone situated on a table in the hall.

His index finger nervously twitched as he hurriedly dialled 999. A loud click sounding in the receiver earpiece signalled he was through to the emergency services. In his anxious state he found himself stumbling over his words as he hurriedly replied to the questions asked by the frustratingly calm operator. Then, after what seemed an eternity, a different voice came over the phone that relayed to him a series of checks that needed to be performed on his father while the emergency services were on their way.

Once the green receiver was placed back in the phone cradle he sprinted back upstairs to reach his parent's bedroom. The door was swung open and he was to find his mother sitting on the edge of the bed lovingly holding her husband's lifeless hand to her wet face.

'Is he all right mum?' he rasped in a desperate call while darting to his father's side.

'No, he's gone, Jim.' she replied calmly, 'There is nothing we can do for him.'

'But there must be, let's try mouth to mouth, heart presses, anything, we just can't do nothing Mum!' he cried in desperation.

'It's too late; he must have quietly passed away in the night. He's cold.'

'No he can't be dead, this can't happen, not to my dad!' Jimmy grasped hold of the lifeless body frantically attempting to haul the heavy leaden weight upright, but with no success.

'What on earth are you doing Jimmy? It's too late, don't you understand there is nothing anybody can do for him now?' she explained to her emotionally torn son.

Her words served to make him realise his efforts were useless. Dropping to kneel at the bedside, he placed the side of his flushed warm cheek against his father's cold exposed upper body, a flow of tears trickled down to slowly form into a puddle in a small hollow on his father's unmoving chest.

He became fixed to this position up to hearing the approaching sirens.

Leaving his mother to be alone with her dead husband, Jimmy returned to his own bedroom to collect a dressing gown so he could be seen to be decent when answering the door to the emergency services.

A post mortem performed on the fifty-two year old later in the week concluded the cause of death was a leaking heart valve which was responsible for bringing on a silent heart attack.

'The best way to go, at least he didn't suffer,' some sympathisers had proffered to the bereaved family, but their well-meaning words did nothing to assuage the guilt Jimmy junior was experiencing on his father's passing.

In the dark days preceding his father's untimely death, Jimmy needed no one to point out he'd not been a great support to his father. Even though he was racked with guilt he understood the situation that existed between father and son wasn't all down to his shortcomings.

Jimmy senior would never rest, he was at it 24/7. The business was given overwhelming attention, much like a spoilt member of the family; it had to have every need and want pandered to. This alone, Jimmy believed, was the indisputable evidence needed to explain the cause of his father's ill-timed and premature death.

A will had been made leaving the entire business in the hands of Jimmy junior. Unfortunately, he did not have the slightest interest in continuing in his father's footsteps. He'd argued terribly with his insistent mother. He did not want to end up like his father; in a box by the time he was fifty-two.

'Let's sell up Mum. There are other field maintenance contractors desperate to take over the business. I'm certain we would get a good price,' he had once suggested.

'You don't understand do you Jimmy? The only value in the business is the machines and the contracts. I suppose you wouldn't know or, even more, be remotely interested to learn that some of the school contracts are due for tender again and it is important we protect the goodwill your father earned over many years by providing a high level of service and value for money to the taxpayer. I will not stand by and see all of his hard work wasted,' she lectured as if explaining the situation to a juvenile.

He resisted the temptation to engage in a blazing row with his mother, he was not going to change her mind on the matter, in spite of the business being willed to him. His mother's insistence in keeping the business in family hands was mostly pragmatically based. They both needed a regular income; her to pay the bills, loans and mortgage and him to finance his social activities.

The following two years witnessed contracts lost, machines poorly maintained and workers losing their jobs. The slow demise of the business subsequently created an unbridgeable rift between mother and her irresponsible son. The crux of her frustration was not having sufficient income to settle all manner of bills dropping through the letter box, while her son was still enjoying the life of Riley.

Eventually the sole contract in force was for the fields and ground maintenance for Ludford High school with Jimmy junior being the sole employee of "Jimmy Melia and Son Grounds Maintenance".

A baking hot summer's day provided the back drop to a scene that was to change Jimmy's life forever. During the hour lunch break, Ludford High pupils were seen to be scattered around the playing fields sitting in small friendship groups, most were eating their lunch with one hand and texting using the other. There were girls who had taken up making daisy chains from the abundant flowers spread amongst the long blades of grass eager to place the lovingly made garland around the necks of their latest beau, be it male or female. Scattered amongst these happy groups were short sleeved, tie-less boys from all year groups having fun playing football or just innocently chasing about on the lush welcoming surface.

Jimmy Melia fully understood he should not be using the small tractor and mowing equipment at a time when pupils are about. He was aware of the obvious dangers and chose to ignore them. The warming sun's rays had put him in a mood to finish the job early so he could get to the pub to quench his thirst.

He donned the compulsory yellow hard hat and safety specs, lit a cigarette while making a start on mowing a part of the sports field not yet occupied by pupils. The steady up and down mowing pattern eventually drew the machine closer and closer to the sitting groups. Gradually the heat of the mid-day sun beating mercilessly on his hard hat caused the dusty grime to mingle with beads of sweat to then trickle down from his forehead into his eyes.

Squinting through the dirty scratched safety spectacles, he scanned around to notice if any teachers were about on duty. There weren't any. He clearly understood he would rightly be stopped from finishing the job if he were to be spotted by a member of staff. The consequence then being, he would be frustratingly delayed in getting to his primary destination-the pub. This uneasy thought served to speed up the sequence of up and down mowing, which in turn, caused groups of pupils to quickly gather up there bits of belongings and to reluctantly disperse as man and machine neared their seating positions.

The presence of the noisy machine not only disturbed the lunch time harmony, but provoked a rising of angry calls from lots of pupils marking their annoyance. Melia, on his part, choose to switch his mind off to their vocal and animated protests.

It was after he had inconveniently disbanded five or six of the lounging groups he heard a loud mechanical noise coming from the towed mower which then jammed to a full stop. Initially he couldn't fathom out what had caused such a failure, and then he heard the sound of a dreadful scream fill the air. Melia peered in the direction where the noise had come from, he took in the sight of a young boy lying prone and motionless with his arms splayed open on the grassy, daisy patterned turf. A long spike of some sort was sticking out of his neck projecting vertically in the air.

He was shaken by another high pitched scream which served to be a trigger for other deeply shocked boys and girls to join in.

Needing to see for himself exactly what was going on, he leapt from the small tractor to race over to where the rolled up sleeved figure lay in the centre of an increasing frantic crowd. He proceeded to roughly push through the gathering till he was able to take in for himself what had happened to the hapless pupil. An upright one inch wide metal strip had pierced into the back of the boy's neck precisely where the ridged line of the spine is exposed. Crimson bright fluid was seen to be soaking into the open collar of his white shirt and to then form in rivulets which turned the ends of his blonde hair to red. A sense of horror gripped his stomach on recognising the long narrow dull grass stained object to be a sheared section from the mowers cutting blades which must have come away and flew off like a piece of shrapnel when the mower hit the obstruction, probably a brick or something similar.

A year nine girl then broke the tension of the watching crowd.

'You've killed him. Look everybody, this man has killed Nathan,' she manically screamed.

Then without warning, pupils started to lash out at the person they understood to be responsible for the accident. Others added to the tragic drama with their wailing screams whilst a small contingent from the swelling crowd raced to the main school building to get help.

The increasing ferocity of the slaps and punches to his body felt like he was being swarmed over by a mighty army of giant ants and even more, was incapable of fending them off. Panic set in causing a high dose of adrenalin to be pumped into his bloodstream. This was flight or fight time; he chose flight.

To get free of the surrounding frantic mob, Melia used the cover of his arms to protect his face leaving his body exposed to absorb the impact of the sharp blows raining down on him. He forcibly pushed through the tightly packed sea of shouting snarling faces and once free to then sprint in the direction of the works van situated two hundred metres or so from the incident. Nearing the dark green and golden livered van he pulled from his jacket pocket a bunch of keys, one of which he knew to be the ignition key.

A swift glance back revealed there was no one who had given chase, what he did see however, was a small group of hurrying teachers being frantically danced around by anxious pupils as they neared the scene of tragedy.

With his head spinning with all manner of things that had gone on in the previous five minutes, he sped away from the school premises to a destination he'd not, as yet, given any thought to.

Chapter Four

The hand of fate had determined this was to be the time when Jimmy Melia's and Bruce McCoy's paths were destined to cross.

McCoy was on a real high, he'd just been successful in being transferred from the uniform ranks to CID. This change in career direction was the fulfilment of a long held ambition and had been earned strictly on merit unlike a few in the upper echelons in the force, who'd curried favour or worse, to get to where they were.

While he was in uniform others recognised in McCoy the potential to go much further in the police. The encouragement he received from influential grounded superiors persuaded him to take the sergeants examinations at a young age. To his absolute delight, he predictably passed with flying colours, this vital step forward served to open the door to enter the plain clothed ranks within the year.

His first real assigned case in the CID was to be part of an investigating team leading enquiries into the tragic death of a thirteen year old Ludford High School boy. After a string of interviews were conducted with pupils and staff, it soon became apparent how the accident happened and more importantly, who was responsible.

Establishing that a groundsman by the name of Jimmy Melia, had swiftly absconded from the school site soon after the incident, an APB was put out to all cars.

A police visit to his mother's home confirmed he was neither there or at the yard where all the machinery was usually kept.

The police were hoping, as so often happens in this type of case, that Melia most likely fled the scene in blind panic. Soon, he would come to his senses and hand himself in at the nearest police station. They waited, while still conducting searches, for three days with no reported sighting or personal contact made by Melia.

It was to be on the fourth day during a night shift that DS McCoy picked up his phone to receive a late call which unbeknown to him, was destined to have a profound bearing on his life not only then, but much later in the future. The muffled nervous voice heard in the crackling ear piece was keen not to reveal his identify. This became of secondary importance when McCoy heard the man had information they were frustratingly waiting on. He suggested the police may want to check out a static caravan sited on the Riverside residential caravan park to help them in apprehending their target, Jimmy Melia.

This unexpected tip off required little further contemplation by a superior ranking CID officer to put into immediate action an operation for the absconding groundsman's arrest.

Four apprehensive CID officers were seated in a cautiously driven slow moving unmarked car as they descended on the near full moon lit caravan park at twelve midnight precisely. Part of the operation included having uniform back up positioned outside the site to prevent entry and to ensure nobody left without authority.

The small group of darkly dressed officers stealthily approached the plot number given by the mysterious caller while the dimly lit site revealed the majority of residents had already turned in for the night.

Prior to arriving at the caravan site, the plain clothed officers had used the time to cover the twenty mile journey to discuss and finally agree an action plan. Two of the more experienced officers were assigned to awaken the target occupant, followed by his arrest. Furthermore, mindful not to risk the chance of Melia making good his escape from police custody, the remaining officers were to stand back to closely monitor the arrest and be ready to be called upon if things happen to go wrong during the young grounds man's planned detainment.

A hard, solid rap on the frosted door glazing panel followed by a loud police instruction to open the door was met with a wall of silence. Suddenly, noise of something similar to that of an opening stiff latch echoed around the quiet site.

A window towards the end of the forty foot long static caravan slowly creaked open allowing a dark slim male adult figure to squirm his way out, followed by a clumsy fall on to the damp turf below him.

Calls for the absconding suspect to stop were ignored. Unhesitatingly, McCoy was the first to react to give chase along the edge of a steep sided river bank. To the escapee's dismay, he recognised one of the pursuing officers was rapidly closing in on him. Melia skidded to a halt at the edge of the riverside, his mind spinning about what he should do next to flee the attentions of the dark racing figure coming up fast towards him. A decision was made to take his chances in the waters of the shallow lazy flowing river.

Melia was in the throes of readying his body to make a bold leap from the river's edge, when he was hit hard by the pursuing dark clad copper who'd hurled himself at speed in his direction. The impact of the two males colliding heavily together sent the grappling bodies flying off the edge of the banked up side to then fall with an almighty splash into the slow flowing river.

The wind was forcibly knocked out of their bodies as they heavily crash landed in the pebble strewn river bed. The icy cold water soaking clothes and skin adding further shock to their nervous systems. The fall had caused McCoy to lose his grip on the fugitive, which paradoxically, then gave each of them precious time to clear their lungs of foul brackish tasting water through bouts of hoarse coughing and guttural spluttering. Through straining bloodshot eyes, Melia spotted the hunched outline of a copper who had become momentarily distracted by a pressing need to clear his throat and lungs from river water. Being careful not to lose his footing on the slippery pebbles forming the riverbed, he approached the coughing figure with his right arm tensed like a coiled spring with the intention of propelling a clenched fist to the side of the struggling man's head.

The contact was sweet. McCoy's head violently spun round with the force of the vicious punch dislocating his jaw from its right socket. His cry of agony was abruptly cut short as he tumbled backwards to find himself yet again submerged under the cold water. Before having any chance to come to his senses, Melia had flung himself on top of the immersed detective with the undisguised intent to prevent him from escaping the unwelcoming depths. McCoy sensed the presence of the hard riverbed pressing against his back while being kept paralysed by the immovable pressure being exerted on his shoulders.

When he was ever to cast his mind back to this particular episode in his life it would be the unshakable image of the hard, mean eyes burning down on him amidst the air bubbles being released from his nostrils as he struggled for his very existence in that cold underworld of the river bed on that near fatal night.

With his oxygen depleted lungs becoming desperate for a fresh charge, McCoy's natural body mechanism involuntarily drew in what it had hoped to be air; instead, his lungs were forced to accept a large gulp of water. In response to the foreign invasion, his brain went into sudden panic mode to automatically switch the nervous system to the primeval will to survive.

Gladly, for McCoy at least, the protruding mound of the patella on his bent left knee proved instrumental in releasing him from Melia's murderous grip. A sharp thrust upwards from his enforced prone position made hard contact with Melia's unprotected testicles, making him reel about roaring in pain clutching his injured parts. Free from Melia's murderous intent, McCoy wasted no time in springing up from the shallow depths to take up an unsure wobbling stance.

This brief interlude, or voluntary standoff, gave precious moments for their individual bodies and minds to partly revive and compose themselves.

McCoy's silence was greeted as a sign of cowardice by his adversary. This, of course was not the case. The dislocated jaw, a near hypothermic bodily state and the fact the lungs were still disgorging water determined in this temporary numbness McCoy would remain silent.

'What's up copper, had enough? Want some of this?' Melina taunted.

McCoy ignored his mocking words. He was more concerned about the stupid, yet serious, escalation in events as he eyed Melia grinning while with openly brandishing a four inch razor sharp flick knife.

Sounds in the background gave warning of the imminent arrival of the other arresting CID officers who'd decided not to enter the river further upstream, as McCoy had done. However, in having chosen to track the escaping manslaughter suspect along the river bank, their progress had been hindered by a series of barbed wired fences.

'Give up, Melia. Don't be a silly boy, throw the knife down. You're in enough trouble as it is,' called one of the three shadowy figures, standing to his left on the steep riverbank.

Due to the casting shadows of the riverbank trees, the trio of CID officers were unable to see the fear of being caught and then spending time in prison deeply etched across Melia's twisted face. McCoy too had noticed the subtle change and as he did so, Melia made a sudden dash to the opposite side of the riverbank to reach a place where dairy cattle came to water.

Here, there was to be no steep bank to negotiate, however, he'd not bargained for the deep muddy water filled ruts left by the countless animals who'd previously visited that spot. No sooner had he stepped from the shallow rivers edge and taken two or three strides he felt the hand of McCoy swipe past his flaying denim jacket. Instinctively, Melia swung round to make a slashing movement with his flick knife; its downward trajectory, which McCoy saw for less than a second, doing the bidding of its master.

In spite of having a dislocated jaw, a shriek emitted from McCoy's purple tinted lips, the honed edge of the flick knife had left him with a long thin deep gash down his face.

In moments, a fast flow of warm blood filled his right eye socket to then continue to run down his cheek in separate strands before soaking into the cotton fabric light blue shirt. He spent no time worrying about the extent of this new injury as he strode through the rutted surface even more determined to prevent Melia's escape.

Desperate to put some distance between himself and the freshly bleeding copper, Melia neglected to take the necessary care to avoid the cattle made water filled holes. Inevitably, a particular deep rut was the cause of him tumbling heavily on to the patchwork of muddy earth.

Thankfully, for both their sakes, the bloodied knife slipped from his grip during the unexpected fall. If it hadn't, chances are, Melia would have lost his head and used the knife to fend off McCoy while they viciously fought each other in the stinking cloying mud.

The intervention of the three sodden wet officers soon put an end to any foolish ideas Melia still held about any thoughts of making an escape. A couple of hard fist blows to the ribs, followed by a number of cracks from two telescopic truncheons deemed Melia to be satisfactorily neutered.

Over the coming days word got out about McCoy's show of initiative and bravery in apprehending Melia. This earned him immediate respect and status from other and more experienced officers. His bold acts too did not go unrecognised by the station's Chief Super who sent down instructions it must be DS McCoy who should be given the further opportunity to tie up the ends of the case and secure a conviction. This, McCoy recognised to be a God-given chance to make a first good impression and he had no intentions of wasting it.

The subsequent wider investigation in to the school boy's death revealed that no maintenance had been carried out on any of the vehicles or machinery since the death of Jimmy's father. Tests carried out on the mowing equipment showed a number of cracks in the cutting blades together with loose or missing rivets which had been designed to hold them securely in place. The lack of checks on the machinery confirmed it was only a matter of time before disaster struck.

Similarly the business's public liability insurance had been allowed to lapse. Monies were owed on vehicle loans, yard rental and he had run several credit cards, including his deceased father's business card, up to their limit to the tune of several thousands of pounds.

This was on top of being charged for corporate manslaughter, attempted murder, serious assault on a police officer, absconding from the scene of a crime and resisting arrest.

McCoy's detailed presentation of the police investigation at the Crown Court resulted in a unanimous jury conviction and a prison sentence of nine years.

While serving his sentence Melia's mother lost her home to pay off credit cards, loan companies' demands and compensation claims. Tragically, she had to spend the short time she had left of her life in sheltered accommodation, shamed, ailing and penniless.

Jimmy Melia would soon begin an alternative adult education course run by hardened inmates. The teachings of which would both change his outlook on the world and his once easy going character forever. There was also plenty of time to brood about how McCoy had mercilessly interrogated him during police interviews and more importantly to him, blamed the keen DS for breaking his mother's heart and being the main cause of her early death.

During the first year of his sentence Melia became a father. He had a son who was given birth by one of his many young female friends he used for casual sex. To the girl's credit she raised the boy with the help of her family and Jimmy's ageing mother when she was alive in the early years of her grandson's life.

On release seven long years later, looking older with his once proud raven black hair turning grey and distinctly thinning, the mother of his child was waiting for him at the prison gates. Even though they never did get round to getting married, the three of them were initially happy just to be together. But this wasn't without many years of struggle primarily due to Jimmy having a prison record which sadly meant he was viewed with suspicion when applying for any type of work. Invariably he relied on the occasional bits he was offered by people who knew him from old, but mainly he got by on selling secondhand cars and dealing in scrap metals. Later in life he was hit by another tragedy when the mother of his only child eventually succumbed to a long term addiction to alcohol by the time she was forty-nine. His adult son later moved out to set up home with a woman who would eventually bear him a baby boy.

Much later in life an acquaintance of Melia's got to know about the circumstances which resulted in him being imprisoned. He was overjoyed when this same person took the gamble to offer him a "jack of all trades" job at a golf club.

Chapter Five

Days before the 10k charity run Sally enjoyed the messages of encouragement from many of her regular shop customers. One such well-wisher had made it his business to call in on her.

'Hello Sally, are you all ready for the run then? I've seen you in training pounding the streets. I don't know how you do it girl,' a greying and balding portly male in his late fifties teased.

'With a little bit of training Jimmy, you could do it with me.' Sally said with a wink of an eye.

'You've got to be joking, just look at my beer belly, it would take me years to get fit,' he laughingly responded.

'Well, I believe it's never too late and at our age it is important to do some physical exercise.'

'I'll take my chances. How many people do you hear of who eat like bloody rabbits and keep themselves super fit and still croak it at a young age?' conjectured the man.

How she knew this to be so true, becoming distracted into thinking now about those dear friends gone at such a young age.

Jimmy was a regular at the "Dreams Come True" charity shop. With the golf club only paying him just above the minimum wage, he wisely watched how he spent his pennies.

'I didn't realize your husband was a police officer. I saw his photograph in the *Bladdington Bugle* receiving a retirement present from the top brass.' he said, taking Sally somewhat by surprise.

'Yes that is right. I have never broadcast what Bruce did for a living. You never know if he might have upset someone along the line and they turn up here and want to take their revenge out on me. I don't know why Eric Carter had to print that his wife, me, was taking part in a 10k charity run. What has that got to do with his retirement?' questioned Sally.

'I don't know Sally, maybe he was just thinking it would be good publicity for your charity event.'

'Maybe, but I don't know.'

'You must be excited though Sally, having him at home with you with all that free time to spend his money.'

'So you have read he got redundancy as well as retiring?' Jimmy didn't answer her. 'He's been very lucky,' she continued, 'we'll never have any money worries, not like some when they come to retire. Not everybody will finish their career with such a good pay off. I didn't when I stopped teaching. Do you know, Jimmy, what is sad for me, he wanted to carry on, can you believe it. He was so desperate to continue working. Made me think he didn't really want to be at home with me at all.' Sally conjectured whilst watching the passing public through the main shop window.

'Do you intend to keep on doing this job?' His enquiry served to break her thoughts from what lay ahead of her and her husband.

'No, now Bruce is reluctantly stuck at home he wants me to finish so that we can spend more time together. The job has been advertised but as yet, a suitable replacement has not been found. I'll just hang on until we find someone.'

'Whoever it is, they will need to be an angel, just like you, Sally.'

'Oh, don't be so daft Jimmy. I do what I do because it comes from the heart. I can see the charity does make a real difference in supporting many desperate families getting through tragic situations.'

'I'll have these two please, Sally.' Jimmy Melia placed a pair of forty-six inch waist trousers and eighteen inch neck shirt on the counter.

Sally looked at each of the labels to see the price and when she came to put the purchase through the till her mind froze, and no matter how hard she tried she could not think how to operate the till.

Melia watched her dainty neatly manicured fingers hover nervously over the tops of the till keys seemingly unable to execute the movement necessary to complete the transaction.

'Is everything alright Sally?' he questioned while looking in on her apparent struggle.

'Yes, yes, I'll be fine in a second or two; it's just one of those senior moments.'

Eventually she called out to a staff volunteer, who was busily steam ironing in a back room, to come to the till. The woman appeared behind the counter to stand alongside Sally.

'Jill, can you please deal with this gentleman.'

Sally did not bid her regular customer farewell, she chose instead, to leave her colleague to complete the transaction while she darted off to the same back room the steam ironer had come from.

'That will be six pounds please, sir,' the woman requested having keyed in the two items.

Melia handed over the cash.

'Strange, has that happened before to Sally?' he enquired.

'All the time I have to tell you, I'm sure she is losing her marbles, it's been happening for quite a while now. I think it's high time she left and allowed one of us volunteers to take over, but I suppose we are not good enough for her,' whispered the woman.

The two items were carefully folded up and placed in a plastic carrier bag, a slam of a door indicated the portly man had left the shop.

Sally McCoy had sought solitude in the small shop toilet. Her nose had reddened from being wiped with a coarse paper tissue. She used the same tissue to soak away the tears running over her cheeks as she inwardly berated herself, for the umpteenth time, for her stupid forgetfulness. Her heart ached with the realisation her condition was undoubtedly, becoming worse.

Chapter Six

'Did the run go all right, DS Grey?' enquired DCI Dick Starr early Monday morning.

'Yes, well no. I'm not sure,' she waffled.

'Flippin' heck, you have just given me every possible answer there, Cora.'

Out of the corner of her eye, Grey had noticed Cooper silently mouthing the words, 'Please don't tell him,' which he further supported by showing his palms pressed together as in prayer anxious for her to support his plea.

'Yes, I mean it went as well as we could have expected, didn't it Max?'

Cooper glared hard at Grey as to question why she thought it necessary to switch Starr's attention on to him.

'Em, yes, it all went well. We both finished the run and got our medals,' replied Cooper rather bashfully.

'Well done Max, but I have to say you do not look too well on this email photo I've got here,' said Starr gleefully wafting a printed photograph about. 'Yes, Eric Carter sent it through early this morning. He even left a small note saying he was so concerned about you at one stage that he was close to calling an ambulance. Hey, and they call this a fun run?'

Starr tossed the photo over to Grey. Her first glance at the image caused her to immediately burst out laughing.

The coloured picture showed both of them in full running gear. Grey could be seen flashing her taut stomach muscles, with the rest of her body looking lithe and athletic. Only a slight blushing of her cheeks indicated she had been involved in some form of physical exertion.

To her side stood a sweat banded Cooper. His long pale thin legs appeared to be slightly knocked kneed and deficient of any muscle definition and furthermore, looked lost in the high cut red nylon shorts which only just about covered his left testicle from being exposed. The dreadful tatty pink printed tee shirt did him no favours by making his green complexion look even sicklier than he probably was. To cap it all, Grey looked to be propping up the ailing runner with his arm stretched around the back of her neck in clear need for someone to support his shattered body.

'That's not fair,' Cooper wined, 'Carter shouldn't have sent you the photograph. I just knew what would happen. I couldn't help getting a stomach upset that morning could I? But at least I didn't jib out like some would,' Cooper said pleading a weak defence for himself.

'I forgot to mention,' Starr followed on, 'Eric said the picture will be in the *Bladdington Bugle* this week together with photographs of the other competitors. This copy can go up on the notice board in the public foyer. Maybe we can print off another copy with a bit of a write up and send it off to the monthly police federation magazine. It will be good for the station to get some publicity for both of your magnificent efforts in supporting the charity.'

'Right with that out of the way, you'll be no doubt pleased to hear, the pair of you are back under my wing. I have put aside a little time so I can learn about what you have both been up to during my enforced six month absence.

Chapter Seven

'What's that burning?'

Bruce McCoy was relaxing in a leather recliner chair reading a book only then to be disturbed by a strong acrid smell coming from the kitchen. With the aid of the heels of his stocking feet, he propelled the projected section of the seat back to form it into an arm chair once again. He then rose from this seating position, placed his opened book page down on the seat and headed for the kitchen.

The sight to greet him was a stainless steel pan on the gas hob releasing spiralling vapours of fine blue smoke into the atmosphere. A turn of the control knob cut the gas off, Bruce then immediately grabbed hold of the Bakelite handle to move the smoking pan to another unused gas ring to allow the ruined contents to cool.

'Sally, where are you?' he called having since left the kitchen to stand at the bottom of the staircase. The blue smoke circulating in the kitchen had started to drift along the ceiling through the open door and into the hallway causing the smoke detector to fill the house with ear splitting high decibel bleeps.

Sally appeared at the top of the landing to see Bruce standing on a wooden chair he'd carried from the kitchen to press the disarm button on the smoke detector fixed into the high ceiling.

'What's happened Bruce?' she enquired while making her way down the carpeted stairway.

'It's the pan of pasta on the hob; it's over heated and started to burn the stuff inside. How could you forget Sally? What were you doing upstairs when you knew you had a pan on the go?'

'What are you talking about? I've not been in the kitchen. It must have been you who left the pan on the hob. It certainly wasn't me!'

'Don't be daft Sally. I would know if it was me who'd started cooking the pasta. You started tea because you said you wanted to do it. Remember?'

'No I don't as a matter of fact,' she sharply retorted, 'I was in our bedroom making the bed so don't start having a go at me and I've been at work all day. What have you done to help out around the house? Bugger all as usual I bet,' she uncharacteristically snarled back at her husband.

'Whoa, what's happening here, I did offer to knock something together when you came through the door, but you said, if you want to remember, you will do something for us. Is this how it's going to be Sally now I have finished work? Because if it is I'll get a job at B&Q so I can be out of your way,' he snarled back in return.

Sally suddenly burst in to tears; this was not a normal reaction for this once emotionally strong, bright woman.

'I'm so sorry Sally, I didn't mean to hurt your feelings.'

He moved to take hold of her in his arms to form a close embrace. This was not just a sniffle cry; Bruce felt her body swelling as if purging a deep emotional grief.

'What on earth is the matter Sally, is it me? Please tell me if I have done something wrong.'

'Haven't you noticed Bruce,' Sally whimpered with her head pressed into the fabric of his shirt.

'Noticed what, my dear?' he replied softly.

'I'm worried Bruce, I seem to be forgetting all manner of things and not only that, I feel that I am losing my self-confidence.'

'Don't be daft Sally, you are wonder woman, everybody says that about you. Who at your age does, or is remotely capable, of doing all the things you do? Go on tell me one person,' he said trying to dispel her worries. She did not respond directly to his question.

'What you and they don't see is, I have been covering things up. You haven't even noticed have you, Bruce? You have had too much on your mind. And no wonder with you being in hospital and then followed by the stress of taking retirement you didn't really want. I deliberately kept you from my petty problems.'

'Have you been to the doctor's about this,' he asked.

'No, I haven't. I don't want to end up like my mother pumped full of tablets and she still had full on dementia in the end.'

'What the heck are you talking about Sally, you haven't got dementia,' he said, suddenly aghast at his wife's stark assessment of her problems, 'You have been doing too much. We agreed for you to finish teaching because you said you did not want the unrelenting pressure and expectations any more. You have to admit though Sally, the work you do for the charity has now become all consuming. Yes, before you say anything, it is for a good cause and the money raised has helped a lot of families but at what cost to your health, Sally?'

'Look Bruce I love my job, it isn't that I overwork, I just think I'm destined to go the same way as my mother and her mother and there is nothing I can do about it.'

At that point she faced her husband, her bright blue moist eyes appearing convinced of her fate.

'That's absolute bloody rubbish. Look at all the running you do, going to the gym twice a week and watching everything you put in your mouth. You look ten years younger than you are. Your mother never looked after herself like you have done and no doubt, your gran was the same. Sally, you have just been doing too much. Tell you what, lets book a long holiday, anywhere you want, it's your choice.'

Bruce was desperate not to accept his wife was falling victim to her family's genetic history. Suggesting a holiday was his way of putting out of mind any more foolish talk about dementia. Sally had expected Bruce to react in the way he did, he would have to face the truth of her situation one day but at the moment he was prepared only to bury it.

'Yes, it sounds a good idea Bruce, but not just yet.'

'Why not?' he whined like a spoiled child.

'As soon as someone has been appointed to take over my job I promise we will get the first plane out. I cannot leave the shop shorthanded Bruce, you know that.'

'Okay then. Look, you go and sit down and I will make us some tea.'

'It's not ...'

'Sally shut up; just go and do as you are told for a change.' Bruce pecked her gently on her damp cheek and pushed her in the direction of the lounge.

He headed for the kitchen to set about cleaning the scorched pan and at the same time gave some thought to what he should make for their evening meal.

During the relative quiet moments he spent scrubbing away at the stubborn burn marks from inside the pan his mind drifted off to start a count of the number of instances to which he had not previously attached any relevance. Sally not remembering birthdays, appointments, and things when they were both out food shopping and her increasing reluctance to drive the car at busy times or at night.

During lunch break the following day, Sally had eaten two rounds of wholemeal chicken sandwiches and downed the 250 ml tomato juice drink at the same time as checking if any more emails had been sent to the shop and were urgent enough to require her immediate attention. One particular message had been sent by the *Face2Face* social network site to alert her that there was a visitor awaiting her attention. She gazed up at the wall clock to see that she still had about fifteen minutes of her break left.

Usually Sally would start back to work again, but after what had happened the previous evening at home she thought maybe she was working a little too hard. Taking heed of what her husband had said, she decided to open up her online personal *Face2Face* account to see who the visitor might be.

The opening account page displayed a smiling image of her along with some not too personal details in the profile box. A casual surfer would be able to freely access her public domain section to see snaps taken of those individuals and families who had benefited from the charities fund raising efforts, alongside supporting testimonials sent through from grateful recipients.

Sally was mindful to ensure her married and personal life was kept separate from her professional duties in running the charity.

Having read the name of Barry Sproston, who wanted to be accepted as a friend of Sally McCoy's, her mind was unable to attach any relevance to the man and why he wanted to become another one of her friends.

'Come on think,' Sally urged her frozen memory. 'He must know me or why would he want to become a friend,' she agonised to herself whilst staring at the man's name up on the screen. Unable to free her mind of the mental block, she copied the name down on a post-it note before logging herself out of the account. Her mind would sometimes drift to thinking about the stranger's name during the remaining three hours left to work.

Later that same afternoon, a woman who had participated in the 10k run on the Sunday, came into the shop to chat with Sally about how much she enjoyed the race.

'I was just behind you at the finishing line, I thought it was like something out of the Olympic Games when I saw you and your husband crossing the finishing line with hands aloft. I hope you don't mind me saying he is a very handsome man and he looks so fit,' the woman said in an envious manner.

The woman's recollections proved to be the key to unlock her mind. She realised now the significance of the name she had written on the post-it note.

'Well thank you for saying, but that was not my husband; he's not into running and that sort of thing. In fact the man was the father of a boy we are currently supporting whilst they are over in America.'

'Oh, I am sorry, But if you don't mind me saying I thought at the time he cannot be her husband, he is far too young for her.' she said in all innocence.

'Well thank you for that observation and that will be four pounds please.' said Sally haughtily, while handing over the plastic supermarket bag containing the customer's purchase.

The woman eventually left the shop having first twirled the squeaky paperback book stand around a few times to see what new books were on show. When she had gone, Sally retrieved the yellow post-it note, mentally read over the man's name then wrote next to it a prompt he was the man whom she met at the run.

Before Sally had arrived home, Bruce had left a note on the hallway table to let his wife know that he'd popped down to the pub early doors with a solemn written pledge he'd have no more than one or two small drinks.

Sally suspected her husband was still struggling with his addiction. The note he'd left for her to read amply announced this fact in spite of being warned by the consultant he was putting his fragile liver at great risk if he continued to drink.

For Sally this situation had a strange irony, here was she trying to save young lives, while her husband was trying to lose his.

She let out a long sigh as an acceptance of his alcohol dependency and the sad fact he was unlikely to change. Having placed the charity shop purchased Prada handbag on the same semi ellipse antique display table top where the note had been left, she headed for the kitchen to see if he'd left a meal for her. The absence of any cooking smells informed her senses he'd likely not got around to making anything. A quick glance around the expensive kitchen soon endorsed her doubts. She wasn't in the mood to make anything for herself just at that time.

Alone in the large four bedroom Victorian house the tempo of the day gradually evaporated from her body making her become pleasantly sleepy. She had been fitfully drowsing for about twenty minutes, resting in one of the extended recliner arm chairs when a bleep sound disturbed her from falling into a deep slumber. She recognised the sound to be a warning from her mobile phone that it was in need of a recharge.

The recliner was first pushed back before going to retrieve the handbag she had earlier left on the antique table in the Staffordshire Milton tiled hall way.

She stepped into the kitchen to place the handbag on the black granite work surface. Pulling back the long zip, her fingers delved around to find the mobile phone amongst the clutter of items, one of which was a yellow post-it note which had stuck itself to the phone's plastic casing. Initially, Sally paid little relevance to the yellow coloured note and proceeded to push in the charger lead to the charge point on the phone and then to rest the plastic casing on the hard mirror finished surface. She then turned her attention to the yellow piece of paper to read the scribbled words.

'Again, you have done it again!' Sally called out in the empty house. Her frustration at not being able to retain simple things, even when written on a note, was crucifying her inside.

Gladly her brain was able to make some sense of what had been written in her own hand. Knowing Bruce would be out for at least another hour or so, she decided to make a cup of tea and then to plant herself down in the study room to open up her *Face2Face* account.

The fibre broadband connection soon had the seventeen inch monitor screen displaying the same homepage graphics viewed in the shop only a few hours previously. Her small hand positioned the mouse over the visitor's name and in a click, provisionally accepted him as a friend. A photograph had been attached to the worded content showing who she soon recognised to be Barry Sproston, next to an adult female, she assumed to be his wife and a very sickly looking young boy having fluid tubes and sticky patch sensors attached to various parts of his body. All were seen to be unsmiling, but there again, Sally considered, they haven't got too much to smile about in their circumstances.

Drawing her attention from the sad photograph, Sally began to read the message:

Hi Sally,

Really enjoyed the run and especially the part when we crossed the line together, I will treasure that incredible moment in my mind for ever. Sorry I had to dash at the end, I was worried about missing the plane and I needed to get to the hotel to shower, change and book out. As you can see from the photo, I'm back with my family now, they really are the most precious people in my life and I missed them so desperately when I was back in England.

The consultant oncologist tells us things are not so good at the moment, but they seem confident they can save our son's life. Dear God, please let that happen.

I have been in contact with my insurance company and they say not to worry. I hope they are right. I will keep in contact to let you know how things are going. A BIG, BIG thanks to you and the fund raisers.

All our Love

Barry, Debbie and our precious son, Wilson. xxx

She read the text again, and then again. There was something niggling at her subconscious mind. She wasn't ungrateful for Sproston having taken the time to inform her of his son's progress and thought it was good of him to thank the charity for the help they were able to afford him and his family.

Why then, she considered, had Sproston been keen to introduce himself totally unannounced at the fun run and the need for him to be accepted in her *Face2Face* friend's account? Surely he should have been making his thanks to the people who reviewed the family's plight at head office as it is they, and not her personally, who decide who does or doesn't get the charity's financial support.

Sally stared at the emotionally worded message flickering on the screen while she mulled things over.

Eventually she came to the conclusion it's likely he has acted with good intentions and she was probably trying to read into something that wasn't there.

She typed a brief reply in return to wish his family every good fortune then touched the send icon.

Yes, she accepted it was brief and lacked some of the feeling contained in the senders original message but she was satisfied it was enough. Her final task was to close the PC down.

Sally had fallen into a deep sleep when Bruce McCoy pressed his cold naked body next to her warm pyjama attired frame. His damp whisky breath loudly exhaling against the exposed nape of her neck was the cause for her being silently awoken from her slumber.

She became acutely aware of his shuffling about as she held her body rigid on her side of the bed patently aware of what her husband's desires were once he had consumed an excess of drink, and this was going to be a night when those instincts were to be denied their release.

He soon tired of his attempts to rouse his wife. On her half, she felt a sense of relief when it became clear he turned away to move to his side of the bed. Once he was snoring, Sally carefully raised her head to look at the red numerals emitting brightly in the darkened room which showed the time to be 11:15.

Resting her head back into the hollow of the soft warm pillow, her mind filled with a sense of pending grief. It didn't take a crystal ball to see that her husband would, sooner, rather than later, become yet another alcohol related death. Her fate, alas, was to be cared for by unfeeling strangers in some damn awful nursing home.

Bruce would never see the tears that trickled down his wife's face to then soak into her pillow, nor feel the deep sadness in her heart. Sleep eventually arrived to take her off into another more peaceful world. But like everything mortal, it would only be temporary.

Chapter Eight

Sally's body clock roused her around seven. She manoeuvred to her right to see if Bruce was still asleep, the snoring sounds even before she caught a glimpse of his face confirmed he was deeply under an alcohol induced sleep.

After quietly folding back the duvet on her side of the bed, she tiptoed to the main bathroom to have a shower. Having dried, dressed and applied fresh make up for the day she silently descended the stairs to the kitchen. Breakfast done, sandwiches made she was ready to start a new day. Usually Bruce would be about and getting under her feet before she set off for work. This morning, in particular, was to be an excuse for not giving him a farewell peck on the cheek since it was he who had made the decision to over indulge the previous evening, to be then followed by a long sleep into the late morning for his body to lessen the debilitating effects of the expected hangover.

Her arrival at the shop was usually timed for around eight thirty, this was so she'd be there first to open up, followed by the unpaid voluntary staff at nine. More pertinently, Sally discovered her mind seemed more lucid in the early morning and less so as the day progressed. Therefore, it became important for her to appear busy and organised at this key time of day to prevent others from thinking she had a problem.

During the half hour before nine, she would set up the till with a float, make a list of things that needed to be done around the shop that day, such as change of window display, removing old stock that wasn't selling and finally check for any post or emails requiring her attention.

During this precious thirty minute slot she'd normally check over the incoming emails. On this particular morning she spotted a message alert from *Face2Face*.

There was nothing that couldn't wait in the list of emails so she decided to access her social network account before the other two lady volunteers arrived in ten minutes' time.

Seeing the opening page of the *Face2Face* site filling the screen, she typed in her email and password details to gain access to her personal account. The person trying to make contact was Barry Sproston. Her immediate thoughts were he probably just wanted to thank her for the message she sent the previous evening.

She found this assumption to be correct in part, however, her concerns were drawn to what else was contained in the message.

Hi Sally,

Thank you for your good wishes, you will never know how much those kind words meant to Debbie and my precious son, Wilson. Sorry to burden you with our plight once again, but we have received terrible news. The hospital's consultant says neither he nor any of the other medical staff can do any more for my son.

There is an oncologist who practices in an exclusive private hospital who has had some success at treating the type of illness Wilson has. This man is likely to be his last chance for survival but the doctors here say he is too ill to be moved to the other side of America as the journey alone could be enough to kill him.

Our consultant oncologist here has spoken to this doctor and he is prepared to fly out to help save my son's life. The trouble is that the private hospital requires compensation payment to cover the cost of his absence on top of his personal fee for treating Wilson. We have been told this will be in the thousands of dollars and they will not sanction his services until they receive payment upfront.

I have phoned my insurance and they categorically state it is not company policy to release payments for treatment without an official hospital document showing a detailed breakdown of all the charges made. We are so desperate Sally, I can't bear the thoughts of losing Wilson, I don't think I could go on in this life if he was taken away from us.

Please, please, please Sally can you think of any way to help my family?

All our love,

Barry, Debbie and Wilson. xxx

A tsunami of emotions swept through her. Again she felt the sensation of warm tears for the second time in less than twelve hours.

'What if it was my little boy?' she agonised, 'I would try anything to save him!'

Her desire to have a family in the fertile years was cruelly denied to Sally when a massive abscess was found on one of her ovaries. To prevent wider infection the gynaecologists recommended removal whilst dismissing the idea that trying a course of powerful antibiotics would be a less drastic alternative to clear up the infection.

The remaining poorly functioning ovary coupled with Bruce McCoy's low sperm count, which the doctor had said was most likely down to his high drinking and low nutrition diet, determined she'd remain childless.

Seeing fresh faced year seven pupils starting their lives at her secondary school served to be an annual painful reminder of the loss of a nurturing role she so wished had been part of her life.

Not having children did have its compensations. There was always plenty of disposable income. Her pay combined with the police salary meant the two of them were able to purchase a very desirable house on the outskirts of Bladdington, change both cars every two years and enjoy exotic holidays around the globe.

Sadly for Sally, these outward trappings of affluence were scant reward for what she so desperately once longed for in her life. All in all, she felt incomplete as a woman. It was only the passing of the years that had served to gradually lessen the ache of loss.

Looking through misty eyes she typed in a reply:

Dear Barry, Debbie and Wilson,

I am desperately saddened by your awful situation. I am hopeful a solution will soon appear to solve all of your problems. Keep on at your insurance company, surely this cannot be the first time they have had to deal with this sort of situation. I will be thinking of you.

Kind regards

Sally McCoy

She clicked on the send icon and immediately her message disappeared from the screen. The sound of the shop doorbell ushered in the arrival of a volunteer. The familiar ringing noise broke Sally away from the computer screen and to move her thoughts to the pressing matters of running the shop. Within the hour her mind would block her memory from thinking any further about the content of the message she'd read earlier that day.

Bruce McCoy eventually raised his heavy head from the pillow at around 10:30 a.m.
'Christ, I feel bloody awful, what time is it?' he dry throat croaked.
'Ten thirty. That's me for a bollocking when Sally gets home tonight!'
McCoy dragged himself to the bedroom en suite to first use the lavatory before carefully stepping on to the unexpected dry base of the shower tray. The main reason for this was easy for McCoy to understand, Sally had not showered in there that morning and probably used the main bathroom so as not to disturb him from his drunken condition.
'She must think I am a right wanker for getting into the state I did last night. There is no hope for you is there, Bruce McCoy?' he said to himself.
His senses were suddenly jolted by the initial stream of very cold water spraying down on to his straight sandy hair. His feet shuffled his upper body away from the chilly flow pouring from the shower head until it was warm enough to step back under it again.
When he'd finished showering, a decision had been made to give a shave a miss; for no other reason than he just couldn't be bothered.
The late morning ablution left him feeling cleaned but not refreshed. The hangover was a good one and from previous experience, it would take up to late afternoon before he was beginning to feel anything like his old self.
The hallway grandfather clock chimed once prompting McCoy to pull his shirt cuff back to look at his wrist watch to see a visual representation of the time.

It was going to be, yet again, another long day. The two rounds of toast, mug of milky coffee and two extra strength pain killers had done nothing to take the edge off his throbbing head and the debilitating nauseous side effects.

Colleagues and friends at Mansefield police headquarters had chipped in to buy McCoy a year's membership at the Old Quarry golf club for his retirement present. Bruce had often mentioned he would like to take up golf once he finished in the force, suggesting it would be a good opportunity to get in a little exercise and to meet people other than coppers and crooks.

He slipped on a light jacket, got the car keys out from the kitchen drawer with thoughts in his head to start making use of his new membership at the club. It was not to play golf, mind; he only wanted to sit and relax in different surroundings and hopefully get into conversation that didn't involve anything to do with police work.

Subconsciously, his true motive was that he craved another drink or more and it was nothing to do with the hair of the dog thing.

The year old Mondeo diesel estate drew up in a vacant space in the tarmac covered car park. McCoy removed his jacket and tossed it over in to the back seat, locked the car and headed for the club's grand entrance while taking in the beautiful cloudless azure sky accompanied by a pleasant warm breeze.

A uniform concierge was on hand to check his name against the long list of registered members.

'I see it is your first visit, Mr McCoy.'

'That's not strictly true, I was here three weeks or more ago at a Police Federation function.'

'Yes, if I correctly recall, wasn't it held for the presentation of a bravery award and someone's retirement?'

'Yes, that is correct.' confirmed McCoy.

'Will you be wanting to play today, sir? I can see from the screen you haven't booked a space.'

'No, I won't be swinging a club quite yet. I still need to get in a lot of practice before I embarrass myself on the green.'

'We do employ a golf professional, very reasonable rates, I think he charges £90 per hour.'

'Let me have a think about that.'

'Hope you have a pleasant visit Mr McCoy.'

'Thank you.'

McCoy pushed his way through the light oak framed fully glazed double doors to find himself in the plush carpeted bar lounge furnished with high back soft leather chairs encircling highly polished mahogany tables. Expensive exotic plants and large ceramic features filled in other parts of the floor space. One of the walls had been chosen to display framed smiling photographs of past club presidents alongside shelved relics of silverware which had been either won by current or long forgotten members. McCoy saw this must have been a quiet part of the day, as there was only he and three other males present in the bar lounge.

At the bar he asked for a double whisky and ordered a chicken club sandwich.

'I'll bring your order to you when you are seated sir,' said the rather elderly hard looking bartender. McCoy collected his drink and strolled over to a table where someone had left a daily paper. While he was engrossed reading the news the *Daily Telegraph* had decided its readership wanted to consume, a white china plate with the ordered sandwich along with a bed of attractive salad leaves was placed on the table.

'Thank you,' said McCoy.

'Will there be anything else, sir?'

'This is fine thank you.'

The bartender returned to the door leading through to the kitchen.

When he was close to the last page of the newspaper, McCoy was disturbed by a cacophony of loud voices entering into the once peaceful bar lounge. He took little notice of the disturbance and continued to read an article taking his attention but not for long.

'Jesus, I don't believe it. It's McCoy, Bruce bloody McCoy. What the hell are you doing here?'

A broad Scottish accent filled the room as much as the man's large presence. His high ruddy complexion and purple toned long ears suggested the man was in his late sixties. The sagging jowly jawline was less to do with heredity and more to enjoying life's excesses; the bulging waist line seemed to support the suggestion.

'It's old dog, Jock Mackie. I thought you would be long gone by now,' McCoy jokingly said whilst both men happily greeted each other with hard playful slaps and vice-like handshakes.

Jock Mackie had climbed to the rank of a uniformed sergeant within four years of being in the force. He had no interest in applying to transfer over to CID even if his superiors said he had the right sort of mentality for that work; he still preferred to do his bobbying on the streets.

Later on in his long police career he did diversify and amongst his experiences he could cite he was once a firearms and driving trainer, a member of the mounted unit and in his final years, schools' education programme leader.

Early into his fledgling career as a DC, Bruce McCoy applied for temporary transfer to Glasgow CID so he could work with the detectives who policed the hard streets of the city and border towns. During his three year stay in Scotland it was to be Jock Mackie who would take this green young detective under his wing both on a personal and professional level. Bruce was indebted to the guidance, encouragement and straight talking received under Mackie's tutelage when he eventually returned back south. They had initially kept in touch, but like most relationships which are separated by great distances, they eventually peter out.

'You still look the same Bruce, that scar is hardly noticeable now, how do you do it?'

'Don't be daft Jock; you still look good as well.'

Both men were lying. Not only had the toll of being a committed police officer been etched deeply across their faces, but the shift work, often long punishing hours and unrelenting stress had not failed to have some effect on their health and personal relationships.

'What are you doing down here in this neck of the woods?' asked McCoy.

'We've been coming here for the past three years. It is a fantastic course and as you can see Bruce, I am here with some of my mates, who I must add are not ex-police.'

'Look, let me get you and your friends a drink, it's so good to see you Jock.'

'No, you sit down here, I'll get you one. What will it be? A large whisky, just like old times.'

'Aye, go on then.' replied McCoy, happily slipping into a Scottish accent.

Mackie moved off to buy the drinks while explaining to his golfing friends he hoped they wouldn't mind if he spent a little time with a long lost friend.

He returned to seat himself facing McCoy in one of the other comfortable chairs.

The two men chatted away furiously each eager to get their snippets of gossip and family news in first. Bruce also mentioned his recent retirement but nothing about his stay in hospital.

'How are you finding retirement?' enquired Mackie.

'Bit soon to tell really, I'll know in a few months time I suppose.'

'You don't sound too happy about it, Bruce.'

'Well, being truthful, I didn't want to finish, I feel I was pushed out.'

'Don't be daft, they probably had to cut staff and from what you tell me you have come out on top, so enjoy the time you have left with Sally, you never know what is around the corner.'

'That's the problem Jock, I can see what is around the corner for me.' replied McCoy in a sad tone.

'Well, are you going to tell me then?' pressed Mackie.

'It's Sally, I think, no, I know, she has started with dementia.'

'No, it can't be possible, surely she is too young. Has she been seen by the doctor?'

'She won't make an appointment. She's not stupid; she saw it all with her own mother and the same with her gran. They too started to suffer when they reached the age Sally is at now,' McCoy paused for a short spell and then continued, 'Let's have another drink, same again?'

'Aye, why not.'

The fleeting remaining hours of the afternoon consisted of further reminisces, what Jock had spent his pension lump sum on and thoughts of what Bruce McCoy was going to do with his windfall.

'I've always left the finance side of things to Sally, she knows all about investments and that sort of thing. But soon I want to be spending. I don't want to have a stack of money around when Sally ends up being cared for in some rip-off nursing home. The bastards will try to rob us of every penny we have.'

'Aye, and they say all the crooks are locked up, hey' replied Mackie showing his understanding of this one time young detective's plight.

Bruce McCoy glanced down at his wristwatch to note the time.

'Bloody hell, it's gone four o'clock, I best be getting back Jock, I want to be in when Sally gets back from work. I'm not in her good books as it is.'

Both men stood upright to face each other across the divide of the coffee table.

They both hugged and heartily shook hands. An exchange of phone numbers was the last act before the two men went their separate ways.

The bartender had appeared to be busying himself while in actual fact having the call to do very little. The conversation between the two ex-police officers was enough to occupy his attention that afternoon.

Chapter Nine

Becky Melia had been allocated the covert task of reporting on the movements of Barry and Debbie Sproston as they took some time away from being at their leukaemia afflicted son's bedside at the Cristoforo Colombo Childrens' Hospital situated close to the Florida Sands Hotel in Miami.

Through her large lensed designer sunglasses she watched them both stroll hand in hand along the picturesque Brandon Park beach in the late morning sunshine. While maintaining a watchful eye on the couple, who by this time had decided to relax on an outcrop of granite stone to take in the crystal blue surf and open their faces up to enjoy the sun and the warm sea breeze, she removed a mobile phone from a pocket in her high cropped shorts.

'This is the time to do it. They are sitting on some rocks and it would take them at least twenty minutes to get back to the hotel,' Becky Melia whispered into her inexpensive Nokia.

'Right, I'm on my way. Let me know immediately of any changes,' responded James Melia.

Melia received the call while seated in the near empty air conditioned residents' lounge area situated on the ground floor of the Florida Sands Hotel. He was seen vacating the lounge wearing a pair of quality tailored beige coloured trousers with a matching large money belt unobtrusively fixed to his waist. A long sleeved dark blue thin cotton shirt was worn to purposely hide the garish tattoos covering both arms.

He would normally be proud to boldly show off the artistry of his chosen ink piercing doctor, however, good sense said he best cover up as the strangers who he'd planned to deceive today, may have a different opinion about the merits of body art. Finally he slipped on a pair of Police brand sunglasses before reaching the hotel's reception desk.

A young woman in her early twenties greeted him wearing a smart light blue two piece suit uniform.

'How can I help you this morning, sir?' she pleasantly enquired in an accent similar to Hannah Montana.

'Hi, good morning to you. I have decided my family would like to see much more of Florida so I need to hire a car for a few days. I need my passport from you so I can have a look around at vehicle hire centres to get a car at the right price,' Melia said while trying not to show his full features to the girl.

'We can do that for you here if you want sir, a car can be brought over to you within the hour,' she said brightly.

'I think I would prefer to look around first myself, I might even go for one of those big 4x4s I've seen rumbling down the boulevards. It might help to make me look cool for change.'

The receptionist politely laughed at his reply.

'That's no problem sir, but they are expensive to hire. What is your room number?'

'423.' he answered convincingly.

She then left the reception desk to retrieve the passport from the secure holding situated behind the hotel room swipe card repository.

Her smiling face reappeared with her focus being on an opened page of the burgundy passport.

'Just some security questions I need to ask you sir. Please can I have your full name, date and place of birth and your address if you don't mind sir,' she asked, conscious not to allow the passport to be taken before being satisfied she had fulfilled all the required checks.

Becky Melia had recently been employed by an agency to clean the offices of Oakwood Engineering situated in Moulton. Her evening contract hours were from five thirty to eight and she was, more often than not, the only person around the offices during these times. Only occasionally did a supervisor show up from the employment agency to perform obligatory checks that all the tasks agreed on the cleaning contract were actually being done. The supervisor was aware that Oakwood engineering never had cause for complaint, in fact Becky often found waiting for her a small gift of chocolates, sometimes it would be a bottle of wine or even just a simple "thank you" card in recognition of her thoroughness.

During the past ten years Barry Sproston worked at Oakwood Engineering as a fabricator/welder. The shop floor and office personnel had generously raised funds through sponsorship and collections to support Sproston and his wife Debbie so they could be at their son's bedside while he was receiving treatment for leukaemia at the Cristoforo Colombo Childrens' Hospital in Miami.

Becky Melia soon made it her business to get to know where the employee personnel records were kept, but it sometimes happened one or two of the records were left out on workdesks probably with every good intention for them to be put back in the filing cabinet the following day. It was on one of those times the risky task of having to finger through a filing cabinet drawer searching for a particular person's file was gladly cancelled when she inadvertently spotted Barry Sproston's details sitting on top of a pile of documents. Conscious someone might unexpectedly appear from nowhere, she rapidly made a record of his notes into a pocket size notebook. Also, as luck would have it, she noticed in a plastic A4 size admin tray about twenty sheets of business headed paper. She took two sheets from the top of the pile and rolled the paper to form a tube being careful not to create any unnecessary creases, to then hide it away in a faux leather shopping bag she carried to work.

The hope was that having gained important access to Sproston's personal details, coupled with the uncanny likeness her husband and Sproston both shared, these two vital elements were likely to be enough to deceive those whom James Melia planned to meet on this long awaited hot day. The two main players behind the deception were confident if they were successful in executing their plan, then the final part of the scam should fall neatly in to place.

In the privacy of their hotel room Becky Melia had listened to her husband recite Barry Sproston's personal details out loud for the last time in readiness for what he might be asked for by the receptionist. Any mistakes meant he would not get his hands on the passport and worse still, could find himself arrested by the Miami police.

After providing the receptionist with the answers to her questions, Melia felt the gripping sensation of his stomach churning accompanied by his knees starting to involuntarily twitch as he tried to hold together the brazen subterfuge. On the surface though, he appeared to be calm and quite normal.

The young receptionist carried out the final check by comparing the features of the man standing in front of her to the photographic image bonded in the passport.

'There you are sir, here is your passport.' She closed the document to hand it over. Melia then undid a security pocket zip sewn into his trousers and slid it snugly in place followed by pulling the zip firmly closed. The sound of his heart pounding throbbed in his ears as he turned to leave the hotel through the wide black tinted glass reception doors, but it would be the sound of the receptionist calling him back that would momentarily paralyse him in his tracks.

'Oh, I'm sorry sir, I nearly forgot, you have to sign as proof that you have taken your passport from the hotel.' The receptionist disappeared to collect the signing out book. Melia neglected to realise he may have to sign for the passport and hoped she would now overlook to check his signature against the one printed on the inside of the back cover.

Returning with a blue ledger style book she opened it past the crinkly worn full pages to an unfilled space below a row of previous recorded signatures and dates.

Signing his name "Barry Sproston", he breathed a deep inward sigh of relief when he gladly watched her close the book without checking the signatures to scurry back to the reception desk after wishing him a good day.

Melia performed another check to feel that the passport was still in the security of his trouser pocket, pleased to sense his unusually sweaty palm confirmed it hadn't gone astray in the hundred or so metres he'd covered since escaping the clutches of the charming receptionist. The next destination was the East Seaboard Trust Corporation situated on 214 East First Street. The mobile phone in his other trouser pocket thankfully continued to remain silent as he neared his destination.

It wouldn't be too long before he entered the air conditioned interior of The East Seaboard Trust Corporation. Reading the signs hanging from the ceiling, he nonchalantly then strolled over to the near empty customer service area grateful for the welcome relief from the hot humid mid-day temperatures.

He purposely lingered for a while in the background until he saw a particular young female bank clerk available at one of the ten or so service counters. Careful not to appear to be in a hurry, he casually walked over to the glass screen to calmly present himself to the young clerk.

'Hello sir, what can we do for you today?' she said showing off an amazing set of pearly white straight teeth.

'I want to open a bank account, please. My dear mother-in-law wants to send money over from the UK to support me and her daughter whilst our son is receiving treatment for his leukaemia at the Cristoforo Colombo Childrens' Hospital.'

The girl's cheery expression changed to one of sympathy on hearing the man's reason for wanting to open an account.

'I am sorry to hear of your son's illness, sir and I hope he will be well soon. We will do our best to be of service to you during your stay in America.'

'Thank you,' replied Melia.

'You do understand, sir you must be able to present to the bank certain documentation to permit an account to be opened in this country?' she said wearing her business head.

'Yes, I think I have everything with me you need. I do hope it is possible to set up an account quickly.' he said in a worried tone.

'If everything is in order then it shouldn't take too long, sir. And as we are not too busy today, we may as well do all the necessary paperwork in one of the small annexe rooms. If you stay where you are sir I'll close the counter position and then come round to take you to the room. I won't be a moment.'

The green lit open sign above the glass partition changed colour to red to read closed. The young clerk appeared from a security door to escort Melia to the chosen annexe room. While sitting in one of the two customer padded seats, he observed the attractive young bank employee peering intently at the computer monitor screen while nimbly tapping in the key details to permit a new bank account to be opened.

'We are ready to start now Mr Sproston,' she said with a bright smile. 'Do you have your passport with you so I can take your details, please?'

He unzipped the trouser pocket to retrieve the passport to then hand it over to her.

'Thank you, it won't take long to type in the details.'

Amidst the sounds formed by the pressing of the individual keys he said, 'I think I will need to have the account open for maybe one month or slightly more.' He deliberately paused at this point waiting for her inquisitiveness to enquire why this was so.

'Why such a short period, Mr Sproston?'

'I don't think my son will make it; the doctors have said it will be a miracle if he pulls through,' he said mournfully.

She lifted her attention from the screen to face Melia.

'Miracles do happen, Mr Sproston. The hospital does have a wonderful reputation; he could not be in better hands,'

'Yes, I suppose you are right. I'm a little depressed after seeing my son struggling to hold on to life for so long. It can really get to you at times.' Melia swiped the back of his hand across his right eye and cheek in the feign act of weeping.

'I can see you are upset, Mr Sproston. I will be as quick as I can so you can get back to your son's bedside. Do you have with you evidence of your place of work and national insurance number?'

'Yes I do, I have a letter from my employer in England verifying my employment status and my national insurance number.' Melia removed a folded A4 paper from his money belt and passed it over to her. He watched carefully as she spread the paper flat to read the details set down in the confirmation letter that had been typed up by his wife on the business headed paper she had taken while cleaning at Oakwood engineering.

'Everything looks fine sir. I'll have to take a photocopy of the letter for security purposes and also it is federal bank policy to contact your employer in England so they can confirm the details.' She left her seat to step over to the fax-cum-photocopying machine to make a copy.

Melia, in the meantime, anxiously checked the passing of time on his wrist watch and was somewhat relieved the mobile hadn't rang for him to receive an urgent call from his wife.

Returning to her seat and passing the original letter back to him, she said it was necessary for her to ring the hospital to confirm the reason for him being in the USA.

'I expected you to have to contact the hospital, so I took the precaution to have the details with me.'

He again reached into the money belt to get the note paper with the hospital phone number and ward number details along with a bundle of dollar bank notes. She momentarily ignored the money sitting on the desk top and began dialling in the handwritten number. She put the receiver down having listened to the ward manager confirming they had a patient in the name of Wilson Sproston, who was daily being attended to by his parents, Barry and Debbie Sproston.

'The last thing that needs to be done now is for you to deposit a sum of $500 to open the account, and I expect that is the amount you have on the table Mr Sproston.'

'Yes, that is correct,' he said nudging the secure banded notes towards her.

While she was counting the money he said he would be using the account to make online money transfers for medical services his son was receiving. He further explained he would need a current account card to make purchases and cash withdrawals to support their daily living expenses.

'I expect you have an email account sir, so if you want I will show you how to access the banks internet banking service, after that I will leave you to put in your security passwords while I arrange for a current account card for you to collect tomorrow.

In the hour Melia had successfully returned Barry Sproston's passport back in the security of the hotel and within twenty-four hours was able to access his own personal internet account and be in possession of a card which would allow him to draw cash from any ATM machine and make expensive purchases.

Chapter Ten

Warming in the kitchen oven was a luxury vegetarian lasagne which was the main of a £10 readymade meal deal he bought from a local supermarket on his journey back home from the golf club. He'd put the white wine in the chiller compartment with the sweet part of the deal opened, ready in its packaging sitting in the microwave waiting for a touch on the start button.

Bruce McCoy had just enough time to have another quick shower, a thorough clean of his teeth to remove most of the smell of alcohol, a belated shave and put on a fresh set of clothing when he heard the house key turn in the door latch. Bruce was in the kitchen when he called out to his wife.

'Is that you dear? You're a bit late tonight. Had a good day?'

'Yes, thanks have you? That smells nice. What is it?'

Sally placed her bag in the usual place and hung her coat temporarily on the newel post before making her way through to the kitchen.

'You've been busy.' said Sally in surprise.

Bruce moved towards her and planted a kiss on her cheek. He then stepped back to watch the food cooking in the oven through the heatproof clear glass door.

'I'm not just a pretty face you know. Not only are you going to have a lovely vegetarian lasagne my dear, there is treacle sponge and custard and a bottle of white wine in the fridge.'

'Well Bruce McCoy, I never knew you were a secret Gary Rhodes.'

He followed by bowing his head in an exaggerated fashion.

'I'm not really. When I was coming back from the library today I spotted a meal deal offer so I thought why not? The rest, as they say, is history.'

'Is it nearly ready? I'm starving.'

'Coming up right away my dear,' he answered cheerily.

Whilst the two dined on the meal deal feast, Bruce again, asked Sally how her day had gone at the shop. She wasn't going to tell him how foolish she felt having to call for assistance when her mind froze using the till on at least four occasions. During that same afternoon Sally came upon a bundle of perfectly serviceable clothes still with their price tags on in the textiles recycling bin. She'd annoyingly gathered up the clothing items and placed the untidy pile on the counter to accusingly look around, to ask what was going on to the other shopworkers.

In response, they initially looked at each other in bemusement, and then one of the co-accused ladies said she had watched Sally put the clothes in the recycling bin herself. She did not say anything to her at the time, for after all, she is the boss.

Finally when she was about to lock up for the day, her eye caught sight of a bundle of unopened post she'd picked up early that morning. Her plan was to deal with the letters later, but of course, she forgot. That was the reason her arrival home had been so delayed.

There was something else that was niggling her sub-conscious, it happened during that same morning, she was sure of that, but no matter how desperately she tried to think about what was bothering her, it refused to come to mind.

'Yes, it's been a good day. We have sold lots of stuff and people have even called in to make donations in lieu of not taking part in the fun run. Aren't some people so kind Bruce?'

'Yes, they are dear,' he agreed.

Sally must not have remembered the previous night and morning's events because she would have surely had him over the coals by now. He wasn't certain whether he should be relieved or saddened. He may have got away from explaining his late drinking escapade; the sadder of the two situations was the growing realisation Sally had serious problems.

When it was her turn to enquire about what sort of day he had, he resorted to telling a pack of lies with great conviction. One thing for sure, he wasn't about to disclose he'd spent the morning nursing a humongous hangover and the afternoon having a good jolly at the golf club with an old lost friend.

'Any ideas yet on how we should invest my redundancy and retirement lump sum? We must have a holiday soon like we said and I think we should be a little reckless and have a big splash on something special,' he said excitedly.

'I'm working on it Bruce, I've been on the internet researching what decent deals there are around at the moment. I don't think it would be wise to tie the money up for longer than three years even if we do lose out on a little bit extra interest by doing so.'

They looked silently across the table to become locked in each other's gaze; both understood the real reason for her reference to the period of three years. Bruce may not make it primarily due to his drinking and sadly, she will likely be here but no longer occupying a world she was once familiar with.

'Let's make a toast,' Bruce cheerfully proclaimed. It was his way of breaking the sudden sense of despair that had descended upon them.

'To the happy times ahead. And of course, not forgetting my gorgeous wife; Sally McCoy.'

He lifted the fluted wine glass to his lips and took a deep draw. Sally raised her glass to purposely only wet her lips. She'd had enough of seeing the effects of alcohol to the extent of taking away any possible enjoyment she could get from drinking.

Bruce cleared away the table while Sally went to their bedroom to put on a change of clothing. Eventually she came down the stairs to enter the lounge to see that Bruce had spread himself out on the long settee and was fast asleep with the television playing to itself. She picked up the remote control resting on the arm of the settee and aimed the sensor at the large flat screen TV to silence the voice of a newscaster reporting on more depressing events happening around the world.

Sally placed the control back on the arm and then quietly closed the lounge door to shut off the rasping snoring noises from invading the rest of the house.

They both had no plans for the night, Bruce will probably be in the land of nod for at least another hour. Sally considered she might get changed yet again into her running gear in a hour or so and do a steady three mile run, nothing too taxing as she was feeling unusually tired. The exercise would clear her head and a nice long soapy bath afterwards would ensure a good night's sleep.

To fill in the hour before changing into her running gear, Sally decided to spend the time on the computer in the study. Her personal password was written on a post-it note stuck in the corner of the monitor screen. It was upon seeing this innocent yellow piece of paper she strangely became a little uneasy and apprehensive. A recent previous experience etched in her increasingly confused mind must have made some association to the inanimate sticker. Dismissing any thoughts it must be of some importance, she proceeded to type in the password.

The PC screen filled with her chosen browser provider with most visited sites saved into the favourites menu across the top of the screen. She had been drawn away from accessing the OK magazine site on noticing a new email icon flashing in her mail box.

A left click revealed it was a notification from her *Face2Face* account of someone wanting to make contact with her.

A click on the favourites bar brought to life the home page of *Face2Face*. The same password written on the note facing her on the screen was typed in to access her own personal user account. She now understood why her brain had alerted her conscience to the yellow sticker, reading the name Barry Sproston, jolted her memory bank enough to recall she had once written the same name on a similar note.

Another left click allowed his message to be opened:

Hi Sally,

I cannot tell you how ecstatic we all are, Wilson especially. The leukaemia consultant has been given leave of absence so he can fly over here to start Wilson's treatment immediately-we hope it isn't too late.

The £22,000 you have agreed to pay the private hospital upfront for his services is an unbelievable gesture. They require payment before he is allowed to fly out and you have said this will not be a problem as there are sufficient funds in your bank to cover the cost and can make an internet transfer from your account. My insurance company have promised they will reimburse you once all charges at the end of treatment have been agreed and finalised so there is no worry in getting your money back.

With events happening so fast I left the hospital leaving details of the private hospital's account behind-stupid me! But it should not be a problem. I will give you my bank details so you can send the transfer to my account, then I can transfer the amount to the hospital later tomorrow. As promised I will not tell anybody about your unbelievable kindness, least of all your husband, even though his unexpected windfall will be saving a young person's life.

Here are my bank details:

Account name:
Mr B Sproston
The East Seaboard Trust Corporation

*214 East First Street
Miami
Florida*

*Account Number: 91828374
Sort code: 31 89 13*

I cannot say thank you enough times Sally. You truly are a unique human being.
I will contact you again in the morning to let you know if the transfer was successful.

Love Barry, Debbie and Wilson xxx

Sally stared at the individual words flickering hypnotically on the screen with her brain spinning in total confusion.

Needing desperately to get some sort of order back in her head, she left her swivel seat to head for the kitchen. On passing the shut lounge door she could still hear the sounds of rhythmic snoring. Standing at the sink, she picked up a wine glass that had been left to dry on the draining board, to fill it to the brim with water from a filter jug. She downed the full glass in one and started to refill the glass when she caught her mirrored reflection in the darkened kitchen window temporarily created by the onset of dusk. She closely peered at her own image and started to whisper to herself:

'What have you done? I must have agreed to help him this morning. I cannot go back on what I promised. That poor boy, that poor family need me. Should I tell Bruce? No, he wouldn't understand, he's too black and white. He said I will get the money back from his insurers and Bruce would be none the wiser.'

Sally took a swig from the glass without turning her gaze from the reflection.

'What if this is a con? It can't be. I've met the man and Eric Carter even said that a local newspaper reported on the family's plight. It all stacks up. I will help this poor family!'

Sally sensed a feeling of relief pour over her when she performed the internet banking transaction. The money had gone from the account and was off to another part of the world to do its good work.

Bruce was awoken from his deep slumber by a voice calling, 'I'm off for a run, I'll be about an hour.' Then the door slammed. He laid his head back on the comfortable seat cushion and swiftly resumed the dream he'd been broken from.

Sally, having completed a three mile circuit, was going through a series of warming down exercises, when she noticed the Mondeo had gone from the drive.

A spare key from under the welcome mat was used to let herself in. The door opened allowing her probing hand to reach out in the dark to find the light switch. On the table in the illuminated hallway a piece of carelessly torn lined notepaper was awaiting her attention. Sally could rightly have a good guess at the probable nature of the content scribbled on the paper. She wasn't to be wrong:

'Had a call from Dick, nipping out for a swift one. Love Bruce x

She screwed the paper up into a small ball and dropped it into a wicker waste paper basket on the way up to have the long soapy bath she had promised herself.

This time she did not hear her husband arrive home much later that night and similarly, as before, in the light of the early morning she prepared herself alone for another day's work at the charity shop.

After gently closing the front door she quickly realised her car was parked by itself. Bruce must have either walked or got a lift home the previous night. Pressing a key fob the Fiesta bleeped to let her have access to the driver's seat. She pressed the keyless ignition button to then spend the time up to arriving at the charity shop contemplating whether what she had done to help in supporting the Sproston family's plight was right, alongside feeling a sense of helpless dismay about how quickly her husband had fallen back into his old ways.

Sally parked her car in its usual place along the street. On entering the shop she made her way through to the small office to take a seat behind her desk. A notepad in the office drawer contained all the passwords for different accounts she had so easily before relied on only from memory not too long ago. This was alongside another support mechanism she adopted, which was to stick post-it notes around the outer plastic trim surrounding the monitor screen of important passwords, names and sometimes, just simple reminders.

She copied in the password and while waiting for the slow office computer to boot itself up, Sally struggled to reason why she was able to perform as near to normal in the morning. It was vital for her during this period of lucidity, to perform the bulk of the admin tasks and duties for the day. From around eleven onwards it was like a mysterious demented power had gained control of her mind and was determined to make her look stupid by virtue of the uncharacteristic simple mistakes she made.

Later for no logical reason, the force relinquished control of her mind and handed it back to the real Sally McCoy and then snatched it back again when it felt like it. She understood in her heart it would not be too long before she needed medication and professional support to slow her descent into becoming a bed bound dementia victim.

Checking the new email post there was the now familiar message from *Face2Face*.

The received message was from Sproston which read:

Dear Sally,

You are an angel sent to us by God, we have been truly blessed. Thank you, thank you, thank you from the bottom of our hearts. The money you sent has been transferred to the private hospital's account. The specialist should be here soon to save our son's precious life. I have attached a photograph of Wilson to this email. We can never thank you enough. I will let you know how things are progressing; let's pray to God it will be good news.

For ever in your debt Barry, Debbie and Wilson xxx

Sally quickly opened the attachment acutely aware that the time on the wall clock showed eight fifty five and soon the volunteer staff would be making their arrival known. She peered into the screen to see a sick looking boy propped up in a hospital bed making an attempt to smile and wave his tubed up arm. The sound of the shop door opening was a signal for her to close the distressing image of the sorry child. Mopping her moist eyes she left her seat to greet the volunteers.

Gladly for Sally the day passed without her having to suffer any of her usual embarrassing moments. Her mind had remained perfectly clear and was thankful she was able to perform tasks she had increasingly made mistakes in doing. Perplexedly, Sally wasn't able to switch off from thinking about her decision to support the Sproston family in their tragic plight. It was with some anxiety over the lunch break that she checked for any incoming emails only to disappointingly find no update had been sent from Florida.

The hours slipped by to bring a close to the shop for the day. Sally had been careful to remember to set the alarm while she listened in on the two volunteers outside bidding each other goodbye. The five lever door lock was turned to secure the building and while facing the locked door she unzipped her handbag to drop the key into an inside pocket. Slipping the long leather strap over her shoulder, she then turned to make her way to the Fiesta parked further along the same street as the charity shop.

'Flipping heck, you made me jump Eric. I didn't expect to see anybody there.' Eric Carter stood unexpectedly outside the shop clutching a brown A4 size envelope.

'I'm sorry Sally I didn't mean to startle you,' he genuinely apologised.

'You did give me a start; I was just locking up for the day.'

'It's a good job I have caught you then, but I won't keep you long. I've brought along some of the photographs I took at the run on Sunday. I asked our office junior to print off some of the action scenes and thought they would form a good display in the shop. Some of the same photographs will be printed in the *Bladdington Bugle* this week.'

'Oh, I do hope I look all right, but thank you Eric that is very kind of you.'

Carter passed the brown envelope over to her.

'I won't look at them now; I'll take them home with me and show Bruce. Thank you so much Eric.'

'No problem Sally, by the way, how is Bruce coping with retirement?'

'I'm not quite sure yet, Eric. I think he is still getting his head around it, he didn't really want to finish but I'm hoping he will make use of the year's golf membership his friends at the station chipped in for as a retirement present. It will do him good to meet fresh faces and get involved in something different other than police work.'

'I suppose it will take some adjustment after being full on all those years. But still, one thing is for sure, he will have no financial worries. I'll have to go on till I'm sixty-six or even more, if I make it, and then I'll only get a lousy state pension, this job doesn't pay enough so you can put money away in to a private scheme. Anyway, I'm not going to bother you with that. If you need any more prints just give me a ring at the office.'

Eric reached out to shake her hand and planted a wooden kiss on her cheek.

'I best be going now, things to do and all that sort of stuff. Take care, Sally.'

'And you Eric,' she replied.

Carter turned left out of the shop entrance while Sally headed right to reach their respective parked cars.

Chapter Eleven

Bruce McCoy was to be found at the Old Quarry golf club during the early afternoon of that day. When he was out drinking the previous evening, Dick Starr had offered McCoy the loan of his golf clubs; the very set he'd used only the once about fifteen years ago or more.

Around mid-morning he'd rang Jock Mackie at his hotel. Luckily Jock had no concrete plans and agreed he would share the afternoon with him on the driving range so he could learn some of the basics on how to play golf.

'Bloody hell Bruce, that's an old set of clubs. You need to get some of that money spent on a decent set,' teased Mackie on grabbing hold of a number nine iron from the dusty golf bag Starr had rummaged from his untidy garage for McCoy to borrow.

'I've got to find out first whether I like golf or not. There is no point in spending good money on something that may end up in the back of the shed for years,' replied McCoy while practising a swing with another antiquated club randomly picked from the battered bag.

The day was still, slightly overcast and the temperature in the mid-teens.

Over the next two hours Mackie's tuition included how to form a proper grip and use the correct club for various strokes on the different sections of the green. The constant striking of golf balls down on the range soon caused McCoy's arms and shoulders to ache from using muscles and joints in ways he'd never called on to do previously.

'I've had enough Jock; I'll be stiff as a board tomorrow. Let's go to the bar so I can get you a farewell drink or two.' suggested McCoy in a feigned show of pain.

'Sounds good to me, Bruce. You've done well today, lad. And if you are really determined to play this game well, you'll need to get your hand down and buy a decent set of clubs. When I've buggered off back to Scotland tomorrow you must promise me Bruce, to keep on practising. The course professional here is a good man, you must book a few lessons with him. I think you are a natural, and you never know, it could be your face everyone looks at when viewing the photograph of the next Old Quarry champ. Now wouldn't that be great!'

'It might sound great, but at ninety pounds a lesson I'm not too sure of that.' McCoy had replied. He then had to listen to Mackie jokingly lecturing him that he was probably tighter than any man living north of the border while they carried their bags back to their respective cars.

'You cannot take the money with you, and please take this right Bruce, it's not like you have any children to leave anything to.'

Sally was in the kitchen mesmerised by the large organically grown potato twirling around in the microwave when she was startled by the front door being slammed.

'Is that you Bruce?' she called.

'No it's the Bladdington ravisher, and he's coming to get you.' he replied like an actor in a Freddie Kruger film.

She ignored his feeble attempt at trying to put on a scary voice.

'I'm having a baked potato and salad for tea, do you want the same?'

'Eh, no thanks, love, I think I'll go for bacon butty on thick white bread daubed in full fat butter. I'm starving after playing golf all afternoon.'

He had moved to stand propped up against the door frame to take in the sight of his wife's neat derrière while she stooped down checking on the progress in the microwave.

'Oh, that's good, I'm sure eating that will keep you fit. I'll put you some bacon under the grill at the same time as crisping my potato off. Will two slices be enough?'

'No my dear, four will do, and don't you dare say anything about my cholesterol. If I like it I will eat it and that is that.' Bruce had long been lectured by Sally about his poor diet but his thoughts always were if she wanted to live on rabbit food then that was her choice.

After Sally had switched on the electric grill, she moved to the fridge to retrieve the bacon storage box from the bottom shelf.

'What's in the envelope?' said Bruce having spotted the large brown envelope resting on the kitchen table.

'Just some photos Eric Carter took at the run on Sunday. I've not even looked at them myself yet.' replied Sally while carefully placing rashers on the chrome plated wire mesh sitting inside the grill tray.

Bruce had moved his stance to pull a chair out to sit at the kitchen table. He reached over to the brown packet to unseal the weak adhesive bond holding the flap down he then turned the envelope upside down to shake the A5 sized images on to the table surface.

There were about seven glossy sheets in total, the first to catch his eye was the coloured picture taken of Grey and Cooper at the finishing line.

'My God, who's he, he looks bloody terrible, is he green? He looks it to me, and people call this a fun run!' McCoy's face lit up in humour on seeing the state of the finishing competitor.

'Mind you, though,' he continued to say after further detailed observation of the photograph, 'she's got a fit body standing next to him.'

'Let me have a look,' called Sally while keeping a watchful eye over the grilling bacon.

He held the photograph aloft for her to see.

'Yes, I think those two are from Bladdington police station, both in the CID I believe.'

'Right, I see, yes I think I can recognise them now, they were at Dick Starr's hero presentation and I think he gave them a mention. They look different dressed in formal clothes, but I don't know, the young lady still looks extremely good.' Bruce commented having turned the photograph back to himself for additional scrutiny.

'She's young enough to be your daughter, McCoy.' Sally hadn't realised at first what she had so innocently said. It was only when she caught sight of her husband looking forlornly at the photograph did she fully understand how her casual comment could have been interpreted.

He always made it known, not only just to her, but to others in their circle of close friends, either he wanted a daughter or later once their individual problems had come to light, how he would have loved a daughter. To move the conversation on, Sally asked what was on the other photographs. He flipped through them in turn and then after viewing each one, skitted them along the shiny table top to reach her end of the table. He did keep one in his hand, the one showing his wife and a stranger looking like a scene from the *Chariots of Fire* bravely breasting the finishing tape.

'Who is this then?' He held the triumphal image aloft for her to glimpse at from the other end of the table.

'Oh, er, yes, that is someone whose family is benefiting from our charity. He joined me right at the end of the run. He asked me if we could be together when the finishing line came up. I could see no harm in it so I said yes.'

'Hmm, I don't like the look of him. He doesn't even seem to be tired, look he hasn't even got a sweat on, that's amazing. Just look at the rest of the photographs, even that Grey girl has some sweat on her forehead and she looks as fit as a fiddle!'

'Bruce, they are just innocent photographs, it's not a police investigation you are leading. They are kind hearted people who have given up some of their time to help poor kids and their desperate families. Please don't tell me you find something sinister in that do you?' She finished sharply.

'Yes, you are right Sally, I'm sorry. Are those bacon butties ready yet?'

Bruce immediately lost interest in the photographs; that was part of her life and not his and who she associated with was really of very little interest to him. Police work was what had motivated him. Being a gullible sop for every bleeding heart that came knocking at the door was not his idea of work satisfaction.

Sally, on the other hand thought it best not to mention how the stranger in the photograph had become such an emotional focus in her life since the charity run and moreover, not to tell him about the £22,000 she had sent to his account.

From across the kitchen table while they were both eating their respective meal choices, Bruce described his day, which had included being taught the basic fundamentals of golf and then moving on for a thrash around the near empty 18 hole course, with his old friend, Jock Mackie.

When it came to her turn to recount her day, having had experienced no memory lapses or not being seen to have done anything stupid was success enough for Sally to mark her day. However, she wasn't to tell him about this personal victory. She did go on to bore her husband into a drowsy stupor through endlessly wittering on about how much money the shop had taken, the number of items she suspected as being stolen from the racks and finally, a long reference to the rudeness shown by some customers.

Conversation between the two in the big empty house was soon exhausted and the remainder of the meal time was spent in usual silence. Bruce slid his chair out from under the table and suggested he would do the tidying away and stack the dishes in the dishwasher. Sally said she would make the bed.

Once their individual assigned tasks had been accomplished Bruce made for the sitting room to stretch out on the long settee armed with the TV remote control.

Sally said she did not want to watch any TV and intended to sit in the study to go on-line.

'Have you decided how we will invest the money yet Sally?' Bruce called as Sally was about to head for the study room.

'Nearly, I've, got some ideas but I want to check them out first,' she answered rather hesitatingly.

'Don't tie it all up, we will need to put some aside for things we might want to buy now,' he said while aiming the remote control at the television to change channels.

'Yes, I know Bruce. Now watch your television.'

She heard no more from him until about fifteen minutes had elapsed when the first snoring noises were vibrating through the soulless house.

This was the sign she was waiting for so she could respond to the email informing of a new message in her *Face2Face* account. Unsurprisingly the message was from Barry Sproston:

Hi Sally,

Bad and good news. The consultant says he can do no more for Wilson and he may die in two to three days if he is unable to have a bone marrow transplant.

He and his team spent hours searching through the national register of bone marrow volunteers and, luckily, has been able to identify a near perfect match, isn't that incredible news. But there is a massive downside, the consultant has spoken over the phone to the person and he has agreed to donate his bone marrow but he wants $60,000 up front, that is £40,000. The man is desperately poor and struggles to support his wife and five children and this is the only way he is able to get any decent money. I can't believe someone would want to deny a young person their life for the sake of a few thousand dollars, especially when you have children of your own.

I cannot bring it into my heart to ask you to help us again in our hour of need; it is just too much to ask from another human being. I will keep you informed when Wilson eventually passes and when I get back to England I'll get that £22,000 to you.

Thank you for coming into our lives, you gave us hope but, sadly, it wasn't to be.

All our love,

Barry, Debbie and Wilson xxx

Sally re-read the message time and time again, she could not get it in to her head how someone could be so heartless to deny a loving family a chance to save their only child. Sally had become so emotionally hooked, she was determined, no matter what, to see this tragic scene turn into a happy ending.

She checked to see if Sproston has attached the new bank details for the hospital, there were none. Really, this little detail did not matter. A temporary standing order account had been set up in Sproston's name and all she had to do was to type in the new amount and that too would be on its way to America to aid a poor boy's salvation.

With the transaction completed, Sally spent a few moments in deep contemplation staring at the internet opening page of the McCoy's chosen on-line banking provider brightly filling the screen. Her trance like state was only broken on having a sudden feeling someone was watching her.

'Bloody hell, Bruce you put the wind up me, I thought you were still asleep, why did you have to creep up like that?' she said after unexpectedly seeing her husband standing at the opening to the study.

'I didn't creep up on you, as you say. You were so engrossed on that damn computer the whole house could have been emptied and you wouldn't have known a thing about it. What have you been doing?' he said twisting his head to see what was showing on the monitor screen.

'Just transferring money across accounts so we are not found short when we draw from the current account,' she convincingly answered.

'I'd be seriously traumatised if we found the accounts to be empty. Is that on-line stuff safe? I have heard different stories at the station of some people who have seen their money disappear off to Russia and places like that. Sometimes the fraud lads are able to get some of the cash back but on most occasions, it vanishes for ever, probably in some evil criminal's drug account.'

'Don't worry Bruce, the banks cover for any loss as long as you haven't been stupid like passing on passwords to strangers, but saying that it can be family members who turn out to be the culprits.'

'Quite. Look now you are "on-line", Bruce put a stress on the two short words, 'Jock gave me a website address. Hey aren't I getting good, Sally?' he said jocularly.

'Just get on with it Bruce. A website address for what?'

'Yes, for a supplier of golf clubs. He reckons I will cut out the middle man and get a better deal if I go on the internet. The company web address is: www.golfheaven.co.uk . Can you get that up Sally?' he said excitedly.

They then spent the next twenty minutes discussing the pros and cons of some of the sets of golf clubs shown on the website. Eventually Bruce settled for the set he'd been originally recommended to go for by his friend, Jock Mackie.

'Right that's the clubs ordered and they should be here within forty-eight hours. Let's hope you use them Bruce.' Sally said with a sense of doubt.

'I will, don't worry, I'm not going to be like Dick and use them the once in fifteen years. Anyway, Jock reckons I have good hand-eye coordination and will soon pick up the game. A natural, he said. Can you believe that Sally! Don't forget, I've got the money to spend, and spend it I will. You never know what's around the corner.'

They both stayed in for the remainder of the evening silently watching TV. After the ten o'clock news Sally shook Bruce awake to go to bed. Before ten thirty they were both fast asleep.

Chapter Twelve

Early morning the next day, Sally received a message in her *Face2Face* account to acknowledge her unbelievable kindness together with a mention not to worry unnecessarily about being refunded by the insurance company.

Later that same day during lunch break, Sproston, yet again contacted Sally to say not only had the bone marrow donor arrived, he had since been medically screened and tested and was now being prepared to allow the marrow transplant to go ahead.

Sally felt a glow of internal happiness after reading the update on Wilson's improving prospects. Closing her eyes, a short prayer was recited to herself for the young boy's safe keeping. The sound of the shop doorbell disturbed her deep spiritual thoughts, enough for her to leave the seat to see who had entered the shop, which she found to be the familiar figure of Eric Carter.

'Hello Eric, twice in two days, you may be in danger of becoming a regular customer.' she welcomed brightly.

'I don't think there is much chance of that. Sally, I'm not here to casually browse like some are able to do. I have something here I want you to have a look at.'

Sally was slightly taken aback at Carter's rather unusual solemn manner, she usually found him to be quite perky and boyish on all the other occasions they had met. Carter pulled from his inside coat pocket a similar coloured envelope to the one he had passed over to Sally the previous day, but smaller in size.

'I want you to have a look at this.' he said passing the sealed envelope over to her.

'What is it?' she enquired pensively.

'Just have a look at the photograph. Then I will explain.'

She removed the contents from the envelope and gently placed the photograph down on the glass counter top to focus on an image what clearly looked to be that of parents sitting with an ill child around a hospital bed. Her senses initially took a jolt at the nature of the picture, it looked remarkably like the family she was so involved in helping. She then became anxious he might know something about what she was up to.

'Why are you showing me this photograph Eric?' she enquired in a defensive tone.

'I suppose you could call it reporter's instinct. It's about the runner who was holding hands with you when you finished the fun run. Remember, I gave you a copy of the photograph I took yesterday.'

'Yes,' replied Sally slowly.

'You said his name was Barry Sproston; I made a note of his name when I was asking you questions. And, if you remember, Sally, he disappeared pretty quickly before I was able to get any comments from him.'

'Oh, yes, that's true. He had to catch a plane back to America to see to his poor boy that is being treated for leukaemia over there. Our charity is providing some financial support while he's receiving treatment,' she responded cagily.

'Right, do you remember I said our sister paper, the *Moulton Sentinel*, had carried a photograph of the family and a few column inches about the boy's leukaemia and how they were going out to America to help save his life.'

'I'm not really sure I can remember you telling me about that Eric. Look what is this all about? I'm getting a bit confused here.' Sally sensed her brain swirling and becoming disconnected from her surroundings.

'I'm nearly there Sally. Are you all right?'

Eric jumped forward to grab hold of the woman's slight frame before she was about to crash to the hard floor. The commotion alerted the two volunteers to stop what they were doing in the back room and race to the shop area.

'What's happened to her?' called one of the women seeing the strange man turning Sally's limp body to the recovery position.

'No panic, she's just fainted. Can one of you get a glass of water? She's coming round,' assured Carter.

A volunteer turned to obey his instruction and shot off quickly into the back room. Amidst the sound of running water the other shop assistant's voice was heard to be questioning Carter.

'What happened? What did you do to make her faint? You didn't attack her did you? I think I should phone the police.'

'Don't be so damn stupid, I'm her friend, Eric Carter, I'm a reporter from the *Bladdington Bugle*. We were just having a chat about the run on Sunday when she suddenly started to faint. And no bloody wonder, how warm is it in this place? You can't breathe. Can you open the door to let some fresh air in?'

She saw the sense in his request and gingerly stepped around the crouched reporter to pull the door ajar. A cool blast rapidly swept away the stale, warm dry air helping to revive the fallen patient.

'There you are Sally,' coaxed Carter pressing the glass of clear cool water to her lips.

She sipped slowly while hearing Carter encouraging her to take it slowly.

Gradually her vision cleared, but confusion still reigned in her eyes.

'Where am I? Who are you? What am I doing on the floor?'

Her senses had become inexplicably disorientated and for those few frightening moments, her mind registered she was in the company of complete strangers.

Observation Ward 3, in the A&E department at Bladdington hospital, was to be Sally's next destination.

Meanwhile Eric Carter had volunteered to take on the task of contacting Bruce McCoy. This was, and for him at least, much more important than the other pressing matters he had planned to fill the rest of the day with. However, he was somewhat niggled thinking was it something he had said that caused her to collapse or was it plainly an underlying condition already delicately primed to leap from its dark hidden recesses?

When he'd received no response to his hard rapping on the door at the McCoy's home, a close neighbour told Carter he had seen Bruce load a set of tatty golf clubs in to his car around twelve. That clue was enough for Carter to find McCoy taking practice swings on the golfing range. Fifteen minutes later they were both at the Bladdington A&E admissions enquiry desk.

McCoy was permitted to pass through the double doors to access Ward 3, while Carter struggled to find a seat in the packed noisy waiting room.

After hurriedly introducing himself to the ward desk nurse, he soon learned everything was fine with his wife. The nurse left her seat from behind the ward reception desk to walk close by his side past rows of symmetrically arranged beds until they came to one which had the light blue curtains drawn around.

A discrete opening was made by the nurse large enough to permit them both to get to the bedside.

'I thought you said she was okay, nurse. Why is she not awake? She looks dreadful,' he said in a panic.

'Don't worry Mr McCoy, the doctor has given your wife a thorough check and he found no suggestion she might have received a blow to the head. He believes it was most likely a very deep faint. This can happen to anyone, especially if you are of a build similar to your wife. I'll wake her for you.'

He nervously watched on as the nurse gently rocked the slumbering patient's shoulder. A sense of relief flooded over him as he saw Sally's normally crystal blue eyes slowly appear in the slits of her opening lids and was then able to recognise one of the two people standing over her.

'Bruce, what are you doing at home?' she enquired drowsily and obviously disorientated.

'Darling, we are not at home we are in a hospital.'

Sally was totally thrown by what he had said with her expression changing to one of fear as she took in the alien surroundings.

The nurse placed a warm hand on to hers to then say calmly, 'Don't worry Mrs McCoy, you had a faint at the shop and it was thought wise you should be taken to hospital to have a precautionary check.'

'I'm all right aren't I? I need to get back to the shop they can't manage without me!'

'Forget the bloody shop Sally, our priority is to make sure you are fit and well,' snapped Bruce.

At that point, the nurse suggested she should leave to allow them both to have some privacy.

'I'll be back in about ten minutes, the doctor should have decided by then what he is going to do.'

'Before you ask Bruce, I don't remember a thing of what happened at the shop, it all just seems a blank.' Sally had said once the nurse had gone from the bedside.

As a result of their frank talking behind the privacy of the drawn screen, Sally had reluctantly agreed to tell the doctor about her suspicions she was showing the first signs of dementia.

Bruce assured Sally her car would come to no harm being left parked on a street overnight in the centre of Bladdington before she reluctantly agreed to be taken straight home from being discharged from the hospital.

The Mondeo estate pulled up in the drive around seven, with Bruce turning the key to let them both into the cold house, empty of welcoming voices. Sally headed straight for the dark kitchen and after flicking the light switch, she tossed the letter addressed to her own GP on to the black granite work surface.

'Some good that will do,' she said, with Bruce catching the sound of her moaning as he followed her through.

'Please, come on Sally, the doctor did say you are doing all the rights things to help with your condition,' he said encouragingly. Bruce was not only happy she had at last broached the taboo subject with the A&E doctor, he was glad too she had not been kept in for observation overnight.

'Oh, that's it then is it? We have to refer to this thing as a "condition".

No longer am I a woman, or a wife, I'm somebody else, someone who is no longer loved or even valued as a human being,' she responded staring daggers in his direction her pupils widely dilated.

Bruce stood slightly shaking his head quite stunned at the self-destructive language his once confident, razor witted wife had used to describe her current self.

'What do you want me to say then? We can't just ignore everything and never talk about it you know.' He then paused for a moment to watch his wife turn her face away from him. 'I love you Sally more than anything or anybody in this world,' he continued, 'I want to keep the same you for as long as I can, is that so wrong for me to want? I have thrown away too many precious years not being around you and I realise I can never get that time back, but I'll tell you something my dear, I'm determined what we have left will the best time of our lives.'

Any lingering doubts about her husband's loyalty and love for her, had been dispelled in those passionate words and moreover, relief she would not be abandoned when the time comes to face up to the uncertain but real obstacles ahead.

At last, Sally was able to free her tense body of all the emotions she had bottled up for so long. Her outward show of tears prompted Bruce to call her to come over to his opened arms to receive his warm, loving and safe embrace.

'I'm sorry Bruce I didn't mean to be so cruel,' she sniffled hard into his bony chest. 'It's so hard to bear. I know you and the doctor mean well. I'll have to take all the treatment and advice in good spirit, and of course, I'll always have you beside me,' she said looking up to his face to catch a reassuring smile.

'Don't you ever worry my dear; I and everybody else will always be there for you.'

He stooped his head to place a soft peck on the end of her small nose.

'There now, you go and sit down, turn on the telly and I'll make us something to eat. Any preferences?'

'No, anything will do thanks.'

Bruce stayed in the kitchen while Sally first checked her look in the hallway mirror using a balm tissue. Satisfied, she then made herself comfortable in the lounge.

Chapter Thirteen

Her sleep was to be dreamless and black. It was like her brain needed to have a deep undisturbed rest to enable itself to get things back in order after the trauma of the previous day.

She was eventually woken by her legs sensing the duvet being pressed down. Her eyes opened to focus on a blurred image placing a tray loaded with tea, orange juice and freshly grilled buttered toast with complementary preserves resting precariously on the duvet top.

Over the impromptu breakfast Bruce had said at some time in the day they would have to go into Bladdington to collect Sally's car.

'I hope it's not been damaged Bruce, I love that car.' she said in a worried tone.

'Well if it has, then the insurance will cover any damage or theft.'

'Oh, don't say it might have been stolen,' panicked Sally.

'Enjoy the breakfast, most things in life don't turn out as bad as you expect.'

'I hope so Bruce.' she replied not too convinced it was true what he'd said.

Bruce gathered the plates, cutlery and jars back on the tray to leave Sally to sweep away the coarse toast crumbs from the duvet top and any other tiny bits that may have found their way onto the mattress sheet. She later showered and dressed while he sorted out the mess he'd made in the kitchen preparing breakfast.

The front door bell rang just as Sally reached the bottom of the stairs leading into the hallway.

'I'll get it,' she called.

'Okay,' said a voice from the kitchen.

Turning the brass latch the door opened to show a delivery man struggling to hold a vertical tall square box which had the words: "Golf Heaven" printed along its entire length.

'It's for a Mr McCoy. Please sign for it.' The young man said impatiently while thrusting an electronic signature machine with what looked like a dangling pen hanging from one of the sides.

'What is it? We haven't ordered anything,' she queried.

'Doesn't "Golf Heaven" printed all over the box give you a BIG clue, Mrs?'

His reply was not only deliberately sarcastic, but the look he threw her would indicate he thought the woman to be thick.

Sally was not sure what she should do next because something in her mind seemed to have pressed pause.

'Hurry up Mrs, I haven't got all day,' he angrily pressed while thrusting the machine at her again.

'What's the problem?' enquired Bruce appearing at the door next to his wife.

'There's no problem mate, I just need you or your missus to sign for this parcel so I can get on delivering the other five hundred or more, I've got in the back of the van.'

Bruce grasped the dangling electronic stylus and scribbled a mark across the signature screen.

'You need to watch your manner young man.' Bruce said to the delivery man after handing back the machine.

'Whatever.' he replied snatching at the signature device. He then turned to head for the van still with its engine running without glancing back.

No sooner had the rude delivery man stepped into the driver's seat the dirty white panel van sped off with a rear wheel spin with the driver hanging out of the door window making a thrusting single finger salute as he headed for the next delivery address.

'What an obnoxious man, he deserves the sack,' said Sally after Bruce had hauled the heavy package into the hallway.

'What was that all about Sally? This is the set of golf clubs you ordered for me on the internet a couple of nights ago.'

'I don't remember ordering anything. It must have been you, Bruce.' She looked him straight in the eye to back up her conviction he was the one who'd done the ordering, not her.

'I never use the computer, never mind order stuff. You don't remember do you, Sally?'

'Let's not talk about it Bruce, if you say I did the ordering fine, let's leave it at that, and we were having such a nice morning.' Sally walked smartly away from him and similarly stepped up the stairwell heading to the bathroom, the sound of the door being bolted showed she had arrived.

Bruce accepted this was exactly the sort of thing that was going to happen with increasing regularity, it wasn't her fault, it was just her "condition" and he decided it would be wise for him not to bring it up when she eventually appeared from the bathroom's temporary sanctuary.

Later, Sally observed her husband's beaming face, while totally unaware of her presence, practising his swing in the lounge using his new golf clubs.

'Do you like them, Bruce?' she said breaking his concentration.

'Like them? They feel brilliant, much better than Dick Starr's old set. Thanks Sally for getting them for me,' he said, while taking yet another imaginary swing at a golf ball.

'Tell you what,' he continued, 'let's go and collect your car then we will go to the golf club for something to eat and after that you can watch the master take a few swings on the range with my new clubs,' Bruce suggested with a wide smile and twinkling eyes. Sally looked upon him to see how unusually enthusiastic he was about his new found sport and couldn't help hoping inside his interest would develop and his addiction to alcohol would become less so.

'Sounds good to me, you get the clubs in the car while I'll get ready.'

Thankfully, Sally's car parked close to the charity shop was found to be unscathed.

The lunch at the golf club proved to be excellent after which Bruce was then able to try out his new clubs while she relaxed in the bright afternoon sunshine. A more or less perfect day had been enjoyed by them both.

Back at home that same evening, Bruce received a phone call from Dick Starr to see if he fancied joining him for an early doors drink.

'Is that okay with you, Sally?'

'Go on, I know you are dying to tell him about your new clubs. I've really enjoyed today Bruce, thank you.'

'And I have as well.' He stepped up to her to hold her warm slender body in a tight embrace, 'I love you Sally McCoy,' he said holding her gaze.

'And I love you too, Bruce McCoy.'

She listened for his car to leave before going in the study to see if any more news had come from America.

There was no new message. She felt a sense of disappointment there had been no update on the young boy's progress as she would have expected at such a critical stage in his treatment.

Maybe he has been so involved in Wilson's treatment and there had been little or no chance for him to get back to her.

Pressing the compose message icon a flashing cursor in the dialogue box seemed to be encouraging her to start typing in some text. Her fingers hovered skimming over the keyboard whilst her thoughts concentrated on what she should type. A finger dropped on the 'D' letter to signify the beginning of her first return communication:

Dear Barry,

Sorry, I don't feel I should be bothering you at such a critical stage in Wilson's treatment. I have been praying your dear son will be blessed by God's guiding love through the skill of the doctor's hands. Let the good Lord surround you and dear Debbie with his divine presence so you can feel his warmth and comfort at this most difficult time.

I look forward to your next message.

God bless you all. Sally McCoy.

A quick read again over the text was enough to satisfy her she had been able to express her sentiments using the minimum of words. An audible click was heard in the silent house to signal the message had gone from the screen.

Sally was sitting in one of the soft leather armchairs in the lounge reading a magazine when she noticed the appearance of the front porch light illuminating against the closed lounge curtains. Next, she heard the front door latch mechanism being operated, then a slamming to of the door. Footsteps falling on a hard ceramic floor concluding with the metallic sounds of keys being tossed on to the granite work surface.

'I'm home.'

'So I hear and see Bruce. Did you have a good night?'

Bruce reached for the remote control from the arm of her chair to turn on the TV in his urgent quest to see what the football results were. He answered her while standing rather unsteadily fiddling with the remote buttons:

'Yes, had a great night, Dick's always a good laugh, he mentioned those two young officers we saw in one of the photographs taken at the end of the run. I couldn't believe it you know.'

He stopped at that point, his concentration focussing on trying to make one of the remote buttons work.

'You couldn't believe what Bruce?' It was plain for Sally to see he'd had a few too many drinks.

'Those youngsters are detective sergeants and they are not even thirty yet and what's more, neither of them have done any plod work worth talking about. The criminals must be bloody laughing!'

He spoke no more with his attention being drawn to first reading and then paging over to see all of the night's football results showing across the screen.

'I don't know why you let it bother you, Bruce. You've had your time and done more than your bit. Leave it to the younger ones to take over. This is our time together to enjoy.'

Bruce having read the results important to him switched off the TV and put the remote back on the arm where he had first found it. He turned to the other armchair occupying the room to slump heavily into its soft comfort.

'Yes. I suppose you are right Sally.' he sighed. 'It just doesn't seem fair, though. I had to have the shit knocked out of me on many occasions and not only that, I had to prove time and time again that I was worthy of being considered for a chance to get into the CID.'

Sally started to read her magazine again leaving Bruce to mumble on to himself. Soon she heard the familiar sounds of his snoring. Around ten thirty they were both tucked up in bed.

The following morning, as usual after opening the shop, her routine was to check for any new emails needing her immediate attention. A carefully manicured and subtle red varnished finger nail ran down the long list on the monitor screen searching to see, in particular, if there was a message alert from *Face2Face*. This check revealed there were none.

The two part-time volunteer assistants punctually arrived for nine. They had heard about Sally's collapse requiring a precautionary trip to the hospital. On meeting her in the back office they initially made a kindly fuss of the returning hero and only after seeking firm assurances she was up to doing the job, the shop returned back to normal with a hissing sound of the steam iron at play complimented by the ringing of the shop till and the regular tinkling of the doorbell.

Around mid-morning the area manageress called in at the shop unannounced. On first impressions, the woman was pleased to find the place busy with customers and the displays all attractively presented. She noticed Sally behind the counter trying to serve a gathering queue while looking somewhat frustrated with the cash till. A call to one of the assistants working in the back room resulted in Sally stepping aside to allow a woman to take over the operation of the till. The same person then continued to deal with the build-up of queuing customers up to the point when the shop was empty, bar one. It was only then the woman left the till to continue sorting out the new charity donations delivered that morning.

In the relative quiet and privacy of the empty shop the area manageress strode up to the counter to re-acquaint herself with one of the charities most valued employees.

'Hello Sally, how are you this morning? I thought I'd just call in to see how you are managing.' She held her hand out for Sally to shake. It was to be another one of those unscheduled moments when her mind seemed to shut off all routes to her normal memory.

Sally reached for the stranger's hand to give it an unsure loose shake. Her mind registered that she must be acquainted with the person broadly smiling in front of her, but no matter how hard she tried, she could not make the connection they both shared. This was a time to fudge.

'Yes, I'm fine, thank you for asking,' Sally confidently breezed.

'Was there a problem with the till? I know we have had them in for just over a year. I would have thought everybody should be familiar with them by now.'

'It's been such a busy morning, the shop has been bursting with customers and on top of that we have had to deal with people dropping off bags full of charity donations and of course van deliveries from the main depot. It all takes time to sort the good stuff out from the rubbish. The three of us haven't had a moment to ourselves.'

The area manageress did not touch on the business about the till again much to Sally's relief. Her thoughts had switched to the need to recruit an assistant manageress alongside her continuing failed efforts to employ a new manageress to replace Sally.

'Well I have to say Sally, this shop is the most successful in the group, and that my girl is down to you and your band of volunteer angels. Also, I'm thrilled to say, the 10k run you organised not only raised a great deal of money but made more of the public aware of the charity's work. Did you see the full page spread in the *Bladdington Bugle*? That would have helped our cause tremendously. We cannot thank you enough, Sally. Hopefully we will soon have someone suitable to take over your job, but in the meantime if you need any more help I'll see if we can draft in another volunteer, or maybe I can roll my sleeves up and give the occasional hand,' she offered from the heart.

Sally's thoughts, however where not quite the same; 'No chance, I don't want you snooping around telling me how to run my shop, no thank you.' She quietly mused.

'I think we will be able to manage, but thanks for the kind offer,' replied Sally.

The area manageress held her hand out again for Sally to shake which she did with a little more gusto this time.

'I'll detain you no longer; I can see you have much work to do. I'll pop down and see you again next week. Hopefully we should have some news on the post being filled. Goodbye Sally, goodbye girls.'

The two workers in the back room called out, 'Goodbye.'

Sally let out a long sigh of relief as she watched the woman pass by the shop's display window and disappear down the street.

And then, as if from nowhere, the woman's name and significance came to mind.

'Roz Sanders, the area boss, why couldn't you remember her name you damn fool,' she cursed herself.

Sally took the necessary remedial action to console herself. 'If Roz Sanders was unhappy with me then that's just plain tough. I have given more than 100% to ensure the success of the shop and if she did not like what she saw, the answer is simple- get somebody else in to do the fucking job.'

It was so unlike Sally to have thoughts and feelings of this nature. Maybe it was purely down to her own frustrating problems that she felt this way or was it a fact of reality soon she herself would become a customer and her hard dedicated work as the shop manageress and successful fund raiser would be forgotten in the midst of time?

Chapter Fourteen

At the same time the area manageress was meeting with his wife, Bruce was eating a round of toast and marmalade while scanning through the new car classifieds in the *Bladdington Bugle*. He'd woken up that morning with the idea to start to look around the local main car agents to see what models they have in to tempt him.

He later dumped all his breakfast dishes in the sink, put his jacket on and gripping the rolled up newspaper he'd been reading over the breakfast table, collected his car keys and set off primed with a mission to seek out, what was to be to him, the most special car purchase of his life.

Sally arrived home at her usual time to find her husband sitting at the breakfast table flicking through a glossy car brochure with further publications produced by other "desperate to sell" manufacturers covering the table surface.

'Didn't expect to see you in. No golf today then?' said Sally casually.

'I thought I'd give it a rest, my shoulder is a bit sore from swinging the clubs,' replied Bruce while making a rolling motion with his alleged injured shoulder.

'Been looking at cars then I see.'

'Yes, bloody expensive some of them are, but if I can get a good part exchange price for the Mondeo I suppose it won't be too bad. Can't take it with you. Strange how everybody seems to be saying that to me. Maybe they know something I don't.'

'Don't be daft Bruce it's just the sort of thing people say when they know you have come into some money and you are of a certain age. Nobody means any harm.' Sally laughingly assured.

'I suppose you are right. Anyway, in order for us to have a car with the newest registration the salesmen says it is better to wait till the end of the month. But if I plunge in now with the current reg, I will get a good discount. What do you think we should do Sally?'

In awaiting her response, Bruce drew his attention from an airbrushed picture of a scantily dressed model draped across the bonnet of a car to gaze up at his wife.

Sally's thoughts however were not on cars. She was mentally calculating the amount of money remaining in their account after the two big internet withdrawals. She felt self-assured the money would be back in the account by the end of the month - after all Sproston had promised her faithfully this would be the case.

'Leave it so you can get the new registration. You may save a few pounds but I know you Bruce, you'll only complain later that you wished you'd hung on those extra few weeks. Just be patient.'

'Yes, you are right, Sally. I'll wait.'

Sally left the kitchen to hang her coat up leaving Bruce to select another car brochure from the others strewn across the table.

An hour or so after tea, Bruce announced he was nipping out to see a man who he knew to be in the second hand vehicle trade.

'I don't know much about cars, Sid will be able to tell me which makes or models to avoid, I don't want to be left with a pup when we come to change it in a couple of years.'

He kissed her on the cheek and left the house with a stash of the brochures stuffed inside a plastic supermarket bag.

Around eight thirty she made herself a mug of hot chocolate and sipped at the steaming contents while sitting in the comfy chair facing the blank computer screen.

It was after tapping in the computer password she had previously written on a slip of paper, she noticed in her email in box a notification from *Face2Face*.

She placed the cursor over the internet link contained in the email message, pressed the mouse and in a fraction of a second was on home page of *Face2Face*. The same password was used to open her account to see an awaiting communication from Barry Sproston.

For that moment her mind was a complete blank as to who this person could be. Only after reading his latest message and the pleas he'd previously sent did some of the memory blocks dissolve. Gradually the lines to her memory cleared allowing her to make sense of what she had become involved in.

She reread his latest message while performing a quick mathematical calculation in her head.

Hi Sally,

Your unbelievable message of hope touched both of our hearts. Sadly we are not able to give Wilson your love as he has fallen into a coma. The doctor warned us there would be a chance of his immune system rejecting the donor's marrow due to the blood match being very close but not perfect. Wilson is back in mortal danger and his only chance now is to be put on medication which costs £3,000 a day for a period of five days. If that fails to work then we have lost our son. There's even more, the donor has now fallen ill and had to be admitted to the hospital's high dependency unit. The doctors say this is because the man was in poor physical health when he volunteered his marrow for transplant. This will put on additional care costs which the administrators reckon will be around £5,000.

I cannot believe I am asking-no pleading, if you can find it in your generous heart to send us the £20,000. The hospital will not start treatment until they have received the money in their account. I know the insurance will pay when they receive the final bill. If there was to be a problem I would sell my house to pay you back. You are our only hope Sally.

Love Barry, Debbie and Wilson xxx

Her eyes were filled with tears of sorrow. How cruel and heartless it would be for her to withdraw her support on being presented with such a life or death situation. Sally felt immediately compelled to send a message back to the tragic Sproston family:

Dear Barry,

I cannot tell you how much my heart hurts for you. All I can do is pray to God he will come in your hour of need and deliver your son back to you in good health. I have sent you the £20,000 and trust you will transfer it to the hospitals account. I am sorry Barry, but this is the final amount of money I will be able to send you and moreover, whatever the outcome I will need the money back from your insurers by the end of the month.

I apologise for being so blunt.

My thoughts are with you always. Sally.

The return communication was sent followed by her shutting down of the computer. Picking up her cup of cooling hot chocolate, while being careful to avoid any spillages on the keyboard, she dazedly made her way to the lounge to finish her usual bedtime drink.

What was strangely now occupying her attention in the quiet room, were the colourful recipes printed in a freebie supermarket magazine. Her mind had closed off from the dramatic events which had gone on in the confines of the study only a few moments ago.

Bruce was to be late and Sally would get into the cold bed by herself.

A bright ray of sunshine piercing a gap in the drawn curtains concentrated on Sally's face causing her to awaken earlier than usual. Bruce was still asleep and breathing heavily and did not stir from her movements getting out of the bed. She screwed up her nose at the strong stale smell of whisky hanging in the atmosphere while she collected her fresh clothes to take to the main bathroom to then have her usual shower.

The shower rose had been adjusted to direct shooting warm water directly into her face to try and snap her out of a deep tiredness she was feeling. Her sleep had been fitful and disturbed. Much of the reason for this was due to Bruce tossing and turning for the early part of the night but mostly it was because of the nature of her dreams.

Sally had dreamt she was back again trying to patiently feed her dementia ridden mother in the nursing home. Her mother's face looked angry and refused to take the food offered to her on the heaped spoon. She kept on shouting at Sally to get out of her room and accusing her of taking her belongings. Sally had pleaded for her to calm down and to take her food. Her mother at that point in the dream snatched hold of the plate from her grasp and sent it spinning across into the closed door of a single wardrobe in the side room.

The commotion had alerted an uncompromising looking heavy built uniformed woman to enter the room brandishing a large syringe filled with blue fluid. Her mother let out a shriek seemingly aware of what was to happen next, her hands reaching out hoping to find refuge in her only daughter.

'Don't let her do anything to me, please save me Sally.' her mother had pleaded in a whimper.

'What are you doing, get that thing away from her,' shouted Sally aggressively.

The injection wielding nurse paused to look at Sally through pitiful eyes.

'So you want me to stop do you? Take a good look, I mean a real good look at the sad person you call your mother, trapped with a useless mind in that soiled bed, that will be you sooner than you think.'

Sally turned to stare at the cowering pencil thin creature attempting to hide behind one of the hard pillows. She was distracted from her horror by the nurse moving closer up to her side.

'I know what I could do, I will give you the injection instead. You haven't long to go, and you would spare Bruce from seeing you in this way.' she said mockingly while pointing at the pathetic fragile figure who was once her strong, generous and lively mother.

'Come on put your arm out, Sally. I'll be gentle, it won't hurt, just a little prick then it will be all over,' she assured.

Sally cast her eyes again to look at the slip of humanity she once recognised and so loved. She did not want to end up like that, she'd rather circumvent the dreadful plans the grim reaper had cruelly got in store for her.

The nurse appeared to possess the unerring power to access the deep recesses of her mind whilst she stared at the once hard features transposing into that of a beautiful angel surrounded in a bright light.

Sally was unable to put up any resistance, when offering her arm for the nurse to roll up her sleeve to expose a vein. She watched the woman fit the injection into the grip of her fingers and move to position the sharp silver needle tantalisingly close to the white skin pulsing above a blue raised vein.

'It will be over soon Sally, for you there is to be no long suffering. What I'm giving to you is a gift of love from all of those you have so unselfishly helped. When I have injected you I will release your poor mother and you will then be free to walk in the light at the side of your mother and father.'

Sally watched the needle painlessly entering into the raised vein followed by the movement of the plunger to evacuate the blue contents into her bloodstream.

'It won't be long Sally.' These words echoed around her head as she drifted off to sleep.

Eventually her eyes slowly opened to see two hazy figures approaching her in the blinding glare of a bright light.

'Your home Sally, we are a family again,' her dream induced mind recognised the voice to be that of her father's and the figure standing holding hands with him was her dear mother.

Before she was able to throw herself to seek succour in the warm embrace of her long deceased parents, she had been awoken from the emotional dream by the piercing morning light streaming through a narrow gap in the drawn bedroom curtains.

Sally kept on re-running the vivid dream through her head while the warm shower gently sprayed her face and body.

The drive to work too did little to detract her uneasy mind from that distressing dream. Scenes of her dementia tortured mother she once thought had been suppressed were clearly still lurking just below the surface.

By the time the car was parked in its usual spot along the street Sally had made a solemn promise that she would take steps to end her own life before being unable to save herself from falling into a world of lost souls.

Her day went on to consist very much the same as the previous. There would be peaks of complete clarity; then followed by unexplained troughs of confusion. However, she was acutely aware each passing day brought with it a subtle decline in her cognitive and motor functions.

Others working with her at different times of the week were able to witness Sally's unexplained mishaps and sometimes odd behaviour. From one time being able to perform like a whirling dervish, Sally was now often covertly watched by the daily changing team of volunteers so they could readily be at hand to help her or provide proper assistance to a customer. Similarly, when she was out of earshot, one or two of the regular customers had begun to gossip to other shop staff about her sometimes confused manner.

The time was fast approaching for Sally to have the need to take a daily cocktail of drugs, however, the letter given to her at the hospital remained in her hand bag. She still clung onto the vain hope that keeping fit, solving mind puzzles and eating the so called right food would pay off in the end. Alas, there was to be no slowing of the speeding juggernaut hurtling down on her.

Following her normal routines, Sally saw there was nothing in the email in box to give rise for any concerns that morning and really, she did not expect to receive daily updates from the Sproston family during this critical five day treatment period.

By the early evening of the third day there had been no further communication received in her *Face2Face* account. Sally had grown understandably anxious for news and decided she should send the family a "thinking of you" message, hoping also it might provoke a return update on the success of the treatment.

A sincere but brief message was composed in the dialogue box. Satisfied that her sentiments were not too over the top, she clicked on send. She stared at the screen expecting the message to disappear which was then normally followed by a large red tick to confirm the message had reached the receiver's account.

Neither happened, what instead followed was a screen pop-up that read the Sproston account was now closed and therefore was no longer open to receive any more messages.

Sally thought she must have simply made a mistake somewhere in the transaction process. She anxiously dropped down a fresh dialogue box and re-typed in the same message. Clicking on send, she leaned back in the swivel chair confidently expecting this time, that the same pop-up message would not reappear. Her senses rang out in alarm to see the identical message again flickering on the screen informing the reader the account was closed. She tried again another three times only to achieve the same result.

It was inconceivable for her to believe Barry Sproston would have closed his account at such a critical stage in their relationship. Convinced there must be a malfunction at the operator's end of the system Sally sent an email to the *Face2Face* members' enquiries department querying the closure of the Sproston's account. She received in seconds a polite standard return email stating the requested information would be sent within twenty-four hours.

Sally's mind began running away with all sorts of imaginings until it was broken by the sound of the front door closing and a familiar voice calling, 'I'm home. I've got us some supper, fish and chips.'

From the corner of her eye, Sally watched her husband head for the kitchen. The sound of plates being removed from a pile stacked in the cupboard followed by the unwrapping of paper indicated she would soon get a call to join him. She quickly closed the computer down switched off the study light and followed the appetising aroma coming from the kitchen. Bruce was already tucking into his meal before Sally had been able to sit in her usual place at the table.

'I'm not really hungry Bruce, I've had my tea.' She said looking at the pile of chips and a jumbo sized battered haddock roughly assembled on a white ceramic plate.

'Get it down you girl. This will do you good, much better than that rabbit food you live on,' Bruce encouraged with his mouth full of steaming chips.

'I'll have some, but I won't be able to eat it all.'

'Eat what you can. What have you done while I've been out?' he asked without a break in his words. The couple went on to talk about their individual evening's events, with Bruce being the more excitable of the two, while they dined on the unexpected supper.

'Right, I'll clear away, you go and sit in the lounge and when I've finished I'll bring you in a nice cup of tea,' said Bruce after he had demolished all of his meal and most of what Sally had left.

'Sally, can you come to the kitchen please,' called Bruce about seven minutes after she had made herself comfortable in the lounge.

'What is it you want?' she enquired while reading an article in the *Diet and Health* monthly.

'Just come to the kitchen please.' he calmly reasserted.

She left the settee placing the opened magazine where she had sat and impatiently rushed to his command.

'What is it Bruce?' The back of her husband was preventing her from seeing what was drawing his attention on the table. He stepped to one side to reveal what he was looking at.

'What's happened here Sally? I only found the bits when I emptied the chip paper in the waste bin. They're our new debit cards, why have they been cut up?'

Sally stared at the two debit cards formed from the gathered cut up sections from the waste bin.

'I have no idea Bruce; I've definitely not done it. You must have cut them this morning when I was at work.'

'The post hadn't arrived by the time I left the house today. You must have cut them up while I have been out this evening.'

'No it wasn't me. Why is everything always me, hey? If it's not you it's those bitches at the bloody shop having a go at me and making me feel a fool!' Her face contorted angrily as she spoke.

'Look Sally I'm not having a go at you, you have made a simple mistake, you're certainly not the first to have cut up the new cards instead of the old ones. I'll nip over to the bank tomorrow and order two more,' he said in an effort to calm her down.

'I did not cut the cards, you won't listen will you, nobody listens to me anymore. Do want you want, I don't fucking care.' She then turned to leave the kitchen, ran up the stairs and into the bathroom leaving Bruce with his mouth agape at not only her disproportionate response to the cutting of the cards, but on hearing the very first time she had used the "f" word.

At about the same time Bruce was calling at the bank to order new debit cards, Sally was reading from the computer screen in the shop back room office the return email from *Face2Face* customer services confirming Barry Sproston had closed his account stating no reason why he had decided to do so.

She understood from this moment on she had no way of contacting him and even more, had probably said goodbye to ever seeing Bruce's money back in their account. Sally felt rather odd at the situation, unperturbed in a sense, it was like her brain had lost the capacity to register the full implications of losing such a vast amount of money.

Over the coming three weeks her mind decreasingly attached little relevance to the financial loss as she continued with her personal struggle to cope with everyday routines she once was able to perform as second nature. The near daily change in behaviour did not go unnoticed by those around her.

Chapter Fifteen

The first day of the month arrived with Sally opening her sandwich box to start her lunchbreak at the charity shop. Taking a bite from the thick cut wholemeal sandwich, she found after a couple of chews the dry texture sticking to the roof of her mouth. Separating the two halves of the sandwich expecting to see some evidence of the tuna she had prepared earlier that morning Sally saw neither margarine spread nor a filling; she had packed just plain bread. The partly eaten dry bread sandwich was placed back in the empty sandwich box leaving Sally only the tomato juice drink for her lunch. While taking her drink, she was contorting her mind about how she could have done such a stupid thing as to not put any filling in her sandwich. Her self-berating thoughts were put to a stop when she heard the familiar sound of her husband's voice asking one of the volunteers to tell Sally he was in the shop. Before the volunteer assistant had left the counter, Sally was standing in the door entrance leading into the shop in full view of her husband.

'What are you doing here? I expected you to be at the golf club,' she said in surprise.

'Haven't you remembered Sally? It's the first day of the month, its new car registration day,' Bruce explained excitedly.

'Oh, right, I must have forgotten, sorry.'

'Never mind dear, get your bag and coat you are coming with me to collect our new car; I can't wait!' he said while rubbing his hands together in a gleeful action.

Sally looked at the assistant to say, 'Are you happy to be left to manage the shop by yourself, Sandra? We shouldn't be long'

'Go on, off you go. I feel so excited for you. We've always had to make do with old bangers now we are both pensioners, you are so lucky.'

Sally took on a crestfallen look as the woman's words made her feel ungrateful for what she had in her life.

'Get your things Sally, then we'll be off,' urged Bruce.

Sally snapped out of her sudden pity to quickly gather her things from the back room office.

The Mondeo was parked on the street near to the shop. It didn't take too long for Sally to notice he had been hard at work from the bright gleam reflecting from the car's metallic silver paintwork. Having got into the passenger seat she remarked on the state of the upholstery and carpets which appeared to have been deeply vacuumed and the dash wiped over with an orange scented cleaner.

'You have been a busy boy this morning Bruce, the car looks as good as new.'

'They gave me a good part exchange deal, but it was conditional on receiving my car in tip top condition, I don't think they will be able to find any faults, what do you think dear?'

His words went over her head; her mind had become somewhat troubled with something she was unable to fathom.

Bruce carefully guided the Mondeo into the Audi main dealer's forecourt to stop in a designated customer parking bay. They both strolled towards the large tinted glazed panel showroom to be met by a highly scented, portly salesman who was clearly expecting their arrival. He grasped hold of Bruce's hand like they were long lost pals and next moved on to Sally repeating the same with the addition of a sticky wet kiss on the cheek.

'Right come this way Mr and Mrs McCoy, everything is nearly ready. If you can let me have the Mondeo keys Mr McCoy then my colleague here can give the car a quick once over. Bruce dropped the keys into the open hand of the pin striped navy blue suited salesman, to be then passed on to a similar attired young man in his very early twenties holding a clipboard.

'I believe Mrs McCoy has not seen the car yet?' questioned the salesman.

'No, she hasn't, it's supposed to be a bit of a surprise for her.' said Bruce.

'Oh, how nice, well let's not keep the suspense going on any longer than necessary, please come this way.'

They followed the man to the far end of the show room where a warm breeze wafted in through a space created by the sliding open of one of the large glazed panels. An Audi A5 Quattro convertible sport car with a scarlet red bow tied around its midriff and positioned ready to be proudly driven into the outside world from the carpeted showroom.

The three of them stopped at the stunning white metallic car.

'I believe these are yours.' The salesman turned to face Sally offering her an Audi badged key fob. She turned to Bruce, a little confused, only to see his face beaming.

'Go on Sally, take the key, it's our new car. Isn't she a beauty, just like you?'

Her eyes looked up and down the car pausing at the loving touch he'd obviously asked the agents to apply, in the form of a red bow.

'Do you like the bow? I thought it would be different than having roses. Go on have a sit in it,' Bruce urged.

The salesman went on to show how to operate some of the more technical gizmo's and then left to allow the McCoy's to check the car over themselves while he busied himself with the paper work together with him making a quick mental calculation of the amount of commission he would get from the sale in his pay packet at the end of the month.

Soon the McCoys were sat in two comfy seats at a plush desk facing the blissfully happy salesman eager to sign off the deal.

'I'm pleased to tell you Mr McCoy we have allowed you £9000 on the Mondeo, the Audi is priced at £46,099. So if we do a little arithmetic, I believe the sum to pay, let's say in round figures, is just £37,000.'

Bruce reached to his trouser pocket to pull his wallet out. He laid it open on the table to retrieve his new debit card and passed it over to the smiling salesman.

'That will do nicely, Mr McCoy,' gushed the grinning sales man.

Bruce and Sally watched him insert the card in the card reader and then pass it over for Bruce to tap in his secret four numbers. The machine was then returned.

The salesman's appearance seemed to have lost its sunny smile as he lifted his attention from the card machine screen to face the McCoys.

'The machine won't accept a withdrawal from the card. There must be a simple mistake. Let's try again.' He tapped in the information again and returned the card reader for the numbers to be attempted again.

'I can assure you Mr Cordon, there is ample money in our account, my police redundancy and pension money have been in there for nearly two months waiting for this moment.' Bruce explained feeling strangely uncomfortable about the situation.

The machine changed hands but the result was the same. The salesman's initial smarmy charm appeared to have lost much of its earlier outward gloss. He then held his hand out to Sally who was clutching the key fob to say, 'I'll take them back please.'

She gingerly handed the keys back over to him.

'Here are your keys for the Mondeo, Mr McCoy, I suggest you get over to your bank and sort this out.'

And without as much as a handshake, he raised his portly body from the seat and honed in on a potential fat commission customer hovering around a lower market Audi A5 convertible.

The two exchanged no words while they swiftly vacated the plush showroom with heads bowed until they were both sat back in the confines of the Mondeo. Bruce turned to look at his wife peering at her as if trying to figure out who this stranger was in the car with him.

'What's the matter Bruce?' she asked calmly. Bruce replied with his voice raised;

'What's the matter? I can't believe you have asked such a stupid question. Christ Sally, I've never been so embarrassed in my whole life. There mustn't have been enough money in the current account to pay for the Audi. How do you explain that Sally? You are in charge of our finances.'

Feeling under pressure Sally raised her hands to cup her face to hide from his angry eyes. Bruce pulled her slim hands away from her face and retained his grip on her wrists to prevent her from doing the same again.

'Sally, come on you must know. Have you transferred some of the money into another account and not left enough in this one?'

Sally's eyes started to fill.

'I don't know Bruce, maybe I have, I just can't remember. Please stop pressurising me, my head can't stand it anymore.'

Bruce released his tight rough hold from her wrists for her to cover her face again from his glaring accusations.

What should have been an exciting and memorable occasion for Bruce had ironically only served to confirm he was gradually, but surely losing the woman he had grown into late middle age with. He pressed her no more; his heart suddenly felt heavy seeing her look so small and pitiful.

'Right, Sally get your seat belt on, we're going over to the bank to get this sorted out, it's probably their balls up any way. And I'll tell you another thing,' he continued to say while pulling the shining Mondeo out of the flag lined showroom forecourt on to the main road, 'if that fat bastard of a salesman, Cordon, thinks I'm going back there again after the way he treated us, then he's got another think coming! Christ, I tell you Sally, if I was back in the job I'd find some way to nail him, the ignorant tosser.'

She sat silent and motionless. His threatening words hadn't registered in her head and he recognised this; Sally would always have a go back at him if he used what she called "profane language". This time she was muted.

They arrived outside the Portshire Bank some twenty minutes later with automatic doors welcoming them into the open plan floor area dotted with executive style desks each having a suited bank employee seated opposite animated bank customers. They were guided to join a queue snaking to a customer services desk set in the middle of the open floor space. The queue gradually shrank till it was their turn to vent their spleen on the young woman who was obviously straining this late on in the afternoon, to hold her highly painted face in a false smile for much longer.

'Hello sir, how can Portshire bank be of service to you today?' she brightly enquired despite the lack of interest shown in her eyes. Bruce had got his debit card out from his wallet in readiness to hand it over at some stage during their visit to the bank.

'It's this card,' he said clicking the card hard on to the service desk, 'I have come here straight from making a failed car purchase. I witnessed my card being rejected twice. I know I have money in my account to cover the purchase, haven't I dear?' he turned to Sally to confirm this fact in front of the service assistant. Sally nodded.

'It was embarrassing to say the least,' he continued to say assertively.

'I'm sorry sir, what I will need to do is to check your account's current financial status. It could be that the problem is at their end, it's not unheard of for that to happen,' she patiently explained.

Her dainty French manicured finger nails picked up the debit card from the desk top to then swipe it through the reader. Before revealing what was showing on the screen she asked the normal security check questions. Satisfied with the bank customer's answers, she was prepared to disclose the McCoy's financial details.

'In your joint current account Mr McCoy there is a balance of £18,700.'

'£18,700? You've got to be joking. There should be near to £100,000,' he responded in alarm. Others in the queue close behind also heard his stark reaction and the sums involved. Bruce twisted his head around to take in strange faces with their knowing looks.

'Something is seriously wrong here, and everybody can hear all our business. I want someone senior to look at this and in private please,' his bordering aggressive tone left the young assistant in no doubt he would have his demands met. As things sometimes happen, the branch manager had just finished shaking hands and wishing his goodbyes to a customer when the young assistant caught his attention. Being eager to fulfil the banks motto abounding the floor space he stepped smartly over to the enquiries station.

'Mr Titley, Mr McCoy here has a situation that may require your attention. His account seems to be short.'

Titley saw from the man's agitated body language, he needed to move any conversation they were to have elsewhere from the open plan area.

'Thank you Emma, I will gladly be of assistance to you sir, madam. If you will follow me please and I'll take you through to my office. Would you both like a coffee?'

The assistant had returned the debit card back into McCoy's safe keeping before the both of them traced the branch manager's steps to a closed door set away from prying bank customers. Once seated in the small room, Titley stepped over to the coffee machine.

'How do you like your coffees?' he pleasantly asked.

'I think we will give the coffees a miss thank you. I just want you to look at our account please because there is something seriously wrong.' Bruce was agitated at the man's relaxed blasé demeanour, especially when the subject was about a life changing sum of money missing from their account.

Titley was quick to measure up the man's mood and placed the card cup back in the stack alongside the coffee machine to sheepishly move to take his place in the executive style seat facing opposite the bank's clients.

'Right, let me introduce myself, I'm Bryan Titley, branch manager, pleased to meet you both.' He stretched his hand across the table to shake each of their hands.

'I understand there is a problem with your account Mr McCoy. What seems to be the matter?'

Bruce went on to explain what had happened at the Audi dealership and his subsequent shame of being found to be short of funds.

'How do you think we looked to those people? I bet they had a real good laugh at us when we'd left the showroom.' Bruce was still irked when he replayed in his mind the images of the salesman's podgy, jowly face sneering at their predicament, even if he had missed out on a swollen pay packet.

'Well I am sorry you went through such an awful trial, but let us have a look at your account details. Can I have your debit card please?'

The card was lightly gripped between index finger and thumb while he carefully tapped in the account digits. This done he spun the flat screen monitor around to face the anxious customer's scrutiny.

'Your account is showing £18,700, is that figure not correct then?'

'It certainly is not, is it Sally.' He glanced to his right to secure a signal of confirmation from his wife but all he saw was a look of bewilderment.

'How much do you think should be in there, Mr McCoy?'

'Mr Titley, I can assure you there should be at least £100,000 in the account. I have recently retired from the police and the settlement figure I got has been in for well over six weeks. Sally was still deciding how best we should invest some of the money, but leaving around half of it to buy a car of my, or rather, our dreams. That's right isn't it Sally?'

Sally sensed Titley's gaze too falling upon her while awaiting a response. This jerked her into giving a rather jittery, but decidedly, unconvincing answer,

'Yes, yes, that is correct.'

'Have there been any large purchases or such?' he enquired further.

Bruce was becoming agitated at the man's slow approach in attempting to establish the reasons behind the money not showing up in their account.

'Far from it for me to tell you how you should do your job Mr Titley, but wouldn't the account history, say over the past six weeks for instance, tell us where the money has gone?'

'I was just getting to that, you must have read my thoughts Mr McCoy,' replied Titley defensively.

'Well the sooner you get the detail on the screen the sooner I will know what has happened to my money,' McCoy pressed coolly.

'Yes, yes, I'm doing it right now.' Titley pressed a function key to display on the screen the accounts activity history.

The unexpected spread of alarming figures struck Bruce dumb while he listened to Titley recite from the screen what he could clearly see for himself.

'There has been some very large withdrawals, let's see, yes, there is one for £22,000, another for £40,000, a £20,000 and another for £400. It would seem the large sums have been on-line banking transfers to the same account in America and one an internet sales transaction.'

Before Titley was able to probe further into the McCoy's banking activities, Bruce had made his mind up what had happened.

'It's clear, we've been bloody robbed, someone has got into our account and siphoned off the money. I knew it, I said all along I didn't like this on-line banking stuff, but she said it was safe and the bank would cover us for any losses if anything did happen. It doesn't look so bloody safe now does it Mr Titley? And it looks like you have got a lot of money to pay back to us?' Bruce peered across the table with arms folded to strike a defiant pose.

'Don't be too hasty in blaming the bank, Mr McCoy,' Titley suggested calmly.

'What do you mean? It's clear the bank is at fault. We've sent no money to America, why would we want to do that?'

'Well it would appear your wife may know the answer because according to our records she used her own on-line account to sanction all three transfers to a Mr Barry Sproston.'

'Bullshit, she doesn't know a Barry Sproston, do you Sally?' he argued while turning to her for confirmation.

She meekly answered him with her head kept low to hide from the inquisitive glare of the two males.

'I don't know Bruce. I can't think straight, I hope I haven't done anything terribly wrong. Please Bruce can we go now? I don't feel well.'

'Sally what have you done? Come on I need an explanation now,' he demanded loudly.

Sally then unexpectedly stood up causing her seat to fall back hard on the carpet. Her features had dramatically changed in a split second from a person who had looked beaten and confused to a figure staring and itching for a fight.

'Don't you dare shout at me McCoy, I'm not one of your prisoners you think you can beat a confession out of. I don't know what has happened to your money and what's more I don't even care. I'm getting out of here and don't bother coming after me.'

Both men were aghast at witnessing such a sudden transformation in the woman's demeanour. Before Bruce could rise to his feet Sally was rushing through the open plan bank floor space and heading for the automatic doors to eventually disappear amongst the busy street shoppers.

Amidst the confusion, Bruce switched his mind to thinking how quickly his world had crumbled since blissfully cleaning out the car that very morning. It was like he'd entered a surreal existence where things he once accepted as being normal were now turned on their heads. How much more misery will this particular day want to pile on him before it was through. Titley's voice stirred him from his temporary melancholy.

'I think the best thing I can do at this moment is to print you a copy of the bank statement to take home with you. If it is proved the bank was at fault then, of course, your account will be reimbursed. In the meantime my staff and I will conduct a thorough investigation into your account's transactions which will likely throw up some answers. Should we agree for us to meet tomorrow, say for ten o'clock, so we can discuss the matter further?'

'Yes, I think that is a good idea. I'm sorry you had to witness my wife's out of character behaviour. She has not been too well lately and I think it all became too much for her. I'll see you tomorrow then Mr Titley.'

Bruce left the office with the printed details sealed in an envelope to go in search of his absconding wife.

McCoy was soon back in the bright day light outside the bank building, standing on the tips of his toes and craning his neck to scan between shoppers busily going about their business on the pedestrianised street, desperately trying to catch sight of his wife.

How his whole being really wanted to shout out her name in the hopes of capturing her attention. The idea was easy to dismiss, strangers milling around innocent of his distress would think him crazy if he resorted to such tactics.

After a few moments he moved off to check in the shops along the street and it was only after he noticed an Oxfam shop did he come to think she may have made her way back to the "Dreams Come True" charity shop.

He broke into a fast walking pace anxious to get to the shop as soon as he could, but the closer he neared the more worried he became about what sort of state he would find her in.

The door activated bell sounded and as he entered the shop, which was unusually void of customers, he was greeted by the same woman volunteer he'd earlier met when collecting Sally.

'Hello Mr McCoy, I didn't expect to see you again so soon, you look out of breath, have you been running?' she was prompted to ask after noticing his face was flushed and beaded with sweat.

'Is she here? Is Sally here?' he pressed, ignoring the content of the woman's observations.

'Whatever is the matter Mr McCoy? Of course Sally is here, she arrived about fifteen minutes ago.' she replied.

'Where is she then, I need to see her now,' he demanded.

'She's sorting bags of clothes in the back storeroom.'

Bruce pushed past the startled woman to the open door behind the serving counter to enter the office part of the building. He scanned the small empty room to see there was yet another door leading from the office. He twisted the handle to step into an area filled with wheeled clothes racks, bric-a-brac and bulging black bin liner type bags piled high towards the ceiling. Beyond the black mound he spotted Sally facing away from him nonchalantly emptying the contents of one of the bags on to a sorting table.

He stepped carefully towards her wary she may still be angry and upset.

'Hello Bruce, what are you doing here?' Sally had picked up the sounds of falling steps approaching her. Her face lit up to when she turned to find it was her husband.

Before he was able to utter a word, he heard the sound of the volunteer's voice call out from behind him.

'Are you all right Sally?' asked Sandra worryingly.

'Of course I'm alright Sandra, why shouldn't I be?' Sally answered while thinking what a strange thing to ask.

'Right, okay then, I'll get back to the shop.' The woman turned to return to the counter.

'What was all of that about? She knows you are my husband.' Sally said when the woman was out of earshot. Bruce was too stumped to give her an answer. He then watched while Sally went back to sifting through the contents of the bag, humming some inane tune, like he was not even there.

He could see there was no point in raising either of the incidents with her. Sally would deny any knowledge of what occurred and more importantly to Bruce, he did not want her to have another dramatic episode which only seemed to make her withdraw further into herself.

'I can see you are very busy here, Sally,' he said in an attempt to strike up some sort of conversation.

'Yes, you could say that, just look at that awful mountain of bags I've got to sort through and Susan in there isn't much use,' she said nodding her head disdainfully in the direction of the shop. Bruce had heard Sally call the woman Sandra earlier. Ignoring this detail he said to her he needed to go and see about updating his mobile phone.

'And don't worry about tea, I'll call and get one of those ten pound meal deals, it is not worth the fuss making anything else. Right, I'll be off then, I'll see you later, Sally.'

He lingered for a short while to watch her gather up a black collection bag, then to rip open a large hole to allow all of its innards to cascade on to the sorting table. She continued to happily hum the irritating tune he'd not heard before, and he never did get a "goodbye" from her.

'How is Sally, Mr McCoy? She looked rather strange when she got back this afternoon.' Sandra enquired while moving out of his way from behind the counter.

'She's fine thank you. I think she probably works too hard here. Goodbye!' he replied very business-like. He wasn't prepared to get in to any conversation concerning his wife's welfare, the chances were he'd only be repeated and would only serve to fuel the idle gossip abounding the place.

Back on the streets, he hurriedly strode through the milling shoppers to return to the car park. With each of his rushed steps he could feel one of the corners of the tucked away bank envelope jabbing away at his chest. His main concern was not about the sharp reminder of the envelope's presence; the account statement secured inside of it would inevitably be the cause of much longer lasting and greater pain.

He was glad to toss the offending envelope on to the passenger seat before embarking on the drive back home. A short detour to call in at the supermarket to pick up a meal deal he promised to get for tea was to form part of the journey home.

While browsing the supermarket aisles, the need to later partake in a proper drink led him to supplement his basket with two litre bottles of blended whisky which were on at an irresistible offer.

The items were placed on the conveyor belt for the checkout operator to scan through and place into plastic bags.

'That will be thirty pounds exactly please sir,' cheerfully requested the young female operator.

Bruce removed his credit card and slipped it in to the card slot and tapped in his numbers. He then realised this was the card he used more or less all the time for transactions and not the debit card that was tucked away in another slot in his wallet. Sally had always been at pains to tell him to only use the credit card when a fee is not being passed on to the customer for its use. The debit card is linked to the current account and is used in shops and certain supermarkets who will only accept debit cards and for making cash withdrawals from ATMs.

'Why did she keep so much money in the current account for so long?' he pondered while the girl was tearing off the till receipt.

She broke the pattern of his thoughts on hearing her brightly say, 'Thank you sir, I hope you have a nice day.'

'Thank you for that, because it couldn't possibly get any worse for me,' he replied giving her a reciprocal smile while gathering the two filled bags one in each hand.

Passing along the row of busy checkout stations he became full of worrying thoughts not just about the potential loss of over £80,000 but more to do with Sally's deteriorating condition. Recognising he possessed the investigative skills and had access to police contacts when it came to dealing with likely fraud, but coping with Sally's situation, now that was a different story. He felt impotent, unskilled and strangely cut adrift from her and it would mostly be down to others, not him, to help slow her degenerative descent.

'A penny for them' were the words he heard to disturb him from a near trance-like state.

'Dick, what are you doing in here?' McCoy cried in surprise.

'I might want to ask the same question of you. Is this it now, highlight of the week shopping at Marks?' DCI Dick Starr was filling in his day off with the necessary bit of shopping when he'd noticed his friend nearing the supermarket's revolving exit. He managed to stop him in his tracks before leaving the building.

'Have you got time for a drink, Bruce? The café is just there.'

Bruce pulled his sleeve back to check his wristwatch.

'Yes, why not, Sally won't be home for another hour or so. I promised I would make tea for her.'

'Wow, you have soon fallen in to the little house husband, I bet you have started to wear a pretty apron too. If all those hard nuts you put away over the years could hear this they'd think you'd grown into a right Jessie.' said Starr jokingly.

'Well what about you with those yellow marigolds you've got sticking out from the top of your bag?' replied McCoy teasingly.

Starr put on the pretence of looking around furtively checking if he had been seen by a member of the underworld.

'You don't think I've been spotted do you Bruce?' said Starr pushing the rubber gloves from view while feigning an anxious manner.

'Come on you old dog, let's go and get those coffees,' laughed McCoy.

They strode side by side giggling like school boys making their way to the café.

'You find us a place Bruce and I'll get the coffees, and here, take my bag as well please,' said Starr passing over his single shopping bag.

Bruce located a table away from the few customers already in the café. He tentatively placed the three shopping bags against the wall so the contents would not spill out on to the carpeted floor. Seated at the table he took the opportunity to get his mind in some form of order, he was desperate to share his burden with another soul.

Five minutes of relative mind relaxing solitude was disturbed when he saw Starr with two coffees perched on a tray anxiously looking around trying to see where he was to sit. Bruce raised his hand beckoning to where he was. Starr spotted him and hurried forward being careful not to spill some of the contents of the two cups in the tray.

'Sorry Bruce, the tray is as slippery as hell and I couldn't help the coffee slopping over the tops of the cups.' said Starr as he placed the dripping cups on the table.

'Don't worry, I've done the same many times when I've got the coffees for me and Sally,' empathised McCoy.

Before another word was spoken the two men took an eager sip from their cups.

'Bloody hell, that's hot!' cried Starr pulling his lips away from the brim of the cup.

'What do you expect you silly sod, it's just come out of the machine,' laughed McCoy.

'Well how's it going then Bruce lad?' enquired Starr while blowing cool air across the surface of his steaming hot drink.

'To be honest Dick, until today, everything was going great,' he replied watching the twirling vapours rising up from his coffee.

'Why? What's happened today, Bruce?' Starr easily read from his friend's demeanour something had served to rock him.

'I really don't know where to start Dick,' he replied in a solemn tone.

'Try the beginning Bruce, it's always the best place,' encouraged Starr.

Over the next ten minutes or so, McCoy spoke about his excitement at the prospect of collecting the new car, then the disappointment and shame at the show room followed by the shock of being told he'd lost most of his redundancy and pension lump sum from their account.

'Christ, Bruce, what a nightmare!' gasped Starr.

'That's not all Dick.' McCoy expressed in a resigned manner.

'What, there's more?' Starr said in an unbelieving tone.

'Yes, it's Sally, she's away with the fairies Dick. No, no, that isn't fair of me to say that.' he said eager to retract any misunderstanding concerning her condition.

'She is showing the early signs of dementia type symptoms, her mother and her mother in turn suffered badly for years with the same illness. The bank manager reckons it was Sally who had sanctioned the on line transfer of money from our account to a person in the name of Barry Sproston, in Florida.'

'Florida? Why would she want to send money out there? And more to the point, who the heck is Barry Sproston?' quizzed Starr.

'God knows, this is something I desperately need to challenge Sally about but she seems so fragile at the moment I'm afraid of making her illness even worse. But the fact of the matter is, the money is no longer in my account and like a pair of bloody fools we saved very little and lived our lives spending mostly for today. We thought the pension lump sum I would get combined with both of our pensions would be enough to allow us not to have any real money worries. That's all changed now. The worst case scenario is we'll just have to sell the house and downsize and get money that way.' Bruce could have also mentioned that at some stage in the near future he'd have to find residential nursing costs for his wife's care. The very thought made him shudder.

'I'm so sorry for both of you Bruce. This should have been the time of your lives. You have both worked bloody hard and deserve to enjoy what retirement brings.' Starr said with genuine feeling.

'I've not given up on getting the money back. No way. If I can prove to the bank our account has been somehow infiltrated then we stand a good chance of getting it all returned. The bank printed me off an up to date statement this afternoon and Titley, the bank manager, says they will urgently conduct their own investigations and he will be in a better position to tell me more when I meet with him tomorrow at ten. But I have to say Dick, I'm not optimistic.'

'You must let me know what goes on Bruce. This very well could result in a police matter and it has happened on my patch.' Starr reached out to place a firm hand on McCoy's left shoulder and shook him warmly and encouraged him further by saying, 'Let's try and look on the bright side, the chances are this time tomorrow, the bank will have it all sorted and you'll be able to get back to enjoying your life again.'

'I do hope so Dick. It's must have been fate to meet you today, I feel so much better now I've been able to talk to somebody I can trust, you know what it is like to be a copper Dick, we don't have many true friends to turn to when there is a crisis in our own lives.'

'Yes, I suppose you are right Bruce.' he replied while making a mental note of how few people he could count on as being true friends; less than a handful.

Starr gathered the coffee cups containing only the cold left over dregs and placed them back on the wet tray to give a nonverbal sign it was time to part company.

'I think it is time to go home Bruce so you can get the tea on, you don't want to be on the end of a real bollocking when Sally comes in if it is not ready on the table,' Starr said teasingly.

'I'll give you a ring tomorrow sometime to let you know how I've gone on. Fingers crossed, hey,' Bruce stood facing Starr making the same finger gesture for good luck.

'Yes, fingers crossed.' replied Starr copying the same marker sign for good luck.

After shaking hands their respective plastic shopping bags were first gathered to leave the cafeteria and then finally they exited the supermarket through the revolving door to go their own separate ways.

Chapter Sixteen

The chive cream cheese filled chicken breasts wrapped in streaky bacon along with honey and rosemary coated roast Maris Piper potatoes were cooking in their individual silver foil containers on the middle shelf of the oven on a moderate heat. In the microwave sat the mixed stem broccoli and mange tout awaiting a press of the start button to begin a three minute cooking cycle. Chilling in the fridge was a lemon zest cheesecake and a bottle of Italian Pino Grigio white wine.

Away from the kitchen Bruce relaxed the best he could in the lounge sipping a large whisky poured from the litre bottle he'd bought that afternoon. The alcohol allowed his stressed mind to loosen off some of the tight knots that hitherto stubbornly prevented him from thinking clearly. Lying open on one of the settee cushions was the A4 size statement printed by the bank's manager. The regimented printed words and figures shown in their respective columns informed him nothing really except to be reminded of the life changing sum of money that was now so obviously absent from his account. He understood he'd have to question Sally about the missing money, however, if she volunteered the information freely herself he would be saved from being accused of interrogating her just like one of his criminal suspects. In order of importance he relegated the money issue below the need for her to seek and receive medical support. Taking a gulp from the crystal whisky tumbler signalled he'd made up his mind after the meal he would persuade her to make an appointment to get her the best medical help the NHS can offer. But first he would have to question her to see if she had received any response to the hospital's letter she'd promised to drop off at the doctors' surgery.

Bruce noted by the grandfather clock in the lounge, Sally was about fifteen minutes later than usual by the time he heard the front door key sliding in to the lock. He'd made sure prior to her arriving home he'd stored away the incriminating bottle of whisky followed by swilling out and drying the drinking glass and had it sat back in the crystalware display cabinet situated in the lounge. He stood in the kitchen listening carefully to all the familiar sounds marking her homecoming. She saw him awaiting her appearance wearing a broad smile.

'I've got the tea on, as promised. Have you had a good day?' He moved to her to gently press his lips on hers. He may as well have kissed a pillar of concrete for all the affection she gave in return. This was not like Sally, and furthermore her face looked deeply worried and confused.

'Everything all right Sally? You look a little bothered, is there a problem at the shop?'

Bruce braced himself as it seemed to him, nowadays he was unable to predict how she would react to such a question. Her response was not immediate. She seemed too concerned about an old crack in one of the hall floor tiles butting up to the kitchen opening.

'I don't know Bruce; I had a strange thing happen to me on the way home tonight ...'

Bruce interrupted her in mid-sentence. 'Look come and sit at the table, everything will be ready in a few minutes and you will be able to tell me all about it then.'

The microwave start button was pressed, to then allow three minutes for the food to be taken out of the oven and served up on the warmed plates followed by the wine being poured into two high stem glasses. The veg was finally served to fill the remaining space on the plates.

The first mouthfuls of the meal had been eaten when Bruce prompted Sally to finish what she had earlier started to say before he served up.

'I don't believe I'm saying this,' Sally said facing her husband having carefully placed her knife and fork back on to the plate.

'Saying what my dear?' Bruce did the same with his own utensils.

Her head now bowed she recalled what had happened to her.

'I got lost on the way home from work tonight, for the life of me my mind went completely blank. I just didn't know where I was. It was dreadful. I couldn't even think what our house looked like, Bruce. I didn't know what to do, I was panicking. I pulled over and had to totally relax and clear my head then out of the blue it all came back. I thought I'd lost my mind.'

A large tear trickled down her cheek momentarily pausing at her jaw for her husband to then watch it falling on to the shiny table surface making a large splash. He pushed his chair back to leave his side of the table and stepped to the back of her to give an assuring hug. She continued to talk while he held her in his embrace.

'Bruce, I don't like what is happening to me. It wasn't only just getting home tonight, there was something else today. I know what happened was serious and I somehow know you were involved. What did we do together today, Bruce?'

He released his arms from around her shoulders to go back to his chair and from across the table linked eye contact with her. This was not the right time to start some in depth analysis of their situation. Sally needed to relax, enjoy the meal, have a glass of wine and later in the evening would be a better time to find answers to their combined current problems.

'We'll talk about things later, hey Sally, lets first enjoy this lovely meal I've been slaving over all day, I've also prepared a lemon cheese cake that is to die for. Oh, and I didn't tell you did I? I bumped into Dick Starr today ...'

Sally continued with her meal and appeared to have perked up and even laughed a little when listening to some of the true and not so true yarns from his past dealings with criminals and rogue police officers.

The dish washer was loaded with the few plates and utensils cleared from the table. Sally collected their still partly filled wine glasses and moved to the lounge for Bruce to join her after his chores. Bruce then dealt with the unenviable task of carrying out to the wheelie bin the near to bursting waste bag carefully prised from the kitchen peddle bin. When he was just about to lift the lid on the wheelie bin the kitchen waste bag burst sending the mixture of card, food waste and tea bags down his trousers and all over his suede shoes.

'Fuck, fuck, fuck!' he cursed under his breath while taking in the unappetising mess he now stood in the centre of.

With the lid of the wheelie bin raised enough to permit the dripping ragged remains of the peddle bin bag to be dropped and signed off with yet another verbal curse.

His next task was to retrieve the shovel and yard brush from the shed to clear away the remains of the bag spillage from the bin storage area followed by a change of trousers and shoes. Later a fresh bin liner was fitted inside the peddle bin and while cleaning his soiled suede shoes over the kitchen sink he made a solemn promise to himself he would never allow the peddle bin to get that full again, ever.

What he'd expected to have taken only five or six minutes had been stretched to twenty or so by the time he was able to join Sally in the lounge where he noticed she had nodded off. He thought to disturb her sleep would not be fair, even though he'd probably had one of the most testing days of his personal life, he considered it trivial when compared with what the future held for Sally.

Gently, he closed the lounge door to leave her to rest for a while in the calm of the still house. In the meantime his attention had been drawn to the open door leading into the study and soon was sitting at the swivel chair which was mainly occupied by his wife. Around the plastic trim of the seventeen inch monitor screen were stuck a number of Post-it notes each having been scribbled on with messages, simple words or numbers. While reading the nature of what had been recorded on the notes Bruce sadly recognised this to be an *aide-mémoire* gallery to be further evidence of Sally's declining mental capacity.

While scanning the stuck on rectangles of paper in a clockwise direction his pupils suddenly froze at a particular note then followed by his fingers reaching up to sharply snatch the slip from its low tack bond on the plastic surround.

'Barry Sproston, I don't believe it!' he angrily hissed to himself after reading the very name of the man who was now in possession of his hard earned money.

As he folded the note in half and slipped it in to his trouser pocket he wondered if Sally had recorded her login name and password on one of the same coloured slips. Systematically he scoured the remaining stuck down notes, to eventually pause at a different coloured note than the others, bearing Sally's login details.

The noise of the lounge door handle being lazily turned indicating Sally had stirred and being anxious not to cause her any more distraction than necessary, Bruce swiftly got from the seat and was out of the study and in the hallway before his drowsy wife was able to form any suspicions.

'What have you been up to Bruce? I thought you said you were coming in to the lounge after you had cleared the kitchen,' she said blearily rubbing one eye.

'You won't believe it Sally, the bloody peddle bin bag burst just as I was about to lift the wheelie bin lid. The stuff went all over me and on the path, so it has taken me a while to clean everything up, get changed and put in a new bag. When I'd done all that I noticed you had fallen asleep so I left you alone to have a little peace.'

'I have told you before not to let the bag get too full, it's not the first time that's happened on you, it serves you right, McCoy,' she laughed.

Bruce was pleased to hear she'd remembered the other times the same thing had happened also she looked and sounded in better spirits.

'I'm going upstairs to change now I need to get out of these clothes. I won't be too long.' She passed him in the hallway to get to the oak stairway, having first planted a soft kiss on his dry lips and said that was for making her such a lovely meal.

'Thanks Sally, but I really didn't do much you know, it all came out of a box,' he replied rather sheepishly.

'It's the thought that counts Bruce,' she replied taking to the stairs.

He watched until she had turned right on the landing to then walk a short distance along the landing to get to the bedroom. The sound of the door closing prompted his re-entry to the study to remove the note with her login details from the screen trim. As with the previous note, he folded it in half so that the sticky strip bonded to each other.

Bruce was sat on the settee watching the television with a full glass of wine perched in his hand when Sally eventually joined him in the lounge dressed in her pink fluffy dressing gown.

'You've been a while dear,' he said not taking his attention from the reality TV programme playing on the screen.

'I thought I'd have a shower, is that all right with you sir!' she responded sharply.

Bruce swung his attention from what he was viewing to look at her having taken up an aggressive stance.

'Sally I honestly didn't mean anything when I said that, come here and sit next to me and I'll give you a cuddle,' he appealed to her while trying to defuse her unreasonable anger. Her response to his request wasn't immediate. She fixed him with a stare and Bruce in return did not divert his glance away from her.

'Come on dear, sit next to me, this is a right laugh watching these idiots, I've topped your glass up so we can just sit and relax for the night.' he semi-pleaded.

Without saying another word she moved to sit beside him, he threw his arm around her neck to pull her in closer, where she meekly followed while showing no sign of resistance.

They both watched the remainder of the programme with no conversation between them, the only sounds heard were of his laughter alone.

The morning showed Sally to be her complete self, but this was not unusual for her at that this time of the day. Bruce too had made sure he got up at the same time, purely to put his mind at rest that she was both mentally capable to drive and cope with the demands the shop would place on her that day.

'I may pop in to see you later today Sally, I'm going into town to look around for a pair of golfing gloves,' he phrased in such a way careful not to raise her suspicions.

'That's fine, but I may not be able to stop and chat, there is so much stuff to sort out. Goodbye then.' A quick kiss on his stubble cheek was to leave him watching her from the house entrance getting into her car on the driveway, reverse and head down the avenue to work. When she was out of sight he turned to go back in the house armed with the intentions to tidy away from breakfast and at the same time, hoping she doesn't forget how to get there.

After he completed the chores, a call made to their doctor's surgery was luckily timed for him to be given a cancelled appointment for twelve o'clock that day.

It wouldn't be too long before his mind switched from worrying about Sally to thinking what he will learn at the ten o'clock meeting at the bank.

Two minutes to ten, Bruce presented himself at the customer services desk to inform a cheerful young assistant of his appointment to see the manger.

'I'll have to leave you for a moment sir, so I can tell him you have arrived. I know he is expecting you.'

While she was gone, Bruce looked uneasily around at the different large printed boards boldly advertising the bank's products.

She reappeared accompanied by Bryan Titley. After the customary handshakes McCoy was lead again to the same office where they'd first met the previous day.

'Take a seat Mr McCoy, would you like a coffee?' Titley enquired.

'Yes thank you, white and two sugars please.'

'Mrs McCoy not with you today then I see?' he said during the pouring of the hot water into the two card cups.

'No, she is the manageress at the 'Dreams Come True' charity shop. They are apparently so busy, she didn't want to take any time away.'

'Yes, I know of the charity, I took part in the 10k fun run a few weeks ago, and I can tell you Mr McCoy I don't know how anyone can call that fun, I ached for days after I can tell you. Well here is your coffee,' he said gingerly handing over the hot floppy sided card cup. They both took a sip from their respective drinks before Titley recommenced the dialogue.

'You will have noted from the account statement there really wasn't much information to go on except for the amounts drawn and when, how it was drawn and an abbreviated destination code.'

'Yes, that's right,' replied McCoy.

Titley then slightly turned to focus part of his attention to what was showing on his PC monitor. He ran his finger across the bright screen checking he was sure of his facts before he spoke.

'We can now tell you the three sums of money were sent as an on-line transfer from your wife's internet account and received by The East Seaboard Trust Corporation Bank in Miami, Florida to an account held by a Mr Barry Sproston. Do you know of any reason why Mrs McCoy would want to transfer money to this person?'

'I have never heard Sally mention this man, nor can I think of any logical reason why she would possibly want to,' he calmly replied. He wasn't about to say a yellow slip bearing the same name written across it had been recently removed by him from his wife's monitor screen. 'Could the account have been hacked into and the money drawn off that way? Being an ex CID officer I know we have departments specially trained in investigating this type of crime.'

'After you left yesterday, I informed the bank's fraud team and they have since looked closely at your wife's account activity. They could see no evidence of the security being breached by hackers or other groups normally associated with this type of theft.'

'So what you are saying Mr Titley, is that my wife operated on her own free will in making these transfers.'

'Yes, that would seem to be the case.'

'Can the money be transferred back from the bank in Miami?' McCoy earnestly pressed.

'The fraud team have contacted the East Seaboard bank to discover the account to which the money transfers were paid into only opened recently by a British national we understand to be Barry Sproston. Apparently his credentials satisfied all the banks personal fraud and validation checks before being sanctioned to hold an account in the USA. From the account records the sum of $10,500 was drawn using different ATM machines in the Miami district in $500 sums and from the dates shown the withdrawals were made most days over a three week period.'

'What about the rest of the money, can the bank get that returned?' pressed McCoy understanding that the money drawn in cash was definitely lost.

'Hang on there is more.' butted in Titley, 'Whoever this Barry Sproston character purports to be, he must have expensive tastes. He made purchases from a jewellers totalling just over £50,000, that amount would be easily gobbled up even if the person bought just one Rolex watch, or a couple of cheaper Omegas. An unscrupulous shop owner wouldn't be bothered to ask any questions about the amount of money being spent, especially when paying by debit card, as long as the funds are cleared when the transaction is made, that is all he is bothered about. Where the cash comes from is of no concern to them. Either Sproston, if such a man exists, bought the items solely for himself, which I somehow doubt, or he intends to sell on later to get clean money. Who knows?' he said with the fingers of both hands clasped together as he lolled back in his executive chair.

'So by my reckoning that's just over £60,000 gone. Where is the rest?' McCoy could feel his heart pumping hard in his chest as he struggled to take in the full impact of what was being reported by Bryan Titley.

'The balance of £21,500 was divided into two separate lots with £11,500 sent by an on line transfer to a bank in England and the remaining £10,000 moved on the same way to a different account also in England. The day after the transfers were made the account was closed.' Titley reported sombrely.

'There must still be the account details held by the two receiving banks in England.' questioned McCoy.

'Yes, you are correct but the American authorities will not release this level of information unless the situation becomes an official police investigation instigated by the American or British authorities.' He replied. 'You are, or rather were a police officer Mr McCoy, and you will acknowledge the difficulty in tracking down the person or person's perpetrating this crime and they would have had over three weeks to cover their tracks once the money had appeared in those two accounts in England. My bet is that the money has likely been moved on yet again, maybe some drawn in cash transactions and possibly by debit card to make some expensive purchases to be sold on to innocent people to make cash. Unfortunately, I too get to hear of this sort of dreadful thing happening, but all banks are adept at burying unwanted attention which could create bad publicity for them.'

'So the bottom line is all my money has gone then?' said Bruce looking deathly white hardly believing the words leaving his lips.

'Seems likely, I think the only chance of getting some of the money back is if the person behind all of this gets caught pretty rapid.'

Bruce wasn't yet prepared to let the bank off the hook and silently racked his brains desperate to come up with a logical or legal reason to get the bank to accept some responsibility for the massive loss.

'Please correct me if I'm wrong Mr Titley, but my understanding has always been that banks have a mechanism for checking large cash movements in and out of personal bank accounts and anything they see as suspicious they contact the customer, that's right isn't it Mr Titley?'

He looked square in the face of the bank manager who appeared to remain stubbornly calm amidst the gravity of the proceedings.

Reading from the information shown on his monitor Titley was about to present a confident answer.

'Yes, you are perfectly correct, the large sums of money received into your account a couple of months back originated from two payment transfers from Bladdington council and the police pensions scheme. A member of the bank's admin team recorded on file they checked your age Mr McCoy and understood one payment was for severance of service in the form of redundancy and the other was from police pensions in settlement of your lump sum payment. Also we have a recorded message from when your wife answered the phone confirming you had taken retirement and she too advised the bank there would be one or two large transfers out of the account for the purpose of future investments. Furthermore, looking back over the past ten years your account regularly shows large sums being withdrawn for what appears to be payments to car dealers and holiday companies. Maybe one could rightly argue greater scrutiny and vigilance in your account dealings could well of have prevented some of the loss taking place, but the pattern of your account use had been noted together with the fact Mrs McCoy had previously warned us large sums will be withdrawn at some stage, most then would reasonably agree nothing unusual happened which should have alerted us. I assume you check your account regularly Mr McCoy, did you not notice the money had disappeared?'

Bruce picked up his coffee to finish off what was left, and then disposed of the empty cup in a waste bin partially filled with other used cups. Sheepishly he went on to respond to Titley's query.

'I'm embarrassed to admit Mr Titley; I have always left all the money dealings to my wife, so I never had any reason to check our accounts. As long as I had cash in my wallet and the credit and debit card worked when I needed to use them, money available to buy new cars and foreign holidays twice a year, I was content to be blissfully ignorant of my wife's financial management.'

'Have you asked Mrs McCoy about the on-line transfers and who this Barry Sproston guy might be?' Titley probed further.

'She isn't very well at the moment so I don't want to push her too hard on the subject.'

'When your wife is better, she might be able to provide some answers. My own feelings are you need to involve the police in this matter as soon as you can.'

Bruce had already decided to take this course of action before Titley had suggested it.

'Moving on to a different matter, I am on your records as being the principal account holder?' McCoy asked.

'Yes, that is correct,' he replied after checking the confidential account information on the screen.

'I want you to put a block on my wife's internet banking facility and to limit any withdrawals on her debit card to a maximum of £50 a day. Also while I'm at it, alter her credit card to a £300 limit but I still want mine to be kept to the same.'

McCoy observed Titley's finger tips move across the keyboard to make his requested changes to their different accounts.

'That's all done for you now Mr McCoy, I think you are wise to make these temporary changes until you have got things sorted out. The banks fraud department will continue to investigate your loss, but in the meantime I strongly advise you report the matter to the police to get them involved and we can then work closely together to hopefully bring this person, Barry Sproston, to justice.'

'I'll keep you no longer, I'm sure you are a busy man and thank you,' said McCoy taking to his feet.

'I'm just sorry we can't do more for you, no doubt we'll be seeing you again sometime in the not too distant future.'

Both men stood up to shake hands followed by McCoy leaving the office to make the journey over to the his doctor's surgery with Titley ambling over to the coffee machine to dispense, yet again, another caffeine loaded drink feeling relieved the sensitive meeting was over.

Chapter Seventeen

After acknowledging his arrival with the practice receptionist, Bruce selected two leaflets from the patient information rack before opening the glazed door to find a vacant seat in the packed waiting room mostly filled with elderly patients. While waiting for his name to appear on the LED patient information screen, he occupied his time to read the two leaflets, one of which was about dementia and the other was on available support agencies specifically for Alzheimer's sufferers. What struck him the most when scanning through the detail of both of the information leaflets there had been liberal use of images of really old people to somehow portray that these type of illnesses only impact on a certain age group. He pictured Sally in his mind while looking at a printed image of a grey, sad and wizened looking woman. He thought it so unfair his wife had become a victim of such a dreadful infliction as most would understand this is only something that was supposed to happen near the end of one's life. He folded the two A5 leaflets and slipped them into his jacket inside pocket and then sat impatiently with his arms folded fleetingly looking up at the red lit LED screen to wait for his name to start scrolling across the display.

After seeing a number of people rise from their seats pleased at last to have seen their name appear on the appointments board, soon it was to be his turn to walk through the same door to access the private corridor lined with one's chosen doctor's consultation room.

A knock on the door received a call for McCoy to 'come in'.

Bruce had been a patient of this particular doctor for twenty years. More recently his last visit resulted in him being referred to Bladdington hospital due to concerns relating to his liver. He entered the room to see the familiar face of his doctor quickly scanning over his patient's notes before the start of the consultation.

'Hello Bruce, please take a seat,' Doctor Jones welcomed cheerfully.

'Hello Doctor Jones, thank you,' replied McCoy making himself comfortable on the plastic steel framed chair.

'How are you? You certainly look better then you did last time I saw you.' enquired the doctor.

'Yes, I'm fine now, thank you.'

'Have you managed to keep off the drink?' Jones questioned while closely peering at his patient to detect for any outward signs of deliberate deception. Bruce understood he had to tell the truth, after all, he was once a copper and everyone knows the police don't tell lies.

'I've certainly cut down Doctor Jones, I've tried to cut it out altogether but I just can't at the moment.'

'Well Bruce, I'm not going to sit here and lecture you, as long as you keep your drinking in check I don't think you should have any serious problems in the near future. Later on in life, who knows what effect it will have had on your health. Anyway, I don't think you have come to see me about your drinking, what is it I can do for you today, Bruce?'

'I'm here to see you about Sally,' Bruce paused for a short spell before continuing,' I think she is suffering from dementia and it's getting worse. I have asked her to make an appointment to see you, but I can tell she is very reluctant to do so. This is why I'm here today. By the way did you get the letter from the hospital? Sally said she would drop it off at the surgery. She fainted and it was thought at the time she might have banged her head. She got the all clear, but while we were there we spoke to a doctor about Sally's dementia type problems. So we expected he would have made a note of his observations in the letter address to you.'

'No, sorry Bruce, I have not seen any letter from the hospital. Maybe Sally has not got round to dropping it off.'

'Hmm, I wonder,' said Bruce thinking it was more likely she had deliberately delayed taking the letter in.

'Tell me what you have observed to make you believe she is suffering from dementia?' asked Doctor Jones.

McCoy went on to describe recent incidents and her odd behaviour which had given rise to his concerns. While he was recalling the different events, Doctor Jones was partly occupied reading through the medical notes the practice held on Sally McCoy; being especially interested to absorb the details recorded in her immediate family's history.

After Bruce had exhausted what he could bring to mind, he and the doctor spoke generally about the effects both short and long term on dementia victims. Jones also mentioned family history could be another factor beyond the control of drugs but he was at pains to stress it didn't mean the situation was hopeless.

'She needs to make an appointment as soon as possible to see me Bruce. Treatment of this type of illness has come on leaps and bounds in recent years and the sooner we get her on a tailored treatment programme of medication and therapy the quicker we can give Sally her life back.'

'I do hope so doctor, I don't know what I would do without her,' he said choking on his words. He'd been able, up to this point, to hide his emotions but his inner resolve melted away to show he had become upset. Doctor Jones placed his hand on his shoulder in a comforting gesture.

'Just get Sally here Bruce, and then we can start to help her.'

'Thank you Doctor Jones, I feel after this talk there is a lot to be hopeful for. Thank you again.'

Bruce wiped away the wetness from his eyes with the back of his hand while striding across the surgery car park to his Mondeo.

'You silly sod, get a grip of yourself man,' he chided himself once in the privacy of his car.

Bruce McCoy considered himself to be the sort of person who had little time for those who weren't afraid to openly show their inner feelings. 'Only Jessies and women do that sort of thing,' he would often be heard to say when he'd previously witnessed such displays. Sadly, due to his own personal circumstances, he was now just only beginning to understand and appreciate some situations occur in life where it is nigh on impossible to fully contain a physical display of emotion from breaking out.

He'd soon have to switch his mind off from the deep re-evaluation process of self, to focus on getting his head straight in readiness to meet his friend, DCI Dick Starr, which was to be his next port of call.

Chapter Eighteen

On the way over to Bladdington police station, McCoy gave Starr a call from his hands free mobile phone. There wasn't much happening in and around Bladdington to urgently concern the police so Starr would be free to greet him, 'Just tell the desk sergeant you are there to see me and he will give me call.' Starr had said before McCoy terminated the call.

The car was left in a pay and display municipal car park near to the police station. Pushing through the public entrance heavy double doors McCoy strode over to an unmanned reception desk.

He then waited patiently for a while to be seen by the officer whose job it was to deal with enquiries from the public. Looking around he noticed a scruffy hand written notice next to what appeared to be a white bell push. He pressed the button once as per the written instructions. Another minute passed and still nobody appeared, so he pressed the button twice this time with longer bursts.

On this occasion the public bell alert system did its job by summoning the desk sergeant to his post. McCoy easily recognised from the middle aged man's stressed features he was not a happy bunny.

'Can't you read man, it clearly states ring once and not bloody twice. I've a good mind to tell you to go and come back later,' he spouted in a display of unreasonable anger.

No matter how hard he tried, McCoy failed to prevent an unfortunate grin from forming on his lips after witnessing the officer's oddly amusing, but pathetic and inappropriate methods he chose to deal with an enquiry from the public. The officer hadn't failed to notice the sudden appearance of a smirk on the person's face giving him eyeball from the other side of the enquiries counter.

'Find it funny do you mate?' questioned the pumped up desk sergeant.

'No officer, to the contrary, I find your actions pathetic and embarrassing to the good name of the police force at large,' calmly answered McCoy.

'I'm not having you speak to a police officer like that, I've a good mind to have you arrested,' he threatened.

'On what charge may I ask?' McCoy calmly enquired.

'We'll think about that when you are in one of the cells.' he replied with a grin.

The desk sergeant reached under the lip of the counter edge to press an alert button. Within seconds an obvious office bound male appeared with the white buttons of the police issue nineteen inch neck shirt positively straining to hold in his vast beer belly.

'What seems to be the problem officer?' the unfit, obese man enquired.

'This person has been very insulting towards me,' he replied in a pitiful tone.

'Oh, has he now?' said the desk bound officer.

McCoy in the meantime had re-positioned himself to having his back to the enquiries counter while the conversation between the two officers was going on.

'Please would you turn round sir, I believe you have been insulting to a police officer,'

McCoy turned to face his accusers with a certain look to show he was in no mood to be messed about with any more.

'Well blow me, if it isn't Bruce McCoy,' cried the desk sergeant's on-call support buddy.

Bruce peered closely at the smiling round jowly face features but struggled to bring his name to mind.

'I'm Jack Stones, don't you remember? We did our police training at Mirelands at the same time. It's not bloody fair, look at you, you've hardly changed at all Bruce.'

'Of course I remember you Jack, great rugby player I recollect.'

'Aye, that's right. I went on to be a member of the police "All England" rugby team. Great days they were,' he whimsically reminisced. 'What happened to you after we finished training?' he continued.

McCoy was anxious to meet Starr and was already frustrated by the unnecessary delays, he therefore decided to keep the conversation short.

'This and that, ended up being a DI, and I have been retired for the last couple of months. In fact what brings me here today, I have an appointment with Dick Starr, he's an old friend of mine. He must be thinking by now I've not turned up,' he said deliberately turning his head to look directly at the sour face sergeant.

His erstwhile friend was quick on taking up the hint. 'Right, sorry Bruce. Ralph, just go and find DCI Starr and tell him his friend, Bruce McCoy, is waiting in reception. Go on, hurry along,' he instructed clearly eager to make a show of his seniority.

The desk sergeant did as he was told but first threw McCoy a dirty look before disappearing to find Starr.

The desk sergeant had stayed out of sight after tracking Starr down. He had decided to eavesdrop from behind the enquiries desk partition, on the three men laughing and joking just like the coming together of weary dogs of war. The reception area later fell quiet on hearing the click of the electronic security door closing on the three noisy veterans.

Starr led McCoy to his side office away from one of the main open plan layout of desks and computer work stations.

'It must be bad news Bruce because you wouldn't be here now if it was any different,' Starr conjectured as he made himself comfortable in his seat behind the untidy desk.

'It would seem Mr Starr, your powers of deduction haven't waned despite your advancing years,' replied McCoy trying to make light of his situation.

'What have the bank said to you then?' quizzed Starr.

'The bank's fraud department contacted the bank in Miami and apparently this guy, Barry Sproston, claimed to be a British National and was able to open a USA account with the credentials he provided.' Before he could continue to further explain the bank's investigation, Starr had butted in.

'I understood a bank required at least to see a passport, a national insurance number and evidence of your employment status before they even considered allowing someone to open an account,' probed Starr.

'That's right Dick, but he must have had the correct documents with him at the time, be them kosher or counterfeit, to convince the bank officials of his authenticity. I cannot believe he would chance detection by using his own personal details, unless his name isn't Barry Sproston and the passport was in fact stolen or otherwise. But what puzzles me is how he got through the employment validation. They surely must have checked the details before sanctioning his application.'

'Quite,' replied Starr striking a pensive pose. Bruce took this as a cue to continue with his story.

'They said around $10,500 had been drawn by ATM, £50,000 spent at a jewellers, with the rest, about £21,000, being transferred using internet banking to two separate banks over here in England; a day later the account was closed,' explained McCoy dejectedly.

'Surely there must still be a chance for the American bank to contact the two in England and get the money transferred to your bank over here.'

'I wish it could be so simple as that Dick, the money was transferred to the banks over here more than three weeks ago and its bound to have been taken out of both accounts by now and most likely closed.'

'It looks like these crooks were careful not to be traced. And even if the accounts have been closed they wouldn't have been so stupid to open accounts using their true identities,' pondered Starr.

'They must have left a trail somewhere Dick, I don't think we are dealing with some villainous Russian internet scammers. My gut feeling is that someone, somehow got to know about Sally's deteriorating mental state and persuaded or even worse, God forbid, forced her to make the transfers. This guy Barry Sproston, I think is real, I don't believe for a moment that is his proper name and possibly with help of accomplices, has been successful in deliberately targeting Sally knowing she had access to large sums of money.' conjectured McCoy.

'Yes, I agree with you Bruce. It doesn't take much for a criminal mind to sniff out an opportunity to make easy money. At the golf club if you remember, Eric Carter took a photograph of you receiving your distinguished service medal from the CCC and he also wrote a bit of a spiel about you taking redundancy and your pension. It doesn't take much of a mathematician to add up what your pay-out might have amounted to.'

'Yes, you are right Dick. I suppose it was common knowledge to an opportunist prepared to take an interest in those sort of things. But how did they get to Sally?'

'Have you asked her anything about this yet? She is the one who is likely to hold most of the answers,' said Starr.

'The truth is Dick I'm worried to start quizzing her about what has gone on. I'm afraid she will go into a shell and make her illness even worse. I have to be patient and wait for the right moment to ask her.'

'The trouble with waiting Bruce, you know as well as I do, the more time we leave things the greater chance of the criminal getting away with it.'

'Yes, I know you are right Dick, but Sally is more important to me than losing the money.'

While McCoy looked rather distant in his thoughts, Starr was talking about getting the incident recorded on Bladdington station's books.

'Right, before we go any further we first have to get down on paper the full facts as we know them to be at this stage. I'll then go upstairs to see Palfreyman to get him to sanction my team to investigate the case.'

Starr left his office to search for the official forms used to record a reported crime. When he reappeared clutching the necessary sheets both men put their heads together to fill in all the details in the required spaces.

Satisfied they had covered all the main issues each then added their own signature at the foot of the last form. While Starr was quickly gathering up the completed sheets he told McCoy he'd call him later to let him know how he'd got on with the super.

Having guided McCoy through to the station's reception and bid farewell to him under the watchful eye of the peeved desk sergeant, Starr returned to his office to make a quick internal call to his chief super to seek permission to see him. This he reluctantly gave, but with a caveat he'd only got ten minutes at the most. Starr gathered up the completed crime incident paperwork, slipped his jacket on and then made his way to Palfreyman's office on the second floor.

Starr was duly summoned to enter the plush hotel specification office after he'd given a sharp short rap on the door, to see Richard Palfreyman giving his uniform coat a brisk stiff brushing.

'Going somewhere, Sir?' enquired Starr.

'Yes Dick, I'm in a bit of a hurry, it's the damn awful Mayor Making ceremony at the town hall and to top it all, I've had to cancel a game of golf so I can be there. What is it you want to see me about?' he said sounding ruffled.

'I have a matter that concerns Bruce McCoy.'

'Bruce McCoy? He'd retired the last time I heard, why should you want to see me about him? he questioned amid the continued sounds of bristle against serge.

'It looks likely someone, somehow has been able to get at his wife to remove £82,000 from their account. The sum was more or less what he got for his pension lump sum and redundancy.'

Palfreyman had removed the fluff free jacket from its wooden hanger and after slipping it on rolled his shoulders to adjust the fit to his liking.

'Seems to me Dick, it's the bank's problem and not ours.'

Starr went on to read out to him the points he and McCoy put on the incident report sheet including the outcomes of the meeting McCoy had had with his bank manager. Afterwards he explained the difficulties Sally McCoy was experiencing due to the onset of dementia type symptoms.

'It's my belief, Superintendent Palfreyman, someone or an organised group have deliberately targeted Sally McCoy. The banks have only limited powers to investigate what looks like to me to be a case of criminal deception and fraud. It should now become a matter for the police to investigate so we can force the bank's arm to provide us with more details about the origins and destinations of the account transfers,' concluded Starr.

Before Palfreyman responded to what he so far understood of McCoy's plight, he moved to face a wall hung mirror to start carefully grooming his thick grey hair.

'So what is it you want from me then Dick? I haven't got much time for any pussy footing about. I've got to get to the bloody town hall.'

'I would like to ask your permission to head a small team to investigate this matter further, Sir.' said Starr.

'We already have trained officers who deal with this sort of thing Dick, why would you want to get involved? Palfreyman pressed while peering at him for the first time from his plush seat positioned behind a mahogany dust free desk.

'I understand they are tied up in dealing with all the metal thefts currently running rampant in the area. No doubt Sir, you will get some flak from those councillors attending at the Town Hall later on today who are especially angry, and justifiably so if I may say, about the theft of bronze memorial plaques from the Cenotaph in Victoria Park. We also mustn't forget you haven't so far, been successful in making any arrests of those who were responsible for stripping the lead from around the roof of the town hall's stately ballroom. I believe it cost close to a million to have the water damage put right.'

'We haven't made any arrest yet Dick, let's get that right.' Palfreyman was keen to stress on the yet. 'But I'm confident my team can deliver, you wait and see Dick!'

It gave Starr a perverse sense of satisfaction to see Palfreyman rattled. He was bound to be grilled later that afternoon about his officers' perceived poor performance in combating the malicious and unethical stealing of metals on his patch.

While Palfreyman was distracted in running ideas through his head on how he could put a spin on the unsolved thefts, Starr spoke further to argue his case.

'During my absence Sir, you moved DS Cooper and Grey from violent crime to the fraud team. Am I correct in assuming you are still keen to groom these two officers for promotion to DI?'

'Yes, I will not deny the fact, Dick. Their outstanding performance in apprehending that Italian madman, regardless of any thought of injury to themselves, did not go unnoticed. We need to promote those individuals who possess the right sort of calibre to drag policing, kicking and screaming, into the twenty-first century. You don't have a problem with that do you DCI Starr?' he somewhat defensively questioned.

Starr fleetingly pondered would this be an appropriate time to put the deluded man right about Max Cooper's senior officer credentials, he wisely decided it wasn't, but another time, maybe.

Ignoring the question whether he had a problem with his assessment, Starr continued to manipulate the metal theft situation to suit his own ends.

'I will of course head the investigation but I would want you to agree in permitting DS Cooper and Grey in taking a real lead role in this case. The experience gained with the fraud team may prove to be invaluable to help bring about a conviction. And let's not forget Bruce McCoy in all of this, he gave fantastic devoted service over many years, we owe it to the man to catch these criminals.' finally appealed Starr.

'Yes, I can see your suggestion has merit Dick. I'll be able to inform the elected members I have a dedicated team of CID officers determined to bring about custodial convictions for the metal thefts and at the same time it may turn out we become the knights in shining armour in coming to Bruce McCoy's rescue. Furthermore, the County Chief Commissioner will be very pleased to hear that DS Cooper and Grey are on track to make DI by the time they are thirty. I do believe one of them will make an excellent CCC themselves in the not too distant future, now that would look good on this station. Do you agree Dick?' he asked. The worried look he wore was now replaced with a broad sunny smile.

Before Starr was able to conjure up a suitable diplomatic reply, Palfreyman had suddenly noticed the time showing on the small gold plated carriage clock sitting on the table.

'I'll have to leave you Dick, go ahead with what we have agreed and be sure to allow Cooper and Grey to do their bit. We older officers must do all we can to nurture natural talent and not put barriers in the way of modernising the police force. They represent the face of the future and we'd all do well to remember that. Keep me informed. Goodbye, Dick.'

Palfreyman left Starr alone in his office while he dashed to the front of the station to be collected by a chauffeur driven car for the short journey to the town hall.

Before returning to his own much less plush office, Starr allowed himself to linger a little while to take in the surface trappings gracing Palfreyman's private chamber.

At some stage during the visual perusal he took to his boss's luxury upholstered seat. From this position behind the large table he casually lolled back viewing the nature and content of the photographs carefully positioned around the four walls. Some of the once familiar faces taken in the black and white and others later in colour, he was sad to notice, had grown into old age or sadly passed on to the next world.

Being sat comfortably in the plush seat usually occupied by a man of much lesser ability than himself, would at one time, cause bile to rise from his stomach when he gave thought to how he'd been cheated and even more, betrayed, by those who were supposed to have looked after his career. However, the unavoidable time he took off to allow the nasty wounds to heal from the near death experience in apprehending Allessandro Placino gave him ample opportunity to critically assess his past life's experiences and, importantly, what he wanted in the future. Being in the surrounds of this very room allowed his subconscious mind to coldly evaluate what it would have probably been like for him to have been the actual person whose place it was to be seated in the chair he was temporarily sat at.

Belatedly, he gladly accepted his personality was out of kilter to those who, at any cost or sacrifice to their own personal life and that of the immediate family, were prepared to fit in to the new police doctrine of being all things to all men.

The old adage, "Be careful what you wish for", sprung to his mind as a blank sheet of paper was torn from an A4 notepad. Over the next fifteen minutes, Starr cleared his mind so he could solely give some thoughts to a framework of action points for the purpose of the investigation into the unlawful taking of his friend's nest egg.

Starr gave McCoy a call late that afternoon to let him know he would be leading a team to investigate the loss from his account.

'I don't think Palfreyman was too keen at first to agree to assigning a relatively high profile team to the case, but by the time I'd finished explaining how both he and the station could come out of this in a good light, especially when he'd be able to maintain a high profile in other crime investigations around Bladdington, he did not see any reason to put a block on my suggestions,' relayed Starr.

'That's great news Dick, you're a true pal.' gushed McCoy.

'I've drawn up an action plan for us to get started on tomorrow morning, is there anything else you can think of that you haven't mentioned before?'

'Yes, I have a slip of paper, well two in fact, which I removed from around the edge of Sally's computer monitor screen. One had her password and the other had the name of Barry Sproston written across it. I think he has been able to get to Sally through some sort of social network site either here at home or at the shop. I don't get a feeling someone has been liaising with her at the shop simply because they all seem to be totally pulled out there.'

'Will you be around your home tomorrow, Bruce? Or have you plans to meet up with your new chums at the golf club,' Starr asked teasingly.

'No, unfortunately I won't be meeting up with them because tomorrow is, Bridge day,' he said in a put-on posh voice.

'Good, I'll send DS Cora Grey around to your house about ten. You'll like her, she knows her way around computers much better than us pair of dinosaurs. She'll be able to quickly suss out if Sally's been got at through one of those sites.'

Bruce brought to mind the image of the athletic Cora Grey propping up her green looking male companion on completing the 10k run. Oddly, he felt an unexpected tingling glow at the prospect of meeting the girl in the flesh. No sooner had Grey's image appeared in his mind, it was quickly extinguished to be replaced with the happy face of his wife with hands held aloft crossing the finishing line with a young man he never did get to know the name of. Maybe the person in the photograph displayed along with other action pictures taken of the run on public display in the charity shop was of no significance, but his police instinct suggested he first needed to take steps himself before he was able to dismiss any possible suspicions he might unjustifiably hold.

Starr continued to divulge aspects of the plan he'd drawn up in Palfreyman's office.

When they eventually bid each other farewell, McCoy set his thoughts to preparing tea in the company of a large whisky.

Chapter Nineteen

No sooner had DS Cooper and Grey appeared in the CID meeting area the following day, a familiar gesture guided the two to join their commanding officer in his own office.

'No need to sit down,' Starr instructed, startling the young officers from taking a seat in the functional office.

'You will be pleased to know, my young disciples, we have a new case to investigate. All that marvellous experience you gained being in the fraud department while I was away for six months will now be put to good use. And, oh yes, I nearly forgot, Mr Palfreyman, upstairs will be taking a special interest in how you both perform. I think it's because you set the bar so high in the Esme Fellow's investigation he now expects the same level of success. I have given him concrete assurances you won't let him down.' The DCI enjoyed seeing the look of trepidation in their young faces.

During Starr's enforced absence both Grey and Cooper had attracted a disproportionate amount of praise from various high ranking officers for their perceived detective abilities in wringing out the facts concerning the death of Esme Fellows. This honeymoon period coincided with a move, designed to broaden their increasing knowledge and skills, to the fraud department where nothing ever really happened. It turned out to be a long and lazy six months where neither of the budding high flying detectives learned much nor were put in situations which took them out of their comfort zones. Starr was back and things were about to change.

'We've got to get a move on, some scum bag has managed to coerce Bruce McCoy's wife into near emptying their joint account of £82,000.'

'Bloody hell, that's a lot of money, how did the dozy cow manage that?' Cooper asked disdainfully.

'Eh, have you met Sally McCoy before, DS Cooper?' Starr queried straight faced.

'Eh, no Sir, should I have done?'

'If you had had the opportunity to come in contact with her, I don't think you would have been so damn disrespectful in using the phrase, what was it now? Oh yes, "dozy cow". Or is it DS Cooper, you might know more about the circumstances how she happened to lose the money and are not letting on? Please be at ease to put Miss Grey and myself in the picture,' Starr said calmly.

Cooper was most definitely not a morning person, it was usual for him not to become fully awake until around ten thirty, with the time being ten past eight, his brain was still stuck in sleep mode. Rattling Starr's cage this time of the day did not bode well for the young DS.

'No Sir, I have not met Sally McCoy and I don't have any inside information on how she may have come to lose the money. I didn't mean to call her a "dozy cow", it was just my gut reaction to her being the one responsible for the money going missing,' Cooper said sheepishly.

'It is my belief DS Cooper, the woman had been deliberately targeted due to someone knowing she was falling to a dementia type illness. Many would have read Bruce McCoy received a good pay off when he retired from the police, it was printed in both local rags a few weeks ago and it may appear a cunning and criminal mind has been able to construct a devious plan to get at the McCoy's bank account.'

'How was the money taken, Sir? £82,000 is a lot of notes to stuff in your pockets,' asked Grey.

'The branch manager at Portshire bank said the money had been taken out of the account in three transactions using internet transfer to an account in the name of Barry Sproston, in Miami, Florida. The bank's own fraud department have checked their systems for any evidence of attempted hacking and found none. They have concluded Sally McCoy knowingly made the transfers and therefore cannot claim compensation for the loss.'

Over the next fifteen minutes the two young detectives digested other important details Starr had been made aware of when he'd previously met with Bruce McCoy. When he'd finally finished repeating what he so far knew, he presented the action plan he'd drawn up in the comfort of Palfreyman's office the day before.

'I don't buy it is a chance hacker who is behind the scam, my gut feeling is it is a lone person or a group of villains local to this area who are behind it all. The Miami connection may also prove to give valuable clues too, but to what extent, I don't yet know. This is where I expect you two to shine if you want to impress the man upstairs and make it nigh on impossible for him not to make you both up to DIs. Before I allocate the tasks do either of you have any questions?'

Both remained quiet. They understood the long honeymoon period was over and the spotlight was being firmly held by Starr to either show them up in a good or bad light. The results of their actions would determine which light it was to be.

'Right then my busy little bees,' recommenced Starr, 'Cora, I want you to go over to Bruce McCoy's house to see what you can find on his wife's computer. He's expecting you but give him a phone call first. The details are in a new folder I've called "Miami", you'll find in the "C" drive.

Max, you'll have the envious pleasure of accompanying me on a trip over to the Portshire bank to grill the McCoy's bank manager, Mr Titley. Give him a call first to let him know we are on our way and after you have done that book us a pool car. You'll find the bank's phone number in the same place I told Cora. Right chop, chop, holiday time is over, we've got work to do,' Starr coaxed enthusiastically.

By nine o'clock the three detectives had vacated the station to set about their assigned tasks.

The telephone call from Cora Grey had startled McCoy from his regular whisky induced sleep. After the call he leapt from the warmth of the double bed worried he might not have given himself sufficient time to look fresh and alert for her arrival, which was due to be around nine thirty. While taking a quick shower the realisation he'd again got himself in such a state not to hear, or even sense, his wife leaving for work that morning became a bitter disappointment to him. The demon whisky was bit by bit taking back control again; if he continued to go down this route he'd find himself back in hospital, but this time he may not be so lucky.

The dreadful business concerning the money alongside that of the worries he had about Sally, somehow provided him with a good excuse to return to his old drinking ways.

'I'll pack in once things get sorted,' were the empty words he'd consoled himself with when he woke up in the mornings with a dull nagging headache. At the back of his mind, he didn't need anybody to tell him he was kidding himself.

At the time agreed earlier on the phone, he heard the doorbell ring. McCoy left the kitchen to walk down the hallway noting the shadowy shape of a female form standing behind the door. He felt a little nervous, and yet quite excited at the prospect of meeting the young detective sergeant as he turned the brass latch to open the front door to welcome her.

'Hello, you must be DS Grey. I recognise you from the photograph my wife has at her shop of you and another officer together at the end of the 10k run,' he said while offering his hand.

'Oh, that photograph, I look awful, I hope it isn't in a prominent position for all and sundry to see,' she replied bashfully.

'You don't look awful at all, it's a good photograph of you, but the guy standing next to you, DS Cooper I think his name is.'

Grey then interjected, 'Yes, that is Max, he's quite funny really, didn't do any training and having a shed load of beer and a curry the night before wouldn't have helped him,' laughed Grey.

'Whatever am I doing keeping you on the doorstep, do come in Cora. You don't mind me calling you by your first name do you?'

'No, of course not. That coffee smells good,' she said detecting the aroma wafting along the hall way from the kitchen.

'Would you like a cup before you start? It should be ready now,' he said like an eager teenager on his first date.

'Yes thank you Bruce. It's okay for me to call you Bruce? Or should I stick with Mr McCoy, Sir,' Grey said sensing she may have overstepped the line when it comes to addressing senior officers.

McCoy laughed at her apparent unease on how to address him.

'Cora, please call me Bruce, even when I was in CID I didn't buy into all that grand title stuff. Look, you go and sit in the lounge and I'll bring you a coffee through. How do you like it?'

'Just black please.'

He took two saucers and coffee cups out from the wall unit and set them on the work surface and proceeded to pour the piping hot coffee from the filter jug. Into his cup he poured a little cream and ladled in two heaps of sugar. He carried both of the saucers gingerly in to the lounge and placed Grey's black coffee on a small table positioned at the side of her armchair. McCoy sat with his coffee to face her from the other armchair in the room.

For a few awkward moments they both looked at each other from their respective seats neither knowing what to say. Cora would break the silence.

'I understand Sally organised the race and competed too. That is brilliant for a woman of her age.'

'Yes, she does fantastically well. She used to be a PE teacher so keeping fit and trim has always been a big part of her life. It's just a shame how cruel nature can be. You do know she is suffering from dementia?'

'Yes, DCI Starr has fully briefed us on the situation. I'm so sorry,'

'These things happen in life Cora, she looks after herself and falls victim to what is hiding in her genes and others, who heavily drink and smoke, seem to go on to live for ever. Doesn't seem right does it? Anyway drink your coffee, and then we will have a go on the computer to see if we can get any clues or answers from there.'

After some idle chit chat mainly about the Allessandro Placino incident, they returned the empty cups and saucers to the kitchen and then on to the study. Bruce allowed Grey to take the main swivel chair facing the keyboard and computer screen while he was prepared to stand and just watch.

'I'm no good on computers, I have always had others who did this sort of stuff, there really was never any need for me to get skilled up,' McCoy said in an apologetic tone.

'I don't expect for you to know a great deal about computers, iPhones, social network sites and the internet as they are all part and parcel of today's generations growing up experience. Your growing up experience was different to your own parents. Things just move on, nothing stands still,' explained Grey being sensitive not to be blatantly patronising to the older person in the room.

McCoy understood things had moved on in some respects but what hadn't changed in his job was the need for a sharp analytical mind and keen eye for detail, coupled with a tenacious drive to secure a safe and proper conviction no matter how many hours it took. Things seemed to him to have gone soft, maybe he had become a dinosaur, which he understood to be a disparaging term to describe those who continued to operate using certain unapproved methods and taking retirement may have saved him from suffering a desperately disappointing end to a long career.

The blue glow emitting from the screen suddenly lit up the relative darkness in the windowless study A flashing text box was requesting a password to be entered to permit access to the array of programs stored on the computer's hard drive.

'Can you let me have Sally's password, Bruce?'

The slip of paper with it written on was already in his hand to pass to her.

'Thanks, now let's see what she has written.'

Grey looked at the words which spelled out "Dreams Come True". She proceeded to type in the individual letters to fill the oblong box while being careful to apply the case sensitive key when tapping in the D, C and T letters.

They awaited a short while to allow the full array of desk top program icons to fill the screen.

'Right we are in,' announced Grey valiantly.

'What are you going to do first?' probed McCoy feeling quite tense about the prospect of finding out what his wife had been up to with him being in total ignorance of her actions.

'We need to establish if somebody has been able to communicate with Sally either through email or a social network site. Let's start with looking at what emails she has had sent to her.'

She placed the cursor over the email box icon and pressed left click on the mouse to access a short list of messages. Reading the subject titles she saw most were junk mail and messages from internet businesses the McCoy's had previously made purchases from. Amongst the list were three email alerts from *Face2Face*.

'Who or what is *Face2Face*, Cora?' asked McCoy quizzically.

'It's one of about three popular social network sites, mostly used by insecure teenagers who are desperate to make friends with people they don't know a single thing about. The problem is when things can and do go wrong, their desperate parents somehow expect the police to intervene. Social sites can be a great way of keeping in contact with friends and family, but as you know Bruce, there are those out there who see it as a God sent opportunity to exploit innocent and naive people.'

'It all sounds too risky and dangerous to me. Why should Sally receive, what was it, yes, three emails from them?'

'We'll soon find out. What's the betting when I open up the emails we will see the name of Barry Sproston somewhere in the body of the message?'

He offered up no odds. However, inside he sensed a tensioning of his chest and the sound of his heart starting to beat hard in his ears at the prospect of seeing the man's name appear.

A click on the email alert revealed the content of the message which read:

'Keeping you connected with those who mean the world to you! Face2Face'
'Barry Sproston, a friend of Sally McCoy, has a message waiting for you. Please access your account asap. Best wishes from:

Face2Face

Ignoring the increased pounding which had moved to his head, McCoy asked Grey to open up the remaining emails sent from *Face2Face*. She carried out his request for them both to see the messages all read the same as the first one she opened.

Grey glanced to her side to immediately notice a change in McCoy's outward demeanour. He was angry, though he spoke no words as yet. Rather than attempting to console him she clicked on the internet link sent with the email message to fill the screen with an eye catching *Face2Face* home page.

'We need to get into her account. Do you know what the password might be?' Grey said looking directly at McCoy to give him a jolt from a myriad of emotions cascading through his mind.

'I don't know what it is, why don't you try the same password you used to open the computer?' suggested McCoy.

She carefully one finger typed in the same password she'd copied previously from the post-it note and surprisingly, had the same success.

'I can see Sally's not big on security, it's important she uses a different password for each site she uses on the internet,' commented Grey in a rather patronising manner.

Bruce did not want to hear her say that. A so called "normal" person would find it near on impossible to store in their memory all of the passwords and combination of numbers, never mind someone who was experiencing a decline in their mental ability. Grey might be one of those lucky ones who escape getting dementia in later life, on the other hand, she could just as easily succumb as Sally had done. This was not the time to challenge her lack of sensitivity and he wisely chose to encourage her to see what was saved in her account.

Grey scrolled down the chronological sequence of messages received and returned by Sproston and Sally McCoy. She allowed sufficient time to permit each of them to silently read every word to gain a full understanding of how such a situation was contrived to result in the £82,000 being taken from the account.

McCoy's head was spinning with all manner of thoughts after taking in the significance of the vignettes that had been skilfully played out between Sproston and his wife.

'I can see how Sproston played Sally. The bastard conned her by promising he'd pay her back using the money from an insurance policy and as we now know, she fell for it hook line and sinker. But just thinking about it,' said McCoy pausing for a short spell before continuing to say, 'He definitely had some inside knowledge of Sally's illness. Seems to me he chanced a hunch Sally would be unable to put up little resistance once he started tugging at her heart strings. The photograph showing him with his wife sitting with a tubed up kid in that hospital bed I would think to be his trump card. A blind man could see the whole thing reeked of being a set up, but poor Sally wasn't able to see through it. The man must be pure evil to use his family to pull off such a stunt. And guess what Cora? I have seen his despicable face before today,' he revealed in an almost casual manner.

'How's that? Have you met him before?' Grey asked rather disbelievingly.

'No, I haven't had the pleasure of his company. Sally has a photograph of the two of them pinned up at the shop, Eric Carter gave her the photo along with a ruck of others he'd taken at the run a few weeks ago. I didn't take any real notice of the picture except to wonder why a man, who is maybe twenty-five or thirty years younger than Sally, would want to find it so important to cross a finishing line hand in hand with her.'

'Did you also notice the dates when Sproston first and last made contact with Sally?' Grey questioned.

'No I didn't, tell me.' he replied in an anxious tone.

'His first contact seems to have been at the 10k run and that happened a little over two months ago.' She then took hold of the mouse to scroll the messages back to the top and then scrolled down again slowly this time taking notes of the dates each message was sent.

'Contact through *Face2Face* was made a couple of days later. And if I keep scrolling down you can see within three weeks he had managed to take the money. Once he had achieved what he was after, the account was closed, thus preventing Sally of any means of getting back in touch with him. What a slimy toad,' she said as if the words were of poison.

'It looks like she made a few attempts to contact him and then nothing over the next four weeks. Either she gave up or she just simply forgot what she had done. Why in the hell didn't she let me know what was happening?' McCoy anguished.

'Maybe she truly believed him when he promised he'd have the money back in the account. If it transpired the money had been returned, you'd be none the wiser and you would have got your new car, and Sally would have been happy she'd been able to support a family in their hour of need. Or another scenario might be she did not tell you what she had done because she was scared how you might react,' suggested Grey.

Grey's inference that Sally could be possibly afraid of him cut him no differently than if she had actually plunged a knife into his heart herself. Dealing with criminals, yes, he'd readily admit, he was tough and uncompromising, but his relationship with Sally, now that could not have been more different. She was and still is his emotional harbour, her loving, caring happy nature filled his life with light, in spite of the problems he created for himself. His love for her was unconditional; it always has been and always will be. Before he went on to reply, McCoy realised he was in danger of becoming too sensitive about things being said about his wife, there would be other's, besides Cora Grey, who will later make innocent remarks relating to Sally's part during the course of the investigation.

'My personal feelings are Sally has become incredibly forgetful and sometimes struggles to bring to mind events that have previously happened only a few days or even hours ago. Maybe being struck with the realisation there was no chance of getting the money back into the account shocked her already fragile system which in turn, may have programmed her brain to shut off any thoughts about what had gone on,' McCoy conjectured.

'Yes, I would tend to agree with you Bruce, but it may make things more difficult when Sally is questioned at some stage.'

'Let's wait and see how far we can propel the investigation forward before considering approaching Sally for her input,' McCoy suggested.

'Fine, let's leave it at that then. What I think we should do next though, is to pay Eric Carter a visit to get a copy of that photograph of Sproston and Sally together, we don't want to cause Sally any unnecessary alarm by turning up at the shop to ask for her copy pinned on the wall,' advised Grey. McCoy was happy to go along with her suggestion.

Grey turned her attention back to the monitor screen.

'I can't see there is any point in opening Sally's internet bank account to see what had gone on there, so I think it is time to close everything down here and when I get back to the station I can open up my computer using Sally's details to make a copy of the emails and the messages in *Face2Face*.'

'Yes, that's a good idea and if it's okay with you Cora, I'd like to be with you when you meet Eric Carter, I've nothing else going on today.' McCoy understood she had every right to refuse his request on the grounds she was on official police business in pursuance of a reported crime. Grey didn't appear to have hesitated when she gave him her answer. 'You are welcome to come along Bruce, you probably know Mr Carter much better than I do.'

'Great, thanks, I'll leave you to get on in here and I'll go and switch the coffee-maker off and lock the back door.' While McCoy busied himself doing the tasks he set for himself, he felt some sense of relief knowing the perpetrator behind the stealing of his hard-earned nest egg had left a trail to be picked over by those skilled at unravelling this type of crime. All that was required now was a keen eye for detail, tenacity of approach, together with that essential ingredient called luck, then McCoy would feel somewhat more optimistic Sproston, or whoever else he was, had little time left to enjoy their freedom.

The current serving female CID officer accompanied by a retired member of the police force pulled up in a small car park situated at the rear of the tired looking premises of the *Bladdington Bugle*.

'This place looks like it could do with a lick of paint,' commented McCoy while getting out from the passenger side of the unmarked police car.

'These are hard times for small regional newspapers, I bet they hardly keep their heads above water,' Grey said after she had locked the car and had started to walk to a rear door entrance to the building.

'We're in luck, Carter's car is here, let's hope he's not too busy to see us,' said McCoy while catching up to Grey before she turned the handle of a tatty door, having long flaking strips of ageing blue paint curling away from the surface, to gain access to the building. They walked a short corridor to reach a reception desk fronting the street entrance which must have only just had a newly printed stack of that week's issue of the *Bladdington Bugle* placed there. Drawing in the not too unpleasant smell of fresh print, they waited patiently for someone to deal with their enquiry. The noise of a door banging against a hard wall broke their concentration from looking at the vast range of photographs obviously taken over many years covering the walls of the tired reception area.

Pushing her way through the door's tight opening was a stout woman holding a large string bound bundle of newspapers in each hand. Without being asked Bruce moved forward to relieve the woman of the two heavy loads and to then stride over the short distance to the reception counter to raise both bundles to above chest height and release them to hit the hard surface with a resounding slap.

'Oh thank you sir, you are so kind, I'll swear this place will be the death of me,' the grateful woman breathlessly remarked as she manoeuvred herself to face the two of them from the other side of the reception desk.

'Now, how can I help you? Do you want to buy a copy of the *Bugle*?' she asked with her hand moving in the direction of a pile of newspapers closest to her.

'No, not today thank you. We are here on official police business.' Grey flashed her warrant card to confirm her identity, while McCoy hung back to the side of her.

'We don't get many police visits, in fact I cannot remember if we have ever had one,' the woman said worriedly.

'There's nothing to be bothered about, it's just a routine visit which we hope will assist us in our enquiries. We need to see Eric Carter; his car is parked outside so I assume he is working on the premises.'

'Yes that's right, Eric was in his office last time I saw him, I'll give him a call for you. Can I ask what your names are please?'

'DS Grey and Bruce McCoy.' answered Grey.

Carter soon appeared in the reception area to greet the familiar faces. After exchanging pleasantries Carter asked how he could be of service to them.

McCoy thought it proper for Grey to start the proceedings, as after all, she was the one representing the law, and sadly for him, he was no longer privy to that role.

'Recently you gave to Sally McCoy copies of the photographs you took during the "Dreams Come True" charity run,' said Grey.

'Yes, that's right. There was also one of you as well if you remember, has that poor guy recovered yet?' Carter replied with a suggestion of a snigger.

'Oh, you must mean DS Cooper; yes he did in fact look terrible when he eventually crawled over the finishing line. He was not too pleased when he saw the same photograph in the police federation magazine. Max is convinced DCI Starr was behind it all, I didn't dare tell him it was me - he'd kill me!'

The three shared the same laugh as they brought to mind the image of the dire state the young DS had got himself into.

Before Cora progressed to the next point, Carter suggested they should move from the reception area and on to his office.

'It might be a bit pokey in there but at least we'll be able to discuss things in private.'

Once piles of stationery and other paraphernalia had been shifted about to unearth two other seats Grey was able to continue, 'I was hoping you would be able to run off another copy of the photograph showing Sally and the other runner beside her at the end of the run.'

'Yes, I can do that for you, it's just a moment's job with the new technology we have got nowadays. I remember at the time Sally telling me the man's name, Barry Sproston, yes that's it, she said his young son was receiving treatment for leukaemia in a hospital in America; Miami I think. Our sister paper, the *Moulton Sentinel* ran a feature on the families plight which included a picture showing the family gathered around a hospital bed.'

While Carter turned his attention to opening up a file on his desk computer to access the picture Grey continued to ask him a further question, 'Do you remember anything in particular about Barry Sproston?'

While the professional colour printer was making its usual noise churning out three copies of the photograph Carter replied, 'I meant to mention something to you Bruce on the day I collected you from the golf club to take you to the hospital to see Sally after she had fainted in the shop. But I thought it best not to say anything because I could see how worried you were about her, naturally. And you know how things are when you are so busy you meet yourself coming back, it just simply went out of my head and I never did get to tell you what was bothering me at the time.'

Bruce had only expected to simply collect a photograph from Carter. He'd now become somewhat anxious in a positive sense, that he was about to learn more revelations about this man Sproston.

'I think now is a good time to let me know what was bothering you, Eric,' urged McCoy. Before he revealed his previous untold concerns, Carter reached over to the printer to pass two of the photographs to McCoy and Grey and kept the other one flat facing up on his desk. The three of them would occasionally drop their gaze to take in the bodily and facial features of the man, while Carter relayed his own fix on the situation.

'It was while I was asking Sally a couple of questions, I noticed Sproston making a rather quick getaway. I remember Sally putting this down to him having to get to the airport to catch a flight back to America.

'I thought it strange how someone who was a beneficiary of the funds raised by those who competed in the run didn't possess the good grace to say a few words at the end. And that's not all.' Carter paused for a moment or two with Grey and McCoy fixing their attention on him awaiting earnestly on what he was about to say, 'When the shots I'd taken had been printed off I was able to take a good look at Sproston and there was something that did not ring true about this man. I vaguely remembered the picture of the Sproston family prior to them jetting off to America to give their child, Wilson one last fighting chance of beating blood cancer. You know, I wasn't totally convinced the Barry Sproston I took a shot of at the end of the run was the same Barry Sproston pictured in the *Moulton Sentinel*. Yes, their features were similar but not identical.'

'Did you later compare the two photographs?' McCoy pressed.

'I had every intention to do so, but like I've already said there is always too much to do too much of the time in this place, and it just simply slipped out of my head. Anyway, why is this man so important? Has he been up to something? Does it involve Sally? Is that why you are here now?' enquired Carter while scrutinising their faces for any tell-tale signs that might give him possible clues.

'You must have already guessed Sproston might have some involvement concerning Sally and I would appreciate it if we just left it at that, thanks Eric,' McCoy answered.

'Yes, sorry Bruce, I don't want to come over as being an insensitive fool, sorry.'

Carter understood McCoy's wife was experiencing problems of some kind based on what was said when they journeyed together to the hospital to see her.

'Is it possible while we're here to get hold of the other photograph so we can make a comparison between the two?' asked Grey.

'Sure, I'll give Trevor a call at the *Moulton Sentinel* and ask him to upload the image onto our internet system and it will then be a simple matter of printing it off here and Bruce, while I'm making this call, just do us all a favour and make us all a coffee, you'll find the cups and other stuff over there.' Carter nodded his head in the direction of a cluttered tray sitting on a small table. 'You might want to think about giving the cups a quick swill, they've not been cleaned for a while.'

The motley collection of chipped cups had a skin of blue mould floating in all but one, which was understood to belong to Carter. Grey had no stomach to clean the disgusting mugs and agreed with McCoy that if he dealt with the deep cleansing, she would make the three coffees which were to be whitened with cheap powdered milk.

After Carter had finished his call, he accepted his familiar mug from Grey and took a sip of the beige fluid without showing any signs of displeasure. She on the other hand, grimaced on tasting hers, and so did McCoy.

'By Jesus, Eric, how do you drink this muck? You need to buy some decent coffee and proper milk. I'd hate to think what it's doing to your insides,' McCoy said screwing his face up to take another reluctant draw from a chipped mug which had a local undertaker's logo printed on it.

'Done me no harm, you just have to get used to it. Right then, I've got the image on screen now. Do you want to come round and have a look at it first before I print it off?'

They both left their seats while still clutching their individual photographs to walk round to the other side of the only desk in the room and stand either side of the seated reporter to all stare looking at a clear full screen image of a mum, dad and young boy taken in a hospital setting.

'The question is does this man bare any resemblance to the one in the photograph?' conjectured Carter. For a few silent moments each of them stared at the computer monitor screen then back to the photograph and back again.

'I think it's the same man,' determined Grey while looking at the two males taking a few more glances before offering their opinion.

'I agree DS Grey, there is a definite likeness, but I'm not hundred per cent sure it's the same man. Like I thought when I first saw him at the run, I suppose,' said Carter.

The two who had offered their views turned to face a pensive looking McCoy in eager anticipation of his verdict. He rubbed his clean shaven chin in outward deliberation with one hand and the other holding the photograph closely to his face scrutinising each and every detail of both of the individual male's features.

Finally, he was able to express his own personal evaluation.

'Yes, I have to agree, on first glance, one could say the man is the same person in each of the two images. But if you look closely at the male sitting on the hospital bed,' he paused for a moment to allow the other two to focus their attention on the screen, and then continued, 'his ears are a different shape and size than the person shown in the photograph. That's not all, I think they have slightly different shaped chins. The Barry Sproston who finished the run with Sally, his is squarer. Have a good look, see what you both think,' encouraged McCoy.

They checked McCoy's assessment against their own.

'Yes, I think you are probably right Bruce, and now that I'm taking in more of what I'm seeing, I think one has higher set cheek bones which changes the appearance of their eyes, albeit only slightly.'

McCoy did not respond to Carter's updated analysis and waited to hear what Grey had to say.

'Well I have to say, to me, they look the same person but we could be here all night debating the issue and time is moving on. I think the best thing to do now is for me to report back to the station with both photographs and let others have a look at them. Is it too much trouble to ask you Eric to send an email to the station with the attachment of the *Moulton Sentinel* photograph? We should still have the one you sent us from the run.'

'I'll do it straight away, and while I'm at it, I'll re-send the run photo just in case someone has deleted the original message,' he replied.

As Grey moved away from the desk thinking business was concluded, McCoy asked Carter to do something else for him, or rather to help the police investigation.

'I assume you will know the reporter who wrote the article about the Sproston's plight.'

Not lifting his head away from focusing on the screen typing up the email to Bladdington police station, he answered, 'Yes, of course I do, it's Sam Hodson, he's a good mate of mine, been in the job for years and I tell you, he doesn't miss much,' he replied with his words containing more than an air of respect for the man.

'I know you already have a lot on your plate Eric.' McCoy paused to await the reporter's not too unexpected reply.

'Tell me about it,' bemoaned Carter while concentrating on getting the requested email out of the way.

'Do you think it might be possible he had made a note of Sproston's home address and details of the hospital his son is being treated at in Miami?'

'I can certainly enquire for you, and knowing Sammy he'll have it tucked away in his notebook somewhere and I suppose you will want that emailing to the station as well, hey.' Carter was only too pleased to assist the police knowing he would later use this situation as a lever for a favour to be returned if, and when, a juicy story broke out in Bladdington.

The two visitors gave their individual thanks and bid their farewells to leave their mostly filled coffee mugs to again skin over to form a replica unpleasant blue floating crust for some other poor soul to scour out in the future.

Chapter Twenty

DCI Starr and DS Cooper had taken up the same seats as McCoy and his wife had previously done when they too had met with the bank's branch manager in his office. Titley had handed the two officers a coffee from the machine and while he was blowing across the top of his, Starr commenced proceedings.

'We are here to inform the bank that the police regard the money taken from Mr and Mrs McCoy's account as fraud and therefore will be investigated under the powers of criminal law,' he said in a quite officious manner.

'Yes, I expected that would be the case. However, as I've already explained to Mr McCoy the bank cannot take any responsibility for the money being drawn from their account and moreover Mrs McCoy appears to have used her internet banking account to sanction each of the withdrawals,' calmly explained Titley.

Starr understood the bank were not in the slightest bit interested how Sally had succumbed to being persuaded to transfer the money. If it was the bank's money that had been taken, well, that would be a different matter.

Starr looked towards the seated DS Cooper, who had taken up a slouched pose with his eyelids showing they were battling against the onset of drowsiness, for him to make the next point they had both agreed to cover during the journey from the station to the bank.

'Eh, yes, sorry, right,' he said fumbling over his words. He watched Starr's reaction shaking his head in disdain as he pulled himself together.

'Right Mr Titley, we are initially taking the assumption that the person we understand to be Barry Sproston is a British national. To open an account in America the applicant must be able to provide the bank with information that authenticates their identity,' questioned the now openly alert Cooper.

Before Titley answered the two officers watched him as he took another long draw from his card coffee cup to top up on his caffeine fix.

'Yes, you are quite right DS Cooper, for the bank to sanction the opening of an account they would have to see a passport or a photo ID driving licence, national insurance number and a testimonial letter from the person's employer, which of course the bank would take steps to verify. And also details of their place of residence whilst in America. Usually a sum of around $500 needs to be deposited before any cards can be issued,' answered Titley.

'The bank must have been satisfied with everything to permit the account to be opened then,' said Cooper.

'Clearly,' replied Titley.

'So in their records they must have a copy of the employer's testimonial showing Sproston's place of work and taken details of where he was living or staying at the time.' continued Cooper.

'Not only that,' butted in Titley, 'the passport would have been scan checked against the records held by UK passport control to confirm that it wasn't a forged or a stolen copy. Whoever processed the application would have certainly checked Sproston's likeness against the photo in the passport.'

'It would help us greatly with our enquiries if you contacted the bank for them to send an email or fax us a copy of Sproston's employer's testimonial and place of residence as soon as possible to Bladdington police station,' requested Cooper. There then came a short lull in the meeting after which Titley asked if there was anything else he could assist them with.

'Yes there is,' said Starr, again looking at Cooper because this was a question he should have asked the bank manager. 'The two accounts the money was transferred to in this country, we would like to have the account holders names, account numbers and the bank addresses. I suppose the bank in Miami can send this information along with what DS Cooper has requested.'

'I'm confident our fraud department can persuade our colleagues across the pond to part with the information you have asked for,' smugly replied Titley.

'I don't wish to detain you any further from dealing with our requests and I look forward to receiving what we have asked for bright and early tomorrow morning Mr Titley,' said Starr while pushing his seat away in readiness to leave the room.

'Oh, I don't think it will be as soon as that, it may take three or even four working days to get everything sanctioned. Banks have to operate in a certain way DCI Starr,' he said reacting quite officiously to the officer's demands.

'Hm, I see,' said Starr rubbing his face stubble while mulling over the manager's remarks. 'I've always considered the ways of the banking industry very strange,' Starr continued, 'if you don't mind me saying Mr Titley,'

Cooper was at this time moving to exit the room because he understood the manager was about to hear a lesson from Starr's gospel of home truths.

'Why is it banks are soon onto the little people if they go overdrawn by a couple of quid and then clobbered with a penalty letter demanding thirty pounds which they must pay immediately or invoke another exaggerated charge? Little wonder they greedily make billions in profits each year, and who for? The equally greedy shareholders.

'The same can be said about the bank's attitude in dealing with Mr and Mrs McCoy's situation. They have all but lost their life savings, and in reality Mr Titley neither you nor the bank give a toss do you? Because it's not the bank's money that's gone. You even have the temerity to state the bank is completely blameless, how smug is that? I have advised Mr and Mrs McCoy to contact the banking ombudsman on the grounds you neglected to inform the principal bank account holder, who you should certainly be aware of, is Mr Bruce McCoy, of the large amounts being taken from his account and deposited elsewhere in the world.

'Now what does it say on those flashy boards hanging from every available nook and cranny outside in the customer area, ah, yes, that's it, *"The bank that will always stand by you whatever life brings"*. Most laudable, I must say Mr Titley. The McCoy's and I will be looking forward to you upholding what you purport to stand for. What we have asked for we will receive at Bladdington station early tomorrow morning please.' Starr concluded by tossing his personal business card onto the desk.

His straight talking had left Titley in no doubt were he and the bank stood as in Starr's mind there is little point in appearing to be meek and wishy-washy if you need to get something to happen. This was such a situation and he was determined to get what he demanded.

We'll make our own way out thank you.' The two detectives forwent handshakes to leave Titley numbed and dumb struck.

Titley had been deeply shaken by the strength of the "no bull shitting" words expressed by the senior police officer because he more than understood they contained an element of truth. Leaving the comfort of the executive seat, he stepped over to the coffee machine and pressed his preferred selection button to drop another cardboard cup. While the hot water streamed from a nozzle to cover the powered mix of coffee granules and milk he anxiously thought about what DCI Starr had left him with.

He would have to make certain Bladdington police received the details from the bank in America by the following morning or his arse would be on the line. Starr was right when he mentioned the McCoy's should have been better served by their bank and he knew if there were to be an internal investigation by the po-faced wonders encamped at the head office into the management of their account, the buck would undoubtedly stop with him. Titley wasn't prepared to be the sacrificial lamb whose only reward was to be a downgraded move to a simple cashier; he'd worked too damn hard for too many years to have his status and pay snatched away from him now.

Taking to his comfy seat again, he earnestly started to make a series of telephone calls to pull in past favours.

On their return from the *Bladdington Bugle*'s offices, Grey had agreed with McCoy that Starr wouldn't likely protest if he accompanied her in the incident room back at Bladdington police station. First though, McCoy would have to present some ID to be allowed to be signed in and for a visitor's badge to be issued.

Grey had pressed the white bell push button to summon the duty desk sergeant from his comfortable seat hidden behind a dividing partition.

'Hello Ralph, I'd like Mr McCoy to be given a visitor's badge so he can join me in the incident room,' cheerfully requested Grey.

Ralph was the same desk sergeant who had been previously embarrassed the last time he came across McCoy.

'I need to see some ID before I can sanction a visitor's pass,' he sharply demanded.

'That's not necessary Ralph, I can personally vouch for this man, just let him sign the book and give him a badge.'

'No can do ma'am, rules are rules. No ID, no pass,' replied the bolshie desk sergeant.

'Ralph, just do …' Grey had started to say having clearly become irritated by the sergeant's intransigent attitude, but was prevented from venting her frustration further by the tactical intervention of the retired detective inspector.

'It's not a problem DS Grey. I have my driving licence with me.' McCoy opened his wallet to remove the pink plastic card and place it down on the counter with Grey vexedly looking on at the anally challenged sergeant.

He gathered the licence from the counter and began to perform a lengthy scrutiny front and back in the obvious hope he'd find something wrong, which would then deny McCoy entry. Whilst McCoy understood the infantile politics behind the desk sergeant's actions, Grey's next reactions would be solely based on what she was now witnessing.

'For Goodness sake Sergeant Bowyer, what is up with you? Give Mr McCoy his licence back and stop playing silly buggers. I want him signed in now!' demanded Grey.

Her reactions did little to modify his manner. He tossed the licence onto the counter to then say sneeringly, 'You do realize you only have ten days before your licence runs out. Now you are no longer one of us I wouldn't expect any favours if you get pulled up if you let it run out.'

'Thank you, Desk Sergeant Bowyer, I will be mindful of your caring advice and make sure my licence is renewed on time,' McCoy calmly replied.

While the desk sergeant signed him in and issued the visitor's pass Grey had built herself up into a simpering rage. When they were about to make their way to the incident room Grey turned to the desk sergeant to tell him she would be seeing him later.

As the two walked down a fluorescent lit corridor leading to the incident room Grey started to apologise for the sergeant's unfortunate behaviour.

'I'm really sorry about that Bruce. I understand Bowyer can be a bit stroppy and grumpy at times, but you can rest assured I will be having a stern word with him for what happened out there.'

'Just leave it Cora. It won't make a spit of difference if you do tackle him. Maybe he's harbouring some sort of long held resentment, I've seen it often enough in all ranks during my time,' said McCoy.

On entering Grey quickly scanned around the faces in the mostly empty incident room to see if Starr and Cooper had arrived. She turned to face McCoy to suggest she would make them both a drink while awaiting their return from the bank.

'Yes, that will be good,' confirmed McCoy.

While he waited for Grey to hopefully improve on the awful concoction they sampled in Carter's office, he strolled around the modern, bright incident room reading the various familiar police issued notices pinned up on walls or stuck on the sides of filing cabinets with blue tack. He was mindful not to disturb the four female admin staff who were staring into eye straining computer monitor screens covering assignments initiated by other senior CID officers. His attention was drawn to a commercially bought notice board where he paused for a while to carefully read the "thank you" letters sent in by grateful members of the public.

Amongst the assembly of different coloured notes was a letter from the station's chief superintendent, Richard Palfreyman, personally thanking Starr and his team for their outstanding work in the investigation which resulted in the DCI taking six months off work to recover from gunshot wounds. Similar letters of congratulation were randomly dotted around the board sent by other force chief supers from different parts of the country.

McCoy understood how important it was for the police to have their often dangerous and unpalatable work appreciated, much of which goes on without the person on the street having a clue of what is going on in their neighbourhood or town.

'Your coffee is here Bruce, it should be a lot better than the last one we had.' called Grey.

'Thanks,' he replied and moved from the notice board to collect his drink.

'Ah, that's better,' McCoy responded on taking the first sip from his mug. 'Do you know Cora, incident rooms across the length and breadth of this country were once bastions of maleness. Female CID officers hadn't been invented when I first entered the force, makes me sound really old doesn't it?' Grey didn't answer while she raised her mug to her lips.

'Not only that,' he continued. 'The room would have been a right tip: files left all over the place, dirty cups, empty whisky bottles on tops of desks and filing cabinets and when everybody was in, the air would have been blue with cigarette smoke. The only technology around then was a desk telephone and if you were important enough, you might have a mobile phone which was as big as a brick. I believe they are collector's items now.' Grey gave a smile while thinking how significant her mobile was in her life with its immense capacity and capability.

McCoy continued, 'I look around this room and there must be at least twelve PCs all of which have easy access to a whole range of criminal records. Many of the victims slaughtered by the modern "Jack the Ripper" would have been spared their fate if the police had had such a powerful database back then.'

Grey was about to mention that any system is only as good as the quality of data loaded into it: if you put crap in, you'll only get crap out, when she suddenly called out to say, 'Crikey, that reminds me I need to check the emails to see if Eric Carter has sent the copies of the two photographs and with a bit of luck, he might even have got us the information we asked for from the *Moulton Sentinel* reporter.

McCoy peered over her shoulder as she carefully searched through the long list of emails sent to Bladdington Police admin message box to find what she was looking for. They both simultaneously read Carter's message to find he had in fact been successful in contacting Sammy Hodson.

'That's good news, I'll print some more copies of the photographs and then save the images in a PowerPoint folder. I will do the same with the details he sent of the hospital in Miami and Sproston's home address.'

McCoy watched the young DS carry out her intentions as if it was second nature. The photo prints had been run off and she had literally seconds to spare after completing the flashy PowerPoint slides, when the incident room door burst open in typical Starr fashion.

'Oh, hello Bruce, I didn't expect to see you here,' said Starr in surprise. Cooper sheepishly stood in the door opening while the DCI bid his friend welcome.

'I have nothing on this afternoon, so I pestered DS Grey to accompany her back to the station. I hope you don't mind.' Starr didn't see the need to reply, the fact was McCoy was here, which went against established protocol and his police instincts. He wasn't however about to ask his friend to leave, but this was to be the last time he'd sit in on an official report back and briefing.

'Right we'll get started then, two more coffees please Cora, and Max, you'll do the reporting back for us,' ordered Starr.

During the journey to and from the bank, Starr had been successful in building up McCoy's reputation to close legendary status. Being mindful of what Starr had said about the man standing chatting, Cooper whipped out his notebook to re-familiarize himself on what had gone on at the bank.

The four incumbents sat with their individual mugs to face the forty-two inch wall hung plasma TV screen awaiting the results of each other's visit that morning.

Grey was first to open up the proceedings. She firstly explained how Sally McCoy had been duped into transferring money from her account to that of Barry Sproston's.

This, she further described, was craftily executed through them both being members of *Face2Face.*

'What in God's name is *Face2Face*, Cora?' piped up Starr.

'Briefly, it's a social network site which allows people to keep in contact and make new friends. I would say most people are members of this site or one of their competitors. Anyway Sproston must have managed to coerce Sally into accepting him as a friend and, of course, the rest is history,' she explained.

'What's wrong with telephone calls, letters, or even good old fashioned meeting people in the flesh? How can you accept someone to be one of your friends when you know bugger all about them? The world is going bloody mad! Are you pair members?'

Grey side-lined Starr's question and continued to explain how Bruce was able to identify Sproston from a photograph attachment received by Sally McCoy, showing him to be with a woman while comforting a sick boy in a hospital bed, as being the same person he recognised from the photograph taken at the end of the run.

Later she expands on how Eric Carter's suspicions led him to recall to mind a similar looking hospital photograph printed in the *Moulton Sentinel* a couple of months back. This directly led him to finding vital information concerning important addresses they would need to follow up later.

Grey passed copies of the two photographs over to Starr and Cooper; these would be the same images as the ones she intended to bring to life on the flat screen TV.

'We have previously debated the apparent likeness between the two men shown in the different photographs over at the *Bladdington Bugle* offices. Before I tell you what we thought, I would be interested in what you two think,' she posed.

The two men aped similar actions to those who had previously first viewed the pictures. A minute or more elapsed before an opinion was aired.

'They definitely look alike, a bit like twins who bear a close resemblance rather than being identical,' offered Starr.

'I think it's the same person. What were your conclusions?' asked Cooper directing his question at Grey.

'Well, like you Max, I said the same. Bruce wasn't convinced and probably Eric Carter was similarly unsure. Really, if we had more photographs of each of the men then it might help in removing some of the doubt we obviously share now,' said Grey.

'That's not likely to happen Cora, so until we come up with evidence to the contrary we will have to assume it is the same man. What else have you got to tell us?' pressed Starr. McCoy had chosen to remain silent throughout the short debate. Even though he had definite views concerning the subtle differences between the two Barry Sproston's, he rightfully understood his position in the group.

Next, the PowerPoint slide illuminating the two addresses recovered from Sam Hodson's notebook appeared on the screen, this was followed with suggestions from Grey on what needed to be done next.

'Keeping in mind what DCI Starr just said, today or tomorrow one of us will have to visit Sproston's home address,' Grey suggested before being interrupted by her superior officer.

'Hmm, Cristoforo Colombo Childrens' Hospital, Miami,' said Starr, slowly reading out aloud each individual word showing on the screen. 'I'll go and see him upstairs and hopefully give him a heart attack after hearing he's got to foot the expense of sending one or more of us on a jaunt to Florida. I can just see his face now,' said Starr with a mischievous grin drawn across his face.

'Can I continue, Sir?' Grey irritably said.

Sorry Miss Grey, please do,' replied Starr rather sheepishly.

'We need to establish whether it is his proper address and if he is back or not. I think it would be wise to have some uniform backup ready as he might not be too pleased to find the police knocking at his door, especially with him knowing he has robbed one of our former colleagues. On the other hand, if we discover that the family have not yet returned from Miami, we can contact the hospital to establish if Sproston is still there or not. Will we have to liaise with Interpol London to have permission granted to contact the hospital, Sir?' queried Grey.

'Not in the first instance. If it is only a matter of establishing if the suspect is actually there, then it is okay to go ahead. It will, of course, become a different matter if we require an arrest to be made, but don't let us jump the gun yet,' replied Starr with McCoy nodding his head endorsing the DCI's stance.

'Is that it Cora?'

'Yes Sir.'

'Right then DS Cooper, it's your turn under the spotlight,' chirped Starr.

Cooper flipped open the page in his small notebook to read the scrawled and mostly unintelligible words made during their meeting with Bryan Titley.

'Besides DCI Starr giving the branch manager a long lecture on the bank's questionable ethics together with threats of being hunted down by the financial ombudsman, we are more than hopeful of receiving early tomorrow morning, an email which should provide the investigation with some tangible leads,' reported Cooper.

'Do you think it would be a good idea to reveal the nature of what we have asked to be sent to us tomorrow, Max?' gently prompted Starr while showing he was mildly amused at Cooper having had the balls to have a go at him in a roundabout way.

'Yes, sorry. We were able to establish that Sproston needed to have been able to produce his passport, NI number, details of where he is, or was staying at in Miami and finally a testimonial letter from his employer before being allowed to open an account. I sense Mr Titley will pull out all of the stops in order for us to proceed with the investigation without any undue delay,' he concluded in a bright flourish.

'Well done, DS Cooper,' praised Starr. Cooper slumped back in his seat thankful the ordeal was over.

'Right then, right then, there are things we can be getting on with today. We will have to be patient and wait till tomorrow comes before we can tackle the rest.' Starr continued with his rallying cry to say, 'and don't get too comfy there DS Cooper, you are coming with me to check if our friend, Mr Sproston is about. Cora, can you put the two photos on the white board and add what we know so far, and when you have done that, you can drop Mr McCoy off. I'll give you a call later Bruce.' Both men gave each other an affirmative nod.

Chapter Twenty-One

'Turn left here, Sir,' directed Cooper. Starr obeyed his instruction to steer the unmarked police car into Elmwood Drive, situated on the rural outskirts of Moulton town. Following the car from a discreet distance, was another unmarked police vehicle having two uniformed occupants in tow as back up.

'What's the number Max?' Starr's attention was drawn to noticing the neat rows of early forties semi-detached houses on either side of the road. The design architect of these houses clearly understood at that time, how unlikely it would be for the purchasers of these houses to eventually aspire to car ownership. Therefore no provision was made for a driveway or the possibility for a garage to be built in the future. Come evening time either side of the road would be filled with modern vehicles owned by three or more, car families.

'Number fifty-nine, that will be on the left' Cooper pointed out having noticed how the house numbers were ordered.

Starr then said in a low solemn voice, 'I can see it.'

'We've only just past number twenty-one, how can you see fifty-nine?'

'Bet you it's the house which has that Mountain Ash tree in front of it with all of those yellow ribbons tied around its trunk.'

The wager wasn't taken up by Cooper. The vehicle pulled up slowly outside the front garden gate of number fifty-nine. From the passenger side window Cooper was able to see that messages of hope and good wishes were also gathered amongst the greying tied ribbons bound around the slender trunk.

The officers left the vehicle to walk up the flag paved path leading to the Sproston family front door. After Starr had rung the bell and rapped the brass knocker, he glanced around his immediate surroundings to note nothing looked neglected. This led him to conjecture either Sproston had in fact returned from America, or someone, such as a neighbour or family relative was looking after the place. He repeated the ringing and rapping again, but still no response.

'Do you think we should try the back Sir?' asked Cooper.

'You go Max. I don't think anyone is here, but it will do no harm in trying.'

Cooper disappeared around the corner to reach the waist height wrought iron gate which would delight any crook, thief or vagabond on being presented with such easy access to the rear of the semi-detached house.

'Oi, what the bloody hell are you doing! I'll set my dog on you. Go on, shift, get away from here or I will call the police.' Starr was startled to hear the cacophony of loud and aggressive shouts forming a duet with fierce animal snarling noises.

The sound of running footsteps preceded Cooper, with Starr then watching his partner scampering past him in clear haste to get to the car. On the opposite neighbour's path, separated only by a dwarf wall, was a short, skinny framed, balding man in his late seventies, being dragged along by an overweight male Rottweiler dog seemingly locked in a single minded pursuit to sink its teeth into the intruder.

Cooper's joy on reaching the car immediately turned to great dismay, Starr had previously activated the central locking and so what followed next was a couple of frenzied laps around the car with the older gentleman just about managing to keep the raging cur from his next meal. Cooper made for the pull up style nearside passenger door handle on recognising from amongst the wild choking snarls, the sweet sound of the central locking mechanism operating. Looking out from the safety of the passenger side window Cooper saw a pair of black manic eyes along with a set of white frothing jaws opening and closing like portcullis gates, clearly not yet convinced an enemy of the pack had escaped its attention. Seeing his partner's terrified look from behind the passenger door glass Starr slipped the car keys back into his jacket pocket.

'Calm down Arnie, what the heck is the matter with you?' the neighbour chided while pulling the dog down from clawing the car's paintwork. Only after the man had promised treats and a long walk did the dog eventually calm down.

Starr thought it wise to remain behind the neatly trimmed privet hedge until it was safe to start questioning the pensioner age man.

'Hello Sir, I'm DCI Starr and the person in the car is DS Cooper.'

The dog had not previously sensed or smelled the other intruder and so set off again with a repeat of its theatrics on eyeballing yet another uninvited threat to his pack.

'Quiet boy,' shouted Starr. The dog immediately stopped barking and cocked his head to one side looking quizzically at this strange animal. After a few seconds stand off a rumble could be heard to start in the dog's chest moving towards its throat.

Starr called again, but this time a little more softly, 'Quiet boy, that's it, quiet boy, sshh.'

The animal dropped to lie flat on his stomach on the cold pavement with his once erect and alert ears formed flat to the sides of his head. In the final act of submission the dog laid his head between the gap of its outstretched legs to be then followed by a long sigh of resignation.

'Well blow me down, how did you do that? That's bloody marvellous. Do you know since we took Arnie in from the dog rescue centre, me and Madge have been trying to get him to do as he is told without any success. You come along and he obeys you. Why do you think that is?' said the pensioner aged man while scratching at the wisps of grey hair springing from his bony cranium.

What Starr really wanted to say was that it's his undoubted charisma and charm he was fortunate enough to be blessed with when it came to dealing with both women and animals alike, but thought better of it as he was here on serious police business.

'Before I proceed to give you an explanation for our being here, I think it would be wise if we conducted our business from where we are standing. We wouldn't want to disturb Arnie again, would we, sir?' explained Starr.

'Yes, I agree officer. What is it you want?' the old man asked.

'We are here to see Mr Sproston, and we can't get anybody to answer the door.'

'Well you won't, they're still with Wilson at that leukaemia hospital in America. They've been gone close to two months now. In fact Barry rang last night to check if everything is okay,' the man then paused which allowed Starr to come in.

'Did he say when the family was likely to return?'

'Barry said there is no hope for his son and he doesn't expect him to survive beyond the next forty-eight hours. Such a damn shame, he is such a lovely boy. God knows how they will cope. Anyway why are you asking about the Sproston family?' the old man pressed Starr.

'Just some enquiries we are following up. Are you at liberty to tell me if you suspected the Sprostons had any money worries?'

'This thing about them having to have Wilson treated over in America was a massive worry for them both. Debbie had told Madge the treatment was going to amount to thousands and they may have to sell the house to pay off the private hospital bill. The bosses and the shop floor at the engineering company he works for have raised a lot of money to help them and I believe the charity "Dreams Come True" are supporting them with their accommodation fees. But, in spite of all the tremendous generosity shown by many people, it was never going to be enough to cover all the costs, Barry told me this.'

At this point in the dialogue Arnie could be heard snoring with Cooper preferring to keep a watchful eye on the beast similar to that portrayed in the film, *The Omen* while listening to the exchanges between the two men from the safety of being behind the partially wound down passenger window.

'It's clear to me then Mr Sproston will be facing a hefty bill at some stage. Do you have a contact number so we might speak to him?' asked Starr.

The man was slightly taken aback sensing things were more serious than he first thought.

'Barry's not in trouble is he? He's a decent man and a good father, why would you want to speak to him?'

'I don't believe Mr Sproston is in any trouble but we are pursuing a line of enquiry and it is important we are able to make contact with him. Do you have a phone number or an address we could have?' Starr understood he had told a necessary white lie in order to prevent the man from becoming over protective towards the Sprostons.

'Yes, yes Madge has all of that stuff. If you wait here I will go and get it for you. Come on Arnie.' the man tugged at the lead connected to the dog's studded collar to awaken the slumbering animal. The dog reluctantly opened its eyes followed by a real struggle to stand upright on all fours.

'Let's go, lad.' The dog paced slowly behind the man up the garden path and through a gate into the back garden.

'Right Cooper, you can get out of the car now, Arnie's gone!' Starr said in a teasing manner.

'That thing needs putting down. Did you see the size of its teeth?' questioned the DS while straightening his jacket with the palms of his sweaty hands.

'If you had remained still the dog wouldn't have chased you. But by running away, he understood you to be a nice piece of fleeing sirloin and, I must admit, he looked pretty well determined to get you.'

'Tell me about it. I bloody hate dogs!' emphatically stated Cooper.

Starr chose to say no more on the subject of canines with his thoughts having turned to wondering how anybody in their right mind might think this insipid young man could ever enhance the quality of policing in the Bladdington constabulary, or any other constabulary come to that.

Two or three minutes later the old man was seen to open the back garden gate holding aloft a piece of paper and then to walk swiftly down the path calling out, 'I've got want you want officers, Madge had got it all written down in a book.'

He handed the folded slip to Starr, who then opened the note flat to read the name and phone number of a hotel in Miami and Barry Sproston's employer's address.

'Glad to help, officers. Now then, Barry's lawn looks as though it could do with a trim and oh, I nearly forgot, Madge had watched from the front window how manfully you were able to calm Arnie and she has asked me to ask you, DCI Starr, do you fancy coming over here to give Arnie a few lessons, we will pay you of course.'

'I would love to help but I'm too busy at the moment. Have a look in yellow pages, you'll find dog trainers in there. Again, thank you for your assistance. Goodbye.'

'Goodbye officers.' reciprocated the old man, who then stood there for a while to watch the silver unmarked police car move off. He did not notice the second police car leaving.

During the journey back to the station Starr took the opportunity to delve into what his younger near contemporary might be thinking.

'You heard what was said back there DS Cooper, I'd like to ask you what your thoughts are.'

'Yes, I have been considering what the neighbour told us about Sproston. He certainly paints him as being a solid family man who must be going through hell and back. How do you cope with the awful prospect of losing a child? I wouldn't want to start to even imagine such a thing,' sympathised Cooper. 'At this very moment I can't believe him to be capable of carrying out such an act, he seems such a decent fellow,' he concluded. Starr then picked up on one of Cooper's points:

'On the surface I would tend to agree with you Max, but one thing this job has taught me is that you can never take anything at face value. The jails are full of con men who have, at some stage, been very adept at convincing people into believing they were not capable of the crime they were eventually found guilty of committing.'

Cooper's mind re-ran what the dog handling man had said about the near certain prospect that Sproston would have to sell his house.

He then went on to say, 'We can state for certain he needed a vast sum to pay for his son's treatment and £82,000 would go a long way towards settling the bill. In desperate times people do desperate things. Who really knows what we are capable of ourselves if faced with such a situation? He may have also done all of this without his wife knowing a thing about it. It was only because Bruce McCoy had planned to buy a new car on the first of September that the loss from his account came to light.'

'Quite,' Starr said momentarily locked in some deep thoughts.

'At the moment he's still our man, what I'd like you to do next, Max is to get onto the airports to check if Barry Sproston went through passport control on the day you bathed yourself in glory and maybe two days after that just in case he caught a later flight out. Also don't forget to ask them for his passport number. While you are doing that I'll ask those lovely ladies in the canteen to rustle up a cup of tea and a bacon and egg bap, I'm starving, I bet you are too Max. When you've done you can have your break.'

Cooper understood the day he needed to check with passport control was the same one when he just about managed to complete the 10k fun run. Starr was only being his usual sarcastic self.

Soon they would be back inside the station with Starr striding off to the canteen and Cooper sulkily walking to find his desk in the incident room knowing he'd probably be in for another long night.

Chapter Twenty-Two

Grey had dropped Bruce McCoy off in Bladdington town centre. It was getting towards mid-afternoon and he would just have enough time to buy a Costa latte and a leisurely read of the *Daily Telegraph* before walking over to the charity shop to share a lift home with Sally.

Starr appeared back in the incident room having used his charm to get one of his "admirers" to make him two bacon and egg baps before shutting up for the day. He was about to devour the remains of the second bap when he called over to where Cooper was sitting.

'Any luck, Max? Hasn't Miss Grey returned yet?' Starr asked without creating a break between the two questions.

'To answer your first point Sir, yes I've managed to contact passport control, and if you look around Sir, it's obvious DS Grey has not yet returned.' Cooper hadn't eaten since having an early morning bowl of sugar puffs. This had caused his blood sugar levels to drop off quite steeply by this point in the day, hence the rather narky reply he gave to his superior.

'No need for the sarcasm DS Cooper, you'll get that privilege if you ever get to my rank and not until. I can clearly see she is not here, I thought she might have called you to let us know what she is up to,' explained Starr.

'No, she hasn't called. Do you want me to get on with what I've been able to find out, Sir?'

'Yes, yes. Right, Max let me know how you got on.'

The police have access to a dedicated service provided by passport control for enquiries such as Cooper made during the time his boss was away topping up on his daily calorie intake.

'Have they closed the canteen yet, Sir?' Cooper enquired looking up at the clock to see it had gone four.

'Well it does shut at four Max, you should have asked me to get you something.'

'You didn't ask me if I wanted anything, Sir.'

'Well you should have done. Look it's not the end of the bloody world, just nip out to Pizza Plus, you can get what you want from there.'

Later Cooper took up his boss's suggestion and deliberately stayed there longer than he normally would have to even up, to his mind, the scores.

'Right, am I ever going to learn what you got from passport control? Come on DS Cooper, what have you got for us?' chivvied Starr.

'They have no records of any person named Barry Sproston, leaving the country late July. However, it is logged that Barry, Debbie and Wilson Sproston flew out to Miami during the beginning of July and according to their records have not yet returned to the UK. They did say the updating of records is not done in real time, often there can be a short delay.' explained Cooper.

'Did you get his passport number?'

'Yes, I've written it down here for you.' Cooper passed the yellow note over to Starr for him to see the long number.

'Could it possibly be that when Sproston appeared at the end of the run he planned it to be a fleeting visit only and might have used a fake passport to retain his anonymity? It wouldn't make any sense for him to draw attention to himself by using his proper passport. Anyway, that is something we all need to think about. Well done Max, you can go and have your break now and I'll see you back in ten minutes.'

Cooper slipped his jacket on to leave his boss to make the call to Miami. He had no intentions of having a ten minute break; it would be more like fifty minutes before he was again back at his desk.

Starr had calculated that the time in Miami was around about mid-day so he was confident someone would still be managing the hotel's reception desk.

He read from a creased piece of paper the details of a neatly hand written telephone number to then prod in each of the digits into the land line phone.

Listening carefully to the ringing tone there then followed a loud crackling noise as if the receiver was being roughly handled, then he heard a sweet heavily accented female American voice:

'Good afternoon, this is Florida Sands hotel. How may I help you?'

'Hello, I am Detective Chief Inspector Starr and I am calling from England.' Starr pronounced his words slowly to ensure she too could understand some of the vagaries he might have in his own accent.

'Hello sir, I will be pleased to help you if I can.'

'Thank you, my officers are conducting enquiries in England which requires me to establish if you have a British National in the name of Barry Sproston staying at the Florida Sands Hotel. He will be booked in with his wife, Debbie.'

'I'm sorry sir, we are not allowed to give out this information over the phone, I'm sure you understand we do this to protect the customers' right to privacy.' she pleasantly explained.

This was near to another white lie time. 'It's good to hear the hotel has a robust policy on preventing this information being accessed by those who may wish to use it for no good purposes.' said Starr.

'Thank you, sir.'

Before the receptionist was allowed to continue to extol more of the hotel's policies Starr said, 'I have spoken to a senior Interpol police officer in Miami and he has kindly informed me that if I am able to quote the personal ID number printed in the passport they could see no reason for you to bar the UK police from the information it seeks to acquire.'

The line fell quiet for a moment. Starr obviously wasn't able to see the young receptionist reaction on first hearing the words: "UK police" followed by "Interpol". She had become fearful a bomb might have been planted in the hotel by some dissident group.

'Is everything okay?' Starr knew she was still hanging onto the phone because he could hear short shallow breaths.

'Yes sir, sorry. Read the number to me and I will check it against the passport, if it is here, of course.'

'Good, the number is: 174234569.'

The sound of the hard plastic receiver being placed on the reception desk surface filled the ear piece at Starr's end of the connection. He loudly drummed his fingers on the desk top while he waited to hear the sound of her voice again.

'Mr Sproston's passport is in our safe keeping so, obviously, he is still staying with us. Is there anything else I can help you with, sir?' the receptionist enquired.

Starr saw no harm in trying his luck.

'Yes, there is something. Are you able to recognise Mr Sproston and his wife Debbie?'

'Yes, they have been staying here for a while now. They have a very poorly son being cared for at the Cristoforo Colombo Childrens' Hospital next to the hotel. I do hope everything turns out well for them, they are such lovely people. I suppose it won't do any harm telling you this, will it sir?' she said suddenly worried she may have done something wrong.

'No, no, you have been more than helpful, but I will ask you to do one last thing for me though.'

'What's that, sir?'

'Please don't let them know about our little conversation, that's all.'

'I won't tell a soul, sir.'

'Goodbye then,' bade Starr.

'Have a nice day, sir.'

Then the connection went dead.

Thirty minutes after Starr had made a second international call, the quiet of the incident room was to be broken by the noisy entry of both Grey and Cooper apparently laughing about something that had gone on in the Pizza Plus restaurant.

'Glad to see you are both back safely. I was just about to send out a search party, I was terribly worried you'd both been kidnapped by a crazed terrorist group.'

The look of laughter on their faces gradually faded to be replaced with a show of embarrassment; both understood they had taken some liberty to extend their break unreasonably.

'Right, sit down both of you and I will let you in on what I have been able to discover from the calls I made during your long and worrying absence,' said Starr.

He went on to recall the conversation he'd had with the hotel receptionist confirming Barry Sproston was still in residence there, followed by what he learned when he made the second international call.

'Similar to the reaction I got when I made the call to the hotel. The hospital was a little cagey at first, but at the mere mention of Interpol they surprisingly become most cooperative. I could easily have been someone holding ulterior motives. You have only just got to go back to recall the devastation Placino reeked at Bladdington hospital to understand what I am saying.'

Both of the openly alert officers nodded their heads in mute agreement.

'They confirmed they do have a patient in their care in the name of Wilson Sproston, and that he is being supported daily by his parents, Barry and Debbie. They have been at his side for the past two months,' reported Starr.

'Looks like we've got our man.' piped up Cooper. 'It all seems to fit. The neighbour told us Sproston's wife was worried they might be forced to sell their house. Siphoning money from Sally McCoy's account would negate the need to take such a drastic step.'

'Aren't you overlooking something, DS Cooper?' said Starr.

'What?' he replied.

'The date of departure passport control gave you coincides with the length of time the Sproston's have been in America. However, reasonable doubt as to the man's authenticity creeps in when he was photographed by Carter taking part in the charity run after his initial departure from the UK, but passport control have no record of his return or jetting out again after that period. To pull off such a stunt he'd have to go to the lengths of getting a fake passport. It's our job to establish whether he did or not,' asserted Starr. Feeling the sudden effects of an adrenalin rush he moved on to press the hitherto silent Grey.

'What are your thoughts, Miss Grey? You've not said much, not even why you were so late getting back to the station after dropping Bruce McCoy off.'

She wasn't able to prevent the sudden feeling of warm blood expanding the tiny capillaries covering her cheeks to give an outward red glow.

Grey wasn't about to divulge why she was late back to the station. It was best to keep the DCI in the dark as he would find it difficult to approve what she had got up to, to be actual police work.

On the journey back to report to the station after dropping off McCoy, she spotted PC Stephen Dale on walking patrol. Later, she would try to reason with herself why a "not to be denied" sexual impulse overrode her professional responsibilities at that time. When the car pulled up alongside the tall, handsome and masculine constable the passenger side window lazily came down followed by a Marilyn Monroe accented voice calling out, 'Hello, officer. I have a problem I'm sure you will be able to help me with.'

The constable stopped dead in his tracks to then stoop down and peer through the passenger side window inquisitive to see who the person was in the car.

'Cora, I didn't expect to see you!' said Dale in total surprise. His eyes then dropped to notice her skirt had been hitched up to reveal a tantalising glimpse of her black stocking top. The look on his face showed he had so predictably swallowed the bait she had set to snare him with.

'Get in Dale, I'm arresting you.' she then demanded.

'What am I being arrested for?' enquired a grinning Dale as he was about to open the passenger door.

'For being a naughty boy, now get in!' He removed his helmet and obeyed the temptress's order.

Rather than leaning over to her to give her his usual strong embrace, he lingered for a second or two to stare into her "undress me eyes" slightly taken aback by her unexpected show.

'Right, PC Dale, I've got about thirty minutes, you know all the nooks and crannies around here, guide me to somewhere we won't be seen.'

Dale wasn't about to miss the chance of fulfilling one of his sexual fantasies, and quickly directed the unmarked car to where a secluded block of garages was situated to the rear of recently built upmarket apartments.

'Will we be all right here?' Even though she was seriously aroused, Grey did not want to be caught in the act.

'People who live in these apartments are all at work, so this time of the day there is never anybody about. And if you look around there are no CCTV cameras. Any more questions, officer?'

'No, come to me you naughty boy.' Grey rushed to press her hot full lips against his while their free hands gently caressed each other. There would be no frenzied tearing off of clothes and underwear followed by a thirty second bout of mad bonking which usually left the lovers completely exhausted, as typically depicted in some blockbuster movies.

Grey was more than happy to be pleasured by the intense sensation brought on by his experienced fingertips gently, ever so gently, passing teasingly close to her erogenous zones. Her arousal was heightened even further by the heady masculine smell of his skin, absent of any moisturiser or after shave. These precious shared moments endorsed her willingness to allow herself to be put under the spell of what her heart desired - a real man.

Before Grey later dropped Dale off where she had earlier spotted him, they had both agreed to meet up again that evening on the proviso Starr didn't have other ideas about what he wanted to do with her time.

'I have been listening Sir, and I was delayed in getting back to the station because Bruce McCoy wanted someone to talk to. He says he doesn't have nor need many friends but he did number you, Sir, among those few he really valued.' Grey looked up at Starr to see if he'd taken in what she had said. His silence confirmed to her he had indeed.

'I used my professional judgement to spend some time with him. Without going into any unnecessary detail, I'm sure Sir, you will give some credence to my situation.'

Grey's explanation was in part true. Her chat with McCoy during the journey from the station to Bladdington town centre did touch on the worries he held about his wife's future and how the loss of the money might impact on both their lives. However, the unplanned tryst with her beau was wisely not touched upon.

'I think we need to deal with the facts we have at hand,' said Grey with a renewed sense of purpose. 'Having established Barry Sproston is still in Miami and visiting his son in hospital, I believe the next step is to have him arrested and questioned.'

'I'll do that Sir, I fancy a trip to Miami, the weather's been crap over here this summer,' spouted Cooper enthusiastically with his hand held up in the air like an eager school kid.

'You don't think for one moment Palfreyman is going to sanction you, DS Cooper, to jet out to Florida with your dad's stretched yellow budgie smugglers packed away in your case in the hope you might get some time on the beach, even if you are one of his blue eyed fast track boys,' Starr answered sharply to dismiss any suggestion of a jolly at ratepayers' expense.

'Let's get onto Interpol, London and they can arrange with the Miami police to take Sproston into custody. We can then question him from here using a RIVA video link,' casually mentioned Grey. Starr followed her suggestion by first throwing her a confused look and then asking,

'What the bloody hell is a RIVA video link, Cora?'

'What, you don't know what RIVA is? It's an acronym for: Recordable International Video Access. Wherever have you been for the past two years, Sir?' Grey responded with a smirking grin on her face.

'No, Miss Grey, I don't know anything about RIVA, and more to the point young lady, nor do I have to,' he replied curtly. 'I have subservient people like you in my team whose job it is to be aware of resources that can be useful to drive an investigation forward.'

Grey should have expected such a put down; she was dealing with DCI Starr after all.

'Sorry, Sir, I didn't mean to be disrespectful,' she said unnecessarily apologetically.

For the next two minutes the two junior officers gave as good a spiel as a keen RIVA sales rep would give to get a new customer to sign a three year contract.

'Right, I understand now. Yes, I agree, that's a good idea. We will be able to question Sproston under the watchful eye of the arresting officers in a Miami police station. Palfreyman will certainly be happy if it all goes well,' concluded Starr.

Then, out of the blue, Starr announced they were both allowed to finish for the day.

'We've got a lot done today and, with a bit of luck tomorrow we should have the details Titley promised he'd have for us. Right, you two young people get off and enjoy whatever you have planned for the night. I'll get onto Interpol and hopefully tomorrow we will be able to view our friend Barry Sproston on a RIVA video link.' He then playfully gave Grey eye contact as a sign both he and she had made their individual points with no grudges held.

The two swiftly left the incident room chatting and faces beaming. Cooper was able to go ahead to join his friends for a couple of pints before the 7:45 p.m. kick off.

Grey's intentions were of a different nature. She planned to fill a hot bath seductively scented with aromatic oils to be later shared with PC Dale. On the way home she called in at Marks and Spencer to buy cinnamon and orange infused candles she planned to strategically place around the bathroom. The purchase of a readymade three course meal for two and a bottle of red wine was included to add to the evening's romance she so eagerly anticipated.

Starr remained at his desk to tap in the chief superintendent's internal number. He chanced Palfreyman would still be in his office and hadn't done an early bunk to join one of his golfing pals. His call resulted in an invitation to join the chief super in his office.

'Hello Dick, what can I do for you? But be quick, I've got to leave the station soon to attend a council meeting,' he said rather impatiently.

Starr's thoughts were, "Of course you have". He was no more rushing off to a council meeting than he was going to have his back, sack and crack done.

Starr went on to explain the day's events and his planned intentions.

'I was mindful not to put any pressure on the budget, that is why I suggested to my younger colleagues we need to use the new technology at our disposal. After all we've had RIVA in for nearly two years now, and they both agree, it would enable us to interview Sproston with no expense incurred.'

'Well done Dick, very good planning and sensible use of our diminishing resources. But you would have thought Grey or Cooper might have come up with the idea to use, what is it called again, Dick?'

'RIVA video link, Sir,' pronounced Starr proudly.

'Yes, RIVA. Anyway Dick, I've got to dash, can't keep these councillors waiting. Pass my congratulations on to the young DSs, we mustn't forget Dick they are the future torch bearers.'

'No, Sir. I won't'

Starr remained while watching the man put on his civilian style jacket and then slip out of the door.

From the quiet of the chief superintendent's office Starr rang the Interpol head office in London. Having then been directed to an appropriate person, Starr carefully gave a full and detailed explanation why he decided it was necessary to use the Interpol service and what he wanted the police in Miami to do for him.

'It's best we don't rush into these things, DCI Starr,' suggested DCI Brian Wilding, the Interpol liaison officer, 'I will certainly make contact with the Miami Police Department and put to the assistant chief of police what you have requested they do for you. On the surface it appears to me to be the most appropriate method in establishing if your suspect is guilty of what you have alleged. I don't think the police over there would want to become too heavily involved, after all they have their hands full dealing with all what goes on in their own patch,' he said.

'So you don't think it is too unreasonable for the Miami police to have Sproston arrested and then have it arranged that we can talk to him using a RIVA video link say, for around about twelve mid-day tomorrow British time?' queried Starr.

'Depends on how busy they are. I will try and push them to meet with your arrangements, after all we tend to pull out all the stops when we receive similar requests from them.' explained Wilding.

'When can I expect an update from you then?'

'Just give me a few moments to think things through. You have given me the man's name and his passport number, the hotel where he is staying at and the hospital his son is being treated in. So it's just a matter of locating him and then the police will simply take him into custody and wait for the British police to make contact. And if what you tell me is true that this Sproston guy seems to be a non-violent type, then it should all be reasonably straightforward, huh, but we are probably both long enough in the tooth DCI Starr to understand things don't always go to plan. Anyway, I will give you the direct phone number and contact name of the assistant chief, or whoever else they may wish to be the contact person to liaise with once I have established the arrangements. If you give me your email address, I will send you the details as soon as I have them at hand. That will save you hanging around waiting for a call from me.'

After giving his appreciation, Starr then bid farewell to his London based contemporary. He then looked at his watch to see it was now close to seven o'clock. For a brief moment he toyed with the idea to give Bruce McCoy a call from Palfreyman's swanky office, but dismissed this thought preferring the option to make a personal call on his friend on his way home.

Starr noticed the Mondeo estate parked on the drive as he pulled up outside the neat Victorian period home. Having pressed the doorbell he then turned to casually glance around the other meticulously maintained properties facing the McCoy's house. The noise from the door latch being operated caused him to again turn his attention to face the door.

It was Sally who answered his call and she looked at him blankly.

'Yes, what is it you want?' she said coldly.

'Hello Sally, I'm here to see Bruce. Is he in?'

'Sorry but I don't know who you are.' she said looking somewhat confused at the stranger standing at the door. Starr was aware of her condition so acted as if her address was normal.

'My name is Dick Starr, Bruce and I were in the police together,' he explained.

'I've never heard him mention you before. Never mind, I'll have to leave you for a moment while I get him for you.' She closed the door shut on him to leave Starr rather bemused about her odd actions.

He was again disturbed from his gazing around the property by the sound of the latch being turned once more, this time to reveal Bruce McCoy standing in the opening.

'Sorry about that, Dick,' McCoy apologised while stepping out of the small entrance porch and then carefully closing the door behind him.

'We'll talk outside if you don't mind, Dick. You can see, Sally is getting no better, I have got to get her to see the doctor, it's no use the way things are going. But that is my worry and not yours,' said McCoy.

Starr wasn't about to offer his sympathies. There was little point in raking over what they had previously discussed concerning his friend's wife.

'Right, let's get down to business, it's been one hell of a busy day, but one I believe will bear fruit for us,' reported Starr.

'That sounds great Dick, don't keep me waiting.' urged McCoy.

The two men strolled around the large back garden in the failing evening light while Starr recalled the day's events, some of which McCoy was already aware off, and others he would be pleased to learn about. McCoy listened intently to what was being said and at the same time forming a picture in his mind of the places and characters visited and met that day.

'So, tomorrow looks like it's going to be another full on day for your team. What I would do to be involved,' said McCoy disappointedly.

'It's a pity Bruce, but you know that is not possible. And while we're on the subject, and please take what I'm going to say next in the manner it is intended.'

Before Starr could finish, McCoy interjected, 'I know what this is all about Dick. I understand and accept I took a bit of a liberty when I went back to the station with DS Grey. It wasn't her fault; I'm guilty of compromising her position. It won't happen again.'

'Good, I knew you would understand,' said Starr relieved this potential tetchy point was out of the way.

'I would ask though Dick, you will keep me informed on how the investigation is going. It just isn't the business about the money being taken; it's more to do with why Sally was seen to be such an easy target. I'm absolutely convinced there has to be a local connection somewhere along the line behind such a cruel deception.'

'The video link interview planned with Sproston will hopefully go ahead as planned and then we will all get more answers.'

Feeling his stomach give off a rumble, Starr pulled up his jacket sleeve to glance at the time on his wrist watch.

'High time I was making a move, it's been a long day and I intend to call in at the carvery on the way home, I'm looking forward to a nice pint of real ale and a good English meal,' Starr enthused rubbing his hands together in anticipation.

After heartily shaking hands the two men went about filling in the remaining waking hours of that particular evening.

Chapter Twenty-Three

Around seven thirty in the morning, Starr was seen to be busying himself printing off copies of the email sent by the Interpol liaison officer, DCI Bryan Wilding, concerning the arrangements he'd agreed with the Miami Police Department. He had done the same with the email attachments sent from the Portshire bank. While he was again scan reading each of the sheets he'd printed off, he caught the sight of Cooper and Grey surreptitiously sneaking into the busy incident room. Both, he couldn't fail to notice, looked worse for wear, each of them no doubt, having enjoyed a late night for very different reasons.

Amidst the din of the early morning idle chatter his recognisable voice was to be heard above that of all others.

'Don't think I haven't seen you pair crawling in late, but don't worry, I've seen to the emails from Interpol and Titley. Just get yourselves a nice cup of coffee and when you are both quite ready, hopefully, you'll decide to join me in my office. But please don't rush.'

The two young detectives kept their heads down as they headed to their individual workstations. When they were seated Cooper leaned towards Grey to whisper,'

'What's got into him? The miserable sod needs to get out more.' Cooper didn't feel in the best of moods either because he was nursing a lager induced hangover after seeing his team be victorious the previous night.

'Be quiet Max, he might hear you,' warned Grey.

Her inner demeanour couldn't have been more different to that of her colleague and friend. Her night of passion had gone according to plan and furthermore, she had awoken before Dale, and the time spent staring at his face and heaving broad chest whilst he soundly slept on, aroused her to a such a point she wasn't about to let the man leave her bedroom until he had "performed" once again for her.

After a couple of minutes had elapsed since their public bollocking, Cooper and Grey stood up from their seats to leave their workstations to enter Starr's office and then sit in polypropylene chairs he had positioned around his desk.

When he saw they had settled he started the meeting by saying, 'If you don't mind, I will make a start. In front of you I have placed copies of the emails and attachments received this morning. You will notice not only has Titley delivered most of what I asked of him yesterday, so has DCI Bryan Wilding at Interpol. Read through the stuff and then I will sit back to listen to what you both have to say.' Starr folded his arms and lolled back in his budget purchased swivel chair to watch them both avidly reading through the printed material.

'Right, my gallant knights in shining armour,' roused Starr on seeing their young faces staring back at him. 'Tell me what we, the defenders of the law, should do to drive this investigation forward. Miss Grey, would you like to volunteer?'

Cooper sensed his body relax relieved the DCI hadn't picked on him to be, yet again, his whipping boy. Grey, on the other hand, was quite happy to voice her ideas which had been mostly formed from what she had just read in both emails.

'It's fantastic news you were able to get the cooperation of the Miami Police Department in agreeing to arrest Sproston, and then if all goes well, have him set up to appear on the RIVA video link for us to then question. You must have pulled a few strings, Sir,' praised Grey.

'I cannot take the credit for what the MPD have agreed to do for us,' said Starr in a serious tone, 'DCI Bryan Wilding is the officer who had acted on our request, he should be the person we need to thank. It was Wilding, not me, who must have pulled a fair few strings to set this up so quickly and that is not to mention the late hours he obviously put in to make it all possible.'

Grey and Cooper both understood the barb contained in the last part of his speech was meant for their benefit.

Undeterred, Grey continued to offer her thoughts, 'Thinking about the information Titley sent through, one of us will need to visit Barry Sproston's place of work to verify if the copy of the testimonial used to open the bank account is genuine or not. Also we can arrange for one of the support staff to contact the two banks here where the money was transferred to from the bank in Miami.' Grey then turned to her equal status partner to give a non-verbal cue it was his turn to be under the watchful scrutiny of the man looking impatiently at him from his position of power.

Cooper immediately straightened up in the chair accompanied by the sound of him clearing his throat from a taste of alcohol induced bile burning his gullet.

'Yes, by all means make a call on the factory,' he started off suggesting,' but maybe this needs to happen only after we have completed our interrogation of Sproston at twelve. It looks highly probable he is our man, but as we have already established, we do have some evidence gathered from passport control and his neighbours which leaves us with some flickering doubts. We have previously discussed the possibility of there being "two" Barry Sprostons, so we need to confirm or eliminate this particular suspect today.'

Cooper glanced at Starr through his bloodshot eyes instinctively awaiting a put down remark. It came, but not in the form he expected.

'Bloody hell Max, you look damn awful. I'd only want to look how you look now if I'd been locked up in a knocking shop for a month. Go and get us all a cup a tea, and while you are there, ask June to make you a breakfast bap that will sort you out. And before you go Max, I agree with what you said. Well done.'

In Cooper's absence Grey was told she was to lead the interrogation of Sproston with Cooper acting as co-interrogator. Starr would have no role to play other than to observe or step in if something blindingly obvious to him needed to be covered.

Chapter Twenty-Four

Hotel Florida Sands six o'clock in the morning, GMT -4 hours. The sudden hard aggressive thumping against the hotel door number 423 startled the occupants in the room together with those once slumbering along the same corridor.

The man and woman occupying the room at his time were sitting on the balcony having a drink when they heard the commotion.

'Who the heck can that be Barry?' said the man's startled wife, Debbie.

'God knows. I best go and see who it is.'

'Be careful Barry, you know how violent this part of Miami can be,' she warned while watching her husband stride over to the door. He took the precaution to peer through the spy glass fitted into the door before deciding whether to welcome the unexpected caller or not.

Before he was able to press his eye into the small circular lens, another set of hard banging rapped against the flimsy wood panelled door followed by aggressive shouts outside on the corridor.

'This is the Miami Police Department, please open the door Mr Sproston, we have a warrant for your arrest.'

Sproston sensed a grip of fear run through his body as he nervously obeyed the MPD's demands. The door was only slightly ajar when, to his horror, he was confronted by a group of tall, armed fully uniformed officers wearing sunglasses, bursting into the hotel room intent on making sure Sproston was going nowhere.

Amidst the confusing din created by the uncompromising American law enforcers, the hysterical calls of Sproston's wife were heard, "Leave him alone, leave him alone. What's going on? He's done nothing, please somebody help!' Her desperate cries were to be of no consideration to the early morning intruders.

In a matter of moments Barry Sproston was legged over by a Hispanic officer, who had then followed up by forcibly pressing him down hard so he became flat against the room carpet. The officer was determined to keep Sproston in this position by using a black leather gloved hand positioned at the back of his skull to grind his face into the rough short piled carpet. While in this prone position another officer then took a tight hold of his left arm and forced it up sharply towards his shoulder blade. Sproston let out a cry of pain, but before he was able to protest about his treatment he heard the sound of a handcuff being applied to his wrist and the ring then closed so tight it caused him to wince as the metal clasp dug into his skin. His arm was then yanked down for the other cuff to be attached to his right wrist in the same uncompromising manner.

Next, he was roughly dragged onto his feet by two officers who then released him to find his balance without the aid of his free arms. Seeing her husband was momentarily released from the clutches of the police, Debbie darted across the room wanting to be close to her shackled husband. An arm held out by one of the policemen barred her way from making the contact she so desperately wanted to feel.

'Sorry, Ma'am, he's under arrest.' the man said in a long drawl.

Barry Sproston spoke next having had a little time to compose himself.

'What am I being arrested for? This is just shear madness, I've done nothing wrong.' Sproston pleaded to the stone faced officers.

'We have a warrant for your arrest, sir. It has been issued by Interpol on request from Bladdington Police, England.'

'But he's done nothing, this is so wrong, let him go!' the woman painfully pleaded and at the same time, being forcibly barred from touching her husband by the robot-like policeman.

Sproston again spoke up after hearing his wife's loyal defence of him.

'What am I being charge with? What have I supposed to have done?' The man behind the black reflective lenses saw the first signs of rising anger in the British man's features. He took his time to answer, appearing to take some perverse joy from the shackled man's predicament.

'It states here, sir, you have fraudulently taken a sum of £82,000 from a police officer's bank account. The British police want to question you through some kind'a video link at eight a.m. today, sir.' The officer looked up from the sheet he'd recited the charge from to face the pale and sweating alleged felon.

Sproston saw his own image being reflected back to him from the officer's dark sunglasses to see it wasn't possible for him to hide his confused, angry expression brought on by the absurd accusation.

'You must be joking, this isn't some sick wind up is it?' he asked with a half grin spreading across his lips.

'No, sir. This is no joke! We have to take you down town now so we can get you processed and ready for the British police.'

'You make it sound like you are dealing with a piece of meat,' replied Sproston as the other two attending officers each took hold either side of him to then file out of the hotel bedroom.

Standing in chatting groups along the corridor were those who had been awoken by the early morning commotion and now eager to catch a glimpse of the perpetrators. Even though Sproston had kept his head down as he was being hauled down the corridor in the direction to the lifts, there were those who recognised him to be the father of the boy who was critically ill in the hospital next to the hotel. However, what they didn't know was that the poor child had died around tea time the previous day.

Debbie Sproston stood on the corridor outside of their hotel room clutching a handkerchief to her reddened face, watching a cuffed hunched figure being dwarfed by the three dark uniformed mechanical officers moving down the corridor and ever closer to the lifts which would take him on yet another journey into the unknown.

Sleep hadn't been an option that previous evening, both she and her husband had been up all night and between great bouts of grief and anguish at the loss of their only son. They had discussed more of the practical things that either needed to be done or faced at some stage. Every last penny had been spent in supporting Wilson over the past two months and without the generous support of 'Dreams Come True' charity and the good people of Moulton digging deep into their pockets there would have been no way they could have remained at their son's bedside throughout the frequent ups and eventual downs of his unfair illness. They touched on the real possibility that they might have to stomach the sale of their home once the final figure for Wilson's treatment was known. Their first concern, however, was to arrange for their son's shattered body to be flown back for interment in Bladdington cemetery. This was the point of their discussion when they were disturbed by the loud banging on the hotel bedroom door.

Chapter Twenty-Five

'It's a call asking for you, sir,' said Grey after she had responded to the phone ringing in Starr's office close to midday.

'Who is it?' he asked before taking the receiver from her grip.

'Sounds American to me, maybe it's the Miami police.'

'Right, let's hope it is.' Starr raised the receiver to his right ear. 'Hello, DCI Starr speaking.'

'Hello, sir. Pleased to hear you over there in England. I'm Captain Brookes-O'Hara of the Miami Police Department,' the man expressed in a pleasant manner.

'Good morning, sir, and salutations to you over there as well,' reciprocated Starr.

'Thank you. I'm pleased to inform you sir, we have made a successful arrest without incident early this morning and the subject is now in our safe custody awaiting you're questioning.'

'Thank you Captain Brookes-O'Hara. Can you please tell me the contact name at your station we need to use to create the video link?' asked Starr prepared with paper and pen to write down the important details.

'Yes, that will be Lieutenant Jane McAndrew; she looks after the public relations end of things here. Once you have logged onto RIVA, type in her name followed by Miami Police Department South Division. She will first introduce herself, followed by your suspect then appearing on screen. But before I leave there are a couple of other things I feel are important for you to be made aware of.'

'What is that, Captain?' asked Starr.

'Mr Sproston's son died late yesterday afternoon. We understand he had been seriously ill for some time but all the same, it must still be an unimaginable loss to both him and his wife. And since being in our custody he has fervently protested his innocence, so I would expect him to be difficult. Let the officer know at the end of the interview what you would want us to do next, DCI Starr.'

'Thank you for letting us know about his son. He is bound to be stressed with that alone never mind when we start to question him about the alleged fraud.' Starr was turned to thinking it was probably a good idea when deciding it should be Grey to do the questioning while he was still in total ignorance of Sproston's sad loss. He'd likely respond differently to a pleasant looking female doing the probing rather than being goaded by a hard bitten mean looking male veteran like himself.

'We will be ready for you by twelve British time. Well I wish you and your colleagues luck with your investigation and if you need any further assistance please do not hesitate to get in touch with me. Goodbye, DCI Starr.'

'Goodbye, Captain Brookes-O'Hara.' Starr placed the receiver back into the cradle, to wonder how the interview might develop with Sproston having to cope with his loss while being questioned about something he appears to claim to be completely innocent of. Grey would need to stick to the facts and avoid being diverted to that which concerned things of the heart.

'Did you hear all that, Cora?' said Starr turning to her.

'Yes, sir. What a shame. But we cannot allow his situation to distract us from getting the answers we need to either prove his guilt or support his innocence,' she reasoned.

Starr was pleased to hear Grey's sentiments, which went someway to make him believe she hadn't been affected by Sproston's situation.

'That's my girl, that was just what I needed you say. Are you and Max prepared to start the interview?' Starr was eager to get the show on the road as he too was keen to see the probable architect of such cruel deceit.

'Yes, a set of questions have all been typed up, we have marked the ones each of us will ask. Are you okay, Max?' Grey asked her co-interrogator. Cooper nodded his head in the affirmative, and while looking decidedly nervous, he was slightly excited about being the first officers in the station to perform a formal inter-continental criminal interview using RIVA technology.

A decision was made to use the relative quiet and privacy of Starr's office for the interview. Grey and Cooper had taken up seated positions where Starr would normally sit to face a seventeen inch monitor screen. Starr kept himself sufficiently far enough away from the web cam to prevent him from being picked up.

'Right, let's go for it,' he chivvied his young charges.

Grey logged on to the police dedicated RIVA connection to see the home page brightly fill the screen. She then typed in the police officer's name and destination at precisely twelve o'clock and waited in nervous anticipation for the screen content to change.

Their wait was to be only short, three seconds later the smiling image of Lieutenant McAndrew was in view in HD clarity.

'Hello, over there in Bladdington, England. I hope you can hear me. My name is Lieutenant Jane McAndrew.' Two small desk top speakers burst into life transmitting her soft American accent around the small office.

From her position in a room in the MPD, McAndrew took in from her monitor screen the youthful image of the two British detective sergeants.

'Yes, we can hear you loud and clear, Lieutenant McAndrew. Please allow me first to make our introductions,' replied Grey.

'Certainly, go ahead,' responded McAndrew, her reply confirming a definite transmission link had been made.

'This is my colleague DS Max Cooper.' Cooper broke into an awkward grin while making a courteous nod.

'My name is DS Cora Grey, and a "hello" to you too from Bladdington police station, England.' Grey then swung the screen around so that the webcam eye picked up DCI Starr, who's appearance on the officer's screen over in Miami portrayed a look of shock and embarrassment while listening to Grey continuing with the introductions. 'This is DCI Richard Starr, he is the chief investigating officer.'

This moment he hadn't prepared for and initially stumbled over his words. 'Hello, Lieutenant Nell McAndrew.'

Immediately he heard Grey hiss, 'Jane, not Nell!'

'Oh, I am sorry, I meant to say Jane,' he apologised while catching a glimpse of Cooper's shoulders shaking and the pinching of his nostrils to prevent a fit of giggles taking hold.

'I'd also like to say how grateful we are for the Miami police in acting so quickly with our request. I hope someday we can return the favour.'

'Well thank you for that, DCI Starr. You know, I just lurve the British accent, I could listen to you talk all day,' McAndrew said with her face beaming in apparent delight. 'I have your suspect, Mr Barry Sproston sitting beside me and he has been made aware of the reasons behind your request for his arrest. So when you are ready I'll spin the screen around so you can start the questioning,' she continued in a much more serious tone.

Grey, with her co-interrogator wiping the tears of mirth from his eyes, were now back in McAndrew's view.

'Yes, we are ready, thank you,' Grey confirmed.

The images on the screen juddered slightly as the monitor was turned on its base to eventually face the male suspect.

No words where immediately exchanged across the video link while both parties weighed up the opposition before battle commenced.

Sproston's disgruntled unshaven face appeared to completely fill the screen to such an extent as to invade upon one's personal space. The high colour resolution showed him to have dark shadows under both bloodshot eyes with lines radiating out into his temple region to form deep creases. His shiny raven black hair hung in Bryan Ferry style as would happen towards the end of a particularly energetic concert. The DSs needed to have been blind not to see the man looked seriously pissed off.

'I am DS Grey, and this is my colleague, DS Cooper. Please can you confirm your name and home address, sir.' formally asked Grey.

Since his uncompromising arrest earlier that morning, Sproston had given some serious thought as to how he should conduct himself when the British police confront him with their accusations. He was angry for sure, he was mad about the injustice of it all, he was grieving badly for the loss of his son, he had been ruthlessly hauled away from his wife and was now accused by the police, while in a foreign land, of doing something he hadn't done.

However, he consoled himself with the knowledge that the police in Bladdington didn't know this yet, for they clearly believed they had their prime suspect in safe custody and it was now just a small matter of them tying up the loose ends.

Even at this late stage, the high tension abounding his body for the past two hours hadn't shown any sign of diminishing. In fact a fresh injection of adrenalin into his system had heightened his consciousness to defend himself with vigour. He possessed the intelligence to understand he could either harm or support his defence over the next few minutes by virtue of his actions and what he said.

'Yes, I confirm my name is Barry Sproston, and my home address is 59 Elmwood Avenue, Moulton, England,' the stark statement resonated deeply within him. He was longing to escape from the accusing cold looks and dank holding cell of the MPD and to be free to return home to Moulton with his wife and the lifeless body of his son, Wilson.

Grey, having been relieved to hear his reply to be calm and not the aggressive outburst she half expected, pressed on with the interview.

'I understand the police have explained to you, Mr Sproston, why a warrant had been issued for your arrest.'

'Yes, they have,' he replied.

'As a matter of legal procedure I will again read out the nature of the crime you have been alleged to have committed and then I will read you your rights.'

'Fine!'

'Mr Barry Sproston, you have been accused of fraudulently taking the sum of £82,000 from the bank account of Mr Bruce McCoy and Mrs Sally McCoy currently residing in Bladdington, England. I have to ask you now do you understand the charge?'

Sproston appeared to be reaching out of the screen at this point causing Grey to move her seat back a little to escape his imposing presence.

'I understand the charge, but I don't accept it DS Grey. I hope that is clear to the both of you,' coldly replied Sproston.

'I will now read you your rights, sir. You do not have to say anything. However, it may harm your defence if you do not mention when questioned something which you later rely on in court. Anything you do say may be given in evidence. Do you understand?' Her head was bowed while she read the statement from a laminate card, when she looked up to the accused again he too was looking down maybe at some sort of mark created by a previous felon, while he mumbled the word, 'Yes.'

'Sorry, Mr Sproston, I did not quite hear what you said.' pressed Grey.

In response he turned to the webcam for her to then detect a subtle yet obvious change in his appearance. His pupils appeared watery and combined with the presence of the bright lights illuminating the room, caused them to twinkle to belie some external evidence of his inner emotions.

'Yes, yes, yes!' he answered in a raised voice.

Grey ignored his obvious tetchiness to move to one side a little to permit DS Cooper to continue with his part of the charging process.

'What I intend to do now Mr Sproston,' Cooper uneasily started, 'is to read to you the evidence we have so far gathered which has lead us to establish your involvement in having committed the crime of fraud. I will ask you to remain silent throughout the report as there will be additional questions we will want to ask and I'm certain there will be some issues you will want to clarify.'

Sproston must have propelled his seat further back from the probing lens of the webcam due to the image on screen showing him with his arms defensively folded against the sparse background of the soulless room where the video link had been routed to.

Cooper went on to read the pre-prepared detailed report generated from different strands of the investigation over the previous days.

In the midst of Cooper's monologue, Chief Superintendent Richard Palfreyman, was seen by the three incumbents to carefully turn the handle of the office door keenly conscious not to create any noise to announce his arrival.

Having enjoyed some success in not making the door emit a squeak, he tiptoed in exaggerated fashion to take up a position next to his DCI.

'How's it going Dick?' he whispered through the corner of his mouth and at the same time giving Cooper and Grey a look and nod of approval.

'All right so far, but we'll have to wait and see how Sproston responds to what we have accused him of doing before we can gauge how well things have gone,' replied Starr who similarly whispered in reply.

The two elder statesmen watched on as Cooper surprisingly impressed in his controlled diction and the consummate ease in which he was able to elaborate on the case background notes he frequently referred to.

When he had completed the reading of the police report, Cooper moved his chair to allow Grey to take up the prominent position. She too had been taken in by her co-interrogator's presentation, and was now conscious it was her turn to put on a show for the watching VIP audience.

'This is your opportunity, Mr Sproston to question the police evidence. I must remind you that you are still under caution and anything you say may be used in evidence against you in a court of law,' said Grey.

Palfreyman turned to Starr his face positively beaming and whispered to his subordinate, 'That's the way you do it Dick. Stick to the book and you can't go wrong. Those two will go a long way, mark my words.'

This man's uninvited presence was irking Starr by the minute. He really wanted to tell him to piss off out of his office and go and pester one of his plummy mates on the golf course. Palfreyman would likely reject this suggestion, however, Starr consoled himself he just needed to put up with him being there for a little while longer yet.

Sproston, in the meantime, had moved his seating position so his distinctive features again filled the monitor screen. During the hearing of the police account of his alleged dealings and whereabouts, he had satisfied himself that his best policy during this stage of the interview was to remain calm and decisive.

'In my defence I want to place on record that I categorically deny I had any involvement in the taking of the £82,000 from that bank account. I did not take part in any charity run and I am not a member of *Face2Face* or any other social site. Furthermore, I did not open a bank account over here in Miami. I will even give you my permission to check my own bank account, you'll then see for yourselves that I'm absolutely stone broke.' Sproston stared unblinkingly into the screen awaiting a response to his claims from the apparently dumb struck British detectives.

Sproston used this pregnant pause to revisit some of the points of evidence presented to him.

'You say I took part in a charity run at the beginning of July?' Sproston further questioned.

'Yes, we have a photograph of you together with Mrs McCoy taken at the end of the race,' replied Grey.

'Can I have a look at that photograph?' pressed Sproston.

Grey turned to her DCI to seek his guidance on this point. Starr silently mouthed 'Yes' with his rationale being if the man was in custody over here in Bladdington, he would be allowed to view the evidence.

Cooper passed the incriminating image to Grey from the thin pile on the desk. She held the charity run picture up to screen free of hand tremor. She, of course then wasn't able to witness him scrutinising every detail of the professionally taken photograph. He was heard through the desk top speakers to say he had finished.

Grey passed the picture back to Cooper to place it with the other evidence, only then to see the sight of the accused rocking slightly to and fro on his chair with a slight grin formed on his lips similar to that when one has been exposed to a subject of irony.

'Yes, I have to agree with you, that man has an unnerving resemblance to me, you know he may be easily mistaken as my twin brother. Amazing!' he laughingly conjectured.

Grey and Cooper watched on as he showed only the side view of his head while still being able to distinguish the sound of him talking to one of the accompanying Miami police officers.

The British officers were then taken by surprise to watch Sproston move from his seated position to stand upright and then start to remove his sweaty t-shirt to expose his white hairless chest and upper arms.

'Look, no tattoos, no tattoos,' they heard him repeat while watching him perform a 360 degrees turn.

Then, in dramatic style, he unbuckled his trouser belt to then free it from the captive loops in one long yank followed by the undoing of the trouser top button and pulling down of the zip to completely remove his trousers leaving his body naked except for a pair of black boxer pants. Repeating the same pirouette he was able to prove to his accusers his legs too were absent of body art.

During this time the two senior officers had joined their younger and junior contemporaries around the monitor screen to witness Sproston's desperate display of innocence. Once he had dressed he positioned his seat so he could be again seen in full view of the web cam.

What the four different ranking officers saw in England was a set of facial features which appeared to have been miraculously transformed from their previous viewing of the same person.

Sproston in turn, was most happy to view the once smug accusing expressions now having been altered to looks of doubt.

Grey spoke up to try and discredit Sproston's attempt at proving his innocence.

'You could have easily included the wearing of temporary body art transfers to compliment your subterfuge. More and more people are turning to this method rather than being burdened with permanent tattoos they may regret later in life.'

On the surface, Sproston appeared to have utterly disregarded Grey's attempt at putting down his response to disprove his guilt in the fraud. He was however, intelligent enough to acknowledge the young female's observations might be perfectly reasonable if a crook was so determined to hide his identity.

His mind at this point, had switched to having a pressing urge to share with the British officers an incident that had happened at the hotel which had later served to bother him greatly.

'Before we go any further, I would like you all to listen to something I believe will cast doubt on my involvement in the fraud.' The image in the screen showed the man's expression to appear contemplative.

'Go ahead, Mr Sproston. You have our full attention,' assured Grey.

'Debbie and I had decided to take a morning out from being at the hospital. I'm not asking for your pity, but no one will ever understand how much it takes out of you both physically and mentally when so much of your waking time is spent either visiting or worrying yourself sick about what might happen to someone you dearly love. We strayed along the beach farther than we expected and by the time we had stopped at a beach restaurant for a bite to eat, it would have been around two o'clock by the time we returned to the hotel. A strange thing then happened, which I have never been able to provide an answer to. The hotel receptionist called us over and asked if we had any luck in hiring the four by four vehicle I had told her about that very morning. She couldn't fail to notice how Debbie and I looked at each other in total bemusement at what she had said to us.

'I remembered her then appearing to be anxious to prove her recollection of their earlier meeting was not wrong. She removed a stiff backed record book from under the reception desk to flick through the pages to find that day's entries to prove my passport had been taken from the hotel. I took the time to have a good look at the entry made when she passed over my passport, it was then I noticed the signature was not made by my hand. She said she later came across my passport in the box used to place hotel room swipe cards by residents vacating or day tripping. I insisted it couldn't have possibly been me who received the passport from her, but I don't believe I fully convinced her.' Sproston relaxed back in the solid wood framed chair arms folded anticipating a further grilling from his accusers.

During the recalling of the passport incident, Cooper had mulled over different scenarios which might reasonably explain why the passport had been removed from the hotel's safekeeping only then to be anonymously returned in a relatively short period of time.

'We have been sent a photocopy copy of your passport which was being held in the records of the East Seaboard Trust Corporation based in Miami. Evidence of you holding a passport, along with a testimonial provided by your employer which included your national insurance number, were used to sanction a bank account in your name.' He was interrupted mid-flow by Sproston's unexpected intervention.

'It wasn't me who'd opened that account if that is what you are thinking. Before we flew out my own bank had arranged for me to make payments and free cash withdrawals on my credit card as a gesture of goodwill. They also kindly made a substantial contribution to support our stay during Wilson's illness. So why would I want to open another account over here? Have you checked the date on which the account was opened at this East Seaboard bank?' he queried.

'You have pre-empted my thinking Mr Sproston. We need to get hold of the date recorded in the receptionist's record book when your passport was taken from the hotel and to see if it tallies with the time the bank account was opened.

It would be of no surprise to me to find both dates are the same,' reflected the male DS.

During Cooper's continued dialogue with Sproston, Grey recognised the interview was unravelling a number of threads that needed to be pulled together before she too, at least, was convinced of this man's guilt.

'I think we should suspend proceedings for fifteen minutes at this point, I'm sure Mr Sproston is more than ready for a break. Please will you allow Lieutenant McAndrew to come to the screen so I can inform her also,' said Grey.

It only required a few moments for Grey to view McAndrew.

'You have no need to repeat what you have said to Mr Sproston, we'll have him ready for you to interview again in fifteen minutes,' said the pleasantly mannered American police officer. Grey thanked the Lieutenant and then moved out of her seat to gather up the pile of evidence notes sitting on the desk top.

With the video link connection being kept live, the four officers vacated Starr's small office to gather around a desk in the more spacious incident room.

Palfreyman positioned himself to sit next to Starr, he in turn, had rather hoped the station's super had buggered off by now so they could get on without his unwelcome interference. Starr's ire was heightened further when he heard the super start the discussion.

'Well Dick, what do you make of that then? But before you say anything, I have to say DS Grey and DS Cooper, how impressed and pleased I was to see you both conduct your business in such a professional manner. Our poorer cousins across the pond couldn't have failed to have been in awe by both of your impeccable presentations. Well done. If you keep this up, I can see very bright futures for you both. What do you say DCI Starr?' His face had been a picture of delight until he heard the DCI's response to his superior's assessment of the station's first and only young fast-track detectives.

'What I think is immaterial, sir, and if I'm really being honest, all I want to do right now is to plan what we should do next. We only have fifteen minutes and I don't want to keep them waiting at the other end,' Starr answered abruptly.

Both men looked at each other like boxers in a public weigh in. Each had their own simmering agenda; however, this was neither the time nor place for their individual deep seated issues to be openly aired.

Grey made the pretence of coughing to break the sudden tension followed by her giving out copies of the three separate coloured photographs they had of Barry Sproston which were aimed at starting the discussion.

'We have less then fifteen minutes to go; we all saw him in the buff and clearly there were no tattoos to be seen. If we all look at the photograph of him allegedly being there at the run, I can now see there is a difference in the upper torsos. The man at the run, his chest is definitely more muscular. Look at the size of his biceps, he must clearly work out.' She paused to allow the others to check her observations against their own evaluation. 'Now,' she continued with her analysis, 'think back to the Barry Sproston on the video link, he does share a near identical facial resemblance to the person in the photograph but their individual body definition is undeniably different.'

She was happy to hear that there were no dissenters to her analysis from others in the group. In the temporary lull that followed, Cooper seized his opportunity not to be left in Grey's wake.

'As I have mentioned before, we need to conduct further checks with the hotel to firmly nail the date recorded in the record book and see if there is a match with the time when the East Seaboard account was opened. That at least should be easy for us to establish. Similarly, passport control previously confirmed Barry Sproston, along with his wife and son left this country well before the fun run at the beginning of July with the passenger data showing he, nor members of his family have yet returned.'

Thinking Cooper had finished, Starr was about to say something about the testimonial the bank was provided with by the person who had been evidently successful in opening the Miami endorsed bank account, but the male DS jumped in before he had the chance to utter a word.

'There are two or three more things I need to say, then I will shut up,' said Cooper in a rush, with Palfreyman looking on obviously enjoying the level of unbridled animated passion being expressed by the young and clearly enthusiastic, detective.

'We will have to pay a visit to Barry Sproston's place of work to check out the authenticity of that testimonial. Also, now that we seem to have established there could be reasonable grounds to doubt this man's involvement, we should run the image we have taken at the fun-run through our face recognition files to see if it throws anything up, and finally, Sproston said he had access to his own bank account, an audit of all the transactions he and his wife made over the past ten weeks will reveal if any large sums were deposited and if so, we'll be able to see where the money originated from. Right, that's me finished,' concluded Cooper.

'Thanks for that Max, you have raised some good points,' praised Starr while looking in the direction of the clock hung high on the wall. 'Right then', he continued, 'We have a few more minutes left, we need to make a decision on how we intend to proceed in light of what we have learned about Barry Sproston.'

Grey was first to offer an opinion.

'Based on what I have learned during the interview and coupled with my gut instinct, I have to admit to having serious doubts whether Sproston is guilty. It's becoming more and more obvious to me, the stealing of Barry Sproston's identity was critical to the success of this elaborate scam.

Sproston and his wife will soon be returning back to the UK once their son's body has been released and arrangements have been put in place for a carrier to fly him back home. We have established where he lives in the UK and I seriously doubt if he will do a runner when he does eventually arrive back. Thinking about it, if we do end up having any fresh concerns, we can always re-arrest him when he disembarks at the airport. To remand Sproston in the USA will only delay his return, we need to have him back over here asap.'

Starr had his thumb and index finger rubbing down the bridge of his nose whilst he considered the immediate ramifications of her proposal. Palfreyman turned to Starr with an expectant look waiting for the DCI to respond, which he duly did, but not as a sop to satisfy his senior colleague.

'Before we jump in let's consider first what evidence we had to lead us to the position we are at now. It goes without saying the person or persons who committed this fraud have been cold and calculating. With that thought in mind, doesn't it also suggest they would behave in precisely the same way if they had the misfortune to be questioned by the authorities about their alleged treacherous deeds? Sproston might well indeed be one of those characters. He's been found out and is cornered like a rat ready to fight and use any means to chance an escape from custody.'

Palfreyman was then seen and heard to clear his throat in readiness to follow on from the DCI.

'I think DCI Starr's grasp of the situation is clear and correct to me. There are some nasty and cold hearted criminals out there who are well versed in the art of lying to get away with crimes they have blatantly committed. You have just got to look at those evil eyes of his to be convinced of his guilt. Let him spend twenty four hours in American custody, this will give a little time then for the team to chase up on DS Cooper's suggestions,' the Chief Superintendent proposed while giving the junior detective yet another knowing nod of approval.

Starr however moved to express an opinion which served to totally disregard the super's view on how to deal with Sproston's arrest, even if the man was unfortunate enough to have "evil eyes".

'We should let him go and allow him and his wife to get on with organising their flight back home. I'm swayed to go along with what Miss Grey said and we need to chase up those things Max mentioned.'

'But DCI Starr,' interjected Palfreyman nervously, 'you do understand, we can be letting loose a wanted criminal from our grasp. We may never find him again and what will Bruce McCoy say then?'

'Well, we can't rightly find him guilty because he has "evil eyes" now can we, Sir?'

Palfreyman understood that slight was aimed at him. He recognised he did not have Starr's experience or natural detective abilities, but he was his superior after all, and he would later aim to get his own back having been humiliated in front of the young impressionable officers.

'I'm prepared to back my own judgement, and if it proves I have been wrong then you can put it on record I'll personally take the blame,' Starr had continued to say.

'Be it on your shoulders DCI Starr, I will not interfere with the strategic decisions you make. And by the way, I have noticed that you have developed an irritating habit DCI Starr.'

'Oh, and what is that may I ask, Chief Superintendent Palfreyman?' he said, puzzled to be on the end of such a remark.

'You really do need to act more professionally in front of DS Cooper and DS Grey.

Please refrain from calling them by their Christian or surnames when on duty. I have heard you on too many occasions do this. These young people are destined for high office and we wouldn't want them to cultivate inappropriate habits from their time in the lower ranks would we DCI Starr,' he said in a deliberate patronising manner.

'No, Sir,' replied Starr.

'Now we've got that out of the way, I have to leave you as I have other pressing matters to deal with. And by the way, well done DS Grey and DS Cooper, your performance has not gone unnoticed.'

Palfreyman rose from his seat and was heading towards the incident room door when, in the background, he was to hear Starr forthrightly say, 'Max, we've got a minute or so, quickly make us all a brew, and Miss Grey can you check the crime log for the telephone number of the hotel so we can check the dates. Thanks Cora.'

Palfreyman slammed the door to when he left the room causing others working at various work stations to look in the direction of the noise.

They then heard the voice of Starr pipe up, 'I wonder what's up with him? Maybe he's late for his golf.'

Before Sproston was about to reappear on the monitor Starr had very briefly discussed with the remaining two officers the importance of getting the Miami police to hold their suspect for another hour or so to give them sufficient time to chase up and hopefully verify certain aspects which had arisen during the video link interview. They were soon to discover Lieutenant McAndrew had made no objections to their request and quickly dealt with another by passing over details of Barry Sproston's bank account which she had read from his debit card.

The hours' grace was secured, Cooper called the hotel number retrieved from the case file. The conversation subsequently held between the same receptionist, who Starr had originally spoken to, provided him with the date when Sproston's passport was recorded as being booked out from their safe keeping.

'Look, both dates are the same, Sir, like we suspected. Remember Sproston saying how the receptionist later discovered his passport? Looks like the person who first convinced her he was who he said he was, didn't feel so confident to see her again when it came to handing it back in.' Starr was looking over Cooper's shoulder while he spoke to see that the dates indeed did tally with the opening of the East Seaboard account.

'If we assume Sproston is telling us the truth, then we have to accept that there is another person who is fraudulently using his identity. I've asked Cora to contact his bank and get them to email us statements of all the transactions he has made over the past two months. I strongly suspect though it will prove to support what Sproston has already told us, he is in fact broke, and no other substantial monies have been deposited or withdrawn during that period,' conjectured Starr.

'We should have in our possession later this afternoon information from the two UK banks where the McCoy's cash was transferred to from Miami. If we find anything that implicates Sproston's involvement then we can arrest him when he gets back here,' suggested Cooper.

'Yes, we can do that,' mulled Starr, 'And once Cora has gone over Sproston's bank statements, we will be in a better position to make a decision on what steps we should take next.'

Within the half hour Grey had received and read over the bank statements together with putting Cooper and Starr in the picture.

'Just got a bit of cash in his account. The only money in has been from his employer, the "Dreams Come True" charity and a £1000 lump sum from his bank. It looks like he's had to use his overdraft facility and is close to his £8,000 limit on his credit card. This to me doesn't sound like a man who is free of money problems. He's right, he is broke. How the heck is he going to pay the hospital bill?'

'Perfect reason then to try and pull of a stunt like fleecing the McCoy's account. When people are desperate, they tend to resort to taking desperate measures and £82,000 would go a long way to solving his problems,' proffered Starr. 'Time for us to make a decision,' he continued, 'we can't keep the MPD waiting much longer. What do you think we should do, Max?' enquired Starr of his junior.

'To have him banged up over there will ultimately delay his return. I'm not yet a hundred per cent certain of his innocence, but I'm close. I think we should allow the police to release him pending to him agreeing to keeping us informed of his travel arrangements,' answered Cooper.

'And you, Miss Grey?'

'Similar to DS Cooper really, I'm too not totally convinced he is our man, but like you have already said Sir, he might be very good at this sort of thing and the details of the account emailed to us might be an elaborate front to throw potential snoopers off from scenting the East Seaboard account,' she offered to the DCI.

Having taken in his junior's thoughts, Starr considered this moment to be an apt opportunity to pass on his long and hard earned wisdom.

'I've always tried to drill into you two that detective work isn't solely about clues, DNA and finger prints. Gut instinct plays a massive part, especially when it comes to solving some difficult cases. This, I believe is such a case. My instincts lead me to trust Sproston is not the one we should be nailing for fraud, and we will have to do some more serious digging before we get a chance of tracking down the guilty person or parties. We will not delay them in making the necessary arrangements to get their son back home here. I don't think they will abscond and end up having the boy's funeral elsewhere in the world. However, it must be impressed upon Sproston that not only must he keep us informed of his flight times, but once he has landed back in this country, he must report, within twenty-four hours to Bladdington police station. Are we all agreed then?'

'Yes!' replied the other two detectives in unison.

The visual link connecting the two continents resumed with Grey, again feeling strangely unsettled at having to look unavoidably into the man's eyes, informing him a decision had been made to permit his release from custody on the basis of agreeing to two provisos. It didn't take long for him to accede to the Bladdington police demands; Sproston's spirit and physical resolve had become so seriously depleted, he might have agreed to almost anything to escape this oppressive and unjust incarceration.

Pleasantries and thanks were past back and forth between police departments before the link was finally closed. A copy of the RIVA audio/visual interview was saved in a file on the station's hard drive, together with Grey taking the additional precaution of burning a back-up copy onto disc.

Chapter Twenty-Six

Debbie Sproston arrived by taxi to the drab unwelcoming concrete and glass police building about twenty minutes after her husband's uncompromising arrest. In her natural haste to be by his side, she turned up at the enquiry desk looking unusually dishevelled due to having had little inclination to consider her outward appearance in such headspinning circumstances.

From having spent the majority of her time in Miami in the childrens' hospital, where doctors and nurses went about their daily work wearing smiles in spite of having sometimes to share the burden of tragedy with distraught parents, she found herself witnessing a hostile gathering of mixed races either seated or formed in a queue awaiting their turn to be seen by a clinically obese, six foot plus tall black uniformed officer. While awaiting her turn to be seen by the officer, she observed him impatiently fobbing people off with their petty enquiries or being guided with the aid of an agitated pointed finger to take a seat and wait. Eventually, her turn arrived to have her enquiry heard by the sweaty man.

'Yes, ma'am, what can I do for you?' he said while ignoring her physical presence to instead focus on adding scribbled notes on a headed note paper positioned on the scratched and worn foyer top.

'I've come to see my husband, Barry Sproston. He was taken away by the police earlier this morning,' she appealed to his ignoring eyes.

'What for?' he asked.

'What do you mean, what for?' she asked not fully understanding what he meant. He lifted his face to look down at the five foot one inch, thirty something female through black lazy bull frog eyes as he suspiciously weighed her up.

'You from England?' he questioned.

'Yes.' she slowly replied not really understanding why he would want to ask her that.

'You know David Beckham?' he said with a half-smile forming on his lips.

'Look. Please don't take this the wrong way officer, but I'm here to see about my husband, not to have a cosy chat about a damn footballer.' she said not caring if he didn't like the sharpness of her reply.

'What has he been charged with?' the officer asked, reverting back to type.

'They said he'd taken some money, £82,000 I think it was, from an account over in Britain. He couldn't have done it; he's been with me all the time we have been over here. I also want to make a complaint about the way he was arrested by those three horrible police men. They...'

Before she was able to finish what she had to say on the matter, the desk officer cut her off.

'I'll give you a complaints form to fill in ma'am. I can see the name of Barry Sproston on the arrest log. I will let an officer know you are here. If you would like to take a seat, there is a coffee machine in the corner. Next.' The officer turned his attention away from the woman and prepared to give his next customer a similar level of service.

She filled in the complaints form to then sit impatiently while half listening in on the steady stream of complaining humanity coming and going from the waiting room. Two hours later, she still hadn't been seen by a senior officer, she was about to leave her seat to approach the desk officer, when a side door opened to reveal her husband being ushered out of the door for it then to be closed smartly behind him.

He stood for a moment looking quite nervous and unable to find his bearings. The sound of a familiar voice calling his name directed his attention to find his wife rushing towards him. They first tightly embraced to seal their joint welcome and then broke away to separate but still clutching together through the tenderness of their hands.

'Is everything all right, Barry? She looked up at him with deep concern across her face.

He did not hear her, his mind had turned to take in the sights and noises of the multi-cultural mix of angry and worried souls filling the oppressive waiting room, along with an unnerving sense of having unwanted attention being drawn to them.

'Let's just get out of this hole.'

He tightened his grip on his wife's hand, and was taken somewhat by surprise when she unexpectedly pulled her hand from his grasp.

'What's the matter Debbie?' he said, suddenly bemused by her actions.

'I've got to pass this complaints form in before we leave. I'm not letting them get away with the way they treated you, Barry. No way!'

Before he could stop her from carrying out her threat she was gone from his reach to be seen by him marching up to the enquiries desk. She slid the filled in form across the scarred foyer surface to then say, 'I've written down my address in England. I hope to hear from the Miami Police Department what they intend to do about my husband's dreadful treatment at the hands of their bully officers.'

Using his fat finger tips, the sloth like officer pressed on the surface of the incriminating report to slide it lazily to one side of the foyer top.

'I'll see that it gets all the attention it deserves ma'am,' he said tiredly.

"Thank you officer.'

She returned to nervously re-entwine her fingers back into her husband's hand to gladly retreat from the burgeoning mass awaiting the attentions of the MPD.

The desk officer had carefully noted the two English visitors hurriedly disappearing through the exit door, before reaching over to the freshly written complaints form. Without fear of being seen by prying stares of those seated nearest to the enquiries desk, he gleefully proceeded to crush the thin paper into the palm of his right hand to reduce it to the size of a large marble. He then turned to aim the paper ball in the direction of a green painted waste bin.

'Slam dunk! That's my baby. Next please,' called the desk officer flush with success of again, hitting the target.

Chapter Twenty-Seven

The time arrived for Cooper to accompany Starr to Oakwood Engineering to check out the authenticity of Sproston's employer testimonial.

A phone call had been made earlier to inform the head of Human Resources department to expect their arrival and it was to be the same person who would pleasantly greet them in the company's modern reception foyer some twenty minutes or so later.

Starr first introduced both of them while casually flipping open his warrant card.

'Welcome to Oakwood Engineering. My name is Miss Fran Jones and I'm the Head of HR,' a smartly dressed woman in her mid to late forties said chirpily.

'Please come this way detectives and I will get a cup of tea arranged for you both.' She led the two men away from the female staffed reception desk to pick up a windowless but brightly fluorescent lit corridor to the right. She stopped at a sapele varnished door with a plastic engraved plate displaying her name and position within the company fixed at eye level. After Miss Jones had stood to one side to allow the two visitors access into her office, she then directed them to the thick upholstered wooden framed chairs. They watched her close the door behind them and then walk round to her own desk to take up her usual seat.

'Julie will be here in a moment with a pot of tea, but while we are waiting for her, how can we at Oakwood Engineering be of service to you?' she seemed to ask with a clear intention to please.

'It's to do with Barry Sproston. You will be most abundantly aware he is over in Miami with his wife supporting his son while he is in hospital,' said Cooper.

'Yes, that is correct. He's been on compassionate leave for over two months now, such a tragic situation to have to cope with. Nothing bad has happened has it?' the woman anxiously queried.

Cooper sidestepped her question and started to remove from the inside pocket of his jacket, a folded A4 sheet.

'I have here a typed testimonial allegedly provided by Oakwood Engineering, which was then used to fraudulently open a bank account with the East Seaboard Bank in Miami. The account holder used this situation to then dishonestly coerce a person into transferring a sum of £82,000 into that same account. Please do not discuss this matter with any other person but we would appreciate your help if you would just cast your eye over this letter.'

He stretched out his arm to pass the thrice folded letter to her. She then laid it on the desk and pressed it down to flatten the creases followed by hooking on her spectacles to silently read each and every typed word.

They watched the woman remove her spectacles and placed them on the desk to indicate the letter details had been studied.

'I expect you will want me to make a comment,' she said while looking up at the two officer's serious faces.

'Yes, that would be helpful, Miss Jones,' urged Cooper.

'I can safely say this typed testimonial did not originate from this company. Yes, I'll agree it's our headed paper and I can clearly see the water mark we use. However, when a letter is sent out by someone or on behalf of an individual, it is company policy to have the originator's initials typed usually on the left hand side and near to the top of the letter. This letter has no such markings. Also, when a letter is ready to be run off it is sent to the main office where it is then produced using a laser jet printer. This letter, I can easily see has been printed using a typical ink jet printer most people have in their homes nowadays. And more than anything else, DS Cooper, I can see my name is there as the signatory, but I can categorically state it was not signed in my hand.'

The three incumbents were disturbed from their thoughts by a young office trainee clattering through the door carrying a tray full of cups and saucers and a white china teapot. 'Thank you, Julie. Tea gentlemen?' enquired the Head of HR as she rose from her seat to deal with setting out the cups and saucers and the pouring of the fresh brew.

During the drinking of the tea DCI Starr asked how it could possibly happen that an authentic company letter headed sheet had fallen into criminal hands.

'I don't know, DCI Starr. We only have a small admin team, and I'm sure none of them would be so careless as to leave letter headed paper around for just anybody to pick up. When you have finished your tea, the admin office is only a couple of doors further along the corridor and I will introduce you to the girls. Hopefully, they'll be able to provide an explanation.'

It was during the time the three drank their tea, Starr told Miss Jones about Barry Sproston's tragic loss. She was again asked to keep this terrible news to herself during the time they were on the factory premises.

After the cups and saucers were placed back on the tray, Miss Jones showed the detectives the way to the admin office while clutching a small white handkerchief to her reddened nose.

The four women seen to be seated at their individual work stations momentarily drew their attention from what they were doing on the monitor screens to focussing on the two male strangers accompanied by an upset looking Fran Jones now present in the room.

'This is DCI Starr and DS Cooper. They've asked to have a confidential word with you all. I won't tell you what it is about, I'll leave it to the officers to explain.' Miss Jones then turned to make a fast exit from the main admin office.

Before Starr was able to state their business for being there, he heard one of the typist say, 'What on earth's up with Fran? I hope she's not in any trouble.' The four women looked around at each other to see concern on each and every one of their faces.

'Sorry ladies, there is nothing to worry about. The reason we are here today does not concern Miss Jones,' said Starr. 'But we are rather hoping one of you might be able to assist us in our enquiries.'

The women were now fully attentive and keenly alert to be part of a police investigation which made an exciting change from their usual mundane work.

'I will make a start then,' said Starr having seen the admin team focussing their full attention on him. He proceeded to hold out the unfolded testimonial letter enough for them to see the company's familiar letter heading but far enough away from sight to prevent them reading the typed content. He then moved on to say, 'I have been led to understand that all letters are printed using a laser jet in this office.'

'Yes, that's right, it's over there,' one of them said pointing to a dedicated desk in an uncluttered corner of the office.

'Where is the headed paper stored then?' asked Starr.

'We each have our own small pile we keep locked away in our drawers,' replied the same woman.

'So, the only people who have access to the headed paper are you four ladies.'

'Yes, but I think Miss Jones has some kept in her office, I've seen her put a paper in the printer when she has not asked any of us for a sheet,' answered a different office lady this time.

During the questioning Cooper had been carefully scanning around the tidy office area. His attention was drawn to one of the typist silver mesh desk document tray.

'Isn't that letter headed paper in that tray?' he said to a person who looked like to him to be a young trainee.

Her face immediately coloured up.

'Yes, sorry I should have put the paper back in the drawer. Sorry Jean,' the girl said looking sheepishly at the office manager.

'I've told her before DS Cooper, but I suppose we are all occasionally guilty of leaving things out or not putting them back immediately in the right place. This is such a busy office, really we need more staff and bigger accommodation, but I suppose that is of no interest to you.'

'So it is possible then for someone to take a sheet of headed paper without any of you noticing it missing,' pressed Cooper.

'We certainly don't keep a number check on how many letter sheets we use if that is what you mean, but I think we would notice anybody taking a copy if any one of us was in the office. There are, of course, others who work for the company who come in here, say, for a bit of a social chit chat, or maybe ask for a letter to be typed, but I can't think of any reason why someone might want to take a blank headed sheet,' responded Jean.

'Well, someone unfortunately has and then used it to fraudulently verify their identity which then led to a criminal offence being committed,' said Starr.

'Has this anything to do with Barry Sproston?' a rotund woman in her thirties, wearing thick lensed glasses asked.

'Why would you want to ask that,' Starr said in surprise.

'A call from a bank in Miami was directed to this office because Fran was away with her partner on a camping holiday in the Lake District. They asked if someone was available to verify a testimonial letter they had been given to authenticate Barry Sproston's identity. I know Barry very well; we both went to the same school and hung around in a group when we were teenagers. The caller read out what Fran had written about Barry and I was also asked to check if his national insurance number was correct. Well that was easy, I just had to open up the personnel records on my PC. Fran had written him a glowing tribute, which I must say, was fully deserving of the poor man.' She momentarily dropped her gaze from the officer feeling a certain hardness in her throat. 'Anyway,' she then continued after shrugging off her own personal sadness she felt for his situation, 'they seemed happy with what I told them. I have to admit though, I never thought to let Fran know about the call, you know what it is like, you either forget or other things move in to divert your attention.'

'Yes, yes,' empathised Starr while Cooper scribbled into his notebook details of the woman's revelation.

'So getting back to the letter blank being taken from the office, besides the people employed here is there anybody else who would have any business to enter the office,' he continued to question.

The group of females pondered over the DCI's question and looked around at each other as if in psychic communication.

'Well, there is Rob who comes in every Wednesday morning to clean the water drinks machine and replenish the stock. We regularly see different engineer reps from the photocopier company because the damn thing is always breaking down. Besides them I can't think of anyone else,' said Jean as she looked at the other three to confirm she was correct in her estimation.

'Does the cleaner count,' chirped up the young trainee.

'Yes, of course, how could we have forgotten her, the lazy cow? She is nowhere near as thorough as Becky Melia. It was a great loss when she left us a few weeks ago,' lamented Jean.

Starr and Cooper immediately recognised the significance of the timeframe.

'Do you know why she left?' asked Starr in a casual air.

'I think it was to do with going on holiday. She'd usually arrive just as we were all preparing to leave for home. I used to have a bit of a chat with her. She was dead excited about going over to America for a holiday of a lifetime. The cleaning agency later told us she hadn't turned into work to resume her job. They weren't too bothered, there are plenty of eastern Europeans living over here who are prepared to work for the peanuts they offer,' explained the woman, who hadn't yet spoken up to that point.

'How did you all find Becky Melia?' asked Cooper directing his question at the office manager.

'I suppose none of us knew her that well, Becky had only been cleaning here a short while. She was very good at her job and the place always seemed to sparkle when we arrived in the mornings. Yes, she had tattoos on her arms and legs and a row of gold horse shoe shaped piercings in each ear, but should that make any difference to how we feel about individual people? We all found her to be okay, that's right, isn't it girls?' They all nodded to signal they agreed with the office manager's assessment.

'Sadly we shall have to leave you all now, but thank you all for your co-operation. We'll make our own way out. Goodbye.' The two detectives left the room to a chorus of 'goodbyes' with the next destination being Fran Jones's office.

Starr's light tapping of his index knuckle against the ply faced door summonsed a meek call of, 'come in please'. They entered the room to notice Miss Jones clutching a handkerchief as they moved to assume the same seats as before.

'Have you told the girls about Barry's son?' she enquired in a low tone.

'No we haven't. I think you should let them know once we have finished here,' suggested Starr.

'Yes, I will do that. What a tragedy. Barry was, I mean is, a very popular person here and there will be many who will share the pain of his loss. It is so sad. Anyway, what else can we do to help you DCI Starr?' the Head of HR asked while pulling herself to sit more upright in her executive style chair.

'There is one more thing you can help us with. I need the name and the address of the agency you use for the cleaning of the offices.'

'Yes, I can get you that information from my PC now.' During the time she was opening up the relevant file she asked why he wanted the information.

'It's just a line of enquiry we are following,' he replied clearly not wanting to reveal any more than necessary.

'I've sent it to print, so I'll have to leave you both for a moment while I get it from the office. I won't be a moment.' No sooner had Fran Jones left her seat than she was back with the cleaning agency details printed on headed paper.

'There you are gentlemen,' she said passing the crisp white A4 paper to Starr for him to collect from her.

'Thank you Miss Jones,' he said while scanning over the printed details.

After a final brief exchange of thanks, the Bladdington detectives left the busy premises for their next destination. In the meantime, Fran Jones remained in the privacy of her office agonising over how she was going to spill the bad news.

'Is it back to the station now, Sir?' enquired Cooper while "clunk clicking" his seat belt. He hoped the answer would be 'yes' which would mean he'd be able to get home at a reasonable hour.

'No, there is plenty of time yet,' replied Starr while looking at his wrist watch. 'The day is still young, Max, do you have to get to somewhere else?'

Cooper's heart sank at the prospect of at least another two hours of detective work, but his luck might possibly change if the person at their next destination fails to be in. He wisely asked for the address of the cleaning agency rather than answer to Starr's flippant concern.

'Bottomley's, "You have never been seriously bottomed until you have been bottomed by Bottomley's, the cleaners specialising in deep penetration", 21 Clarence Street, Yarnwich. Who the bloody hell thought that one up? You would have been locked up years ago for using such an innuendo laden slogan,' said Starr in a disgusted tone.

'You need to chill out more, Sir. It's only an amusing play on words, most would see it as a bit of fun, Jesus,' Cooper said clearly dismayed and shaking his head at his boss's lack of humour.

Starr ignored his junior's remarks to focus on asking if he knew how to get to their next destination.

'I know where Clarence Street is, Sir,' he answered through a stifled yawn.

'Great detective work, DS Cooper. Palfreyman was right, you have a great future ahead of you son.' Starr replied in deliberate sarcasm. The two officers spoke no more until Cooper drew the car to a stop outside a door having the same business name Starr had previously read from the sheet given to him by Fran Jones.

'Looks like the offices are upstairs; there is certainly no frontage to the business. You wait here Max while I see if anybody is in.'

Starr unclipped his seat belt then strolled over to the green painted solid wood door with a sign screwed into it to advertise the existence of the business. Only after he had failed to find a bell push or door knocker, he sighted a stainless steel inter-com box fixed to the brickwork to the side of the door with a handwritten grubby white label showing the word "Bottomley's". After a single press of the metal button, he waited patiently for a few moments for a reply without success. He pressed the same button again, but this time for much longer. A crackling sound emitting from the small inter-com speaker grill served to heighten Starr's hopes there was someone present in the upstairs office to receive their visit.

'Lay of the bloody buzzer. What the hell do ya want?' were the words he heard emitting from the tinny intercom speaker. Years ago Starr would have had no hesitation in kicking down the door to have been greeted in such a disrespectful way. Alas, times had changed to such an extent it was now deemed politically correct for the police to be unaffected by such a display of attitude.

'My name is DCI Starr, sir. We need to have a word with you concerning a police matter.'

'What police matter?' the man asked in the same blunt tone.

'The sooner you allow us in sir, the sooner you will know what we need to speak to you about. Unless, of course, you are happy for the passing public to know we are here investigating your company's likely involvement in a serious fraud.'

'What fraud? I ain't dun nothing wrong.' Starr had deliberately played the man knowing his words would provoke such a response. A short audible burst crackled from a buzzer to signal the door was open. Starr nodded to Cooper, who had been listening in on what had been said, to join him.

The two men noisily bounded up the two flights of stairs to reach the only door on the small landing. Starr ignored the usual courtesy one would follow by first knocking on the door before being invited to enter; and elected to burst into the untidy smoke filled office like he was taking part in a serious drug bust he'd once become accustomed to in the late seventies. The man sitting behind a desk piled up with stacks of old magazines, papers, empty sandwich packages, a filled ash tray and an old yellowing PC, nearly jumped out of his skin.

This act of bullishness Starr had only moments before planned with Cooper as they entered the building. It was while watching the victim struggling to pull himself together after being terrified out of his wits, that served Cooper with a valuable piece of experience. He could now appreciate the selective use of the power of surprise and how it could provide a sometimes necessary lever to render villains momentarily impotent.

'I hope we didn't scare you, sir,' enquired Starr with a twinkle in his eye.

'Scare me, bloody scare me. You nearly gave me a bloody heart attack.' gasped the frightened man as he turned to noisily rummage around in a desk drawer.

'Got ya!' The painfully thin faced man, whose features made one think he was bordering on anorexia, slammed a light blue inhaler to his mouth to take in a long deep draw. Cooper asked if he was all right and suggested he call him a doctor. The man shook his head as he placed the life saving device on to the desk top to join the other clutter. 'I'll be fine,' he said having been able to recompose himself. 'What is it you want? It must be bloody serious to come into the room like that.'

'We want to ask you about Becky Melia, we are led to believe she was employed by your company when she was a cleaner at Oakwood Engineering,' pressed Starr, pleased to have turned the tables.

'The name doesn't immediately ring a bell. Just give me a moment I'll have to have a look on the computer. So she's been involved in some sort of fraud then has she?' he said while tapping on the keyboard. He did not receive an answer to satisfy his inquisitiveness.

Starr looked around the nicotine stained dingy office not quite understanding how companies and local small businesses in the area would entrust this edgy looking man, who was concentrating squinting at the PC screen, with servicing of cleaning contracts. He was quite sure they would not have signed on the dotted line if they had been sat in these four walls.

'Yes, I've got her here,' he suddenly spouted. 'It says here she was with us for a short while, she always turned up and gladly, no complaints from Oakwood Engineering. She stopped coming a good few weeks ago. I think my missus said something about her going on a long holiday and we did not see her again after that.' He looked up to the detectives in further expectation of another probing question.

'Do you have a contact address and copies of any references you took up?' asked Cooper.

'I can print you off the address she gave us and other personal details we have recorded on the system. I may still have a picture of her on the computer, you know what it is like nowadays, everybody has got to wear one of those bloody stupid ID badges. References though, I can't help you there, we didn't take any. You need to understand nobody wants the job of cleaning in this area, they think it is below them even if they are desperate for work and haven't got a penny to scratch their arses with. We are just glad to get anybody in, that is why most people we have on the books are eastern Europeans and damn good workers they are too,' he said in an expression of pride. He left his seat to retrieve two A4 sheets from an ancient ink printer to then pass them over to the person he recognised as being the more senior of the two officers.

'Thank you,' said Starr giving a quick glance over the personal details and the woman's features, followed then by carefully folding the two papers to fit the inside pocket of his overcoat.

'Sorry the picture of Melia is not clear, it's an old printer and it don't do colour,' explained Bottomley.

'It's a good start; at least we have some indication of what she looks like. I'll keep you no longer; we have other business to attend to so we need to be on our way.' Starr and Cooper gestured a goodbye with a nod of their heads and left the office. The man tentatively listened to their footsteps noisily descending the two flights of stairs. On hearing the slamming of the door, Bottomley, at last, was able to let out a huge sigh of relief in readiness to take another blast from his inhaler.

The police officer's unannounced visit had had Harry Bottomley seriously worried he'd been dobbed in by a snitch over a totally different matter. If the police officers had bothered to look over his shoulder whilst he was finding Becky Melia's employment details, they would have seen the names of individuals who, if they had done a little digging, were those of illegal economic immigrants from outside the EEC being paid at a rate of three pounds an hour, which was less than half he should have been paying them if they were legally entitled to work in the UK. But he and his business partner wife were prepared to take the unlikely risk of them being caught. The tendering process for cleaning contracts was cut-throat and even if the Bottomley's didn't pay the going rate and employed people they shouldn't have, they still struggled to pay themselves a decent wage at the end of the month.

His nicotine stained fingers dug around the mound of stumped out cigarettes piled up in a pressed aluminium Senior Service ash tray eager to find one which still had some life left in it. With the lit cigarette gripped between his dry lips he inhaled hard then slowly released the blue smoke from his congested lungs. It was with some satisfaction he'd not been caught out; well not this time, anyway.

While sitting in the stationary unmarked police car outside the cleaner's business door entrance, Starr unfolded the poorly printed sheets he'd previously put in his inside pocket to again peer at Becky Melia's features and contrast them with the other personal details Harry Bottomley had kept on file about her.

'Didn't miss a day Max all the time she was there. They paid her for four hours work five days a week so she had plenty of undisturbed time to do whatever she wanted really. It must have been easy to have taken a sheet of letter headed paper and to find Barry Sproston's national insurance number. Let's just check out the address she gave and then we shall call it a day.' he said while passing over the image the cleaning company used to authenticate Melia's identity.

Not having had the benefit of seeing the picture in colour, Cooper carefully absorbed the woman's key features: mid-thirties, shoulder length blonde hair which had a skunk like black streak down the centre parting, full clear eyes below a high forehead, the making of dark rings under each eye probably made her look older than she actually was, her lips were full and a neat chin with a pronounced dimple in the middle. She was likely to have been very pretty at one time, but life style choices have a habit of turning even princesses in to bullfrogs.

Once Cooper had passed the A4 sheet back to his partner, he didn't need any external encouragement to ask for Melia's address.

'9 Regent Street, Mansfield. Do you know it Max?' said Starr.

'No, but give me the postcode and I'll put it in the sat nav.'

'MF12 6TG.' Starr watched Cooper tap in the individual digits and seconds later heard a female voice say, 'Go straight ahead and take the first right.'

After a twenty minute drive they pulled up outside an empty terraced house having a letting agent's sign nailed to the external brickwork, debating what they should do next.

The house was only one of the same type to be found in many similar looking streets in the local area which were built during the mid to late eighteenth century to house the massive influx of rail workers needed to provide the skilled and unskilled labour which, history would record, put Mansefield on the map as a major steam locomotive and engineering manufacture. Most of the rail sheds had now gone only to be replaced with acres of desolate, scarred and rubbish strewn derelict land, something Hitler had tried to achieve but mostly failed to do at that time in history during the Second World War.

It was then viewed with a certain irony, amongst those who valiantly fought and lost the battle to stop the Government from handing out multi- million engineering contracts to foreigners, he'd now be so happy his goal had been achieved some fifty years later, without even having to lift a single finger.

The housing stock, had as yet, escaped the heavy swinging demolition balls and the big bucket rubble movers. Sadly though, it was a secret plan of the local modernisers, who had little regard for the communities long railway heritage, to force compulsory purchase on many of the happy residents in their quest to build bespoke four and five bedroomed executive properties on top of the scraped off land where solid homes once stood for a hundred and fifty years or more.

It hadn't taken too long for the two officers to see the property was empty and for some time at that, with the amount of unopened mail scattered across the lino covered entrance hall floor which Cooper easily spotted when he looked through the wide letter box flap in the grubby yellowing UPVC front door.

'Well it's clear she is not here and hasn't been for some while. Should we go now, Sir?' Cooper felt he'd done his fair share of detective work that day, enough in fact to satisfy the most out spoken of ratepayers who subscribe to the common myth that coppers are an idle bunch.

'Not yet DS Cooper. There is no point in putting off till tomorrow what you can just as easily do today.' Starr couldn't help to then hear a low groan emit from Cooper's lips from being in such close confines. He didn't tackle the young aspiring officer for his distinct lack of enthusiasm. But he'd added this mental note to join the long list of other disappointments.

'Tell me DS Cooper, what do you think is the next logical step we should take, seeing that our friend, Mrs Melia is not at home and more to the point, isn't likely to be?'

'I'm not sure, I'm too tired to think, it's been a long day, Sir,' Cooper answered being careful not to make eye contact with his partner.

'Well, I'll tell you then what we shall do. It is obvious to me there are people living in the houses either side of the one Melia lived in, or have you not yet noticed the twitching curtains? I think it would be a good idea if we knocked on each of the doors and enquire if they know of Mrs Melia's whereabouts. What do you say, DS Cooper?' pressed Starr clearly making no attempt to disguise his deliberate patronising manner.

'Yeah, okay. Let's get on with it.' Cooper then stepped out to leave his superior shaking his head in despair.

Starr joined Cooper just after he'd rang the doorbell to the house on the left. They didn't have to wait long for their call to be answered by a freshly shaven headed stockily built man in his late thirties. His demeanour immediately conveyed that of deep suspicion which was further amplified when he said,' Yes, what do you want. Can't you read the sign? You better not be those bloody Jo'vah Witnesses,' he warned pointing aggressively at a triangular shaped sticker positioned in the small glazed panel in a similar cheap plastic door to his neighbours.

Starr pulled out his warrant card with Cooper following suit to establish their authority.

'So you are not Jo'vah witnesses then?' the man said, who had the full length of both exposed steroid built arms covered in a myriad of tattoos.

'No, sorry to disappoint you sir, we are just plain old police officers,' confirmed Starr.

'Ugh,' the man replied using a monosyllabic word of choice.

'We are here to see if you can help us to establish the whereabouts of Mrs Becky Melia. We can see nobody has been living at the address for a while.'

'Why do you want to know?' the man asked cagily.

'We are hoping she might be able to help us with an on-going investigation. And that is all I'm at liberty to tell you, sir,' replied Starr.

'Well then, I'll tell you what shall I, all I'm at liberty to say to you is she don't live there anymore. That's all I know.' With his bulked up biceps crossed tightly across his similarly steroid induced pecks he made no pretence that his limited cooperation was nearly exhausted.

'Do you have any idea where she moved to?' surprisingly piped up Cooper.

'Nope!'

'Did she have any family living with her?' asked Starr.

'Didn't see any,' came a monotone reply.

It was patently clear to Starr this man was not going to give anything away and he couldn't arrest him for that alone. Maybe they would have better luck with the other neighbour.

'Thank you for your cooperation, and I'll bid you good day, sir.' The man saw no reason for him to reply in a similar polite manner, preferring instead to slam the flimsy door in the officers faces.

This display of craven behaviour often made Cooper question if he really wanted to forge a long career in the police force. But pressures, such as that from the stations chief superintendent, seemed to be forcing him down a path that, which he knew deep inside, wasn't for him. Surely, he would often reason to himself and other close friends, there must be jobs out there where one isn't subjected to such naked abuse.

'Right Max, let's make a call on the other neighbour, hopefully we'll meet someone who is less ignorant and better educated.' Cooper followed Starr to cover the short distance to make their next call.

Starr rapped the shiny brass knocker against the striking plate on the door to 7, Regent Street. The door latch was heard to turn with the door slowly opening to the full extent the security chain would allow to then expose a pensioner aged female peering quizzically at the two smartly dressed strangers.

'Yes, what is it you want?' the woman asked nervously.

'We are police officers and we are hoping you might be able to assist us in our enquiries,' explained Starr while the woman was squinting at the two warrant cards being held out for her to inspect. The sound of the security chain being removed from its captive position proved she was happy with who they said they were. The door was fully opened to reveal a bespectacled small grey haired figure wearing an old fashioned full length pinafore in traditional paisley design.

'Hello, I'm DCI Starr and this is my colleague, DS Cooper.' The woman held her rheumatoid affected hand out for the detectives to shake, which they both gladly accepted with accompanying smiles.

'My name is Flo Jackson, and what can I do to help the police?' she said, then her features suddenly changed as if she had become startled. 'Oh, I'm so sorry,' she said in some despair, 'how rude of me, please come inside and I'll make you both a nice cup of tea.'

They followed her to the middle room which she called the sitting room and invited them to take a seat in each of the two cottage chairs. She informed the seated officers she wouldn't be too long in making the promised tea and disappeared into the kitchen. The two men scanned around the walls and furniture in the small room taking in the ageing sepia and black and white photographs held in Bakelite dark brown frames of Flo Jackson wearing overalls along with many other smiling young girls of her generation helping the war effort. Cooper picked up one particular photograph which caught his eye. He looked deep into the image and couldn't help but feel the joy exuding from the two youthful looking faces.

'Is this you, Mrs Jackson, in this photograph?' Cooper called out to her as she busied herself in the kitchen.

'Oh, you don't want to be looking at those old pictures,' she answered. He heard her put something down on a worktop and watched her as she ambled over to him to take a look at the picture he was still holding in his hand.

'Yes, that's me and my Ted, we were only about twenty then. It was taken by a friend at the September Wakes fair. He was such a handsome man was my Ted, I'll never know what he saw in me,' she said passing the frame back to Cooper.

'Well, if you don't mind me saying, Mrs Jackson, I can clearly see what he saw in you; you were absolutely gorgeous. Ted would have had a battle on his hands if I'd been around then,' said Cooper.

'Don't be so daft.' she replied coyly.

'I'm serious, look at the other pictures taken of you and your friends, you are by far the most pretty,' he said further complimenting her.

'I'll have to leave you, or you won't get your tea.' Flo flitted off to the kitchen unable to rid her face of the smile Cooper had put there.

There were many other photographs showing the chronological history of other family members which they both glanced at during the background sounds of her placing china cups onto saucers and pouring hot water into a tea pot in addition to cupboard doors being opened and closed. The sound of the therapeutic rhythm of the brewed tea being poured into individual cups and then being placed on a woven wicker edged serving tray was heard before she reappeared in the sitting room having added three china plates with the top one holding homemade scones. She served her two unexpected guests before settling down in the cottage style two seater settee.

'What is it I can help you with officers?' Flo Jackson asked after she had taken a careful sip from her cup.

'It's to do with your erstwhile neighbour, Becky Melia,' said Starr with his mouth full of the driest scone he had ever eaten. He was tempted to have a drink of the tea to lubricate the arid lump but chose not to risk scalding his mouth in the process.

'I thought it might,' she said adopting a nonchalant air.

'Why do you say that?' Cooper casually asked.

'It was awful when they were here.' Before she could explain further Starr, who had been able to force down his gullet most of the first bite he had of the scone, asked her, 'They, do you mean there was more than Becky Melia who lived next door?'

'Yes, that's right. She was married, her husband's name was James and they had an awful son, Brett. Bratt would have been a more suitable name to describe him. Do you know they played music till all hours, these walls are very thin and you can hear everything that goes on. I hardly got any sleep while they were here, it was making me ill. I'm so glad they have gone. I hope who ever moves in next is more considerate and courteous than the Melias.'

'Can you describe James Melia to us,' asked Starr while giving Cooper a nod to make notes in his notepad.

'Yes, I can remember him clearly, even if my mind isn't what it used to be when I was younger. He was slim to medium build, had black hair, blue eyes; yes, those eyes somehow unnerved me. He had tattoos on his arms and on his legs. What is it with people today that they want to cover themselves in tattoos, even Becky Melia had them. In my day the only people with tattoos were gipsys, sailors and circus freaks. Still, hopefully I won't have long and I'll be free of this mad world to join Ted.' While she paused for a moment, the two officers looked on saddened by the fact this clearly decent woman felt such unease with modern society.

'He kept vicious dogs in the back yard you know; I think he had about four of them. I used to see him put them into the back of a van and not return until way past midnight. The dogs barking always woke me up. I often saw from my back bedroom window one or two of the dogs had nasty bloody cuts, what on earth was he doing with the poor things?'

'What do you know about Becky Melia, Mrs Jackson,' asked Cooper.

She seemed to be mulling over things in her mind before she was prepared to offer a response.

'I think underneath that brash exterior, she was a frightened woman. I often saw her with bruises; I wouldn't be at all surprised if he knocked her about. She was worse when she had had a drink. Both of them were always drinking. I used to hear them arguing a lot, I don't think theirs was a match made in heaven. I'm so glad they have gone.'

'Do you know where they have moved to?' asked Starr.

'I don't, all I do know is that a person from the letting agents knocked on my door and asked the same question. The young woman told me they hadn't paid the rent for four months and the house had been left in a wrecked state. Nice people.' She said no more for a few moments to leave the two detectives to ponder over the picture Flo Jackson painted of the Melia family.

'There is something else officers, that might be of use to you,' she said, which caused the two men to readjust their thoughts back to listening to what this woman was about to say.

'As I said before, the walls in these old houses are paper thin and you can even hear the next door neighbours breathing. A while back, just before they disappeared, I heard them talking, planning a holiday to America, Miami I think they said. How on earth could they afford such a holiday? I don't think he works and I know she was only a cleaner, her money couldn't possibly stretch that far.'

'Did they have people who visited them?' asked Cooper, who felt a sense of kinship with the woman as she reminded him greatly of his own recently deceased Nan, with her kindly ways but inoffensive direct manner.

'It was mostly one man who looked to me to be in his sixties, he seemed to call on them quite regularly, I think I heard Brett calling him granddad Jimmy. They had lots of rough looking people round when they had those wild parties till gone four in the morning. James had a lot to do with that beastly looking man next door to him, Damien Fox, and another across the road; I think he is from Scotland. I don't think either of them goes to work.

Do you know that Damien Fox went over to China and came back with a woman or should I say girl, half his age. Treats her terribly, always shouting at the poor thing, waits on him hand and foot and is most probably beaten by the horrible man. I can't help but hear what goes on. I don't know how these people do it, they always seemed to be having new things all of the time, but where was the money coming from? I have to manage on my state pension and the little bit I get from my Ted's pension.' Flo Jackson continued to ramble on with other matters, such as what the street was like during and after the Second World War, all the rationing that went on and the bombing of most of the loco sheds. The two detectives were inclined to listen to her talking at length about a multitude of things, which had no direct relevance to their investigation, over her ninety years. After they were told her only daughter had moved many years ago to Australia, and then listen to her speak proudly of her grandchildren and great grandchildren, Starr noticed the time to be six thirty.

'I'm sorry Mrs Jackson, we'll have to be getting off now. It has been a pleasure to meet you,' he said.

'Oh, thank you so much for calling in on me; I have so enjoyed having both of you here. Life can be very lonely at times,' she said with more than a hint of sorrow.

Cooper unexpectedly rose from his seat to walk over to the woman to gently clasp her hand in his and lent over to place a tender kiss on her cheek.

'Yes, I too have been humbled to listen to what you have told us about your life. You need to be on the radio, Mrs Jackson.'

'Oh, don't be so daft, people are not interested in what old pensioners like me have to say,' she said with her face abeam at what the young officer had said to her.

'You sit there and talk to DCI Starr, while I'll collect in the cups and plates and do the washing up for you.'

'Please don't bother, I'll do them later,' she replied.

'No, I'm doing this. Just tell DCI Starr what you got up to when you and the other young girls built the Spitfires, I bet you had some fun,' suggested Cooper cheekily.

'Oh, yes we did.' A twinkle could be seen in her eye with a broad smile filling her face as her mind slipped back to those halcyon days.

'Well, Flo, are you going to tell me then?' jovially prompted Starr.

'Yes, yes. I got a bit trapped in my thoughts then. Now where was I?'

Cooper listened in on her life's history from the kitchen while he washed and dried the cups, saucers and plates and put them away in the immaculately clean cupboards. The familiar house décor and furnishings served to transport him back to the times when he loved to see his nan and granddad. When he had clasped the woman's warm, sadly deformed hand it reminded him so much of how he missed both of them. A hardness in his throat temporarily prevented him from swallowing a build-up of saliva as his permanent loss, again, registered firmly in his heart.

Ten minutes later the two officers bid Flo Jackson farewell with Cooper making a solemn promise he would call in on her. As it was now approaching seven, Starr had said to his partner they would have a full discussion about the events of the day with Cora Grey present at eight sharp in the morning. Cooper did not argue with his boss's plans and after he dropped Starr off at the station he would offset the disappointment of missing the evening football match with his similarly devoted football friends by heading to the carvery for a couple of pints and a plate of food which he intended to pile up to the ceiling.

Later, Cooper met up in a different pub to appoint himself as chair to oversee yet another serious investigation, with his friends as chief witnesses, into how his team had contrived to lose such a winnable game. Many pints were to be downed before Cooper arrived at his verdict; their team is truly crap and the manager must be sacked before it was too late to escape relegation. He was to hear no dissenters to his proposed action.

Chapter Twenty-Eight

Around about nine thirty that same night Flo Jackson, who had earlier washed and changed into her candlewick dressing gown, was thinking about going to bed. She had spent much of the time during that late evening going over the unexpected but highly enjoyable visit she'd had by the two detectives, which left her to think there are still some nice people left in this world after all.

The lights had been switched off in the kitchen and sitting room, before she walked to the hallway where she was then stopped from ascending the steep stairway to her bedroom by a loud knock on the door.

'Who could this be at this time of the night? Maybe it's the police again,' were the immediate thoughts running through her head.

Feeling confident in her mind who the callers were, she unusually slid the security chain completely out so it freely dangled down. The door was opened to reveal not the pleasant faces of her earlier callers but the figure of a man she had previously described to the detectives.

'Hello, Flo. I thought it's about time I paid you a visit. It must be two months or more now, and I'm certain you have lots to tell me,' said James Melia. His demon like blue eyes making unnerving contact with hers.

'Oh, oh,' she stuttered in surprise.

'Well aren't you going to let me in Flo? It's gone quite cold out here,' Melia said while stamping his feet and blowing into his cupped hands in a feigned show he was battling against the effects of the low night temperature.

'I suppose so, I was just about to go to bed. Come through, are the rest of the family all right?' she said as he followed her through to the sitting room having first checked that nobody had spotted him going into number 7, Regent Street.

'Sit down James and I'll make you a cup of tea,' she tentatively offered.

'No, I'll stand, but you can sit down,' he commanded.

She unsteadily took to one of the single cottage arm chairs while sensing her mouth had become dry together with her head pounding to every rapid beat of her straining heart.

'Who's been a naughty girl today then, Flo?' he snapped in a contorted snarl.

'What do you mean, I've done nothing,' she replied suddenly frightened by the alarming change in the man's expression.

'You've been talking to the police, haven't you Flo?' he said stepping a little closer to her. She pushed herself further back into the chair to vainly distance herself from his threatening presence, but there was nowhere to escape to.

'Yes, yes, they have been here today,' she nervously stuttered.

'What did they question you about, Flo?' he pressed aggressively.

'They, they asked if I knew of Becky's whereabouts. I said I didn't know,' she answered while turning her head to one side to escape his penetrating stare.

'What else did you tell them? They were here for nearly two fucking hours,' he demanded while simultaneously taking up a more threatening stance by positioning each of his clammy palms on the wooden arms so his contorted features were a mere inch or two from hers. She was distracted by the awful presence of stale whisky fumes filling her personal space due to her confused mind wrestling to conjure up a response to placate the raging Melia.

'I'll ask you again you fucking old bitch, what did you say to the filth,' he shouted with his vile spittle spattering over her turned cheek. She then turned to stare back at him through terrified eyes to stubbornly remain silent.

Frustrated at her perceived lack of cooperation, her grabbed hold of a chuck of thin grey hair to begin violently shaking her head about.

'Tell me what you said to the pigs if you know what is good for you, you fucking old bitch. Do you want to join Ted?'

The mean words hit deeply causing her even greater emotional distress at what she was being callously subjected to

'I, I, didn't tell them anything, I just talked about the war years.' She rasped and somewhat relieved she had been able to say something which might convince the madman to leave her home. But, this wasn't to be the case.

'Fuckin' lyin' bitch. Did you tell them about the dogs? I bet you fuckin' did. What else did you say? They were here for hours, tell me or I will fuckin kill you!'

He then got her by the throat with a single hand, the hard restriction on the windpipe starved the brain of oxygen causing her mind to fall into a fast spin.

Soporific murmurings from the past filled her diminishing consciousness as she sensed her body being inexplicably drawn into a brightly coloured vortex dragging her down, deeper and deeper. In the dull background she heard murmurings of repeated vile threats. It wouldn't be too long before the once familiar sounds of voices not heard for many years would soon drown that of Melia's out.

The motion of the vortex gradually slowed to a stop. A misty shadowy figure then appeared to be approaching her with arms held out. The features of the stranger became sharper and more together for her to recognise them to be that of Ted in his prime years. Before she was able to fall into his outstretched arms Flo Jackson suddenly gasped and thrust her hands to the crushing pain in her chest.

'Let it go, Flo. You have come back home. It's been too long.' Ted's face beamed with happiness as he wrapped his arms around the only true love of his life. The earthborne pain evaporated from her as her soul left her crippled body to be lovingly entrusted to the man she so ached to be with again.

Just before her heart gave in she'd wet herself, so much was the terror this poor frail woman had to first endure before her welcome release.

Melia wouldn't notice she had emptied her bladder. The first sign he had gone too far was when he watched her creased eyelids slowly close followed by a long rattling gasp from her blue tinged lips to exhale her final warm breath across her killer's beaded sweaty face. Her small lifeless head lolled to one side while her thin wrinkled neck was still being tightly gripped in Melia's right hand.

'Wake up you stupid bitch, I'm not finished with you yet,' he unkindly threatened the listless figure, thinking she had only fainted. It didn't take him long though, to realise Mrs Jackson was gone.

Her warm body was left supported by the high-backed winged cottage chair, and on show were the red marks around her neck for the entire world to see.

In the silent sitting room, a surge of panic coursed through Melia's body. He had just murdered a poor defenceless pensioner and if he was to escape detection, his tracks needed to be covered up. Melia's spinning mind began to race with all manner of ploys: set fire to the house, fake a bungled burglary, put her body in the boot of his car and dump it somewhere. These scenarios were soon discarded when he heard loud voices and rap music coming from the house he once occupied and subsequently left owing four months' rent.

A group of local youths had chosen the same night to break into the empty building next door to Flo Jackson's two bedroomed terrace house to have an impromptu rave party. The feral underclass organisers had posted on *Face2Face* social media site a notice to invite all and sundry to come along to create complete mayhem through to the early hours and maybe, beyond.

Melia was stuck, what should he do in the light of the unexpected events? He needed to see for himself what was happening outside on the street. He left the rapidly cooling body in the sitting room to stride over through to the front room and then, taking care to conceal his presence, he gently pulled a drawn curtain to one side to give an interrupted view both up and down the street.

Youths were seen to be milling around like hyenas awaiting their superior ranking predators to become sated from their gorging on a fresh kill. Whilst Melia was covertly hidden in the darkened room he couldn't fail to see that some miscreants had taken an interest in his late reg Audi A5 with one youth trying the driver's side door handle.

Just then he heard the familiar mechanical sounds of a door latch operating followed by an animated figure appearing on the pavement making manic waving signs to gesture the semi-hidden hoards to make their way over to the hitherto empty house. The unfurnished house was soon filled with excited young people eager to get high or become wasted on alcohol over the long night of listening, or more likely going crazy, to music inextricably linked to their particular generation.

The amplifier had been set to its highest level mixed with full booming base to feed the four large speakers. The alternating air pressure waves being pumped out of the speaker cones caused the walls and contents to vibrate in unison to the music in the houses either side of the property. Mercifully, for Flo Jackson, she had been spared the frustration of being subject to this modern anti-social phenomenon and, if one is to believe such things, was so glad to be held tight in the strong arms of her husband.

While remaining secreted behind the curtain and feeling the air vibrate in unison to a sound having its origins in modern black American ghetto music, Melia decided his best option was to get out of the place quickly. The unbearable noise level would ensure someone living close by would call the police, who in turn, were likely to hold fire until they had received five or six further calls of the same complaint. He'd be well away from the address the neighbours were complaining about by the time the police finally decided to arrive.

The Mansefield police eventually got around to dealing with the loud music complaint about two o'clock in the morning. When two marked police cars arrived at 9, Regent Street they were immediately surrounded by a hoard of teenage and older boys and girls. Seen amongst the out of control hoard were individuals holding their iPhones up to the windscreen and side glass excitingly recording the reactions of the two trapped officers. The plan of these amateur film makers was to post their media art on the internet for others of their ilk to laugh and gloat over.

Among the group there would be those who were in such a drunk and drugged up state their feeble intoxicated brains were unable to register that they were committing a serious criminal offence by kicking in the patrol car doors and other metal body panels. One particular youngster amongst this out of control group was kitted out with a short sharp pointed knife which he used to neutralise one of the police patrol cars. The hissing sound of compressed air escaping from the cars punctured tyres could just be discerned above the oscillating vibrating chaos being selfishly pumped out from the 'For Let' two bedroomed terrace house.

One of the officers in the first car to arrive had the good sense to call for back up before venturing onto the menacing street. He watched his colleagues in the car situated a few feet behind them win the battle to get the car door open against the pressure of the hysterical mob. Both uniformed men were then seen with metal telescopic truncheons fully extended while being tightly encircled by a group of mostly males, who'd likely been willingly brainwashed by a combination of anti-establishment song lyrics and an all night long over indulgence in a poison of choice.

Seeing their colleagues, and most probably close friends, in imminent danger, the other officers in the leading car followed suit. There was to be no reasoning with this threatening mob as they proceeded to attack the tight ring of ugly faces with their own similar extended truncheons. This signalled the start of a short but violent two minute spell where usual civilised norms were temporarily lost or ignored.

By the time the white riot vans turned up many had swiftly fled the scene either through fear of arrest or from being incapacitated due to being at the receiving end of a steel truncheon.

It didn't take long for the attending twenty officers to have the two vans full of those who had unwisely deemed it necessary to continue to be openly defiant and deliberately obstructive in preventing the police from carrying out their duties in protecting the local law abiding community. The sound system used by the organisers was unlikely to ever pump music out again due to a particular officer's handling of the equipment. During the fracas this same officer had been spat at full in the face, and moreover, had bottles of beer thrown at him and received two nasty grazes on his forehead and chin from a scuffle with three demented youths.

An hour later two senior uniformed officers were performing a final sweep of the once riotous street. It was then they noticed the front door of number seven was ajar.

James Melia had earlier fled from the property thinking he had closed the front door, but a combination of haste and the noise booming from the house next door prevented him from hearing or seeing the dangling security chain stopping the door from closing due to it getting jammed between the door and the frame.

'Is there anybody there? You have left your door open.' One of the officers called down the darkened musty hallway. The house remained silent.
'Anybody there. We are the police. You need to lock the door.' Still silence.
'We better go and have a look to see if anybody is in. They can't be in bed after all that racket next door and on the streets,' suggested the accompanying officer.
When the hall light was switched on, they saw two doors leading off from the hallway and a flight of steep stairs to the upstairs rooms.
The front room was first checked to see nobody was there, they moved then to the second door to open it to a darkened room. An officer felt around the wall to find the light switch to illuminate the dark space. The click of the switch filled the area with a dull shaded light from a high ceiling fitting, so it took a few moments for them to notice a crumpled figure of an old lady propped up in a typical pensioner style chair with reddish bluey marks around her neck. Throughout their long careers the officers had been called to enough incidents to easily recognise that the woman was not only dead but had met her end in suspicious circumstances.
'Better call in the big boys, Phil. This is a bit beyond our remit,' said the same officer who had found the lightswitch. It didn't take long for CID and other high ranking uniform officers to arrive and have the house and street cordoned off as a serious crime scene.

Chapter Twenty-Nine

The following day at Bladdington police station, Cooper was noted for his late arrival as he bashfully pulled a seat up to join DCI Starr and DS Grey both engrossed looking into a computer monitor screen in the main incident room.

Without casting him a direct look, Starr said, while still reading the information Grey had up on the screen from her task assignment, 'Glad you could make it DS Cooper, I was worried that the heavy day we had yesterday had taken it out of you. But I suppose all that ale you pumped through your system last night and talking football shite with your mates helped to revive you.'

Cooper sensed his stomach clench at his so called superiors off hand remarks. Yes, he was late, tired through a lack of sleep and felt a little hungover, but he was not going to meekly accept another one of his snide comments.

'Well, at least I do something with my life, not like you, even if it is talking "football shite" as you call it.' Cooper replied with no attempt to disguise how he wanted his sentiments to be heard and understood by this sometimes, ignorant man.

Starr didn't appear to flinch and maintained his focus on the bright screen as if nothing had been said by his subordinate; however, he understood that Cooper's jibe contained an element of truth. Maybe he should have found a pub and had a good laugh and a joke with friends he similarly felt comfortable with. He had instead, decided to call in on Bruce McCoy's home to bring him up-to-date, especially the enlightening talk he and Cooper had with Flo Jackson and after listening intently to what Starr had said, McCoy in turn, told the serving DCI about the appointment at the doctors and how he had managed to persuade Sally to attend and how glad he was now she'd finally agreed to take part in a programme of medical and therapy treatment to combat her "condition".

Starr had purposely restricted himself to one glass of whisky. It would have been tempting to keep up with the many re-fills McCoy enjoyed during the DCI's telling and subsequent probing questioning by the retired DI. He eventually left at eleven thirty. He would have loved more of the expensive single malt, but was pleased he hadn't succumbed to temptation. He wasn't about to tempt 'sods law' and take the risk of being pulled over by the flashing blue light of a patrol car and bagged by a young zealous uniformed officer. What a catch this particular DCI would have been for him!

From the lit porch McCoy watched Starr reverse his car out of the drive and to remain there until the vehicle's sharp red rear lights disappeared into the distant dark. Before he turned to enter the silent house again, he pressed the cut glass whisky tumbler to his lips to empty the sizeable remnants in a single gulp. He stood there for a few more moments taking in deep slow breaths of the still late night air while trying to dig out from his alcohol soaked brain if the name of James Melia had any significance to him.

During a long, restless night, McCoy's mind would repeatedly bring in the same name in the form of nonsensical dreams. Having fully awoken into the late morning and none the wiser to who this person may be, McCoy decided it was necessary for him to start some digging of his own.

'I've not briefed DS Grey about the result of our visits to Oakwood Engineering, Bottomley's cleaners, or our trip over to Mansefield. Let's first hear what Cora has to say then it will be our turn,' said Starr turning to look directly at Cooper in a broad smile, he then switched his attention back to the screen again. Cooper shook his head, it was as if the terse comments they had earlier shared had never happened.

'Right, I was able to speak to the head of customer services in both of the separate bank branches. You will not be surprised to learn that the money has completely gone from each of the accounts with both being subsequently closed,' reported Grey.

'Were you able to get from the bank a record of the transactions?' asked Cooper.

'Yes, I've got one of them up on the screen. All withdrawals and transactions have been made using debit cards or on-line payments. There are eight transactions for on-line betting at £200 a time, so that's taken care of £1,600 pounds straight away. The rest of the account was emptied using ATMs at different banks and supermarkets around the county. The other account, the whole amount of £10,000 was withdrawn using a debit card payment to "Gavin's Quality Autos". On our behalf the bank made further checks to track this payment, and you won't be surprised to find out the account is closed and the holder no longer lives at the address held by the bank,' reported Grey.

'Do we have any information on the account holders who received the transactions from the East Seaboard internet account?' Starr quizzed.

'Yes, both accounts were opened on-line using the same name. This happened only a couple of months back; that seems to fit ideally in to the time frame,' suggested Grey.

'Do we have a name and an address?' queried Cooper.

'Somebody with the name of Mrs Brenda O'Flynn, she gave an address in Yarnwich. Maybe she is the person behind the fraud. But, first consider this; would you give your real name and address to the banks and in so doing, make it easy for the police to track you down? I doubt it somehow,' said Grey.

'Banks don't allow accounts to be opened willy nilly, surely they make certain checks beforehand?' said Cooper.

'Confirmation of an address and national insurance number are what most banks are satisfied with. Sometimes they might ask for a passport or driving licence number for additional verification. Anyhow, we need to send someone over to Yarnwich to carry out a few checks for us.'

'Correct, Cora. And by the way, well done in getting the information from the banks so quickly, I know they can be awkward to deal with, even when it's the police for God's sake,' griped Starr. 'Right, we need to move things on,' Starr rallied, 'I'll commandeer one of those new detective constables Palfreyman promoted from the uniform ranks. He or she can get over to Yarnwich to check this Brenda O'Flynn character out. And I'll also let them have a look at chasing up Gavin, the cars salesman. It's my betting he's as bent as a nine bob note. Who'd buy a car from someone called Gavin?'

The two young detectives didn't feel it necessary to add further comment on the DCI's obvious dislike to the car salesman's Christian name.

'Right, we'll all have a cup of tea and then move into my office where Max will go through what happened yesterday, are you okay with that DS Cooper?'

'Yes, Sir,' he answered while in the midst of a wide yawn.

Cooper eventually started to cover what he and Starr had managed to discover over the previous long day, even to the extent of including some of his own thoughts and ideas on how certain events might possibly have occurred.

It was when he was covering what had gone on when they had visited Becky Melia's address, did Cora Grey then finds it necessary to butt in.

'Regent Street, did you say Max?' She pressed with her tone being one of alarm.

'Yes, that's right. We discovered that Becky Melia had flown from that address, so we asked the neighbours either side if they knew of her whereabouts. You look worried, Cora, is there a problem,' queried Cooper.

'Well, it's highly unlikely either of you would have learned about what had gone on in Regent Street last night,' she tentatively suggested.

'No, we don't. Does it have any relevance to the investigation?' said Starr.

'Let me tell you what PC Dale told me and then you'll be able to decide.'

'Don't keep us waiting any longer. What happened?' urged Starr in his usual impatient manner.

'Late last night the police were called to a house in Regent Street. A number of calls were received from angry residents about the loud music and the nuisance being caused by a large gathering of rowdy youths. The two attending cars were surrounded by drunken yobs who subjected the vehicles to a sustained attack; someone had even punctured the tyres. Anyway, they called for backup, but Mansefield police were short on numbers because of the premiership game on that same night, so they asked for Bladdington police to provide them with eight officers and a riot van. PC Dale said it had taken twenty minutes or so before they were able to fully gain control of the street.'

'Bloody hell, it sounds like Beirut. Did anybody get hurt?' Starr asked in earnest.

'One officer was taken to Bladdington hospital for treatment and a few of the others had cuts and bruises. About twenty arrests were made in all; they were taken to Mansefield station and locked up for the night. No doubt, some will be facing criminal charges today. But that is not all,' she momentarily included a pause in her report at this point and without any further prompting she continued to say, 'When a final sweep was made, an officer discovered a front door open next to the empty house that had been used for the rave. They couldn't get an answer so they entered the house and it was then they discovered an elderly woman dead in her chair in one of the downstairs room. PC Dale heard the woman's death is now being treated as murder and to the dismay of the senior officers, all those idiots who were earlier arrested will now be subject to a full murder enquiry.'

'I hope to God it's not Flo Jackson, that would be absolutely terrible if it turned out to be that poor woman.' Cooper seemed to plead while throwing himself back into his seat and running his hand through his hair. He had truly intended to keep to his promise to call in on her, hopefully this might still be the case, but the nagging ache in his very soul told him otherwise. Starr glanced at his male colleague to note his forlorn distant look. He too, was stunned to hear of the woman's possible demise, and if it were to be true, then maybe their visit to her address the previous day might have had something to do with her death.

'We need to find out for certain from Mansefield police the address where the body was discovered, I'll give Bob Stableford a call. Max while I'm doing that, can you fill Cora in on what happened while we were at Regent Street yesterday.'

He then left the two young officers to make the call from the privacy of his office. While he was dialling Stableford's direct line number he pictured in his mind the angry features of Flo Jackson's near neighbour, Damien Fox. He and Mrs Jackson were the only people in the street at that time who knew about the nature of their call. Maybe her murder was totally unrelated to the police being there the previous day; his gut instinct suggested something different.

'Hello, DI Bob Stableford speaking.'

'Hello, Bob it's Dick here.'

'How are you, you old dog, I've not heard from you for a while. I bet this isn't a social call,' Stableford said in a jocular manner.

'You are right, Bob, it's not a social call, it's to do with the woman's body one of your officers discovered at an address in Regent Street last night.'

'Bloody hell Dick you must be psychic, how have you got to hear about it so quickly? I've literally been in my office for a few minutes and only just finished briefly reading the case notes left on my desk by one of the attending CID officers.'

'Ah, ha, that's why I'm a DCI, Bob and you are a DI. No, seriously, a team of our uniform officers were asked to support Mansefield police in quelling the trouble in Regent Street. Apparently there was this football match on and this had stretched your resources. One of our police constables had heard about the body being found and he in turn told DS Cora Grey.'

'Don't tell me, that would be PC Dale. It was clear he was bonking DS Grey when I worked with you months ago, lucky sod.'

'Nevertheless, do you have a name for the deceased?' pressed Starr.

'Please take this right Dick. Why are Bladdington police interested in a dead person found on our patch?'

Starr then spent the next fifteen minutes or more explaining how his interest in the Regent Street mortality had come about.

'Poor old Bruce and Sally McCoy, all those years of hard work and some bastard wipes them out. And by what you have said, it seems there is little, if any chance of getting a penny back unless Bruce is successful in claiming negligence against the bank,' sympathised Stableford.

'So do you have a name of the person? Bob,'

'Yes, sorry Dick, the person is believed to be a Florence Jackson, but as you know, we will have to inform relatives so they can confirm her identity.'

Starr let out a long sigh on being told the two words he was dreading to hear. It was hard to believe that less than twenty-four hours ago she was mostly happy in her own little world, but unknowingly to Florence Jackson, the unexpected visit by the police served to be a dark harbinger of her impending doom.

'I'll identify her, I spent enough time with her yesterday to recognise her features. Her only daughter lives in Australia and she has no blood relatives in this country. I suppose you'll have to sift through Mrs Jackson's drawers for an address or phone number to report the tragic news to her daughter. Who can possibly blame them for thinking this country has gone to the dogs when the family hear she was likely murdered?' Starr lamented.

'Quite,' agreed Stableford, who then moved on to say that the post-mortem was due to be carried out at eleven thirty and it would be helpful if Starr could complete the legal procedure of identifying the body before the forensic coroners started to disassemble Mrs Jackson's frail body into its component parts.

The call ended after Starr had agreed to meet Stableford at ten thirty.

Starr left his office to re-enter the incident room. His attention was immediately drawn to the angst lines of expectation etched across Cooper's face.

'Please say it's not her, Sir,' his whole being seemed to cry out.

'I'm so sorry, Max. It is Mrs Jackson.'

Cooper smashed his fist down hard on the desk top causing others working in the room to be disturbed from what they were doing.

'It's not right, none of this is right, I fucking hate this job. If we hadn't gone around there yesterday then she would still be alive. It's all our fault she is dead,' Cooper angrily spat with tears rolling unashamedly down his cheeks. Cora Grey stood up from her seat to walk around the back of Cooper's shoulders to give him a close hug. She understood no words would adequately explain to her friend-not colleague, the unfairness of this woman's cruel death.

'I know Max, this job can be so bad at times, you can't help but be personally affected by some of the unfairness and injustices life can sometimes throw at you. We owe it to Flo Jackson to find her killer and get him locked up for the rest of his life.'

Cooper then lifted his handkerchief from his ruddy face.

'That's a joke, Sir, the stupid judges will give the murderer a slap on the wrist and he will be out in five years. If I get to the bastard first, they'll be no need for a court case.' Cooper's features hardened as he run through his mind a macabre drama he intended to act out when, not if, he gets his hands on Flo Jackson's killer.

Starr wisely ignored the DS's veiled threat and went on to explain he had volunteered to carry out the identification process at the coroner's lab planned for ten thirty. After much debate and argument between the three officers, Starr eventually conceded to allowing Cooper and Grey to accompany him.

While they were waiting for the time to elapse up to them leaving the station for the drive across town to the coroner's lab, Cooper busied himself by typing up the notes into the case file, while Grey had volunteered to contact the bank Becky Melia had nominated for the paying in of her wages from Bottomley's cleaners. She had by now, become quite adept at dealing with awkward and sometimes deliberate obstructive customer services personnel who had clearly been subjected to yearly rigorous training programmes to instil in their minds that their bank could do no wrong.

Starr on the other hand, wasn't in any mood to brief the pasty, jowly station's Chief Superintendent, Richard Palfreyman, so he had decided to take up the little used opportunity to type an email to report on how the investigation into Bruce McCoy's £82,000 fraud was progressing and also to inform him that an additional detective constable had been commandeered to do some of the leg work. There was little doubt he'd later either be called up to his office or receive an email from Palfreyman to pick fault in some aspect of the investigation. Starr stubbornly consoled himself with the understood protocol - it was the Super's prerogative to give his own personal analysis of a situation. However, in Starr's mind, the indisputable fact remained; the man couldn't tell the difference between his arse or his elbow.

The police visit to Brenda O'Flynn's address discovered her to be a victim of failing sight which was further compounded by her being partly invalided to a wheel chair. Mrs O'Flynn had been a widow for three years and needed home help early morning, mid-day, tea time and finally last thing before she went to bed. Really she should have been in a care home but didn't want to leave the house she had lived in for over fifty years. Her last wish was to be carried out in a box from where she had enjoyed so many happy times rather than taken from a soulless building where they viewed old people solely as a commodity to make big money.

When sensitively questioned about the two suspicious accounts the aged woman made strong claims she knew absolutely nothing about their existence. However, the police were keen to learn that a nephew, in the name of Davy O'Flynn, managed her dwindling finances, daily post and bits of essential shopping.

Chapter Thirty

Ten thirty, the three officers were met at the coroner's reception desk by DI Bob Stableford. After handshakes he assumed the task of escorting the small group to the relatives' room. Care had been taken in the furnishing of the small space to provide a feeling of serenity while in the absence of any obvious religious images. Each of the four officers took a seat to await in silence the emergence of a medically qualified person from the other door in the room. After what seemed to be an age, the watched door handle turned with a pronounced creak to mark the appearance of a smiling pathologist.

'Such a big group of you, Flo Jackson must have been a special person.' None of the attending officers were able to drum up a suitable riposte to his remark.

'I believe in the absence of having a member of the deceased family present, DCI Starr is willing to assist us in the formal identification of Mrs Florence Jackson?' he asked while scanning each of the male officers faces.

'Yes, that's me,' replied Starr taking to his feet. Cooper followed suite. 'I would also like to assist DCI Starr in identifying Mrs Jackson.'

Starr turned to look at Cooper unsure in his mind if the young officer was up to it.

'I'll be all right. I want to do this,' was Cooper's response to his superior's questioning look.

'Please come this way, it shouldn't take too long for the formal identification.' The medical man disappeared into the adjacent annexe room followed by the two volunteers. He strolled to take up the far side position of the shrouded shape lying on steel constructed trolley, while the officers stood rigidly upright on the other side.

'Are you ready?' he asked while gripping the hem of the white cotton shroud.

The two officers nodded in unison.

The shroud was drawn back slowly to first reveal strands of her thinning grey hair followed then by the porcelain white colour of her forehead, closed eyes covered with purple tinged lids, a short nose, thin lips drained of any life colour and her familiar chin sporting the long stray hairs which had been noticed the previous day.

The shroud was sensitively folded back on to the cold body to expose the shoulders, enough for all to see the deep bruising which seemed to encircle her full neck line.

'I have to formally ask you now DCI Starr, are you able to positively identify this person to be Florence Jackson of 7, Regent Street, Mansefield.'

Without appearing to remove his stare from the dead woman's face, he said clearly, 'Yes, I positively identify this woman to be that of Mrs Florence Jackson.'

'Thank you,' replied the man. He then moved to gather the shroud hem to cover the body.

He was stopped in his tracks by a call of, 'No, not yet,' from Cooper. He was unable yet to leave the sad crushed figure and needed to use this precious moment to help assuage his guilty feelings that he was in some way, responsible for this woman's death. There would probably be no time other than this where he would be in her presence to say how sorry and devastated he was that she had been taken in such a callous way.

Starr and the assistant coroner were astute enough to read the situation and both left the room to leave the forlorn figure of Cooper looking down at the lifeless person he had so enjoyed meeting for such a fleeting, but significant moment in his life.

Five minutes later the handle once more creaked to allow Cooper to join the others sitting in the relatives' room. Grey moved to put her arms around him and the men patted him on his shoulders in a way only males can do.

Cooper was beginning to understand policing can be tough at times, so tough in fact, it can take you to the edge and throw you over into oblivion. He was close to that edge.

The assistant pathologist re-entered the room and during the background noise of the trolley being wheeled out, he had invited the officers to stay and watch the autopsy on Florence Jackson. They all declined the invitation as they had all previously opted to drive over to the "Three Nuns" pub for a much needed pint and something to eat. It would be in the surroundings of this thirteenth century public house where they would plan to deal with the sudden unexpected turn in the investigation.

Chapter Thirty-One

'Hi, Debs, this is Bruce McCoy. How are ya?'

After forcing down two rounds of toast and a large cup of black coffee, Bruce McCoy then swallowed four paracetamol tablets to help get rid of his clanging headache.

During each of the heavy thumps pounding his skull he recalled an incident that happened thirty odd years ago which resulted in him having forever to bear a long facial scar. The perpetrator's surname he could readily bring to mind, Melia, but for the life of him, the man's Christian name escaped him. Starr had given him the name of James, however, McCoy's drink addled brain recognised there was some doubt whether this was the same person he had fought in the river so long ago.

There was no point in asking Sally if the man's name rung a bell, so he had decided to contact a trusted female admin colleague he had become close to when he worked at Mansefield police station.

'Hello, Bruce. I'm fine, how are you? Is retirement suiting you? It's same old here,' brightly reacted Debbie Kewley on hearing his familiar voice. She had taken the call in an office that had confidential access to past and serving police officer arrest and conviction records.

'Yes, I'm fine, thanks Debs. I was hoping you could do me a favour.'

'If I possibly can, sure. What is it you want, Bruce?'

'With all this spare time I've got on my hands I have decided to write a book about my career in the police, you know it's the sort of thing people do when they get to my age.'

'Oh, so you are going to be an author then, how exciting,' Debbie Kewley giggled at the other end of the line.

'Well, to be truthful, I've only just started to flesh out what I want to include and that is where I need your help, Debs,' said McCoy, while using the tips of his fingers to massage his throbbing right temple.

'What is it I can help you with?'

'The thing is, Debs, I can remember most of the names and faces of the criminals I had the dubious pleasure of meeting, but there is one name in particular, James Melia, that is frustrating me. Sometime in my career I believe I might have had dealings with this man, but for the life of me, I cannot bring the incident to mind or the date when the arrest happened. It might even be the case I had only a minor part to play in his arrest, I just don't know. I'm hoping Debs, you can find the time to check my arrest and conviction record to see if such a name comes up. It most probably will turn out to be a simple matter of my imagination playing tricks and at my age, I can assure you it happens, anyway, I need to find out one way or the other.'

'I can't see that being a problem, but I can't do it straight away, it's got so busy in here. This business about reducing crime figures against impossible targets has upped our workload enormously, and we both know what a crock that is. I won't bother about asking for clearance, it's only been a short while since you left the force. You do know though, don't you Bruce,' she said warningly, 'you cannot use a person's name in your book without first getting their permission?'

'Yes, yes, I understand that. Thanks for your help, Debs; I'll leave you with my mobile number so you can let me know if you find anything.'

When McCoy finished the call, he made his way to the fridge to remove a carton of fresh orange juice from the bottom door tray and gulp down what remained of the contents. The empty carton was deposited in the stainless steel pedal bin on the way to him lying full length on the lounge settee to try and bring his pounding head down.

Chapter Thirty-Two

Over two pints of bitter, half a shandy and a glass of mineral water, the four officers dined from a two meals for a fiver lunch time menu. It was during this intimate period while sat round a typical oblong shaped pub dining table, when Damien Fox's name came up in the discussion.

'He was the only other person we questioned as to the whereabouts of Becky Melia. And you couldn't say he was exactly cooperative when we spoke to him,' said Cooper while scooping up a fork full of reconstituted mash potato and onion gravy.

'You are right, Max. Makes me wonder if he tipped somebody off about the nature of our call. It's too much to believe it was just sheer coincidence Flo Jackson was murdered on the same night. We did spend quite a bit of time with her, and I bet this was made known to others, probably by Fox, who might have understood she had told us things that could lead to their arrest,' conjectured Starr while running a finger across the condensation on the outer surface of his half empty pint glass.

'Has anybody checked if either Melia or Fox have criminal records?' questioned Stableford as he sliced through the spongy textured gammon steak.

The three blank faces looking back at him was enough for him to see that this had not, as yet, been done. Stableford put his knife and fork onto his plate and slipped his hand into his jacket pocket which was hanging from the back of his wood framed seat to pull out an iPhone. He then proceeded to place the device in an available space on the crowded dining table and began to tap in a number using his right index finger.

'I'll get the station to send us any records we might hold on them. All that sort of thing can be done by the touch of a button nowadays,' Stableford announced proudly.

The three Bladdington officers resumed their meals and continued to chatter about the case, especially Damien Fox's possible involvement, while Stableford spoke to someone employed at Mansefield police station.

After all the plates had been cleared and a fresh round of drinks was being carefully carried over to the table on a slippery wet tray by Grey, did they all hear the unsubtle tune of a *Star Wars* ring tone blare out from Stableford's iPhone to disturb others similarly dining in the upmarket country pub. The DI clumsily prodded the iPhone screen and then raised it to his ear to listen to the call, during which time, Grey carefully placed the round of drinks on the table.

'Thanks for that, see you then, Vicky,' said Stableford with a broad smile forming on his face which hadn't gone unnoticed by his contemporaries.

'Hey, who's this Vicky, Bob? You sounded just like a smitten schoolboy, does the missus know about this?' teased Starr.

'Don't be daft, Dick. I'm old enough to be her dad. She is a lovely, charming lady and that's all. Anyway, more to the point, she has got what we asked for,' said Stableford while trying to divert attention away from his obvious embarrassment.

'What did she say, Sir?' asked Cooper.

'The only James Melia on record got in a ruck of bother in his teenage years, such as being hauled in for being drunk and disorderly, smashing the town hall windows and stealing a couple of cars. In his twenties he was done for handling stolen goods, a case of GBH against a known drug dealer and was taken in for questioning for domestic violence. He never went down but we have his prints and mug shot on record. Damien Fox is a real charmer. He has done a four year stretch for two counts of ABH, knife attack apparently, and he has other convictions for GBH, car theft, and animal cruelty. He has a long record of arrests for being drunk and disorderly in his teens and twenties. It doesn't take much stretch of the imagination to suspect he might have had something to do with Florence Jackson's death.' Stableford then opened up the email Vicky had promised to send for it to appear on the iPhones large polycarbonate screen. After he scan read the contents himself to check if he'd missed out any important details, Stableford then passed it over to Cooper for him to be the second person to read the abridged criminal records of both men.

Once the iPhone had completed the circumnavigation of the table members, Stableford slipped his new toy back into his jacket pocket. This was interpreted as a signal for the small group to decide what should happen next.

'Right, we have all had some time to give some thought about what we should do to propel the investigation. I think we need to get over to Regent Street and take Damien Fox down to the station for further questioning,' suggested Starr.

'Which station Dick? Bladdington or Mansefield? The murder did happen on Mansefield's patch,' questioned Stableford.

'Yes, I have given some thought about that, Bob. We need to stick to the correct protocol or someone higher up might see some political gain in creating distrust between the two stations, and we don't want that to happen. So, Bob, my answer to your question is this; you will make the formal arrest, Fox will then be taken to Mansefield nick and hopefully, your gaffer will agree to one of us being present at the interview to assist in the interrogation.'

'Can't argue with that, Dick, it all seems fair and above board to me,' said Stableford.

The four officers then stood upright in synch to down the remains of their drinks and to the rally cry of, 'Let's go and get Fox!' they left the Three Nuns pub to pile into two cars for the journey over to Regent Street.

Chapter Thirty-Three

The car was driven through a maze of streets all having similar railway company built terraced houses before they arrived at their destination. Besides the familiar police tape cordoning off the obvious crime scene, the officers immediately noticed bouquets of flowers had started to be laid by decent and caring folk on the pavement outside of Mrs Jackson's humble home.

'There must be at least twenty bouquets laid there already, look, some have even tied bunches to the drain pipe with ribbons,' Grey said from the confines of the police car looking in the direction of the sad floral display.

'I can see DI Geoff Fairhurst. He must still be here from being called out very early this morning. He must need the overtime to be here this length of time. With five kids he likely does,' observed Stableford.

Before they planned to gather at Fox's door the three Bladdington officers followed Stableford along the old blue block laid pavement to reach the fluttering crime scene tape. DI Fairhurst was seen talking to a SOC officer when he became distracted by a familiar voice calling out his Christian name:

'Geoff, how are things going here?'

'Hi, Bob. I've expected you to show your face. Forensics have been really busy, I'll take you into the house and show you what they have found.'

Fairhurst turned his attention to take in the presence of strangers standing slightly back from his senior officer, all of whom, he couldn't fail to notice, were attired in familiar CID dress code.

Stableford hadn't failed to clock his colleague's inquisitive look.

'Sorry, DI Fairhurst, these officers are from Bladdington station. This is DCI Dick Starr, DS Cora Grey and DS Max Cooper.'

After a series of hearty genuine handshakes were dispensed with, Stableford allowed Starr to briefly explain to the Mansefield detective inspector the purpose of their attendance at the crime scene.

'I've had dealings with Damien Fox in the past, I didn't realise he lived so close to this address. So you believe he could have had something to do with the woman's murder then?' questioned DI Fairhurst.

'Our intentions are to take him down to Mansefield station for further questioning. If he's hiding anything, we'll have more chance of getting him to talk there,' said Stableford.

'Well good luck then, Fox is an evil, cunning bastard,' warned Fairhurst, 'He stuck a knife in a young lad he accused of looking at his girlfriend. Luckily, the blade just missed his heart but it had nicked a main artery, believe me, there was blood everywhere, it's a miracle he survived. He was out in no time, bloody stupid judge!' Fairhurst was glad it wasn't to be him again who'd likely have to manhandle Fox into the back of a police vehicle to then drag him off to the local nick.

'We won't disturb the forensics team if you don't mind, our priority is to apprehend Fox, hopefully we'll find he's in,' said Starr casting an eye over to the grubby white plastic door where he strongly suspected things would soon kick off.

'If you need any help in arresting him, just give me a shout,' called Fairhurst, while really silently hoping they wouldn't need to have to take him up on his offer.

The four officers walked the short distance from the fluttering crime scene tapes to gather on the pavement fronting Damien Fox's house. Starr purposely rapped loudly against the door then stepped a little away to watch through a small frosted window panel, an approaching large dark figure cussing out loudly.

The door was pulled inwards to give Damien Fox a clear view of the callers consisting of two familiar and two unfamiliar faces. He was also to be the first to express a greeting fashioned in his own inimitable style.

'Fucking hell, it's you again, you just don't fucking give up do ya. You know, you need to see a doctor about your purple face, there could be something seriously wrong with you, and the rest of you can fuck off as well,' snarled Fox.

'Well, good afternoon to you too, Mr Fox,' calmly replied Starr, 'You will be no doubt happy to hear we have reserved a comfortable place for you at Mansefield police station, which we are all rather hoping will be to your liking.'

Damien Fox's limited cognitive ability took a few moments longer than the average human species to decipher each of the purple faced detective's words and then attach some meaning to them.

'What the fuck are you on about? Have you gone mad? You stupid bastard. I'm going nowhere with you lot,' was Damien Fox's eventual answer to Starr's warm invitation.

'I'll ignore for the moment the rudeness of your welcome. However, Mr Fox, I am not prepared to overlook the strong possibility you had something to do with Mrs Florence Jackson's death.

'You are mad aren't you? answered Fox in reply to Starr's suggestion. 'I had nowt to do with her being strangled, but she had it coming, she was nothing but an interfering old bag,' proclaimed the muscle-bound beefcake. Cooper by this stage was seen to be shaking and clenching his fist in anger on hearing Fox's unfair assessment of Flo Jackson and before he was able to throw a similar insult his way, Grey posed the man a question designed to provoke a response he would later seriously regret.

'Mr Fox, I don't believe any of us here have said anything about Mrs Jackson being strangled. The only people who might know how she unfortunately died are currently performing an autopsy on her, and of course, we must include those too who fled the murder scene knowing what they had done. So please tell us Mr Fox, how do you know she has been strangled? I suggest to you, Mr Fox, the person responsible for her death is you.'

Her blunt accusation alleging his involvement had the effect of changing the look on Fox's face from one of bolshie confidence to that of wide eyed fright.

This was to be his "fight or flight" moment; Fox chose flight. He suddenly turned his bulked up frame away from the small gathering blocking any possible exit through the front door to try to evade police capture via the alleys running along the backs of the terrace houses.

Cooper quickly assessed there was a real chance Fox's bolt for freedom might be successful. He wasn't prepared to consider any possibility of that happening. He charged from the group in rapid pursuit of the escaping villain which carried him along the hallway, through a dark middle room, which then led to a kitchen extension and finally back into daylight onto a dirty paved back yard having a steel meshed pen containing four American pit bull terrier dogs being sent crazy by the sudden commotion.

Starr and Grey latched on to the chase, with Stableford darting off to find the back alleyway to block off Fox's escape. DI Fairhurst, who had held back from re-entering Flo Jackson's house, got wind of the unfolding trouble and without being asked, joined Stableford in running round to the backs of the houses.

Cooper closed in on Fox as he tried to scramble over the double padlocked gate set into a seven foot tall alley brick wall. The immense strength Fox had built in his over developed biceps wasn't quite enough to haul his heavy frame over the high wall in one swift movement. His left booted foot found sufficient purchase on a cross bracing screwed into the timber framed gate door to get him closer to disappearing over the high wall. While fixing his handgrip on the ridge shaped coping stone, he heard one of the male police pursuers shout something he failed to understand and then felt the force of hands grabbing firmly hold of his lower leg to halt his final vault over the wall.

'Got you, you're going nowhere you evil bastard!' yelled Cooper in jubilation, he then suddenly shrieked out in pain as Fox sent his deep tread army specification boot hard into the young copper's face. Caught in the throes of agony Cooper lost his grip and being in a temporary disorientated state, his thin frame was sent spinning against the dog pen. An unstoppable stream of blood leached through his fingers to drip like fast running red candle wax on to his shirt and trousers. The caged pit bulls by this time had gathered in a protective pack tight up against the sturdy steel meshing clawing frantically with razor sharp white fangs snapping behind frothed jaws desperate to get at the unfamiliar figure reeling against the metal barrier.

In spite of his injuries, Cooper just managed to pull his senses together to see Fox close to disappearing over the high brick wall. He made a desperate lunge at Fox's trailing leg to sink his teeth deep and hard against the tracksuit fabric and through to the toned flesh of the lower calf. Fox responded to the unexpected human bite with not only a high pitched shriek but was the cause of him to lose grip on the slippery moss covered coping stones. Cooper delivered a sharp yank on a dangling leg to bring Fox back down to earth in an undignified heap on the hard yard surface. Cooper took a moment or two to steady himself while nervously watching the bulked up figure struggling to get to his feet.

Starr and Grey were about to grab hold of the staggering maddened hulk when Cooper thrust his arm out to prevent them from moving in.

'I'll deal with him, I owe it to Flo Jackson,' said Cooper in steely determination.

Fox was then heard to cry out in a sudden burst of laughter on catching his slight framed foe's boast.

'You against me, now that is going to be fun. You think you are some sort of crusader for that old bag, you skinny bastard. You're going to need more than your teeth to stop me, you fucking girl.'

Fox's punch caught Cooper by surprise; his fist caught him in the stomach and sent him flaying against the hard rusting mesh of the dog pen. While he was dropped to his knees winded by the force of the blow he heard Starr warn Fox and then move in with handcuffs jangling to make an arrest, these actions were only to be met with a bout of raucous laughter.

'Come close to me with them old man, and I'll fucking drop you and stick them up your arse.' The wild primaeval look thrown by this close representation of Neanderthal man, communicated to Starr the likely outcome he would again be seriously injured if he made any attempt to cuff the madman.

'Call for back up, DS Grey,' said Starr while wisely taking a step back.

'Already done, Sir. They are on their way as I speak,' she answered.

'You yellow bellied gang of wimps, come on you three against me. What do you say, you skinny bitch?' taunted Fox while jabbing his clenched fists about in a mock boxer's stance.

It was at that very point when Cooper saw his chance to bring this testosterone fuelled show to an end. He kept his head low and body stooped to charge headlong sending the force of moving body hard into the antagonist's stomach. With the surprise attack catching Fox completely unawares, he was unable to prevent the impact of the unexpected high inertia force from sending his heavy torso crashing hard against the solid wooden tall gate in a loud thump. He lay there momentarily stunned. His bald shaven head struck one of the two large Yale padlocks to create a two inch gash with streams of blood filling each of his eye sockets.

While still struggling to get his wind back, Cooper saw Fox get back up on his feet. The maddened ape detected the wavering thin figure and with his mind set on doing some real serious harm, he swung his iron like fist with the overt intent of removing the copper's head from his shoulders. Luckily for Cooper, a large stream of cloying blood pouring from the deep head wound ran down from his forehead to block his vision in one eye.

The malicious swipe missed Cooper's cheek by only a couple of inches and while Fox rubbed his bloodied hand in his eye socket, Cooper summoned up a mass of energy to peel off a punch of his own into Fox's slackened midriff muscles.

The unexpected blow caused him to lurch forward, which created an opening Cooper intended to exploit. This time it would be his left fist to do the damage. With all the remaining energy in his body transferred to one single point his intent was to release it in an upper cut thrust under the exposed square jaw.

Starr and Grey gasped at the sights and sound created by their fellow officer's violent execution. The crack of a fist striking a jaw was heard above the din of the wild barking dogs followed by the heavy body seemingly being lifted from its gravity held position on the yard surface to then fly backwards through the air and to strike hard against the wooden gate and the same padlock causing yet another case for Fox to need more stitches.

While Cooper bent forward to rest his hands on his knees and with Fox out for the count, Starr rushed in to shackle the madman's wrist with his cuffs, while Grey used her set to bind his legs together to the background sound of police cars arriving in the street.

The animated male voices coming from inside Fox's house signalled the worried appearance of Stableford and Fairhurst and shortly after, the first of the uniformed backup.

'Are you all, all right? We could hear the commotion at the end of the alley way. Sounded like all hell broke loose!'

Stableford anxiously pressed while he took in the unlikely scene of Fox all bloodied, lying double cuffed flat on his back and apparently out for the count. The slightly built Cooper was seen to be sitting on his haunches with a pressed blood soaked handkerchief to his nose.

Starr nodded in the direction of the two worried detectives to give a non-verbal sign things were under control. He then took a couple of long strides over to the pen caging the snarling frothing animals.

Starr was then heard to be making low shushing sounds which at first, appeared to have little effect in calming the deranged pit bulls. However, his persistence soon paid off. The dogs' frantic barks were gradually but surely, replaced by low whimpers while Starr continued to assure the innocent creatures they were safe and free from having to fight for their survival.

The gathered group of uniformed and plainclothed officers continued to look on to witness the four dogs eventually lie flat with their stomachs pressed to the faeces strewn concrete pen floor and each in turn, rested their scarred and torn heads onto their front paws.

'Bloody incredible, Dick. How did you do that?' Stableford marvelled.

'These poor creatures are active American pit bull terriers, they are a banned breed and when they are taken from here will have to be destroyed. Just look at the state of them: scarred skin, ripped ears, disfigured faces and made to live in such filthy conditions,' said Starr, clearly dismayed how low some species of the human race are willing to drop to get their kicks.

'Why have two of the dogs got heavy chains wrapped around their necks?' asked Cooper through his bloodied handkerchief.

'That's a dog man's trick to build up the dog's neck muscle structure so it can more easily tear other animals to bits. Unbelievable. Poor creatures are probably better off dead.'

The silent gathered group in the small back yard turned to watch Starr stride over to a battered galvanised bucket which, along with a small shovel propped up beside it, appeared to have been used to give the pen an occasional cleaning. During the periods of the infrequent cleaning the bucket had become full of rain water and with the addition of fag ends and long fermented dog faeces, had created a strong fetid mix.

The silenced group watched Starr tuck his fingers under the steel handle to lift the filled bucket and to then turn and walk over to the unconscious figure.

'You're not going to do what I think you are going to do are you, Sir?' queried Cooper who by this time had got to his feet and sported a big grin across his bloodied face having anticipated the intentions of his senior officer.

In reply Starr said, 'You don't think we are going to wait all day for the charming Mr Fox to have a nice little nap do you, DS Cooper?'

'No, Sir!'

'I'm glad you agree, so I'm sure you will not mind if I give him a gentle wake up call.'

'Not at all, sir' answered Cooper while hardly being able to contain himself.

Starr positioned the bucket three feet above Fox's upturned face and commenced mumbling a few words of encouragement just as he had done with the caged pit bulls.

'Wake up Damien; it's time to wake up. You have been asleep long enough now. Come on Damien, wake up.'

Starr's verbal mutterings served to stimulate Fox's diminishing number of brain cells enough for him to flickeringly open his blood encrusted eye lids. It was during this split second of semi-consciousness that he was finally to be fully awoken from his enforced dreamless slumber by an almighty deluge of ice cold brackish water mixed with soggy cigarette butts and soft unidentifiable clods completely drenching his head and upper body.

The attending officers burst out in combined laughter as they viewed the evil figure of Damien Fox frantically gasping and gagging as he tried to clear his throat of foul tasting water and other bits of debris at the same time as attempting to get to his shackled feet.

When Fox finally managed to regain some of his senses, his blurred vision took in a gallery of strange faces: some outwardly laughing and others with broad smirking grins. It didn't take him long to notice the purple faced detective, he'd twice ridiculed, clutching a familiar galvanised coated bucket.

'Just thought you needed freshening up a bit Damien. But I think once we get you down to the station we need for you to see a doctor, you may have swallowed something nasty, you never know what might have been in this bucket.'

Fox looked down at his chest and could recognise different colours of dog waste splattered on his tight t-shirt.

'You fucking bastard, I'll kill you for this!' Enraged, Fox with the realisation of what had been poured over him.

'If you don't calm down Mr Fox I'll have to set my young detective on you again.' Starr said looking in the direction of the bent nose Cooper.

Fox knew at this point there was no use in struggling or protesting because even with his limited intelligence, he understood he'd been out gunned and even more, humiliated.

After having had his rights read out to him by Grey, Cooper and Fairhurst roughly hauled Fox along to shuffle his cuffed feet through the small terraced house while being watched by his brow beaten internet bride looking on silently. She inwardly wished he'd be taken away for a long, long time. She might be lucky enough to find a kind soul to pay for an economy class one-way air ticket back to her small village in China to pick up her life again as it was before she stupidly allowed her very existence to be crushed by this dangerous man.

'What's all that stuff on your hands and jacket, Bob?' casually enquired Starr while Fox was being dragged from the yard wearing a "Kermit the Frog" printed tea towel tightly bound around his gashed skull in Hulk Hogan style.

'Bloody vandal paint, sticks like shit to a blanket. Geoff is the same. When we got to the back of the houses we found that the ally closed by high metal gates. To get to the back of Fox's house we'd have to climb over them, that is when we both discovered the top rail had been daubed in vandal paint. I know I'm covered in the stuff but it does stop people from getting into places they shouldn't. Anyway, luckily, Cooper's unbeknown pugilist talents stopped our friend from escaping. Bet you thought he hadn't got it in him, hey, Dick?'

Stableford left him to think over what he had said to snatch a pair of Fox's white boxer shorts from the clothes line to then proceed to remove some of the sticky black residue from his fingers and palms. During the cleaning process Starr replied to his friend's observations concerning the detective sergeant's performance.

'Before we got to Fox's house, it was clear Cooper was pumped up because of what had happened to Flo Jackson. Pure adrenalin made him give chase when Fox decided to do a runner and all credit to the lad for stopping him from escaping. But would he have done the same if he knew little of the crime victim? I don't think so somehow. He'd become too emotionally involved and as we know Bob, there is a distinct danger it can then so easily cloud one's rational judgement. Cooper might have been seriously hurt or even killed, don't let's forget, Fox had already served time for a near lethal knife stabbing, who's to say he wouldn't have done the same thing again to Cooper? He didn't know Fox wasn't armed with a knife. He isolated himself from the team, something you never do when dealing with a known violent criminal. This time he was lucky to get away with just a broken nose. But I suppose his heroics will provide him with some bragging rights with junior officers and his football friends. But just think of how the situation could have gone so seriously wrong. We could easily now be looking on seeing Cooper being zipped up in a black plastic body bag.'

'Quite.' solemnly replied Stableford as he moved to re-peg the freshly blackened boxer shorts back on the clothes line.

Before the house was eventually left in solitude, the murder suspects clothing had been carefully placed in clear labelled plastic bags by the same SOC forensics team who had been previously busy in Flo Jackson's humble home dusting and painstakingly seeking for signs to link incriminating evidence to the perpetrator of her sad death. Other black plastic bin bags were used to remove a quantity of unopened cardboard boxes found in the under stairs cupboard suspected of containing electronic Notebooks, iPhones and blue ray players.

The RSPCA had quickly responded to DS Grey's request to have to four pit bulls removed from the address. Their short violent lives came to a grateful end later that same evening.

Finally, Starr, Stableford, Grey and Fox's oriental partner, left Regent Street in an unmarked police car for the journey over to Mansefield police station. The forensics team finally locked up the adjacent houses when their work was done close to midnight.

Chapter Thirty-Four

'James, it's Robbie Kelly.'

Kelly, who lives opposite Damien Fox's rented home, didn't take long to recognise Melia to be a kindred spirit once he had noticed his interest in pit bull breeds and especially that the animals were not being kept purely for walking or aesthetic reasons. Kelly's primary motives for owning such a breed of dog appealed to his own sadistic and base instincts and took little time to form a friendship bond with both Melia and Fox.

The mobile phone was pressed to Kelly's right ear while he viewed, from behind partially drawn curtains from the front bedroom of his run down terrace house, two police officers bundling a shackled adult male with what appeared to him to be a small towel wrapped around his head to stem the bleeding from an obvious scalp wound, into the back of an unmarked police car.

Melia soon recognised the broad Scottish tones of his once opposite neighbour.

'Yes, it's me Robbie.'

'Can you speak, James? I mean is there anybody about who might be able to listen in? 'Kelly queried in a tone which only served to unsettle Melia, especially after what he had done the previous night.

'No, what is it Robbie?' he replied trying to put on a casual air.

'I've just watched the police throw Foxy into the back of a car. Something big has gone on because they have him cuffed and a towel wrapped around his head to cover a bleeding wound. Maybe it's something to do with what happened in the street last night, James.'

'Why, what went on last night, Robbie,' Melia enquired in a sort of naive innocence.

There was a short break in the conversation while Kelly seemed to need a little time to compose a reply.

'Hey, come on James, laddie, what, you don't know what went on?' Kelly said in clear amazement at his friend's feigned ignorance of the previous night's events. 'But I noticed your car parked in the street. I even saw you leave Mrs Jackson's house just before all hell broke loose.'

Melia understood there was no point in denying to his violent friend that he was mistaken with his claim. Before he was able to conjure up in his mind a suitable response which would explain his reason for being in the street, and particularly, as he was seen to leave a murder victim's house the very night she was found dead, Kelly continued, 'When I got up early this morning to walk the dogs, I watched a body bag being taken away and Foxy confirmed it was Mrs Jackson but wouldn't say much else when I spoke to him later that morning. The cops are everywhere. It can't be natural causes or why would the street be barrier taped off and a load of forensic type people coming and going all day? Do you think Foxy might have had something to do with it? We both know she was a nosy cow; she didn't miss a thing always peeping through her curtains.

Anyhow, what were you doing at Mrs Jackson's house last night? Do you think you should let the police know when you saw her so they can work out a time when she was most likely murdered, God forbid.'

Kelly had been quite shaken at the possibility that Mrs Jackson had been murdered. Yes, her snooping and prying behind closed curtains did irritate him at times, but he understood she was a lonely old woman and how else was she expected to fill each long and mind numbing day?

'I was just collecting some mail.'

'Isn't that the job of the letting agents? How could Mrs Jackson get into your old house to gather the letters?'

'Let's leave it at that Robbie, do you understand?' Melia made no attempt to disguise the fact he did not welcome his friend's prying into his reasons for being at the deceased's address.

'You had nothing to do with this, I hope James.' Kelly wasn't to be frightened off by Melia's implied threat. He was a good twenty years older and being raised in a dirt poor tenement block in a part of Edinburgh the tourists were steered well away from, it wasn't the lessons he learned at school that taught him how to live off his wits, he'd been exposed to a different type of "teacher" who had better equipped him in the art of survival.

'Just leave it, Robbie if you know what is good for you.'

'Ha, you threatening me, laddie?' replied Kelly in a half mocking tone.

'Take it how you want, Kelly. But if the police come snooping about I'll know who'll get a cold call visit they will live to regret.'

'Oh, so you suddenly think you are a hard boy, hey. Tell you what, you come round here now and we'll sort this out. Better still I think I'll just walkover the street and tell the police everything they want to know.'

'Go on do that, but I tell you this old man, yours will be the next body bag to be thrown into the back of a meat wagon.'

The threatening words were the last Kelly heard before the line went dead.

From his bedroom window he continued to watch a group of officers getting into another police car with Fox's diminutive Chinese bride in tow. Kelly slipped his mobile back into his pocket while giving some thought to the conversation he'd held with his once friend. The implied threats did not bother him; he could break Melia with one hand if he needed to. It was the realisation Melia and possibly Fox, could have been implicated in Mrs Jackson's death and if so, why should they want to do such a terrible thing?

Chapter Thirty-Five

The noise created by a mobile phone startled McCoy from yet another alcohol induced sleep at around nine thirty in the morning.

He sensed Sally was no longer by him but instinctively turned to her side of the double bed which showed the fine creases made into the mattress cover sheet together with the duvet having been carefully folded back to partially cover his snoring presence.

His early morning vision was never that good and drink seemed to make it worse, so when his searching hand eventually got hold of the mobile phone, he was able at last, to press the green incoming call icon button.

'Hello. Bruce McCoy speaking,' he said in a near undecipherable ramble.

'Hi, Bruce, it's Debbie Kewley. Don't tell me you are still in bed.' A female voice answered brightly.

'One of the benefits of early retirement, Debs,' McCoy expressed, a bit more clearly this time.

'I think I have found what you asked me to look for to help you with your book. Isn't it exciting? It seems you made an arrest of a person by the name of Jimmy Melia thirty four years ago. He was convicted for the involuntary manslaughter of a school boy when a mowing machine cutter blade sheared off and embedded itself in the poor boy's neck, how tragic,' she said in a sympathetic tone. 'It also states here Melia absconded from the crime scene and his eventual arrest a few days later, was made by you, Bruce, in a river of all places. The record also shows you received a knife wound during the arrest. What a brave man you are. Is that the scar you have running down your face? You certainly kept that quiet, Bruce.'

'What was the point in going round telling everybody? One can clearly see the mark on my face, even if it has become less pronounced over the years.' he said.

'Well, I hope you don't mind me saying Bruce, but I think it adds to your appearance. Something like a rugged, tough handsomeness us women find attractive in a man.'

'Come off it Deb's, but thanks for your comments,' he replied to her off-hand compliment.

'Anyway, she continued,' a bravery commendation followed presented by no other than the Chief County Commissioner. Seems to me Bruce someone could make a film out of this, never mind a book,' Debbie suggested enthusiastically.

'Don't be daft, Debs. It's was just police work. Seems so long ago since that happened. I do remember now, he was known as Jimmy Melia, and not James. Like you have already said, that's why I was struggling to bring him to mind.'

McCoy made, what first seemed to be a contemplative pause, only then for him to continue in a lower tone,' If I am truthful to myself, I do miss my job. I never wanted to go in the first place. I was pushed out you know, Debbie. There are others who should have gone before me. I was doing a bloody good job.'

Bruce surprised himself by how easily he opened up to express feelings of morose he'd tried to suppress during each of the mind numbing months he'd been drawing a police pension.

His current existence seemed pointless to him. While he laid his head back cradled into the soft feather pillow looking up at the ornate plaster ceiling, he felt life no longer had a real purpose and all what was left for him was to care for his dementia riven wife on their small pensions. The only crutch he depended on was what he increasingly poured into a crystal cut glass.

The welcome tones of Debbie's familiar voice served to break him away from developing deeper sentimental feelings about his enforced loss.

'I've also taken the liberty to check the electoral role register to see if a person in the name of Jimmy Melia still lives in the area; and there is! I thought you may want to see him first to get permission to use his name in your book. Do you have a pen and paper handy Bruce, so you can write it down?'

'Good thinking Deb's, just wait a moment.'

Bruce placed his mobile on the duvet cover to then lean over to pull out the drawer of the bedside cabinet to rummage around to find the back of an old receipt and a filched stubby brown Argos pencil.

'Right, I'm ready,' said McCoy feeling a strange sense of excitement.

'The address we have is 25, Randle Avenue, Coddington, CW4 9WE. This data is over three years old and of course, it may not be the same person you arrested all those years ago.'

McCoy hurriedly scribbled the details of the address while feeling rather shady for using Debbie to search out Melia's address for other ulterior motives.

'Thanks for that, Deb's you are a treasure.'

'Well, good luck with the writing of your book, Bruce. I'll have to shoot now. I've got a pile of work to get through. Give my regards to Sally.'

'I will, Thanks, Debs.'

McCoy tossed the mobile phone to gently land on the soft duvet cover while he remained lying on his back replaying in his mind the sketchy events from all that time ago.

Chapter Thirty-Six

'I need to see Jack Stephens later about having the car serviced. Seems like we will have to keep it longer than I intended now that our money is gone,' he bemoaned to his wife over the kitchen dining table.

Sally stopped in mid-flow from putting a fork full of tomato based pasta into her mouth to look at her husband in a quizzical manner.

'What?' he said noticing the silent look she was giving him.

'What do you mean the money has gone? You got your pension lump sum and redundancy when you left the police. We can certainly afford to change the car,' she explained as if she did not quite understand why he said there was no money to spend on such an expense.

Bruce lifted another fork full of the pasta he had earlier prepared for them both, towards his mouth and deliberately avoiding eye contact with Sally. While he swallowed the baked creation Sally pushed for an answer to explain his previous remark.

No matter how hard it had been for him to be both understanding and forgiving of Sally's worsening condition that caused her to act so recklessly with his money, it still rankled deeply knowing that their future lives would be less financially secure and some of his and their shared dreams ruined. He was angry, yes, really bloody angry, who wouldn't be, knowing some cold hearted ruthless faceless criminal had taken it upon himself to rob him of a hard earned comfortable retirement?

For a split second, he was close to venting his spleen to reveal his true feelings on how he really felt about the situation she alone had created. Why had she been so stupid and naive to be suckered into such an obviously clear scam? And not only that, why keep it all a secret from him? Then the heady rush to have it all out with her, dissipated as swiftly as it first appeared.

'Sorry Sally, I didn't actually mean gone. We both agreed to invest it in a bond for three years so we can get a good return. There is no problem in having to keep the car a bit longer, we'll just change it when the bond matures,' he said smilingly across the table but underneath he felt guilty for fleetingly allowing his true emotions to come to the surface.

Sally turned her gaze away from him and continued to finish her meal.

Thirty minutes later McCoy drove from his home having told his wife he may be gone for a couple of hours because Jack Stephens would obviously want to show off his prized collection of vintage motorbikes to him as was his custom with any visitor.

McCoy set the inbuilt car sat nav to CW4 9WE and then obeyed the instructions given out by the electronic female voice guiding him to a destination which he'd hoped would start to provide some of the answers to questions which had been incessantly gnawing at his very soul.

After covering the fifteen mile journey the Mondeo estate drew into a patched up concrete 1950s laid avenue, servicing council built properties constructed at the same time. Number twenty five was situated at the end of a block of four mews houses. The car was parked a short distance away from the outwardly looking neat address. McCoy then spent a few moments running through his head a plan of action he drew up during that long day since he'd received the call from Debs Kewley. A long deliberate inhalation of breath was taken as he neared to being prepared as best he could to meet an old adversary. There was one more final thing for him to do, his hand reached over to the glove compartment to reach for a half bottle of whisky, from which he'd previously taken a couple of long swigs during the journey over. One final gulp of the amber fluid from the narrow glass neck, then he'd be prepared to confront what he'd hoped to be a major figure instrumental in his financial loss.

He locked the car with remote key fob, took in a another deep breath and then strode purposely to number twenty five, the sensation of butterflies in his stomach grew more intense the closer he got to the waist height wrought iron garden gate.

Beyond the gate a concrete laid path led up to the original wooden half glazed door which had been installed when the house was a new build in the fifties.

McCoy tapped firmly on the frosted glazed panel and then stepped back a little to await a response. He didn't have to wait long to see a short shadowy figure approaching the door and then to reach up to the door latch.

The door opened to reveal a boy of around aged eleven who distinctively possessed very similar features to the child he'd seen in a photograph contained in an email received by Sally.

'Hello is Mr Melia in?' enquired McCoy in a friendly manner.

'Why, who are you?' the young boy asked wearing a look of suspicion.

'Me and your dad are old pals. I'd thought I just drop by to see how he's getting on,' said McCoy ignoring the youngster's scowling appearance.

'It can't be my Dad you want; you are too old to be a mate of his. It must be my Granddad Jimmy; he's a pensioner like you.'

Charming boy, thought McCoy. He then asked if his pensioner relative was in.

'Yeah, he's around the back in the garden, I'll go and get 'im for you. What's your name, mate?'

'Just tell him it's Bruce, he'll know who I am.'

The boy scampered off having first partially closed the front door on the unexpected visitor. Bruce used his fingertips against the glass panel to gently ease the door open to view a short corridor used to access the ground floor rooms and the stairway.

His attention was soon drawn to a framed photograph hanging from the wall in the flock papered hallway. To get a closer look at the people gathered in the picture, he dared to take a single step onto the fitted carpet. What he saw made his face redden and his heart race faster; the three individuals assembled in a cosy family group were the same individuals he'd become familiar with having so often looked at the photographic image of their deliberately contrived charade to dupe his wife.

He then picked up whispering angry voices behind the door he assumed led to the kitchen and distinctly make out the boy whining, 'I didn't know, Granddad Jimmy. What should I have done?'

'Get outside and keep out of my sight,' an older voice commanded sharply. McCoy quietly stepped back outside the front door.

It then all went quiet behind the white painted panel door for a few seconds, then McCoy watched the door handle drop to reveal the visage of a male form he'd not seen for over thirty years and somewhat more alarmingly, witness the ravaging effects the ageing process can sometimes have on the human body. Gone was the well coiffured shiny black mane that marked him out from other male challengers of his day. Gone was the slim, toned muscular athletic body and gone too were the handsome features betwixt a hint of femininity; the combination of which used to draw woman to him in droves. One striking feature, however, had not succumbed to the passing years, the trademark cold steely blue eyes. This was more than enough evidence to prove that the crumbling edifice before him was (the) Jimmy Melia.

The same Jimmy Melia who once tried to throttle the very life out of him as they both viciously fought in that cold, dank river a life time ago. McCoy involuntarily lifted a couple of finger tips to stroke over the path of the old scar and how close he came to losing an eye or even having his throat slashed, while his mind briefly turned back to that near fatal episode in his life.

It also struck McCoy how similar Melia was once to the adult male in the photograph he'd only moments before scanned over in the family portrait, and how had he missed the family connection he would never understand.

Jimmy Melia, however, was all too familiar with the slim shaded figure menacingly standing at his front door; he'd harboured a festering grudge against this particular detective for a long time. Not only did Melia blame him for the lengthy spell in prison, he was also convinced McCoy's actions were directly responsible for his mother's destitution, decline in health and eventual death. Seeing him at the Police Federation awards evening receiving all those accolades only a few months back, served to pick at the scab of an unhealed ulcer.

'What can I do for you?' Melia enquired while making no attempt to disguise the fact that the unexpected caller wasn't about to be invited into his home for a nice cup of tea and a ginger biscuit.

'You don't remember me then, Jimmy?' McCoy asked in feigned surprise.

'No, should I?' he aggressively responded.

'I know we have both aged a bit, but you must remember me, I'm Bruce McCoy, DS Bruce McCoy as I was known then. You did this to me, surely you remember me for that alone.' McCoy pointed to the scar he'd been made to live with for so long.

Melia ignored the purpose of McCoy's gesture.

'What is it you want? I did my time.' Melia raised his hand to the door latch to signal his intentions to close the door on the visitor.

'I think you know why I am here, Jimmy.' Any pretence of friendliness on McCoy's behalf had too, been dispensed with at this point.

'How the fuck do I know why you are here? Why don't you just fuck off.' Melia made a move to push the door shut but was prevented from doing so by McCoy jamming his foot between the door and the frame. He then positioned his shoulder against the wooden section of the door to give it a hard push, and in so doing, unbalanced Melia's footing to send him crashing backwards onto the hall floor.

McCoy swiftly stepped into the hall way to take up an opened legged stance over the flattened Melia whom he then watched making futile attempts to get back onto his feet. When it looked like he may get to his feet McCoy positioned his foot against his barrelled chest to forcibly send him back down up close to the shut kitchen door.

Melia wasn't about to give up that easily, his arms flayed against the flock covered walls determined to gain some leverage to manoeuvre his obese frame to an upright position. But all attempts were met by the sole of McCoy's shoe.

'You know why I'm here, don't you, Jimmy?' Due to all the exertion, a film of sweat had formed over the long scar bisecting his sallow sharp features, and combined with the effects of the dull light present in the short hallway, conspired to cast a menacing shadow across his old injury.

'Leave me alone, I don't know what you are talking about. You're not a copper any more, I'll have you done for assault, you bastard.' warned Melia looking up at the menacing visage.

McCoy ignored the threats to turn and place a finger against the glass covering the happy family gathering hung in the hall way.

'This person in this picture is your son isn't it, Jimmy? He's the one who has robbed me of my money. Don't fucking dare deny it. He looks just like you; from the same fucking rotten stock.'

Melia turned to rubbing the side of his balding head in feigned injury while slipping McCoy a sly grin. This simple knowing gesture was not only enough to confirm James Melia's involvement but it served to send his blood pressure up close to boiling point.

'I'm not fucking about with you any more, Jimmy boy. I want to know where he lives and I want every last fucking penny back.' Melia's head had been forced to be lain flat against the prickly texture of the cheap hall way carpet with McCoy standing astride him glaring down with murderous intent in his wild eyes.

'I don't know what you are talking about, McCoy. You come to my home, burst into my house and then threaten and assault me. I'll make sure you will get in big trouble for this. Who will look after your sick wife when you are slammed up inside, hey? Not you. Maybe I can go round and give her some warm comfort; you know what I mean, Bruce?' Melia winked.

Having knowledge of his wife's condition coupled with his lewd loaded suggestion was enough for him to grab Melia by his grubby shirt collar, wrench him upwards a few inches and then in a flash, smash a hard clenched fist across his light stubble jaw. The sharp blow stunned Melia but not enough to knock him out. Having held on to the man's shirt, McCoy again roughly lifted him up close enough for Melia to feel his warm cloying spittle spray his face to dazedly listen to prophetic words the retired officer ranted between gritted teeth.

'You keep away from her, or I'll rip your stinking guts out. Do you understand Melia? Do you fucking understand?' he yelled shaking Melia's head around like a rag doll.

The erratic jarring movements of the kitchen door striking against Melia's prone body were enough for McCoy to consider his exit. He took the precaution to snatch the family photograph off the wall before he returned back to his car.

'Granddad, what happened? Are you all right?' the grandson asked earnestly after he had managed to force his body through a small opening between the door and the door frame.

Before McCoy drove off from the address, Melia had had the presence of mind to instruct his distressed grandson to write down the registration number of the silver Ford Mondeo estate car.

McCoy sat in the relative calm of his stationary vehicle for a few moments to settle his nerves. When he calmed a little, his shaking left hand reached over to the glove compartment to reach for the whisky bottle. With the bottle safely in his grasp, he clumsily unscrewed the metal cap which ended up spinning out from his grasp into the drivers' foot well. He couldn't be bothered to search around his feet to find the cap; anyway, he'd reasoned to himself, he'd likely polish off the remaining contents so the need for a cap would become superfluous.

Chapter Thirty-Seven

Four minutes later with the dark of the night ever increasingly moving in, McCoy started the car up to make the journey home.

'He knows, James. He was here tonight by himself. He's on to us.'

'How can he be? You're over reacting, Dad. You didn't say anything to him did you? I know how much you wanted to get even with him.'

'Don't be so damn stupid, why would I want to I tell him anything? But I couldn't stop McCoy from taking the photograph from the hall. Why would he want to take it with him unless he had good reason to? I warned you to be careful, James. McCoy might be addled with drink these days but I'm certain his mind is just as sharp.'

'So no other coppers were with him then?'

'No, like I have already told you, the man finished in the police months back. How do you think you were able to get that amount of money from his daft wife? I'm certain he was acting alone and probably the coppers have no inkling as yet what he has been up to. Otherwise why wasn't it the police who turned up tonight?'

'So the chances are they might not be aware of what McCoy thinks he is on to. Right, just leave it with me, Dad. I'll sort this one out.'

'You're not going to do something stupid are you, James. McCoy might not have involved the police, but we just don't know. We need to lie low for a while, it might just all blow over.'

'Like I've already said Dad, leave this one with me,' assured the son, who had it in his mind that the time was ripe to call in a big favour.

The combined effects of the drink and the re-running of the vivid images spinning around in his head of what had happened during the unannounced visit, meant that McCoy wasn't as attentive as he would normally have been if he was fully sober and less stressed. He therefore failed to notice the speeding black saloon racing up behind him. Only when his neck was violently jolted from a rear impact to his car, was he then fully thrown back into alert mode.

'What the hell was that?' he called out while fighting to keep the slewing car on the road. He turned to look into his rear view mirror to see, what he suspected to be the same dark vehicle, a fast approaching car speeding towards his rear end seemingly intent on repeating the same crazy manoeuvre. McCoy pressed the accelerator hard down to the floor, but he hadn't quite acted fast enough to prevent another hard collision to the rear of his car.

This second impact was successful in forcing the silver Mondeo onto the soft grass verge causing deep tyre ruts and great clods of turf and soil to be spewed high up into the air. McCoy manically fought with the steering wheel to prevent the heavy fast moving metal mass from dropping into a looming stagnant water filled drainage ditch. It was mostly down to the training programme he'd been put through at the start of his police career that he was now able to fight against the car's trajectory to skilfully guide it back onto the solid macadam surface.

The continued presence of the determined chaser showed up in his rear view mirror as both cars raced off towards a newly built dual carriageway bypass. This is where McCoy realised he now stood a better chance of escaping the attentions of the unknown and uninvited dueller.

It wasn't too long before the chasing powerful car took up the outer lane on the by-pass to come up more or less, neck and neck with the Mondeo estate car. McCoy saw from the corner of his eye the driver's hand movement to the left on his steering wheel. He quickly mimicked the same action thus preventing the full impact of the pursuing driver's intention to force McCoy off the road and into the solid concrete support structure of a fly-over bridge rapidly coming up in the road ahead. His trained actions prevented the Mondeo from being concertinaed against the unmoving concrete mass head-on, but not enough for the full nearside of the car to make hard sliding contact with the bridge structure and then noisily scrape along its length causing a shower of bright sparks, mixed with the terrible sound of shattering door glass as the once perfectly formed metal panels were being ruthlessly torn from their spot welded fittings.

McCoy recognised not only had he been lucky to escape death but, or worse still, could have easily been left with serious lifelong debilitating injuries if the driver in the black chasing car had got his way. There was no time to dwell on who might be behind such suicidal action. His priority was to focus on tightly gripping the steering wheel of his own fast moving car and to be mindful of the laws of self-preservation if he was to stand a chance of escaping the attentions of this obviously determined pursuer.

Through the mud splattered windscreen, McCoy noticed that the black car had slowed up ahead of him, maybe with the reason being the driver wanted to catch sight of the tangled wreckage blazing angrily in the dark of the night under flyover bridge.

What did come into his vision was the crumpled near side Mondeo which had taken up the outer lane and closing at speed behind him.

Disappointed in having clearly failed in his plan, the driver pressed the accelerator down hard and swung the car to the right across the white marked lanes to prevent McCoy from passing and even more, part of yet another attempt to force the Mondeo into the steel crash barriers.

McCoy had anticipated such a manoeuvre and sharply braked to avoid the deadly high speed contact between the two cars. It was then, he had decided, to execute a learned manoeuvre of his own. It had been made patently clear to him that there was to be no reasoning with this maniac.

McCoy again neared the dark car while in the outside lane driving at high speed, fully expecting the car ahead of him to perform the same blocking manoeuvre. He wasn't to be disappointed. The vehicle ahead made a twitch of a movement which served to provide McCoy with an early warning of the driver's deadly intention. The Mondeo came up close to the rear end of the black car and as anticipated, the driver slew the car across into the outer lane missing the Mondeo only by a few millimetres.

McCoy smiled to himself, his hand had been forced to reveal to the crazy driver what he had learned when under Jock Mackie's wing many moons ago.

The driver steered his car back into the nearside lane to concentrate on controlling his twitching vehicle which was caused by switching across lanes too quickly. And while he was again preparing to swerve across the path of the battered Mondeo, McCoy had pressed the accelerator down hard to the floor to make the metal to metal contact he planned for. The driver would only feel a hard nudge from the controlled contact of a deformed front wing against the rear panel of his own car before he was about to be sent in to oblivion. McCoy swiftly eased off the accelerator and sharply applied the brakes to keep well clear from the pending devastation lying ahead of him.

The black saloon spun round wildly causing all of the four tyres to scream out in loud protest about their unfair treatment. Blue, belching smoke followed in their wake as the driver's futile amateur attempts failed to bring the large powerful vehicle back under control. The screech of tyres suddenly ceased only to be replaced with the sickening noise of shattering glass and deforming metal as the careering two ton mass crashed side on to the unmovable steel barriers and then dramatically somersaulted over the metal barrier into the southbound carriageway. This wasn't to be the night when the laws of physics would be rewritten. In order to dissipate the great bank of kinetic energy still stored in the car's mass, it required six full body revolutions before all was spent. A cacophony of crashing, breaking sounds in unison with a vivid display of flaying broken car parts accompanied the destruction of the car until the night again, fell silent.

From the safety of the damaged Mondeo, McCoy saw that the black car had come to a stop on its roof straddled across both lanes with one headlight eerily illuminating the northbound carriageway embankment. Whispers of light smoke rising from the stationary metal form gave a strange look to that similar to a race horse after finishing a two mile hurdle race on a cold autumn day.

The eerie silence that is said to fall after such an event was to be shattered by dreadful calls coming from the upturned black silhouette.

'Get, me out of here, I'm bleeding. I can't move. Help me, help me! '

Bruce had already pulled his car over to the nearside lane and loped over the central crash barrier when he had heard the man's mournful cry. Whilst jogging over to the stricken vehicle McCoy had mentally noted that the engine fuel supply had been shut off and the fine smoke coming from the upturned belly of the car was due to the exposed exhaust system. The window glass was no longer in existence and the rigorously test crashed roof had retained its integrity albeit now in a slightly trapezoid shape.

He made his way round to the driver's door to then drop to his knees to catch sight of the desperate male figure seemingly trapped inside his upturned seat.

'Get me out please mate, I can't move. I think I am bleeding to death,' the man's gasped words contained a desperate edge.

Even though McCoy had been initially taken aback at the bloody sight of the man who clearly appeared to be trapped and was surrounded by yellow deflated air bags, this was not the time to start a formal interrogation, no matter what the stranger had done or tried to do.

His first thoughts were to open the driver's side door but when he'd used all of his strength in tugging at the chrome plated door handle only to find it would not budge an inch. The twisted roof and door pillars had caused the door to jam solidly in place; he also discovered the same to be true when he tried the passenger side of the two door model.

The man's pleas were becoming weaker. Bruce understood he had no other alternative but to get inside the car to try to stem the obvious blood loss if there was to be any chance of him being alive when the emergency services finally arrive.

He crawled through the space once taken up by the passenger window, his hands moved gingerly across the once pristine roof lining which was covered in small irregular pieces of tempered glass mingled with sticky blood and other bits of paraphernalia as he carefully twisted his slim frame into the interior. Trapped at the wheel was a thirty something, white, beer bellied male; his drooping bloodied eyelids gave a clear indication he was close to losing consciousness.

'Don't go to sleep, it's vital you keep awake. Do you hear me?' shouted McCoy with his lips only inches from the man's glistening face.

'Yes, yes, I hear you. Please get me out of here. I don't want to die.' The strength of his plea was clearly weak and with traces of blood leeching out of the corner of his mouth and frothing from his nostrils patently spoke of internal injuries. Time wasn't on this man's side.

McCoy hurriedly searched around the injured soft body to eventually find a shard of grey hard plastic, which once formed part of the dashboard, had broken away at some stage in the car's destruction and buried itself deep into the slipping man's left groin.

Each beat of the heart evacuated a large pulse of blood from his limp body which then journeyed down over the man's exposed belly then further over his shirt covered chest and out onto his neck to then divide up into individual small streams of red to trace the deep sweaty contours of his face. The forces of gravity encouraged the flow to meander through a thick thatch of gel groomed hair and then finally, drip like a steady shower of rain to create an ever increasing crimson pool on the beige roof lining.

McCoy understood if the man was to have any chance of survival he needed to act rapidly. The sound of a recent expensive purchase of cotton Bladdington golf polo shirt being torn filled the near silent cabin. McCoy wasn't about to leave this dying man in search of a suitable compression pad. His destroyed top was hurriedly folded into a dense square swab and then applied the best he could, around the jutting piece of plastic.

McCoy found his face sometimes coming into direct skin contact with that of the injured man's through having to retain an awkward and uncomfortable body position necessary to hold the pad securely in place. How ironic it was to find himself in this position, after all, the person he was now trying to save was only up to a few minutes ago, doing his utmost to ensure he'd, be taken from the new carriageway in a body bag himself.

Voices heard circling the accident scene assured the car's two incumbents that help was on the way. The close proximity of a deafening siren drawing up close to the wreckage site showed the news to be true.

McCoy listened intently to hear a scamper of rushing feet which soon transpired to be two paramedics. A young female had no hesitation in getting down on her hands and knees to join the shirtless McCoy in the same bloodied glass strewn space. The accompanying male appeared at the driver's side similarly on his hands and knees.

'How is he?' she asked having quickly assessed who was the injured party in spite of both males being covered in blood.

'Bleeding from the groin, a piece plastic of all things, probably from the dashboard. I've got a pad over it. He is also bleeding from his mouth and nostrils. Looks bad to me.'

'You didn't pull the plastic out did you?' she asked anxiously.

'No, I'm keeping the pressure around it.'

'Good, by the look of things if you had pulled it out he'd be dead now. Are you all right to keep doing it?'

'Yes.' McCoy had become stiff from having to hold such an awkward position, and also sensed the pressure he was once able to apply to the wound was gradually weakening.

'Good, while you are doing that I'll give his body a further check to see if he is losing blood from anywhere else.'

During the brief exchange between the desperate man's potential saviours, the driver had drifted off to a place he was destined never to return from. If he could, he would have told the paramedics they were wasting their time putting him on a saline drip and messing about with a neck brace.

The female paramedic had pushed up hard against McCoy in the claustrophobic space for her head to partially disappear from view to allow a purple surgically gloved hand to search around the man's lower legs and feet hidden in the cramped foot well.

Seconds later she wriggled herself free from the confined space.

'Are you happy to still hold the pressure pad there?'

'Yes, no problem.'

'The fire service will have to get him out, his feet are trapped under the brake and clutch pedals, it's common in RTAs.'

After a short deliberate pause she continued, 'There's something else.'

'What?' pressed McCoy, turning to the young paramedic and noting a marked change in her expression.

'He's got a small hand gun secured in a holster strapped to his leg. Why would he have that? How did the accident happen?'

Before McCoy was able to offer any explanation the male paramedic called out in some alarm.

'He's slipping; his pulse has dropped to thirty and falling. I'll give him a shot of adrenalin, but it will most likely be a waste of time, I think he has lost too much blood.'

He bent down to his canvas medical bag to root out a sealed strip containing an injection and a phial of adrenalin. Checking the amount along the measure lines on the plastic injection tube he moved then to push the needle into yet another vein.

He then took hold of the digital pulse monitor to await an improvement. The flashing green digits displayed a falling pulse rate.

'Give him another dose before it's too late,' urged the female paramedic having been shown the reading by her colleague.

'I will, but it's a waste of time.'

Another shot was pumped into the slipping man. From McCoy's intimate position he detected the shallow erratic breathing rhythm being spasmodically replaced by a rattle sounding deep in the man's throat. A dreadful noise he had become so tragically familiar with when he was in uniform.

'Hang on mate, you've got to hang on. They'll have you out of here soon and off to hospital.' McCoy urged turning to the man's expressionless gaze. At this stage of the slow dying process each of his red crusted nostril openings had taken to blowing large bubbles of blood which gently popped after each weakening breath. The fine spray created by each of those individual burst bubbles settled on McCoy's already blood smeared skin. It wasn't too long before he sensed an indescribable tranquillity that uniquely arrives at the point of death. McCoy removed his aching fingers from the pad, he'd used in vain to stem the man's acute blood loss, to shake the numbness from his hand.

'You did your best to save him, the man would be grateful for that,' said the uniformed female seeing too that the lifeforce had departed from the unmoving body. Bruce McCoy's thoughts were elsewhere and had neither the energy or inclination to show any outward acknowledgement of her oft seen waste of life.

'Let's get out of here and allow the firemen do their job. I'll check you over in the ambulance before the police have a word with you,' she said while starting to reverse her body out of the upturned vehicle.

Soon, McCoy followed suit but not before he'd paused to take in a long look at the strapped in lifeless body with eyes appearing to be staring at the top edge of the shattered windscreen and his bulky tattooed arms flaying out either side of his static chest.

How easily for the situation to have been reversed McCoy profoundly considered in that brief moment in time.

'Would this same man he so desperately tried to save, do the same for me? Doesn't seem likely. So best to move on and get out of this carnage.' he sadly consoled himself as he stiffly replicated the same reverse contorted routine as the female paramedic had exercised.

His slippery bloodied hands supported the weight of his cramped body during his planned exit across the hitherto pristine roof lining, which had been soiled with a broad scattering of broken irregular shaped pieces of heat treated toughened glass with some of the remnants gathered randomly in large pools of glutinous blood where the body now hung like a pig freshly slaughtered. McCoy was conscious to avoid placing his hand in such bloodied areas. When the inevitable happened his feeling hand did not register what he'd expected to be of hard bits of glass. In the pool of haemoglobin a hand sized rectangular shaped object filled his palm and to gain a better look at what the strange object was, he shifted his hand so as to capture the flashing blue light intermittently illuminating the interior of the wrecked car's cabin space. Using his finger tips to wipe away some of the coating of blood on the hard material surface, it didn't take him too long to recognise the object of his curiosity to be the deceased driver's iPhone.

He was given a sudden start when the phone suddenly lit up accompanied by a tinny ringtone of "Land of Hope and Glory". He could see people were busying themselves around the upturned car and paying him little attention, so McCoy decided to touch the red smeared screen to accept the call. He then heard a voice say, 'Is it done Davy?' These short but significant words threw McCoy causing him to hesitate about how he should reply. Any thoughts were swiftly nullified on having noted the unexpected figure of a purposeful looking fireman kneeling down in readiness to scan around the vehicle's upturned interior.

'Bloody hell mate, you just frightened the crap out of me, I didn't expect to see anyone in the car except for the driver. I was told you were being seen by the paramedic.' he said in surprise.

'I was about to get out when my phone rang. You know what it's like, even in desperate situations like this there is an uncontrollable urge to see who is calling you.' replied McCoy attempting to make light of his predicament.

'You best get out quick and let the paramedics have a look at you.'

'Don't worry; I won't be in your way much longer.'

McCoy pressed the slightly raised button on the top edge of the phone to pull up a screen menu to turn it off. He then slipped the phone into his trouser pocket and continued his awkward crawl across the roof lining.

After forcing his body to stand somewhere near erect on his two blood tarnished feet, McCoy flared his nostrils to instinctively draw in the strong, fresh reviving smell of the night air, glad to purge his lungs of the sickly miasma which had filled the deceased man's car.

He next sensed a hand on his sticky biceps and then a gentle pressure which would guide him to the rear open doors leading to a brightly lit interior of a modern ambulance.

'We need to check you over and get you cleaned up, sir,' said the female paramedic.

'No, I'm all right, thank you young lady. Something to wipe this mess off me will do.' he replied while looking down at his torso and arms.

'Well, I think you are unwise, sir. Shock might hit you later; don't forget you have not only witnessed a terrible accident, you have tried to save and then watch the same person lose his life. Just experiencing one of those events alone is enough to greatly upset most people,' she warned, her wide crystal clear blue eyes widening to further stress her genuine concern.

'No, I'm fine thank you, just a wet towel and a few wipes will do.'

'And there is something else,' she unexpectedly continued.

'What's that?'

'You will need to go the hospital to be checked for any possible HIV infection. Just look, you are covered in the man's blood, it takes only a small amount to enter the blood stream for you to become infected.'

McCoy had not even given the slightest thought to this possibility when he raced to the assistance of the maniac pursuer. It would be shear prophecy if the man indeed had been successful in accomplishing his mission after all.

With the paramedic's potential fatal health threat still resounding in his head McCoy noted the presence of a uniformed police officer who looked to be in his late twenties.

The intense bright light being emitted from the inside of the ambulance against the darkness of the early night caused the young officer to readjust his vision before he was able to take in the full appearance of the person the male paramedic had said was the first to have arrived at the accident. He let out a gasp on seeing what appeared to him to be an image of someone in the business of slaughtering animals, but done in such a careless way as to become covered in blood from head to toe.

'Hello, sir. Are you in a fit state to answer one or two questions? I have been informed by the paramedic that you were the first person to arrive at the scene of the accident. Is that correct, sir?'

The officer then glanced tentatively at the female paramedic gathering a wad of antiseptic wipes to allow McCoy to clean his skin of the drying blood and half expecting for her to say something to stop any interference with the care of her patient.

'Yes, yes officer. That is correct.' McCoy replied with the paramedic gently easing the staining from his face with a large damp wipe.

'Did you see what happened, sir?' he further interrogated.

'Yes, the driver had tried to force me off the dual carriageway. He somehow lost control of his vehicle and ended up flipping over the central reservation barrier and then rolling a few times before resting on its roof. I did try to help him, but it wasn't enough,' finished McCoy lowly.

'I'm sure you did your best to help the person, sir. But when you've cleaned up, I'll ask you to take a breathalyser test. It's procedure in all RTAs. And if you are up to it, I'll have to take a statement from you down at the station. I'll come back in a few minutes when you have finished.'

An image of the empty half bottle of whisky resting inside the battered Mondeo's glove compartment flashed in his mind. Even though he was a hardened drinker, the amount consumed would surely show him to be over the limit.

The paramedic observed the officer stroll over to join the assembled emergency vehicles with their blue flashing high intensity beacons flood lighting the smashed overturned five series BMW.

'I couldn't help but to smell drink on your breath while we were attending to the injured man,' the paramedic whispered as she passed McCoy a white NHS towel while he continued with the wipes.

'Yes, there is no sense in denying I had had a small drink, but I can assure you it was not enough to impair my judgement.' replied McCoy while rubbing down his firm torso with the rough towel.

'Huh, they all say that!' she said surprisingly irately. 'If I had my way, there would be no drinking and driving. I've seen too many lives lost through drink.'

McCoy understood there was no point in getting into a heated discussion about her zero tolerance views. Little more was said up to the point where the same constable reappeared at the rear of the ambulance to see McCoy mostly cleaned up and wearing a spare paramedic shirt, which had been kept by for similar messy situations such as this.

McCoy stepped down from the ambulance to accompany the constable to a marked car situated haphazardly with the other emergency vehicles. The rear passenger side door was opened giving McCoy a non-verbal cue as to where he should sit. The constable closed the door sharply and then stepped forward to slide into the driver's seat.

McCoy felt a nervous tension in his bladder as he closely watched the constable tear open a sealed packet to get at a sterile mouth tube which he then fitted tightly into the hand held breathalyser unit.

' I want you to put the tube to your lips and then blow until I tell you to stop. If you fail to do as I ask, you will be arrested for failing to give a breathalyser sample when requested to do so by an officer of the law. Do you understand, sir?'

'Did I understand? I've probably done more of these then you've had hot dinners,' McCoy thought. His memory slipped back so tangibly to his early baptism in policing in the rough, brutal, hard streets of Glasgow. He behaved like a pussy in complying with the young officer's instructions compared to some of the violent aggressive outburst he once had to contend with.

'Keep blowing, make sure your lips are sealed around the tube, keep blowing, keep blowing.'

McCoy soon came to the point of feeling quite faint and could blow no more into the palm size machine being gripped in the constable's right hand.

'Okay, stop now.'

Immediately McCoy let out a gasp followed then by deeply inhaling to recharge his spent lungs as he looked on to interpret the passive look on the officer's face.

'The reading shows a positive test. You are just over the limit at 85; the maximum is 80 milligrammes of alcohol per 100 millilitres. You will now be formally arrested for failing a road side breathalyser test and will be taken down to Bladdington police station for a further test to be taken. Do you understand, sir?'

McCoy just gave a nod to confirm he understood, next thing he heard was the formal arrest citation being read out loud and clear. After handing over the car keys, the constable left McCoy to sit alone in the familiar smelling police vehicle whilst arrangements were made to remove the battered Mondeo from obstructing the highway.

In the relative seclusion of the locked police car McCoy watched the familiar movements of the dark silhouetted shapes busily going about the multi-various tasks they were trained to perform in these often tragic situations. His thoughts then switched to the surreal events on the dual carriageway. Why was the man, now freed from the metal trap and lying motionless and bloodied on the damp tarmac, so intent in driving him off the road? Was it just plain and simple road rage? Or was it something far more sinister?

When he'd had enough of watching the drama being played out around him, McCoy noticed his hands were slightly trembling. Maybe, it was a tell-tale sign his body was succumbing to shock, he wasn't sure. In the relative darkness of the police car he raised one of his quaking hands up to his face to see the presence of purple brown clotted blood trapped under his finger nails. The same organic residue was present in the deep wrinkles and skin folds on the back of his long bony hands. His whole body suddenly shuddered at this realisation.

McCoy so badly wanted a deep cleansing shower to wash away the remnants of the dead man's once life preserving fluids, but for now, he was resigned to being chauffeured to Bladdington police station to face the ignominy of a further breath test and a likely grilling concerning the antecedents of the RTA conducted by his erstwhile colleagues.

Chapter Thirty Eight

'Had your mate here last night, Sir,' was heard the call which broke Starr's concentration as he rushed through the station's reception area.

The desk sergeant had been on duty and skulking behind the reception desk when McCoy was seen by him to be exchanging handshakes and bidding farewell to a uniformed constable at just gone four o'clock that morning.

'Which mate?' irritably enquired Dick Starr on having been stopped in his tracks.

'That McCoy guy, if I remember right he was stationed over at Mansefield. Been retired off now. I never liked the look of him from the first time I saw him. If you ask me the force is best off without his like.'

Starr's journey to work that morning had been fraught by a traffic light failure at a major junction in Bladdington centre. The predictable unavoidable delay coupled with having to tolerate the shenanigans of rude and incompetent motorists, drained him of any or little patience he may normally possess at the start of a long shift. So already twenty-five minutes late, Starr was certainly in no mood to listen to the prejudice ramblings of an inconsequential desk bound officer.

'What do you mean by, "best off without his like". You better explain yourself officer, and I hope it is bloody good for your sake!' angrily barked DCI Starr.

'I ... I ... I, well, I mean, he was arrested for drunk driving, way over the limit I heard, but he somehow passed the test here. Everyone in the force knew he was an alcoholic, that's why he was shown the door. And, and, that's not all.' The stuttering desk sergeant had to pause for a while to catch his breath having not inhaled since Starr seriously rattled his cage.

'What do you mean? That's not all. Stop fucking me about and get it out!' Starr expressed in near rage. The closeness of their faces left the desk sergeant to become yet another victim of Starr's legendary spittle.

Having been able to only gulp in two short gasps of air while deliberately avoiding Starr's manic stare, the desk sergeant continued now in clear desperation.

'I ... I ... was told McCoy was involved in an RTA on the new bypass. A man died at the scene, bled like a pig apparently. Carnage everywhere. Driving like lunatics was what one witness had said. Seems like there had been a chase of some sort with the other fella coming worse off. Maybe the dead guy had upset McCoy, you know how bad road rage can be and with him being drunk at the ...'

'That's enough!'

The sergeant's stark abridged report had shocked Starr, he seriously hoped that Bruce hadn't done something stupid. He'd know more once he'd first finished telling the sergeant he would be disciplined if any of this was repeated to another officer.

The desk sergeant had certainly got the message and was relieved to see the concerned looking DCI scan his card through the ID reader and disappear into the inner sanctum of the station.

Starr was to next burst into the main incident room to see that the mice were indeed playing while the fat cat had been away.

'What do you call this, get to your damn stations and get some work done?'

What he had seen was the sight of small clusters of uniformed and plain clothed officers lolling in chairs and sitting on desk tops idly gossiping. Starr's deliberate loud tone and sharp manner left them to understand something had seriously rattled the DCI.

The main reason for the tardiness of the group was because of what had happened on the new bypass the previous night together with exaggerated reports of Cooper's heroic arrest of the notorious Damien Fox the previous day in Regent Street. Sporting two black eyes, a wide pink plaster over the bridge of his nose and a top swollen lip gave the distinct impression he'd just been through three rounds with Ali. Oddly enough, by the look of the female staff clucking around him, they seemed to find his "new" appearance appealing in a basic instinct sense. Max Cooper was taking every opportunity to enjoy the petting and sensual touching from some of the star struck females. One attractive office trainee even unbuttoned his shirt in a deliberate teasing manner to closely inspect the bruising around his stomach with little protest from Cooper. But, alas, Starr as usual, put an abrupt end to all this welcomed attention.

Seeing the group scattering in all directions around the room Starr called out, 'Cooper, Grey my office now!'

Starr had put his coat on the hook on the back of the half glazed panelled door and then moved to plonk himself down on his familiar chair with the pronounced scowl he was wearing when first entering the station still evident across his face. The agitated movements he made while sitting in his chair created an annoying squeak from the swivel mechanism which added further to his outward show of annoyance as he awaited the sheepish arrival of his immediate juniors.

'Shut the door Miss Grey.' DS Grey did as she was told and then turned to stand next to DS Cooper to face the DCI.

'Right, tell me why all the station is sitting round doing bugger all? You two are amongst the most senior detectives in the room. When I am not in, it's your responsibility to make sure everyone is on task. Have I made myself absolutely clear?' he demanded while noting the extent of Cooper's facial injuries.

'Yes, Sir!' the junior rank officers jointly replied.

'DS Grey, I suspect you have some interesting bits to tell me.'

Starr had no doubts in his mind what the chattering buzz was all about when he had initially entered the incident room, but was keen too to listen to what the young female officer had to say as he'd not failed to notice she had recently taken to arriving to work earlier than other colleagues and would therefore be likely to have learned much more of what had been investigated and reported during the previous shift. Before she started Starr had given a nod for them to take a seat.

'It concerns your friend, Bruce McCoy.' She starkly opened before reporting the main points she had gleaned from those who'd been around over the eventful late evening and night shift.

When Grey had exhausted all she knew, Starr was about to suggest that he along with one of them should drive over to McCoy's house to address a few things that were niggling him from Grey's report, when suddenly the office door burst open to reveal a fully uniformed cap wearing senior figure who was obviously taking no precautions to hide that he was seriously angry.

'What the bloody hell happened yesterday, DCI Starr? I've just had Mansefield Chief Super on the phone making accusations that one of my officers seriously assaulted a man they had in custody. He also said you poured a bucket of dog faeces over the man's injuries and is now rightly worried he might catch a fatal illness. This man Fox has filed an official complaint citing police violence along with placing his life in danger from a possible life threatening infection. I'm seriously thinking DCI Starr, that you have finally lost it,' he shouted in clear rage.

Starr remained seated retaining an air of composure in spite of the way he had been so rudely spoken to. He deliberately stayed silent knowing it wouldn't be too long before Palfreyman needed to let off another blast of steam. He wasn't to be proved wrong.

'Well, don't just sit there man, say something. This is a terrible example you are setting to our younger colleagues,' he starkly accused.

Starr rose to his feet slowly and placed both hands on his desk to take up a leaning pose to look the Chief Superintendent straight in the eye.

'I have to tell you, Chief Superintendent Palfreyman, that man who you alleged was assaulted by one of my officers, was actually doing his best to escape after we had told him he was to accompany us to Mansefield station to be questioned about the murder of a frail and gentle old woman who, unfortunately for her, lived in the same street as that monster,' said Starr expressing each word with clear slow diction.

'For your information, DCI Starr, Mansefield police have released him early this morning pending further enquiries. So maybe you have overseen yet another botched arrest. I have no hesitation in telling you DCI Starr I'm getting quite fed up with the way you deal with things and I'm afraid to say you are becoming something of an embarrassment not only to me but to the whole damn station.'

Those situated in the large incident room had stopped working to listen in on the raised voices coming from the private office.

Throughout the unscripted proceedings Cooper had turned away from the Super's ranting to focus his thoughts, not on the evil Damien Fox, but on the injustice of the baseless accusations relating to Starr's competence and his standing in Bladdington station. Yes, Cooper quite well understood Starr could be sarcastic, rude and much more. But for certain, he had learned that the DCI was a hardworking, no bullshitting copper who got results, and more than anything else, had a genuine heart under that sometimes brash exterior. He was no longer going to allow Palfreyman to continue in his unsubstantiated tirade on his immediate senior officer to pass unchallenged.

Starr watched in surprise to see Cooper rise from his seat and to then turn and confront the station's top man face to face. Palfreyman's loud gasp filled the room on seeing the state of one of his two earmarked protégées. Cooper purposely maintained his fixed gaze so that Starr's accuser could fully take in the nature of his injuries he had sustained during the violent arrest. He then lifted up his loose fitting shirt to reveal two large crude circles of blue, black and red bruising to his stomach and side. All of this was done without Cooper uttering a single word.

Palfreyman then turned his attention back to glare at Starr.

'What have you allowed to happen here, DCI Starr?' His previous angry tone had showed no signs of abating.

Starr's lips were about to move to probably say something he'd later regret, only to be saved by the unexpected intervention of his male junior.

'I'm sorry, Sir.' said Cooper, 'I cannot be party to the slanderous comments you have made concerning, DCI Starr.'

'Max, Max, please sit down.' Cooper had no intentions of complying with Starr's advice and continued. 'These injuries,' he said while pointing to the pink plaster, 'are as a result of Damien Fox deliberately sending his boot hard into my face as I tried to stop him from escaping arrest over a high wall. After I managed to get him down from the wall, he then hit me in the stomach. DCI Starr did try …'

He was stopped mid flow by Palfreyman raising his hand and saying, 'Thank you for that DS Cooper, but I don't want to hear any more, DCI Starr to my office please, now,' curtly demanded the Super while turning in anticipation of leaving the tense atmosphere pervading the office.

Cooper was in no frame of mind to meekly cave in to the Palfreyman's clear desire to move proceedings to the formal confines of his plush office to pour more blame onto Starr's shoulders.

'No Sir, you cannot leave just like that. I feel it is very important for you to understand what really happened yesterday.'

Palfreyman, having read into the steely determination etched across Max Cooper's bruised and battered features, turned to Starr to state,

'I knew it would eventually come to this. This subordination is a clear indication of your poor leadership, DCI Starr. I won't stand for it anymore.'

While Palfreyman fumed, Cooper retained his nerve to make his defence of the DCI.

'Fox received his injuries from striking his head against the gate locks after I was put in a desperate position to defend myself. DCI Starr used what we all thought to be a bucket of clear water, to revive Fox after he had been momentarily stunned. In all areas of this case I, along with everybody else who was there, can only say that DCI Starr had acted decisively. In fact, if you really want to have a go at anybody, it should be me. I'm the one who makes the mistakes, the one who is lazy and content to do only the minimum. I am the one who likes getting off home on time or even better, earlier. I honestly believe that DCI Starr deserves another big medal for all the shit he has to put up with. I don't know how he has stuck being in the police for so long when he has got people from backgrounds similar to my own telling him how to do his job. Well,

I would want to tell them all to bugger off and stick the job up their arses.' On that note Cooper turned away to leave the Super stunned and momentarily speechless.

'I think the young man must be suffering from concussion. Can you see to it DCI Starr that he is taken immediately to the hospital for a medical check-up. We will meet later.' Palfreyman, while still glowing crimson red, then sharply turned to make a quick exit from the oppressive atmosphere abounding the small office space.

The room fell quiet while the three incumbents mulled over the vexed issues raised during the previous tense minutes.

'Are you sure you are all right, Max?' enquired Starr breaking the silence.

'Never felt better, Sir,' he replied, smiling.

'Good, I think it would be best for all of us to keep out of Palfreyman's way for the next few hours. We will pay Bruce McCoy a visit first then we will decide where we go from there. And Max,' said Starr pausing.

'Yes, Sir?'

'Thank you for what you said, it may get you in a little bother, but thanks,' Cooper watched him then give a friendly wink.

He asked the junior officers to commandeer a police pool car while he dealt with the telephone call to McCoy. He couldn't help but to hear the noise level rise after the two DSs entered the main incident room as he tapped in McCoy's number from his personal notebook.

Chapter Thirty-Nine

A fresh intoximeter reading taken at the station an hour or so later showed McCoy to be fractionally under the legal drink drive limit. He had missed a driving ban by the skin of his teeth. Furthermore the detailed statement he gave about the surreal events on the dual carriageway was further corroborated by other road users who had witnessed the deceased driver's shenanigans in trying to force McCoy off the road.

An offer to be taken over to Bladdington hospital for an HIV check was turned down as the station doctor readily agreed it was too early yet to establish if McCoy might have been exposed to the fatal condition. Blood tests to be performed on the deceased driver would soon enough confirm if he was an actual HIV carrier.

A patrol car had then dropped McCoy off at home. In normal circumstances, the police would not provide this level of service for someone who had been arrested and later released. With McCoy wearing a paramedics' short sleeved shirt and evidence of dried blood staining his trousers and parts of other uncovered skin, it was wisely considered by the constable to take him home away from any unsuspecting early rising members of the public.

McCoy took care to slip the brass key into the door latch he then gently pushed the door which thankfully, did not creak to give away his very late return home. Having nimbly slipped off his brown stained leather shoes which he then held on to tightly, he cautiously climbed up the flight of stairs. Every step made by his stocking feet was placed with extreme caution until he was, at last, behind the door of the family bathroom.

Sally rose a couple of hours later to find her husband not by her side. She became momentarily confused as to where he might be. It was then the bedroom door swung open for her to see a smiling Bruce McCoy gaily balancing a tray containing two boiled eggs, buttered toasted wholemeal bread cut into neat soldiers and two cups of steaming tea in their own favourite china mugs.

'Good morning my dear, I bet you must think there is something up with me being up at this time?' he joked as he laid the tray on her duvet covered lap followed by a loving kiss on her cheek.

With the last vestiges of a deep dreamless sleep slipping away she noticed Bruce had shaved, groomed his hair nicely and was wearing a freshly ironed white open neck shirt together with navy blue sharp pressed trousers. She felt strangely aroused to see her husband looking so smart. His smiling face beamed into hers which served to bring on a tinge of guilt when she recognised he was still the only one for her, but never told him so.

Over the many years of their marriage, Sally had become so accustomed to being treated like a spoiled princess by her husband, she rarely, if ever, paid him any attention other than having a go at his drinking, poor diet and a unreasonable commitment to his job. This wasn't to be the right time to agonise over life's little regrets. She was intent on embracing this unscripted moment to enjoy the impromptu breakfast while she listened to her husband's excuse for his early rise. He went on to tell her he had decided to write a book on his career in the police and he couldn't sleep anymore because his head was swimming with all manner of ideas, so he had decided to get up early to write them down on paper before they had a chance to vanish from his mind.

She was happy to hear that Bruce had found something else alongside his new hobby of golf, which she dearly hoped would ultimately steer him away from alcohol.

This intimate special time flew by all too quickly. Sally needed to prepare herself for work and it was with some reluctance she left the company of her husband and the comfort of the warm snug duvet to have a shower while he gathered up the tray items to take them back down to the kitchen.

The washed plates, mugs and cutlery had been left to dry on the draining board while McCoy checked the dead driver's iPhone he'd stashed away in the kitchen's junk drawer away from Sally's chance discovery. He was not too familiar with the design of the touch operated phone but could see that it had received eight unanswered calls and a similar number of text messages. It was his intention, once Sally had gone off to work, to see for himself the nature of the texts the driver had belatedly received and with a bit of luck, other incriminating evidence saved elsewhere on the phone.

Chapter Forty

Background noises of wild dogs barking, snapping, yelping and snarling mingled in with high pitched excited cheers accompanied the nauseating moving graphic scenes being played on the iPhone screen. One man's mean looking mug shown in a group of three, McCoy was already familiar with, and by the sounds of the raucous victory cheers coming from the two shaven headed bulked up males it was easy to understand they were likely to be close friends of James Melia's or at least, fellow pit bull fighting enthusiasts. The barbaric footage, which had obviously been recorded at some illegal venue, showed sickening sights of pairs of dogs being baited with sharp sticks and goaded further by aggressive yells till they were near crazed and then let loose in a crudely built enclosed arena to set about ripping each other apart to the obvious delight of their barbaric owners and invited guests.

When these horrific scenes ended, McCoy touched the screen on another saved folder to yet again become engrossed in watching another video burst taken at a gathering of young adult males and impressionable teenage girls performing hand brake turns in their souped up cars at a venue he recognised to be a main super market car park in Bladdington. The iPhone must have, at some stage in the late night meet, been handed to another person present because McCoy was now looking at moving images of the same man who had attempted to drive him off the dual carriageway before bringing about his own demise.

The sound of the house phone ringing broke him away from what had been so far revealed to him from the dead driver's iPhone during the past ten minutes or more.

The call from Starr was not unexpected and was subsequently kept short. They both had agreed there was little point in going over the previous night's events in any detail as it was best left for when Starr called in at his house.

McCoy placed the iPhone back in the kitchen drawer with the intent to search through the calls register and text messages later on.

While making a pot of filter coffee and getting the cups from the cupboard, McCoy gave some thought to the past adversary who'd given him a daily physical reminder of their first coming together some thirty four years ago. His intuition told him it was unlikely not to be a coincidence that someone later wanted to christen the new bypass with the taking of his life and with what he'd already seen on the iPhone, he was becoming more convinced there was a path which led right back to old Jimmy Melia.

A sharp rap on the original Victorian door broke him away from thinking about the many unforeseen changes that had befallen him since retiring from the police only a few months back.

With welcomes dispensed with, the expected concern was expressed as to how Cooper had succumbed to such facial injuries. After Cooper had offered some brief explanation, McCoy ushered them through to the kitchen. The three detectives each took a seat around the large rectangular shaped kitchen table still talking about what had gone on over in Mansefield while McCoy handled the filter jug to pour coffee into the cups hoping there would be enough to fill four rather than the two he'd planned for.

After the drinks were served Starr turned to McCoy to ask him how he happened to be involved in a fatal car accident.

'No doubt Dick, you or one of you at least would have read the police reports and my signed statement. And that is truly what happened. I have no idea why the man wanted to force me off the road, maybe it has something to do with our account, who knows?' conjectured McCoy shrugging his shoulders.

'Why were you on the new bypass?' questioned Starr.

'I'd been to see a friend over in Coddington, there is no harm in that is there Dick?'

McCoy wasn't about to reveal the real reason why he had happened to be on the bypass that previous night. However, Starr's question had caught him off guard to make his reply sound rather defensive.

'No, no. I didn't mean to imply anything; I just thought it was a bit out of your way to go for a few drinks.'

McCoy understood his remark to be a cloaked reference to being found very close to the drink drive limit.

'We met at that new pub close to the end of the by-pass, "The Salt Panners Rest", I suppose I lost track on what I had to drink. Easily done when you are in good company, we both know that don't we Dick?' said McCoy. 'The man had a gun strapped to his leg; did you read that in any of the reports?' McCoy continued on a different tack.

'Yes, we did. The worrying thing for me,' said Starr, 'Why would he want to be wearing a gun hidden down his trousers if he didn't intend to use it? I understand forensics are carrying out tests on it to establish if the gun can be linked to any other crimes.'

'Do you have the driver's name?' pressed McCoy.

'No. At the moment, we cannot be fully certain of his identity, the credit cards found in his wallet all have different names and it is most likely none of them actually belonged to him. DS Grey has assigned a desk constable to chase up the banks to check them out. Maybe we will be lucky and get an address from there,' reported Starr.

'What about the car registration? That will pull up the man's name and mug shot from the licensing authority.' suggested McCoy.

'That was done soon after the accident,' answered Grey. 'Seems the car was a clone. The crash site investigators soon discovered the tax disc had been taken from another vehicle and the VIN number did not match the registration document. However, it did reveal a match to a black series five BMW that had been reported stolen six months ago from the Bristol area.'

McCoy then got up from his seat with the others remaining at the table thinking he was going to make more coffee. They watched him sidle over to a different part of the kitchen to then slide open a drawer. He was then seen to be holding a rectangular shaped object clasped in his hand as he took to his seat again. The item was released from his grasp and slid over the highly varnished table surface in the direction of DCI Starr.

'What's this, Bruce?' asked Starr being slightly confused at his friend's actions.

At that moment, McCoy wasn't able to bring it upon himself to explain the purpose of presenting such an obvious recognised item.

'It's an iPhone, Sir.' said Grey, which she then followed by asking, 'Is this significant, Bruce?' Even though Grey understood it most likely was, she felt compelled to ask such an obvious question.

'Yes, I believe it is,' he answered with his head held low to prevent visual contact with the others.

'I did something wrong last night. I know I shouldn't have done it, but I did, it's too late now for regrets.' McCoy picked up his cup to drain the last dregs of cold coffee to loosen his dry throat while Starr, Grey and Cooper looked on anxiously awaiting for him to continue.

'The phone belongs to the man who died at the scene last night. It must have been in his pocket or even on the dashboard, I don't know. After it became clear he had taken his last breath and there was nothing else that I could do for him, I began crawling out across the roof lining when my hand came across the phone sitting amongst pieces of glass in a pool of blood. I don't know why I did it, but I must have subconsciously somehow thought it might give me some vital clues to who the person was and why he came after me.'

'Have you been able to get into the phone?' asked Cooper.

'No, I haven't tried.' replied McCoy knowing he'd just told a big fib.

'Bloody hell, Bruce. You do realise what a foolish thing you have done?' blazed Starr.

'Of course I do, Dick. I should have handed the phone in or at least left the phone in the car for the police to find later.'

'Anything that is discovered on the phone which might then help us track down the identity of the dead man or provide other leads will now become inadmissible in a court of law. Any barrister would have a fucking field day and sling the whole case out of court.' Starr angrily said. 'And not only that Bruce, by rights I should arrest you for deliberately removing evidence from a crime scene which might prevent the police from being able to conduct a thorough investigation. I can't believe you have done such a stupid thing.'

'Well. I have and I will have to live with the consequences.'

The temporary standoff was surprisingly broken by Cooper's timely intervention.

'Don't let's forget, who ever owned this phone tried to kill Bruce and it was pure good fortune he didn't achieve his aim. From the witness statements it is abundantly clear the driver had no regard whatsoever for other road users. Innocent lives could have been wrecked while the driver walked away unscathed and even more, be back amongst his low life friends laughing and bragging what he'd got away with. Anyway, why all the worry? Who's to know we have the phone? If there is anything on it that gives us leads, that's great, all we have to say it was down to the team's diligent detective work.'

'I wholly agree with Max.' joined in Grey enthusiastically. 'It seems to me by sticking faithfully to the law it gives criminals a great advantage over us because, let's face it, most don't give a toss about it. We have something in our possession that may well not be admissible in a court of law, but why throw this advantage away to present this person with some sort of victory? I understand Bruce did wrong to take the phone, but after considering all what he and Sally have been through, can any of us say we wouldn't have done the same thing if you really believed that the car accident wasn't by chance but in fact, was part of a bigger picture?'

McCoy chose to remain silent as he and the other two junior detectives looked on at Starr rubbing his chin and seemingly debating the merits of what he'd heard and learned about the inner workings of his apprentices.

Eventually, Starr raised his hand to pick up the inanimate item, which had become the object of his mental tussle concerning police ethics, to then appear to want to get a closer look at it.

'This is a bit like Bob Stableford's phone, is that right Cora?' queried Starr.

'Yes it is, Sir,' Grey replied.

'The way Bob was going on about how marvellous these things are there should be a lot for us to have a look at. Do you agree, Max?'

'Yes, Sir.' grinned Cooper.

'Well, let's not waste any more time, we have a serious investigation to conduct.'

The gathered group were relieved to hear the decision Starr had somewhat cryptically communicated and then had followed up by sliding the phone across the table with the intention for it only to be accessed by the young serving officers to the exclusion of the recently retiree.

McCoy wasn't put out by his friend's actions in bypassing his direct involvement, because after all, he had committed a custodial offence and for the time being at least, the issue appeared to have been put to one side. McCoy also considered it wise not to mention he'd already accessed parts of the phone's memory. It wouldn't be too long before Grey or Cooper came across and shared the same incriminating video clips he'd watched before their arrival.

The minutes flew by while they first intently viewed and then discussed each of the individual saved video clips to form a growing list of names suspected for their direct or implied involvement in criminal activities in and around the area of Bladdington and in particular, the appearance of James Melia, Damien Fox and the presence of the dead driver, who's likeness had been confirmed by McCoy, would later be subject to detailed criminal checks back at the station.

'This text message is interesting. What is your car's registration, Bruce?' asked Grey after pausing at a particular message the driver had fortunately neglected to delete.

'LX63YPU. Why?' he quizzed. McCoy was peering over her left shoulder but without the help of his reading glasses he wasn't able to make out the message that clearly.

'I'll read out what it says: *Payback time Davy. Silver Mondeo LX63 YPU. Most prob head back to Blad. Be quick, make sure dont arrive.*

'So I think we can discount the possibility that the accident was a result of a demented road rage driver. Someone was making it their business to get you removed,' said Grey while turning to look at McCoy. He didn't make any comment concerning her observation but he did ask if there were more messages or calls made after the time of the accident.

She opened up the next message in the list noting the sender's number to be the same as the one in the previous message.

'What does it say, Cora?' urged Starr.

'It just says,' *Is it dun?*. Looks like someone was keen to check up on his "called in" favour,' surmised Grey.

She then read from the screen another revealing message, this time though it was from a different sender:

Davy 4 ur diary. 26th sept. pb meet. 10 start. Croft farm

Before Grey was able to put her interpretation on the message Cooper had jumped in.

'I wouldn't at all be surprised if it's the same Croft Farm on the outskirts of Bladdington. From the look of things they have organised a pit bull fight on the twenty sixth. That's two day's time,' he said after glancing down at his wrist watch to check the date. 'I have to say they have chosen a good place to hold the fight. It's well away from any other properties, and it is a good distance down a long single track lane. No one could possibly hear a thing for miles around. I used to play around Croft Farm when I was a kid, especially for scrumping apples and pears. Some crazy old farmer had it then, he'd often come out of his tumbledown house and threaten us all with a shotgun. Poor sod most likely had Alzheimer's and didn't know it. Pity he had no one around who cared enough to put him into a nursing home. I remember reading the police had found his decomposed body. A postman had reported he had not seen the old man about the place for a few weeks.'

At that point Grey pressed her foot hard onto to Cooper's to make a physical sign he'd been unknowingly insensitive when he made that careless sleight about Alzheimer's sufferers.

Cooper thought it best to quickly move on from the taboo subject and describe how Croft Farm looks nowadays.

'After the buildings had lain derelict for a few years the father of a friend of mine bought and did up the property and eventually turned it into a thriving market garden business. I used to be paid to help out during the holidays and at weekends when I was in the sixth form. They later sold out to a Dutch company who concentrate on bringing stuff in from Holland. What used to be potato fields and grazing meadows have been replaced with enormous storage warehouses and poly tunnels. A perfect venue I would say for illicit entertainment, if that is what some people want to call it.'

'And all this time, I thought you spent all your youth practising in the church choir, Morris dancing and making Airfix models. Only joking, Max!' remarked Starr grinning at his own humour. 'Well done, you have given us information that might prove to be very useful when we plan the next stage of the investigation.'

'What do you have in mind, Dick?' pressed McCoy. After listening to Cooper, he had himself formulated a plan of what they could do next, but protocol would dictate he was in no official position to put his ideas forward for consideration.

Before Starr was able to present his sketchy plan of attack, Grey interrupted.

'I think it would be unwise to re-arrest Damien Fox even if we do have evidence on the iPhone of his involvement in dog fighting. And we cannot possibly take him in for just being a known associate of James Melia. Furthermore, there is a good chance he and Melia will be at Croft Farm on the twenty sixth. We need to devise a plan to utilise a combined uniform and ground force raid on the meeting and hopefully catch them all there red handed. While we are doing this we need to get someone back at the station to get hold of the phone companies to trace the owner of this phone and the call records. Now we have the phone number of the person who gave the dead driver Bruce's registration number, the phone company will have his name and address on their system. Let's hope it is not a stolen phone or a pay as you go.'

'Good thinking, Cora,' praised Starr. 'If we put the frighteners on Fox, it could possibly lead to the dog fight being cancelled and bang goes an early opportunity to nail James Melia amongst others.'

Starr drank the last bit of cold coffee from his cup and picked up a chocolate covered digestive from a plate sitting in the middle of the table. Having filled his mouth with half the biscuit he revealed what his intentions were.

'We need to get back to the station to see if forensics have any news on Flo Jackson's death, then there is the business of chasing up the phone companies and contacting Bob Stableford to see if he has any more news on Damien Fox.' He then paused for a moment looking as though he'd forgotten something important. Cooper came in to prompt his memory.

'There is also Becky Melia, her bank details should provide us with an address. We need to chase up that address we got from the electoral register which showed a Jimmy Melia living in Coddington; he's most likely not our man but it's worth a visit.'

'Right, I think we are done here. Times moving on and we've got a lot to do.' Starr encouraged. He then picked up the iPhone from the table to slip it into his trouser pocket.

'Thanks for the coffee and biscuits Bruce. I'll be in contact later. Let's go you two. You stay there Bruce, we'll let ourselves out.'

McCoy, as instructed by the DCI, remained in his seat to watch and listen with some envy, the discussions going on between the three detectives as they left his home. The front door closed with its familiar sound followed by a car starting up and moving away. The absence of other life forms in the house made it feel soulless and empty, which was little different to McCoy's own assessment about himself.

However, like the departed detectives, he too, had things to do and mull over that morning and not all of it was to do with the visit he'd just had. Maybe it was the combination of having no sleep for over twenty-four hours and moreover, what he'd been subjected to during that time, or even the fact he'd felt marginalised by his once contemporaries that caused the black clouds of melancholy to descend around him and kept him fixed in his seat longer then he'd planned.

Later, when he'd finished rinsing and drying the coffee cups, a mundane task he'd been increasingly relegated to perform since being forced to retire,

McCoy spoke to his insurers. When he placed the phone back on the receiver he slipped his jacket on to walk the two miles into town to collect a courtesy car from a nationwide car rental service. But before leaving, he'd checked for his library card in his wallet, because his first port of call was going to be Bladdington library where he could acquire the assistance of one of the pleasant librarians to help use one of the many computers to access the Google Earth site.

Later he would stride down the library steps in possession of an A4 colour printed aerial plan of Croft Farm to then make a left turn to walk, with some purpose, the short distance to the car rental centre.

Chapter Forty-One

'I think I have a solution to the iPhone situation,' said Cora Grey as the police pool car neared Bladdington station. Starr took hold of the rear view mirror to alter its position so he could see Grey, who was sitting directly behind him in the rear passenger seat, to save him from craning his head around the bulky headrest.

'What's that?' he answered. Starr himself had not neglected to give some serious thought about the phone and it was not necessarily the fact that McCoy had taken the phone, it was more to do with his own internal wrangling that he too did not want to hand the criminals an unwarranted advantage gift wrapped by the law, and no doubt, ably abetted by the screwed up judicial system playing by the book.

'Please let me tell you first Sir, without any butting in,' Grey said with the understanding of how her boss operated.

'Carry on, Miss Grey, don't let me stop you,' cajoled Starr eager to listen to a solution to the oblong shaped presence sitting uncomfortably in his trouser pocket.

'Let's say PC Dale had been handed the phone while he was on street duty by a cyclist who had earlier found it in the gutter near to the crash site. That could easily be believed as Bruce McCoy did say the car turned over a few times before it came to a standstill. It's easy to assume the driver might have had the phone in his hand or even on the dash and it was subsequently lost during the car's rolling motion, and with the side windows breaking, there is no saying where it might have ended up. '

Grey's piece of fiction was greeted with, 'Great idea, Cora,' from Max Cooper and a cautionary, 'Mm,' by Starr.

'I'm certain PC Dale will go along with this. I know he gets seriously pissed off at times with what criminals are allowed to get away with. And don't let's lose sight of one important thing, the driver did his best to force Bruce off the road in the hope he'd do him some real harm.' she said as Cooper made a right turn into the barrier gated police car park at the rear of Bladdington station.

The three detectives, having slammed the car doors shut, then walked in a tight group towards the rear security door.

'See what he says, Cora,' said Starr while he swiped his card in the reader at the side of the door.

'I'll give him a call on his mobile when I get back to my desk.'

Stephen Dale proved to be easily coerced into a little unlawful activity. The implied rewards promised by Grey to secure his cooperation removed all resistance to any possibility of refusing to go along with this unusual request.

During the following hectic minutes, other police personnel were briefed and then issued with some of the lesser important, but still significant operational tasks to complete. One such experienced colleague was left to deal with a handwritten list of instructions relating to the iPhone with which she had been entrusted.

The strategic elements of the investigation were divided up between the senior investigators. Starr planned to go over to Mansefield station to see Bob Stableford to catch up on the interrogation and subsequent release of Damien Fox and for any updates on Flo Jackson's autopsy. Then at some stage in the day he'd be forced to report to chief superintendent Palfreyman to run over his proposed plan for a night raid on Croft farm if they failed to apprehend James Melia in the meantime.

Grey and Cooper later left the station armed with the addresses of Becky Melia and Jimmy Melia.

Chapter Forty-Two

'We'd like to speak to Becky Melia, please,' said one of the two young looking police detectives both holding their individual IDs aloft.

Grey and Cooper found the change of address provided by the bank Becky Melia had chosen to have her money paid into from Bottomley's cleaners.

'She don't live here, mate!' the woman replied defensively with her body position blocking the door entrance and any possibility of an invitation to join her in the lounge of the recently built three bedroom detached house for a nice cup of tea and a chat.

Even though Becky Melia had deliberately told a big lie and furthermore, had acted in a most unwelcoming manner, she found herself being drawn into taking a closer look at the males nasty facial injuries to wonder how he'd managed to receive them.

Throughout the morning Cooper had checked his look every few minutes being that he was unhappy about the angry swellings around his face showing no signs of diminishing. Maybe it was too soon to expect signs of improvement so soon after having a size thirteen boot smashed in one's face. The deep aching coming from the roots of his teeth and the after effects of the hospital visit to fix his dislocated jaw, was a constant nagging reminder of his injuries in spite of taking four high strength pain killers just before setting off for work that morning.

Becky Melia watched Cooper remove a folded sheet of paper from his inside jacket pocket to then scrutinise, with exaggerated attention, at what was on the sheet.

'Strange,' said Cooper slowly. 'The picture of a woman I'm looking at on this sheet shares a remarkable likeness to you. And the number on your front door is the same one we have been given by the bank,' he said while purposely training his swollen eyes on the house number fixed at the top of the door.

As Murphy's Law would sometimes have it, a postman then appeared to the side of the two visitors holding a pile of letters mixed in with junk mail. The woman must have recognised the appearance of the postman as a likely cause of other unnecessary problems she could well do without. Hastily, she held her hand out to take the offered post but was prevented from doing so by the swift intervention of Grey.

'Hey, you cheeky bitch, give me those letters, now!' Her loud demands were followed by making a move to snatch the post from being sifted through by Grey.

The woman's intentions were circumvented by Cooper stepping in to place his slight frame between the two women which inevitably helped Grey to find ample evidence to disprove the woman's denials.

'How odd,' said Grey calmly, 'these letters appeared to be addressed to, let's see now, Mrs R. Melia. Now if my memory serves me well Becky is short for Rebecca. There are two here for her, also a Mr J. Melia and others that appear to be birthday cards to a Master B. Melia. I don't think you are telling us the truth, madam.'

'Give me those letters. What gives you the right to go through someone's mail. You coppers are all the same, no wonder everyone hates you!'

Whilst Cooper became involved in a physical struggle to keep the irate woman from progressing beyond the confines of the door step, he was to hear Grey reply to the accusations spat so venomously from the woman's mouth.

'Let me tell you something Mrs Melia. What gives you the right to fleece a poor woman's account while assuming the identity of a family battling to save their son from cancer? Huh, you say people hate the police, wait till they have found out what you and your husband have been up to. Then you will understand what hate really is,' responded Grey openly demonstrating she too had the capacity to talk with "attitude" when pushed to do so.

The woman appeared to be momentarily dumbstruck and bewildered. The two determined faces giving her serious eyeball at the door only added to stirring up her already confused mind.

'How could they possibly know so much?' she'd heard a little voice echo, while simultaneously running through her mind the assurances given to her after she had reluctantly caved in and agreed to go along with a plan cooked up by her husband and father-in-law: "The police will never catch us, don't worry, Becky". Her bad husband's words didn't seem to her to be quite so prophetic now.

Those who only knew of Becky Melia from the time she had got involved with James could justifiably describe her to be a woman of debatable substance with a penchant to over indulge in alcohol.

But this wasn't always the case. Friends from her early school days would recall Rebecca Simpson, as she was then known, for being one of the most popular and brightest pupils in her year group with high prospects of being accepted at Oxford University to read Biological Sciences. She was also envied for her stunning natural beauty which never needed to be enhanced with layers of makeup, unlike like so many of her contemporaries at that time.

Disappointingly for her devoted parents, and more so for Rebecca, her fate was to be sealed at such a young impressionable age. Her genes had been programmed since birth so, when the time came, she would be unable to resist the dark handsome features and "naughty boy" ways of the local tough heartthrob, James Melia.

When the early heady days of courtship had run its course, Melia set about indoctrinating her mind with his own distorted view of the world. No matter what the situation, he failed to see the good in any one; always appearing more than happy to put people down and seek out opportunities to create an unfair advantage from someone else's misfortune.

Becky, as Melia had christened her, did not always like what she saw but was forced to blindly accept. She'd soon learned to protest would often lead to a severe beating, which he was invariably sorry for afterwards, showering her with flowers and gifts to beg for her forgiveness; until the next time.

Since coming back from Miami, there already rocky relationship had become even more unstable.

James soon discovered he too had become an unsuspecting victim of a scam pulled off by the back street jewellers in Miami. The £50,000 he'd spent of the McCoy's money on a couple of Omega watches and designer heavy gold wrist chains all proved not to be genuine. Where he hoped he'd get £25,000 for the lot, he now had to accept only £5,000 from a gullible young academy premiership footballer. The American dollars drawn from the different ATM points were exchanged for sterling using a criminal contact who was only prepared to give him fifty percent of the face value. Part of the McCoy's nest egg disappeared like water down the drain to satisfy his uncontrollable gambling habit. A substantial lump of cash went to a fellow crook in exchange for a year old cloned Audi A5.

Even though Becky was relieved she had persuaded him to pay three months' rent upfront on the house they were now living in, she was astute enough to realise their ill-gotten gains would soon be exhausted and they'd be back to square one. She wondered how much longer she could be part of this depraved existence. Maybe it wasn't too late for her to make a life of her own. Maybe there was real hope she could fulfil her early dreams of going to university make her dear parents proud of her once again.

'I've been dreading this day, I told him it would happen. Is the boy still alive?' asked Becky Melia with the harsh strains clearly evident when she first spoke to the officers having melted away.

'No, he sadly died a few days back,' answered Grey. Becky Melia said nothing on hearing the terrible news.

'Is James Melia at home?' asked Cooper.

'No, I've not seen or heard of him since early yesterday. He didn't tell me where he was going or even more, what he is up to. He never does.'

What she said was not quite the truth. He had in fact rung her late the previous night to say he would not be home. He gave no reason other than to say it was business and only to expect him when he shows his face at the door. This pattern of behaviour had become a feature during the fourteen years of being together.

'Can we come in? I believe we have a lot to talk about,' said Grey.

A tense interview was conducted in the lounge of the sparsely furnished house. Becky Melia's tactics appeared to be she was protecting herself by mostly playing ignorant of the events being questioned about by the two detectives. In fairness to Becky Melia, she did have the intelligence to understand he was up to no good but had learned, just like a beaten animal, not to quiz him about what he was up to. She just went along for the ride and where the money was coming from, well, that was of no concern of hers, and even if she knew, her position in the relationship dictated her feelings or views would be ignored.

Damien Fox's name was mentioned to her, with the significance of his name being linked to the male detective's injuries and the police arrest for the suspicious death of her one time neighbour, Flo Jackson.

'Oh, that's terrible news. Poor Mrs Jackson,' said Melia drawing on a freshly lit cigarette with a distant look of shock appearing across her face. 'We must have given that poor woman hell. James loved the wild drunken parties we had. He'd always insist on inviting all of his awful rough looking mates and wanted to have the music turned up loud to all hours. No one dared complain, except little old Flo Jackson. That poor lady was the only one in the street who had the guts to stand up to James. I'm ashamed to admit I was really horrible to her at times. What a bitch I've become.' She reached down to the side of her arm chair to a box of tissues with the purpose to wipe away the tears that had formed in the corner of her eyes. That done, the damp tissue was tucked under the cuff of her cardigan sleeve followed by an extra-long draw on the tipped cigarette to wait for the next question.

'So you do admit to taking the headed paper from Oakwood Engineering?' pressed Grey towards the end of the interview.

'Yes, I'd be a liar to deny it. I felt terrible taking the sheet, the people who worked there were so nice and incredibly friendly towards me. The only reason I took on the cleaning job was for the sole purpose of getting hold of one of those damn letter headed sheets. James said if I failed, his whole plan would go up in the air. You wouldn't believe how much pressure he put me under to get what he wanted but he never did give me a reason why he so badly needed it. What is sad for me, I ended up really enjoying working there; I hope I didn't get anyone in to trouble.'

Cooper started the engine with Grey sitting to his side in the passenger seat.

'Seems to me her main excuse was that she was kept in the dark, how could she possibly not know that both the Sproston's and their ill son were being used as a smokescreen to get at Sally McCoy? I don't think her pleas of ignorance will convince a jury she was just an innocent accomplice,' suggested Cooper.

Grey answered him with part of her mind occupied in thinking about what type of reception they were about to receive at the Coddington address, which had earlier been confirmed by Becky Melia to be the home of her father-in-law.

"If she decides to support the case for the prosecution then she might get away with just a light slap on the wrist. That business about her taking the letter headed paper, I think the jury would accept her plea that she was forcibly coerced into taking it based on the fact she did not knowingly understand the purpose of its intended use.'

'Looks like she might get away scot free then. Doesn't seem fair to me,' bemoaned Cooper while preparing to obey an audible satellite navigation instruction to take the next right in fifty yards.

'Her biggest worry, I think, is when James Melia eventually finds out she has let the cat out of the bag. If we don't get to him first, then I wouldn't at all be surprised when we visit her again, we'll see her in a hospital bed. Why do woman fall for that type of man?'

'You tell me Cora, you're a woman, or haven't you noticed!' he playfully answered with her responding with a couple of light slaps to his left shoulder.

Chapter Forty-Three

'He'll have to face charges of police assault, contravening the 1991 Dangerous Dogs Act and being under suspicion for dealing in stolen goods. The charge we really wanted to stick on him, forensics weren't able to find any incriminating evidence to place him at Mrs Jackson's house, so the chief super said we had to let him go.'

The old friends had initially met up in the modern brightly lit reception area of Mansefield police station, before moving off to a small office used by the duty desk sergeant.

'Hell's bells!' Starr called in frustration.

'There's more, Dick,' said Bob Stableford as he spooned coffee granules from a jar belonging to the desk sergeant into two unwashed cups.

'Fox has filed an official complaint citing undue police violence during his arrest. Can you believe it?' he said more in anguish than disgust.

'Nothing surprises me. We have taken the precaution to photograph Cooper's injuries and have a copy of the hospital report after he had his dislocated jaw put back in place. In the end Bob, it's his word against the three of us.'

Starr wasn't going to allow this deliberate side show to derail his actions, even if it was plenty enough to get Palfreyman jumping about and making all sorts of derogatory comments about his leadership.

'What's the verdict on Flo Jackson then?' he asked while watching Stableford pour the hot water into the cups.

'Death due to asphyxiation brought on by strangulation. Poor soul. Forensics managed to lift some half decent finger prints from around her neck and the from arm chair. I have a detective working on the database as we speak. We just have to hope whoever did this, had their finger prints taken at some time. The statements taken from the idiots we arrested during the near riot in Regent Street don't give us any further clues.'

After Stableford had ladled in semi-skimmed powdered milk to whiten the coffee, Starr reported, between sips of the putrid tasting hot drink, what he understood to have happened on the bypass the previous night which had, as one of its main players, Bruce McCoy, who had so narrowly missed an early sitting with his maker; a fate the driver had not been so lucky to avoid. He went on to mention that the male fatality was found with a gun strapped to his calf with tests planned to establish if it had been used in other gun related crimes. Then he described the incredible stroke of luck in having the dead man's iPhone handed in to a constable by a cyclist who'd found it close to the fatal crash site.

'RTA investigators are usually very thorough, too thorough for their own good at times when they keep roads closed for hours on end, painstakingly searching for evidence with little regard to the gridlock in the surrounding area. Seems strange they missed it, look at mine, they cannot be described as being exactly small.' Stableford took the iPhone from his jacket pocket to place it in the space separating the two men.

'Just a bit of luck, I suppose,' said Starr while taking a cursory look at the plastic cased object.

Before Starr was forced to leave Stableford's company, he explained the nature of the content saved on the driver's iPhone, expressively: the fact that McCoy appears to have been cynically targeted, and images of Melia, Fox and the dead driver had been saved on video and finally, the message relating to Croft Farm.

'We have someone at the station contacting phone companies. Grey and Cooper should have some news about their visits and I've got to see Palfreyman. Time for me to go, Bob.'

They agreed to keep each other up to speed as they bid each other goodbye at the glazed doors leading to Starr's exit from the reception area.

Chapter Forty-Four

'What do you mean dead? How the heck did that happen? It wasn't supposed to be him.' Jimmy Melia sounded and looked shocked when told the stark news from his tense looking son while they both stood in the bleach smelling kitchen around mid-morning.

'It happened on the new bypass; he was pronounced dead at the scene. I suspected something was seriously wrong when he did not answer my calls or texts.

'I called around Davy's house this morning to see if he was there. His missus told me he had not come home last night; he won't answer her calls, and she is worried sick where he might be. I told her not to worry, he probably had gone over to a mate's house, had too much drink and ended up kipping down on the settee for the night.'

'Who told you he'd been killed then?' It was not just that he was concerned about Davy O'Flynn's unexpected road death, Jimmy Melia was rightly more worried about the loss of income he would suffer from no longer benefiting from the illicit business deals he had nurtured with O'Flynn over the past year or two. He recognised he would find it near impossible to survive on the little he earned from working at the golf club.

'I heard it on Blad FM. The newsreader said there had been a fatal car accident around eight last night on the new bypass. Witnesses had reported seeing two cars involved in a high speed chase, with one of the vehicles ending up on its roof on the opposite carriageway. The name of the dead male driver would not be released until the next of kin had been informed. The female newsreader did mention the car though; a late model black BMW, the same as Davy's car. The driver of the other car was taken into custody for failing a road side breathalyser test. Then, as coincidence would have it, I got a call from Damien Fox, he said he'd been arrested yesterday, kept in overnight and released this morning. While he was waiting to get his things at the discharge desk he overheard a couple of coppers talking about the accident and one of them mentioned Davy O'Flynn's name, so it must be him.'

'What a damn shame. Did you go back to tell Chantelle?'

'Did I bollocks! Let the cops have that job,' sharply replied James Melia.

'I hope she never finds out who he was returning a favour for. This was never meant to happen, James, it should be McCoy who's injured or dead. He'll understand the person chasing him was trying to wipe him out, he's no fool, he won't just go away now this has happened. Thinking back, I shouldn't have called you and Davy would now still be with us.'

'I think he is onto us anyway and I wasn't going to sit back and do nothing about McCoy threatening you.' He then paused for a second or two before continuing, 'There's more, Dad.'

'What's that?'

'The police were round Damien Fox's house asking for my whereabouts; he told them nothing. After he gave them short shrift they called in on that old bitch's house next door and didn't leave, so Fox said, for at least two hours. I bet she wasn't able to keep her big mouth shut. God knows what she told them. I'm glad the old cow is no longer about to stir up any more trouble.' Jimmy Melia couldn't help but to see the dark venom in his son's eyes when he'd spoke about Mrs Jackson.

'Do you mean she is dead, James?' Melia senior asked in obvious surprise at the news.

'Yes, the copper's took Fox in yesterday for questioning, that's the reason he was at Mansefield station when he heard the news about Davy. They released him on conditional bail pending further enquiries.' James Melia then noticed his father peering at him in a questioning manner. 'What?' he said uncomfortable at being the focus of the older man's gaze.

Jimmy Melia had listened in on a gathering group of pensioner aged people earlier that morning worriedly talking at the tills in the local mini-mart about an old lady being found dead in suspicious circumstances in Mansefield and how, on the same night, the police had to deal with an unruly mass gathering of youths in the same area. Not only that, and more worrying for him, an acquaintance of his son, who lived opposite the deceased pensioner, had called him early that morning asking for his son's whereabouts as he needed to speak to James about a call he'd had from him and wanted to sort things out. The caller mentioned he saw James leaving the deceased woman's house the night she was found dead.

'I hope you had nothing to do with her death, James, I know what a bad temper you have got,' he said not breaking eye contact with his son.

'What the fuck are you talking about, Dad? It was probably one of the idiots rioting in the street that night who did it. I think you are losing your marbles, just like Sally McCoy.'

'What were you doing in Mrs Jackson's house then?' He was always able to tell when his son was lying, even if he had missed the formative years of his young life serving a prison sentence. He maintained an unwavering eye contact to spot tell-tale signs he was lying while choosing to ignore the deliberately callous barbed reference to dementia, even if he did admit to becoming increasingly forgetful and confused.

'Look, I only called to ask her what she told the cops. She must have said something for them to be in her house for so long,' he seemed to plead.

'Did you touch or threaten her?'

'I admit I did lose my temper, I didn't believe her when she told me she had said nothing.' Melia senior noticed fresh beads of sweat forming across his son's furrowed forehead.

'Did you touch her, James?' he snapped his tone verging on anger.

'I think I might have got her round the throat to give her a gentle shake. I can't remember. I was frustrated,' he answered feebly.

'You bloody fool; you must have killed the poor woman. She was easily in her nineties. She'd likely know nothing, except for a bit of useless idle chit chat.

You don't know your own bloody strength.' shouted Jimmy on hearing his confession.

'I didn't go round with the intention to kill her. How was I to know she would be so frail?' he whined.

'Trouble with you, you are so used to knocking Becky about. You're a fucking savage; you thought you could do the same to Mrs Jackson. Well you're in deep shit now, you brainless fool.'

The truisms contained in the spat words bit deep and hard enough for James Melia to react in raising his fist up close to his father's face.

'Yes, go on, do it! You like knocking people about don't you Son.' goaded Jimmy Melia while looking deep into his son's demented screwed up face poised with his clenched fist only a fraction away from his high cheek bone. Jimmy then noticed his features soften to be slowly replaced with a rather awkward grin.

With the threat of the clenched fist removed James Melia spoke with purposeful diction to say, 'If I'm in the shit, so are you Father. After all, whose plan was it? Yours! A big idea about getting your revenge at long last, but it looks highly likely McCoy will out smart you again. If I end up inside so will you. Thing is though, I will get out sometime, but you Dad, you'll be taken out in a wooden overcoat,' he followed with an intentional sneer. 'If you know what is good for you, you'll keep your mouth shut, because as you have already said, I don't know my own strength.'

Jimmy Melia was unable to find an adequate and equal response to match the threat.

'I've wasted enough time here, I'll let myself out. Just remember what I said.' James Melia winked at his dumbstruck father knowing he had, in those few highly charged minutes, crossed an unredeemable point in their lives.

James Melia moved to take the brass handle to pull the door half open to access the hallway leading to the front door when he was stopped mid-motion.

A loud rap on the front door glass panel coupled with the sight of two hazy figures peering in for signs of movement jolted James Melia enough for his feet to freeze to the carpet. A strong pull on his shoulder broke him out of his temporary paralysis to yank him back into the kitchen.

A hushed voice then said, 'Could be the cops, get out round the back.'

He yanked at the door handle but the door did not budge. His elbow jarred painfully when the door failed to open; it was locked.

'It's locked, where is the fucking key?' hissed James Melia.

'Let me think, let me think, where did I put it?' his father replied while scratching his balding pate.

Another hard rap on the glass was repeated with the addition of a female voice calling, 'It's the police, please come to the door' which only added to Jimmy Melia's confusion as to the whereabouts of the door keys.

'Fucking hell, hurry up,' James Melia growled lowly. The first signs of panic were setting in.

'I know, there in my coat pocket, I had them when I went to the shop this morning.'

He reached into his outdoor coat pocket which was hanging from the back of a wooden kitchen chair to pull out a bunch of three keys.

'It's the one with the red plastic end,' he said passing the keys over amid another call from the awaiting police on the doorstep.

'Go round the back Max, if someone is here, they may want to avoid seeing us. Be careful,' warned DS Grey.

'The key slipped easily into the door lock, a twist to the left followed by a turn of the handle allowed James Melia to escape the house and find himself then deciding which way to go while pacing on the concrete paved path.

'Oi, where do you think you are going? Stay where you are. It's the police!'

Cooper had appeared from the access ally, which served the middle two houses of the council built block of four mews. Any indecision rapidly evaporated on seeing the blocking stance taken up by the plain clothes copper. A straight run forward across his father's neat garden would lead him to a row of wooden six foot wavy edged fencing panels one of which had the convenience of having a hand built box constructed compost heap situated close by. Melia's fast run combined with the assistance of the springy compost material all contributed to him making a clean hand assisted bound over the high fence.

It was Cooper's intentions to replicate, or better still, exceed the athletic prowess of the escaping male. His well meant intentions were not to be realised; his take off foot had unfortunately fell awkwardly on a wooden rotten edge of the compost box causing the side structure to fall apart with Cooper following in its wake. He fell all of a ruck on to the solid lawn surface lowly moaning while nursing both his new and old injuries.

Melia sprinted off to make himself scarce down the labyrinth of public alley ways forming a pedestrian thoroughfare on the sprawling council estate.

Jimmy Melia stood nervously looking out from the kitchen window somewhat relieved his son had been spared from having to face the two police officers, one of whom, he cagily observed, was engaged in rubbing his freshly injured knee. Throughout this temporary distraction he was aware of a demanding female presence calling for someone to answer her at the door.

Melia opened the kitchen door leading into the hallway to be greeted by another hard rap on the glass panel.

'Hang on, I'm coming,' he called out in an agitated tone directed at the unknown blurred figure impatiently waiting for him to unlock the door.

He was greeted by the young DS holding aloft a warrant card with a non-too pleased look about her.

'I am Detective Sergeant Grey; I understand you are Mr Melia.'

'Who says I am?' he answered defensively.

'I have just come from your daughter-in-law's house, Becky Melia. She confirmed this to be the address of her husband's father. And surprisingly so the description she gave of you turned out to be a perfect match.'

'What do you want?' he reluctantly continued.

'I would like to question you about the whereabouts of your son, James Melia. Can I come inside and talk to you?'

'No. You are not welcome here.' His dark stare into her fresh looking features left her with little doubt the police had no chance at all of being invited into this address.

Cooper, in the meantime had managed to hobble round to the front of the house to position himself next to his female partner. Being only a matter of a couple of feet away from the person who had only moments before gave chase after his son before he was able to escape over the garden fence, Jimmy Melia couldn't fail to notice the extent of the male detective's injuries. In normal circumstances, he'd most likely enquire how he had fallen victim to such injuries. However, the effects of a lifetime of bitter conditioning dictated these were not your normal everyday people- they were coppers, the filth, pigs and any other offensive term the police have been subject to since the days of Robert Peel.

'That was your son, James, who I saw jumping over the garden fence, wasn't it Mr Melia?' Grey looked on in surprise after taking in the context of Cooper's blunt question she'd previously had no knowledge about until now.

'Don't know what you are talking about, mate.' Melia replied nastily.

'I saw him leave your house from the back door,' Cooper responded in disbelief. 'Why would he want to climb over a bloody great high fence? He knew we were the police, only a guilty person with something to hide would want to make such a decision. And, I would appreciate it if you did not call me, mate!'

'He didn't come from my house, mate. I think you disturbed someone trying to break into my house and he made a run for it when he saw you appear from the house entry. Wasn't I lucky you turned up? I could have been another unsolved burglar crime statistic the police don't give two fucking hoots about.'

'Bullshit, I saw a person matching the description of your son leave through your back door,' Cooper said in a raised voice.

'Sorry mate, you're mistaken. How can you see properly through those two shiners?' smirked Melia, who then decided not to let up about the young detectives battered and bruised appearance. 'I bet whoever did that to you enjoyed every minute of it.'

'That's enough, Mr Melia. I have to warn you, if you persist in this manner we will have no alternative but to take you down to the station for further questioning,' snapped Grey having rightly tired of the old man's baiting of her partner.

Cooper wisely elected to remain silent as the temptation to clock the rude, arrogant and provocative man was close to becoming a reality.

'Take me down to the station then. That will give me the opportunity to file an official complaint for police intimidation and assault.' Melia looked on abundantly enjoying the effect his carefully introduced revelation was having on the door step bound officers.

'What are you talking about? We have neither intimidated or assaulted you. How can you possibly accuse us of such things?' said Grey looking rattled and bemused after hearing Melia's allegation.

Melia purposely held his smirking grin for a while longer relishing how easy it had been for him to turn the tables on these unwanted callers.

'Come on. You cannot make serious accusations against us without coming up with the evidence,' said Grey impatiently.

'Who said it was about you two?' he said holding a wide grin.

'I think you are confused Mr Melia. You haven't bumped your head recently have you?' questioned Grey.

'Yes, I have in fact, how deceptive of you DS Grey. No wonder you are a copper,' answered Melia in a sarcastic manner.

Grey and Cooper simultaneously turned to each other, both had had their fill of Melia's mind games and an agreeing nod between the two of them telepathically communicated he needed to be carted off down to the station to have their business concluded there rather than on the door step in the enemy's territory.

Melia wasn't that big of a fool not to pick up on the officers' intentions.

'Bruce McCoy, yes, Detective Inspector Bruce McCoy. I am certain you know him or at least know of him.' He paused at that point to await an inevitable response at the mentioning of this particular man's name.

'What about Bruce McCoy?' pressed Grey.

'He paid me a surprise visit the other evening. Accused me of all sorts of dreadful things. He said I knew something about some money being stolen. He ended up pushing me to the floor, where he threatened and assaulted me. He stunk of drink, not surprising really, McCoy has always been a piss head.' he said with apparent glee.

'Did you want to get revenge on him for what he did to you?' Cooper said, thinking there might be a connection to McCoy being subject to a near fatal car accident on the same night.

'Revenge, what are talking about?' said Melia.

'Just a little thought that's all.' said Cooper teasingly.

'What are you trying to get at sonny?'

Cooper was pleased to see Melia's supercilious grin wiped from his angry face. He would soon turn grey after he had heard what Cooper had to say.

'An attempt was made on Bruce McCoy's life soon after he left this address on the same night you claim he paid you an unexpected visit. A car tried to force him off the road, but things didn't go as planned for the driver and it was he, and not McCoy, who bought it on the Bladdington bypass. We have evidence to prove your son was a known associate of the dead driver. I think it is too much to believe it is all but a coincidence.'

'Well, you're the bloody coppers, isn't it your job to get the proof first before throwing out accusations.' Melia appeared to be rattled. Cooper was determined to press him further.

'And what's more, Mr Melia. Your daughter-in-law revealed to us other serious criminal activities involving your son. Especially interesting to the police is your son's alleged involvement in serious fraud concerning an internet bank account. She even went as far as to admitting being part of the scam with you, Mr Melia, being the brains behind it all.'

The young DS thought it appropriate to insert a pause at that point, the tree had been rigorously shaken, he and Grey were waiting to discover what had fallen to the ground.

'It's lies, all fucking lies. She is nothing but a lying bitch. You must have put words in her mouth. I know how you copper's work. I've been there before. McCoy stitched me up so I served a longer stretch than I should have done and I blame that bastard for breaking my mother's heart and putting her in an early grave. It's like history repeating itself all over again,' raged Melia.

The rushed and stilted police proceedings inconveniently carried out on the doorstep had gone on long enough. The detectives understood Melia was holding back and they would stand a better chance of prising him open back on their own patch.

'We need you to accompany us down to the station for further questioning. Please read Mr Melia his rights, DS Grey.' Cooper's next intentions were to release the handcuffs clipped to a belt loop around his trouser waist.

As the reading of the formal arrest citation was being drowned out by Melia's loud protests about police injustices, a high pitched squeak noise accompanied the opening of a steel wrought iron gate. This event went unnoticed until it was too late.

Cooper froze from what he was doing to see the same man, who had earlier loped over the rear garden fence panel, striding down the short garden path holding a long aluminium baseball bat aloft with unambiguous intent in his wild eyes.

'He ain't going fucking nowhere. Step over there, or you will get some of this!' he convincingly threatened.

James Melia had doubled back on himself with the intention of retrieving his car which had been parked at a discreet distance from his father's house. He was about to start the car up when the sound of his mobile ring tone stopped him from pressing the start button on the dash. The nature of the call received from Damien Fox served to change his mind.

From the protective screen of the high privet hedge, he'd been listening in on the loud exchange of accusations and threats between the law and his father.

Melia could feel the dampness of his palms against the familiar leather bound handle of the long baseball bat he'd only moments before taken from the back seat of his car while he tensely concentrated over what he should do next, both in the light of Fox's mobile call and on hearing further confirmation of his wife's betrayal in the heightened exchange being played out for all and sundry in the neighbourhood to listen in on.

Chapter Forty Five

Fox had been careful to have kept himself hidden in his white van while he patiently waited for the familiar detectives to leave the Melia's newly rented home. He then left it for a further ten minutes before venturing over to knock on the front door.

It was during that same ten minute spell Becky Melia had made the momentous decision to move back into her parent's home and to begin divorce proceedings. Brett would have to choose whether he wanted to go with her or stay with his evil father. Becky answered the door to be greeted by the sight of her husband's best mate. Her heart sank. She asked him through to the kitchen hoping the call would be short and not necessarily sweet.

They both stood in the kitchen while she listened impatiently to Fox describing what had happened to him and how he had become an innocent victim of police brutality and violence. Hence the scalp injuries.

His unwanted presence served to add credence to her decision to leave Melia, she wanted out, and sooner the better. It was at that electric moment of feeling the weight of the heavy chains being lifted from her that had so blighted her life, she foolishly told him about what she had said to the detectives.

Like her own husband, Fox was vastly experienced in coldly meting out irrational violent treatment to, what he understood to be, the weaker sex. The way in which Fox treated his Chinese internet bride was just testament to his sadistic nature. She had sadly become accustomed to his regular beatings and moreover, was able to do little when subject to the man's perverse sexual appetite. Being kept penniless and situated so far away from her own loving family back in the east, he had conspired to make it nigh on impossible for her to escape his vile clutches.

The force of the blow sent her flying backwards onto the cream ceramic tiled floor with her bottom first hitting the hard surface followed by her upper torso flipping back violently. A cracking sound, similar to that heard when a coconut shell is struck by a claw hammer, filled the kitchen. The veil of blackness that had descended over Becky Melia when Fox's brute sized hand made first contact was to be permanent.

Her son, Brett, had bunked off the school premises at the start of lunch break with a sulky group of like-minded friends to arrive at his home ten minutes later. He'd first noticed a familiar white van, the driver of which was a one time next door neighbour, with a mobile phone glued to the side of his head, pulling away from the house frontage. On entering the house he found his mother lying unconscious on the dry kitchen floor bleeding slowly from the back of her skull.

Days later, her bereft parents would have the pain of arranging a funeral for their only daughter.

Chapter Forty-Six

While Cooper was driving back to the station, he listened in on Grey making a call to Starr.

'The damn lunatic threatened us with a baseball bat. By the look of him we needed no convincing that he intended to use the bat if we dared provoke him. We had no other choice but to let Jimmy Melia leave with his son,' Cora Grey said reporting on the aftermath of their visit to Coddington while still trying to control her shattered nerves.

'You both did the right thing, if he can throttle a poor innocent lady to death, there is no saying what more he is capable of,' said Starr.

'So it was James Melia who killed her then?' pressed Grey.

'Yes, it wasn't Fox as we first suspected. Fingerprints lifted from the wooden arms of the chair showed a match to James Melia. Yes, he could argue his prints were there from when he had visited her on a previous occasion. If he was determined to stick to this alibi, it would likely come undone because the team doing the door to door enquiries along Regent Street found someone willing to testify they saw James Melia suspiciously leave Mrs Jackson's house just before the real trouble started. I'm willing to bet the DNA contained in the swabs from Mrs Jackson skin and clothes would show an identical match to Melia's. But of course, we have to get him first to allow us to do this check.'

'What do you want us to do now, Sir?' continued Grey.

'Get back to the station, then we will discuss what to do. By the way, I will put out an APB to be on the lookout for the Melia's.'

'Someone in the name of Barry Sproston is waiting for you in reception Sir. He says you told him to report to the station when he'd arrived back from America.'

Starr had received the call from the desk sergeant moments after speaking to DS Grey.

The swiftness of events following the RIVA link to Miami had made him almost forget about this man and his circumstances. However, on the positive side, not only had Starr become unequivocally convinced of the man's innocence, he had garnered a real sympathy in the way his tragic situation had been wilfully exploited for criminal gain.

'Thanks, Ralph. Tell him I'll be down in a minute.'

When he entered the small interview room situated off the main reception area, Sproston was found by Starr to be aimlessly flicking through a worn Salvation Army magazine.

'Hello, Mr Sproston. I'm DCI Starr.'

Sproston remained in his sitting position as he casually tossed the months old magazine onto the small round table placed in the middle of the claustrophobic room to then glance up to see a hand offered in welcome.

The signs of early grief drawn across the recently bereaved father's features were clear for Starr to see.

'I'm so sorry for your terrible loss. I can't for one moment imagine what you and your wife are going through,' Starr continued sympathetically.

He was relieved to see Sproston then push a hand out to lightly grasp his.

Starr then took one of the other four plastic seats to face the one time suspect.

'Am I still under suspicion?' questioned Sproston.

'No, I believe we are completely satisfied we have sufficient evidence to support your claimed innocence. Since the interview we conducted with you in America we have been able to make substantial progress,' answered Starr careful not to sound triumphalist.

'So, you have someone in the frame then?'

'Possibly,' Starr answered cagily.

'I have had some time to think things over since my son died.' Sproston paused; appearing then to divert his attention to a citizen's advice centre's flyer pinned on a near bare notice board. While Starr gave the man time to compose himself, he was able to fully take in the man's distinctive facial features he had noted on the PC monitor screen during the Miami video link and could now fully appreciate how uncannily similar they were to those of the investigation's main suspect.

'I can only think that this whole thing must have been planned by those local to this area. The press published our plight in detail resulting in someone realising there was an opportunity to make a profitable situation from my family's distress,' suggested Sproston with his attention now back in focus.

'Yes, the evidence so far suggests you have innocently been part of an elaborate scam to exhort a large sum of money from an unsuspecting victim,' answered Starr.

'I have been told someone by the name of Becky Melia might have played a part in all of this. Is that right, DCI Starr?'

Sproston had earlier given the head of personnel at Oakwood Engineering a call to update her on his situation. It was during this genuine emotional exchange when the visit by Bladdington police cropped up together with the name of this particular office cleaner.

Starr felt annoyed such details had been so easily divulged before the police were able to fully carry out their investigations. There could be little doubt much more would have been discussed between the two of them. Therefore he saw no good reason why he should deny the existence of the woman's name in relation to their enquiries.

'That is correct, it took us a while to establish the woman's address, in fact a small team of detectives have made a visit to her home this very morning and I'm awaiting on the results of their enquiries.' said Starr careful not to reveal too much of what he knew at this early stage.

'I know this might sound ridiculous,' Sproston said as if slightly embarrassed, 'but this wouldn't have anything to do with a James Melia.'

Hearing this man's name initially took Starr by surprise.

'Why do you ask?' posed Starr.

'Two things really. For as long as I can remember I was raised by my gran on my mother's side of the family. My mother was only seventeen when she had me and it didn't take too long for her to realise she couldn't cope with a new baby. I got dumped off at my gran's while she disappeared with another man.

It was just before my gran died she told me my mother had become an alcoholic and died of liver failure when she was only twenty-nine. And that wasn't all.'

Watching Sproston tensely running his long set of fingers through each other, Starr understood this man most probably had it tough when he was young by not being able to explain to his teasing peers why he had no mum or dad looking after him and furthermore, made worse by having only an elderly widow caring for him.

'Apparently, my mother, if you want to call her that, was paid a large sum of money, £3,000 if I remember correctly, by a person named Jimmy Melia who she said, owned some sort of grounds maintenance business. The cash was for her to pay for an abortion and a little more money besides. My mother apparently gladly accepted the offer and of course, did not go ahead with the abortion. To this very day I feel everlasting shame and embarrassment to read on my birth certificate my father is unknown. Gran told me my father was someone by the name of Jimmy Melia just before she died a few years ago. By what had been said at the time it wasn't the first occasion the father of this Jimmy Melia had been forced to pay off his son's pregnant girlfriends.'

Starr remained silent watching Sproston mindfully toiling over deep issues which served to bother him greatly in this extended period of contemplation. When he was ready, he then turned to Starr to further open up on what had so occupied his thoughts.

'In my twenties I had often been mistaken for someone named James Melia, I even believe I have actually seen him during the past year in the Golden Square shopping centre in Bladdington. The uncanny thing for me is not only was he a similar height and build as me, his hair was styled near identically to mine. It would also seem the striking blue eyes have come down in the genes in both of us. Seems so ironic now that it was Wilson, my son when he was first diagnosed with leukaemia, who pointed his likeness out to me.' He paused at that point, his soul touched by the stark reminder his son would never be at his side again. 'So if you have moved the investigation on to questioning Becky Melia,' he later continued, 'it is quite understandable that this James Melia, I have been often mistaken for, might bear some relationship to her.'

Sproston then observed Starr pull open the flap of the mustard coloured A4 wallet to remove a couple of items from the loosely gathered contents. He then took hold of two enlarged photographs. While Sproston scanned across each of the photographs in turn the DCI explained their significance in the investigation and especially, the times when the pictures actually were taken. He allowed Sproston some time to take in the image of himself sitting on a hospital bed next to his wife alongside a weak, sad looking young boy having a tube entering his body through his left nostril, and that of a similar aged man to himself with hands jointly held aloft with a woman he guessed to be in her late fifties both dressed in running gear.

'This man is James Melia, isn't he?' said Sproston while not removing his attention from the two coloured photographs.

'Yes, we believe it is,' answered Starr.

'There can be no denying we both share a look and appear to be of a similar age and from what my gran told me about my own family circumstances, it's likely James Melia was another soul brought into this world through one of Jimmy Melia's early life shagging exploits. He shares the same surname as Jimmy Melia, maybe he decided to do the right thing this time and lived with his mother, I'm just guessing, but it seems highly plausible.'

Starr made no comment, he was conscious not to give away too much of what he had gleaned from current police records and what he had already been told by Bruce McCoy concerning Jimmy Melia's past.

The final ten minutes spent in the small interview room was a carefully guarded dialogue pertaining to the overall progress made by the police so far. Starr offered Sproston a card showing the name of a consultant who was able to offer his free services to victims of crime. Sproston gave the printed details a cursory glance before slipping the stiff card into his inside jacket pocket while being accompanied by Starr through to the station's main entrance.

Chapter Forty-Seven

In the relatively secluded car park at the back of "The Parrot and Elephant" public house, an Audi A5 was seen next to a dirty 1990s white Ford Transit van. On one side of the car's rear passenger seat was sat Jimmy Melia having moved from the front to make way for the arrival of Damien Fox. The two occupants were silently watching James Melia from behind the vehicle's dark tinted windows, who had only moments before got out the car to get a better reception for an incoming call on his mobile. His animated gestures made it clear all was not well with what he was hearing on the mobile. When he'd finished the call, Melia strode over to his car with a rattled look. The driver's door was sharply pulled open followed by Melia dropping the full weight of his body into the leather upholstered seat. A thin film of sweat bathed his forehead as he turned to transfix a wild stare in Fox's direction.

Jimmy Melia sensed there was about to be big trouble between his son and Fox and therefore moved to the edge of the rear passenger seat in readiness for what he did not yet know.

'What the fuck have you done, Fox?' shouted James Melia.

'Don't know what you are on about,' said Fox calmly moving his focus on to an elderly couple entering the pub to take advantage of the lunchtime offers.

'What's happened, James?' pressed his father. The son took no notice of him.

'Look at me you bastard,' yelled Melia.

Fox slowly turned to obey the direct instruction.

'What the fuck has got into you?' said Fox.

'What the fuck has got into me?' Let me have a look at your hands.' Melia caught Fox off guard as he lunged out to grasp hold of both of his hands.

'Where is that cut from? That's fresh,' angrily questioned Melia while not slackening his hold on his wrists.

'Van wouldn't start this morning and while I was pissing about with the engine I must have caught it on something. Why? How do you think I got it?' replied Fox vigorously shaking his wrists free from Melia's clutch.

'Hey, come on you two calm down, for fuck's sake. What's got into you James?'

'What's got into me, Dad? That was a call from Brett; Becky has been taken to hospital. He found her unconscious and bleeding from her head, lying on the kitchen floor. He said he recognised your van leaving the house, Fox, just before he found her nearly dead on the fucking floor. What have you done you mad bastard?'

'What the fuck are you on about? I ain't done nothing to her, man. Huh, you call me a mad bastard? At least I didn't kill no old defenceless woman. Now that is sick!' Melia saw an annoying smirk grow across Fox's face at the end of his true words.

Melia's brain was still spinning with what had gone on with the two young police detectives at his father's council house earlier that day, this unexpected development, coupled with Fox's barbed reference to Mrs Jackson's death, all conspired to push him over the edge.

With his right hand obscured from Fox's view, Melia felt around for a familiar shaped object he kept hidden from view in the door glove compartment.

In a blink of an eye, his body spun around on the soft leather seat with Fox hearing the audible click of a four inch flick knife opening fractionally before he felt the keen edge of cold bright steel pressing into the bulge of his Adams apple, enough for a slow running crimson line to appear from under the blade edge. Fox pressed back hard into the passenger seat with his eyes bulging in terror, frantic to remove the sharp stinging presence from his throat.

'Now, Damien you are not going to wet yourself are you?' teased Melia.

Fox was unable to reply to his sadistic taunt for obvious reasons.

'James, stop all of this, now! Have you gone completely stark raving mad?' Jimmy Melia reached out to grab hold of his son's rigidly held arm in an attempt to push the razor sharp blade away from Fox's slowly oscillating Adam's apple.

'Careful, Dad. My hand might slip and I don't think Damien would be too pleased.' James Melia enjoyed watching the bands of sweat pumping from the pores on Fox's face and seeing the carotid vein pulsing rapidly in his neck.

Satisfied he'd tormented Fox enough for him to fear for his life, Melia slowly removed the flick knife pressure from the wet salty skin, with a tight grip on the handle being maintained just in case his friend had any stupid ideas about acting out some form of retaliatory action.

'Fucking hell, Melia. You've seriously lost it man. I …I had fuck all to do with what happened to Becky,' he pleaded reaching up to his throat to check that he was still in one piece. There was no alternative other than for Fox to lie, and more importantly, to be a damn good convincing liar at that. If he'd been foolish enough to tell the truth, then he'd be wearing more than a Glasgow smile right now.

'Why did you have to go to my house when you know the police are sniffing about? What was up with giving me a call on the mobile?' he said angrily.

'I did try your mobile, check your missed calls register if you don't believe me.'

If Melia had taken up Fox's suggestion, he'd have the added pressure of thinking how best to dispose of a murder weapon.

'I decided to call in to see if you were about. I did notice the kitchen floor was wet; Becky must have slipped and cracked her head when I left. You know how she likes the Vodka. She reeked of the stuff when I spoke to her. She was drunk, that can be the only explanation to what happened to her. I'm so sorry, James.' he said, trying hard to be genuine in his sentiments.

'If I find out you have had anything to do with this, Fox, I'll slit you from ear to ear.' The two men stared menacingly at each other with each of them being seemingly determined not to be the first to break away.

'Who's going to look after, Brett? Neither you or I can because of this bloody mess we are in.' said Jimmy Melia seeing it as an appropriate item of concern to break the tense deadlock going on in the front of the car.

'He'll be looked after by Becky's parents, it won't be for too long. Becky's a tough old bird; she'll get over this no trouble.'

'You do understand the family is fucked now don't you, James? You'll spend years in jail and I will most likely see my days out there. I should have left all well alone with McCoy. I suppose he was only doing his job after all,' bemoaned Jimmy Melia slumping back into the rear passenger seat.

'Well, it's all too fucking late now. What's done is done. Our best hope is that we can make a bundle on the dog fight tomorrow night so we can get out of this shit hole country for a long while. You still all right to collect the dog today, Damien?'

Fox really wanted to say, 'Fuck you, the deals off, you psycho!' However, he thought better of it.

While he tried to stem the slow seeping blood from his nicked throat Fox reaffirmed the "fixed" imported champion American pit bull terrier dog was to be collected from a fellow blood sport enthusiast who'd demanded and received £4,000 up front for its services. This large sum was close to the last Melia had at his disposal after he'd kept cash back for placing bets at the bloodsport meeting. This was to be the last roll of the dice to try and make up his recent large betting losses.

Fox climbed into the driver's seat of the Ford Transit relieved to be free from James Melia's increasingly unstable and irrational presence. Before starting up his own vehicle he watched the black Audi leave the pub car park to make a journey in the direction of Bladdington golf club where Jimmy Melia would hide himself away in the course steward's seldom used living accommodation annexe.

Before turning the ignition key he cast his eye over the lightly blood-stained handkerchief he had been holding over the stinging razor cut. After stuffing the stained cloth into his jeans pocket not only did he notice his hands were trembling but his mind seemed to be locked in to replaying the terrifying moments experienced during the knife incident. Melia's father he now remembered as seeing, was similarly shocked by the serious altercation played out in the front passenger seats. From the safe haven of the van, he conjectured what the likely outcome might have been if he'd told Melia his wife had let the cat out of the bag and it was him who was the cause for her to be critically ill in hospital bleeding from the brain. So, rather than having the honed flick knife purposely held to nick the skin of his throat, James Melia would have executed a single swift move designed to inflict a much deeper and harder cut to slice through the throat cartilage to then separate the windpipe from its near attachment to the back of the tongue. He imagined his crumpled body lying on the pot holed car park being drained of blood. The elderly couple he'd seen earlier would have to experience the horror of discovering his brutally discarded remains. Damien Fox shuddered at the thoughts as he pulled from the pub exit and onto his next destination; his brother's house some sixty miles away from Bladdington.

Chapter Forty-Eight

It had been on Damien Fox's suggestion to James Melia that he should approach his older sibling to secure the services of a particular dog which was listed in the banned breeds contained in the Dangerous Dogs Act of 1991. Fox had planned to use the four dogs he kept caged in the backyard of his terraced house for baiting before the main event was to start. This meant the poor souls would at best die quickly from a snapped neck. At worse their worn bodies would be mercilessly torn to pieces over a prolonged period by stronger more savage animals. The RSPCA, if only they knew it, did the four animals a big favour by saving them for a much worse fate.

Before the 'pedigree' brindle dog in Justin Fox's illegal ownership had arrived in England, it had first been smuggled out of America on a cargo boat bound for Northern Ireland. The animal was destined to arrive at one of the small ports dotted along the west coast by "dog men" attached to a criminal group having connections with the once notorious "Farmer Boys"; an organisation which was found to be a major supplier of dangerous dog breeds, especially American pit bull terriers, to the British mainland.

It was usual that the dog would arrive into Northern Ireland already "conditioned". However, if the animal had been temporarily spared the unrelenting cruel beatings along with barbaric body building techniques designed to build up the muscular strength in both shoulders and jaws, to be then finally goaded into ripping apart lesser animals such as, fight-weary injured weakened pit bulls, smaller breed dogs, rabbits and even cats, the task would be gleefully undertaken by those who positively enjoyed and understood what needed to be done to turn these gentle animals into psycho killers. Some Irish sadistic dog men even used badgers, but most wisely avoided these shy protective creatures due to its ability to more than look after itself by inflicting deep puncture wounds with its fang teeth and long scalpel sharp claws used to shred fur and flesh and more than anything else, the reputation for fighting for its life to the bitter end.

Next, the animal would be taken across the border and into Southern Ireland to avoid the stricter animal checking and export controls in the north. Most pit bulls end their long journey to the British mainland by passing through Dublin, eventually landing in a secluded port to be welcomed by either their new owner or a well-paid middleman.

Great fortunes can be paid for these animals, some dogs descended from celebrated champions, can bring up to £60,000 and even higher.

The dog Damien Fox was about to collect from his city banker brother, had been sourced at a price of £20,000. In the eyes of his envious middle to upper class bloodsport pals, Justin Fox should justifiably feel proud of his recently acquired pit bull's success having chalked up seven kills in its last ten fights. The dog, just as importantly, was also making him money, lots of it.

Justin Fox had taken a call from his brother Damien where he had explained the police had taken away his own four dogs and in so doing he would miss out in taking part in the meeting in a couple of days' time. The intelligent successful and wealthy Justin Fox had for some reason harboured a certain irrational guilt when it came to his younger "loser" brother. He'd gladly helped him out in the past, but on this occasion his younger brother's pleadings needed more consideration due to the unexpected nature of his request. After a ten minute discussion, peppered with weak promises and unconvincing assurances, a figure was agreed to be paid upfront for the services of the dog alongside a caveat which ensured he'd receive twenty per cent of any winnings.

A call then to James Melia resulted in the deal being rubber stamped.

Chapter Forty-Nine

Star spotted Cooper and Grey holding filled plates nearing him as he waded through chips, beans, sausage and eggs in the police canteen. Now sitting opposite to the senior officer, Grey unwrapped the cling film covering a bed of salad leaves sprinkled with shredded carrots and beetroot, with a roll of Parma ham skewered with a cocktail stick being the final accompaniment to her choice of lunchtime meal. Cooper, on the other hand, had gone for two large farmhouse white baps filled to bursting with bacon and runny fried eggs.

'You two okay?' enquired Starr while stuffing a fork, speared through four large hand cut chips, into his mouth.

'I'm fine,' said Grey while picking up a single strand of shredded carrot with her index finger and thumb, 'but Max took another fall, didn't you?'

'Yeah, I'm all right though. I'm just thankful that nutter didn't get it into his head to use that baseball bat on us.'

'Well you won't win the pretty boy of the year award by the way you look now, so I suppose it wouldn't have made much difference to your chances if he had actually set about you, Max,' teased Starr.

'Very funny, Sir, not!' answered Cooper while taking a larger than anticipated bite from the bap which caused the egg yolk to burst and then run down from his face and onto his shirt.

Starr ignored his junior's table mishap and while he was watching Cooper clearing the sticky mess from his face and clothing reported in more detail what he'd gathered from forensics regarding James Melia's apparent involvement in Flo Jackson's death. He also mentioned Barry Sproston's unexpected attendance at the station.

Cooper and Grey listened intently to their superior's report and when he'd finished they didn't trouble him with any profound questioning as they were keen to give a graphic account of what had gone on during their unannounced calls at both Becky and Jimmy Melia's addresses.

One of Starr's female admirers employed in the canteen deposited three steaming mugs of tea on the trestle size table just at the point where he was about to suggest a course of action for the illegal pit bull meeting planned for the following day.

'Thank you, Ann, that's very kind of you.' said Starr looking up at the middle aged woman's smiling features.

'If there is anything else you would like DCI Starr, you only need to ask.' she offered with a suggestive wink.

The woman then proceeded to gather up the used plates and placing them on the same serving tray used to carry the mugs of tea.

'Thank you, Ann,' said Starr.

'My pleasure DCI Starr,' she replied with yet another wink. Cooper and Grey were both bursting to laugh out loud at the expense of Starr's obvious embarrassment.

'All right, that's enough. I can't help it that I'm a babe magnet to some of the more mature woman in this place,' he said to the openly giggling young detectives.

'Right, let's get down to serious business.' Starr was keen to put some flesh on the bones of the plan he'd concocted.

During the background noises created by the hustle and bustle of the busy canteen the three leading detectives scribbled down notes on how they expected to organise personnel and other resources for the pending night time operation. An understanding that is wasn't feasible for the stretched police resources to make many arrests beyond that of their primary target was first established but consideration was given to how many uniform officers should be present to provide a suitable level of presence and muscle if things kicked off. Cooper's idea that the RSPCA be on alert to remove the banned breeds from their sadistic owners was included together with the covert use of cameras to record those characters in attendance from across all sections of society who take a perverse pleasure in this so called sport.

Around two o'clock, Starr rose from his seat at the canteen table clutching a flow diagram neatly drawn by Grey outlining each of their specific roles and those of other key players to be executed during the actual operation. She had also made a note of other important operational aspects such as crucial timings when action was to be taken, manpower numbers, type of vehicles to be commandeered and the involvement of other external agencies.

First, Starr would have to run the plan pass the station chief superintendent, Richard Palfreyman and in the meantime, Cooper and Grey would haul Becky Melia in for further questioning.

The unmarked police car drew up outside the rented home for the two detectives to then observe small groups of people looking about as though something bad had recently happened. It would be a neighbour, who had been disturbed from reading a daily paper by the sound of a blaring siren, who went on to tell the plain clothed officers he later watched the ambulance leave having taken away, what looked to him, to be a female adult lain on a stretcher accompanied by a young boy in floods of tears.

A visit then to Bladdington hospital confirmed the admitted patient to be Becky Melia with the extent of her serious cranial injuries requiring a bed in the intensive care ward.

The life support machine keeping her alive was being closely monitored by the medical staff, with Beck Melia's elderly parents and distraught son anxiously looking on for any improving signs in her condition.

The doctor who was responsible for issuing medical care instructions to the specialist trained nurses also alerted Cooper and Grey about his concerns for Becky Melia after he had overheard them saying who they were at the ICU ward's reception desk.

He had ushered them into his office situated behind the reception desk to then starkly reveal that the readings taken from the monitors hooked up to Mrs Melia gave an early indication she was unlikely to recover from the major brain trauma. There was nothing that they could do for her at this stage other than to wait and hope. However, he did go on to express his concerns about the obvious presence of red marks and deep bruising across the right cheek and jaw, which he understood were probably caused by a sharp blow of the hand. This alone gave him justifiable reason to believe the critically ill patient had been subject to a violent assault prior to the injury to the back of the head.

Later that evening, Becky Melia succumbed to a fatal heart attack brought on by uncontrollable electrical impulses in her brain being able to by-pass the sedating effects of the opiate based medication being pumped into her by an intravenous drip in her neck. The following day, an autopsy report provided police forensics with a DNA sample of torn skin found trapped between her two front incisor teeth. Suspecting the woman might have been a victim of a serious crime a senior pathologist had taken the additional precaution to carefully swab the facial wounds. Both samples were to be subject to DNA analysis and then compared against the national criminal records kept by the police.

Damien Fox did not know it yet, but his days of freedom were swiftly coming to an end for a long time. The conviction for manslaughter would attract a fifteen year minimum sentence to the delight of Rebecca Melia's heartbroken parents and her son, Brett.

Chapter Fifty

Barry Sproston was towards the back of a long queue waiting to pay his petrol bill at a mini-mart fuel station. His mind was pre-occupied in thinking about what had gone on between himself and the DCI while patiently shuffling along until finally it was his turn to slide his card into the credit card reader and tap in his four secret pin numbers. The reason for the long line of agitated paying customers was due to a tall raven haired man in his mid-thirties settling his fuel bill and paying additionally for the bulging bag of groceries he'd quickly picked from the mini-mart shelves. Sproston did not notice the man turn from the pay station and then to head back to his car on the station forecourt. He was only drawn to his presence when the man's swinging plastic bag struck Sproston on his knee cap as he clumsily attempted to squeeze along the narrow lane of paying customers.

'Sorry mate,' said the man.

Both the impact of the hard rim edge of a tin of beans contained in the oscillating disposable bag and the sound of the offender's voice startle Sproston away from his immediate troubled thoughts. A look of shock then formed across both of their faces as they individually recognised each other for very different distinct reasons. Those waiting to pay for their fuel who had taken the time to study the individual male features, would say they looked like twins at first glance.

'Hey, your James Melia, aren't you?' said Sproston, his voiced pitched higher and louder than it would be in normal conversation.

The man did not reply but continued to make his hurried exit from the pay station.

Convinced he was the same person who went by the name he had inadvertently called out, Sproston left his place in the queue to pursue the dashing figure through the automatic sliding doors.

'Hey, stop. I know you are James Melia,' called Sproston as he continued to stride with purpose towards the man who'd stopped by this time to search his pockets for the keyless ignition card.

'Fuck off mate, if you know what is good for you.' he warned turning to his accuser.

'No I won't fuck off. I'm Barry Sproston and of course you will know this won't you Melia? Because it was you who stole my identity so you could trick a poor gullible woman into sending you money. How could you be so damn heartless?'

Sproston then reached into his pocket to pull out his mobile phone and start to tap the number pads.

'What the fuck do you think you are doing?' questioned Melia.

'Ringing for the police. What do you think I'm doing? I'm not about to let you just slip away after all the agony you caused me and my family.'

Melia then made a rush for Sproston to get at the mobile phone. In the meantime, Jimmy Melia had got out from the car to stand on the oil stained forecourt taking in the spectacle of his son grappling with another man sharing the same uncanny likeness.

In the animated commotion the phone slipped out of Sproston's grasp to fall close to Melia's feet who then instinctively stamped down hard to crush the mobile between his heel and the concrete laid surface, he then kicked out to scatter the broken parts across the garage forecourt.

'How are you going to tell the police now, you fucking loser?' mockingly sneered Melia.

'I'll not let you leave here.' Sproston replied having taken up a defiant stance with both fists clenched.

'That's very fucking funny, go on, you just try and stop me!' laughed Melia. He then turned to step back to his car wearing a dark menacing expression.

'Don't you dare do what I think you are going to do, James?'

Sproston turned his attention to the balding greying man who he vaguely noticed get out from the car just as Melia made a lunge for him.

'Just shut the fuck up Dad and get back in the fucking car,' demanded his son gesticulating with his right hand to the passenger seat.

Sproston let out a gasp on hearing that James Melia had innocently let slip that this person was likely to be his father.

'I don't believe it. Your Jimmy Melia aren't you?' pressed Sproston.

'What is it to you if I am?' he answered cagily.

'It's not everyday someone finds out who their father is, after thirty-five years of not knowing, and of all places, on a petrol forecourt.' said Sproston in disbelief.

'What the hell are you talking about, you're not my son?' answered Jimmy Melia while being unable to draw himself from thinking there was a remarkable familiarity about this man who was claiming he was his father.

'Do you remember Patricia Sproston? I know it's a long time ago; she was only seventeen when you knew her. She was my mother. I have been told your father paid for her to have an abortion when he found out you had made her pregnant. Well she didn't go ahead with the abortion, she kept the money to herself and when I was born she abandoned me and it was my gran who raised me, but you wouldn't know this.'

Jimmy Melia's face stiffened on hearing a familiar name from his untamed past used by the man to add credence to his claim.

He remembered being very fond of Patricia Sproston. Yes he'd had sex with her on a few occasions but was unaware she had become pregnant. She or most likely, someone from her large family, had told his father in the hopes of making some financial gain from the potentially shaming situation. Jimmy Melia was distracted from the mental images of both his own father he'd ashamedly taken unfair advantage of, and those of the pretty girl he'd once held tight in his grasp, by his son making yet another forceful demand for him to get back in to the car.

'Fucking get in the car dad, or I'll drag you in myself,' he had shouted.

Sproston could see clearly that his revelations had somewhat hit home and had captured the old man's attention. He decided to press on further.

'So by my reckoning that makes you my father, he is my half-brother,' he said pointing in the direction of James Melia. 'And it was your grandson who died of leukaemia in Florida.'

'Don't believe it Dad; he's fucking with your head.' Melia had had enough of this charade and pulled the driver's door wide open to reach into the side glove compartment to retrieve the flick knife.

Clutching the weapon, he stepped over to his alleged half-brother with the same audible click heard earlier in the day alerting Jimmy Melia to his senses.

'He's got a knife!' a voice screamed from someone in the watching crowd.

'Put that knife away James, don't you dare think about using it or I will kill you with my bare hands. By God I swear I will!'

His father's murderous threat stopped James Melia in his tracks with the opened out knife blade only inches away from Sproston's abdomen.

Witnesses to this unrehearsed surreal event quickly scattered desperate not to become embroiled in the potentially fatal stand-off. Someone amongst the dispersing group made a 999 call and then had the balls to shout out to Barry Sproston the police were on their way.

In spite of hearing the warning call, Melia thought it necessary for him to scrutinise Sproston's features while subconsciously securing the menacing presence of the flick knife back into its closed position. Sproston felt a margin of fear leave his tense body on seeing Melia swiftly turn and then get into the car. After he wisely stepped to one side to watch the driver's swift getaway from the garage forecourt, he remained where he stood his mind apparently struggling to take in the full ramifications of what had gone on and, even more, what a worse fate could have befallen him during those crucial three minutes.

He had long paid for his fuel and left the station before the law arrived in the guise of a single car containing two female police officers and a male community bobby. Sproston wasn't prepared to allow himself to be subject to another stressful police interview.

The drive over to the course steward's house at the golf course gave Jimmy Melia an opportunity to off load large chunks of guilt he'd carried from his teenage years. James Melia listened to the long list of regrets his father had allowed to fester in his soul. When James had pressed about what was said, in all places, on a petrol forecourt, his father confessed he wasn't in a position to disprove what Sproston had said, especially because he did admit to having many casual relationships and Patricia Sproston was one of them and after all, no one could deny there was a distinct resemblance between Sproston and what he hitherto, understood to be his only son.

'I wish I had never seen that photograph of Sproston with his family in the *Moulton Sentinel* or even more, never have bought that bloody paper. It was only because you shared very similar looks to him and the fact it was reported McCoy was to get a big pay off, that all of this mess we are in came about. How I wish I could turn the clock back. All those wasted years wanting revenge has screwed my head up and what is even much worse, I've ended up destroying my own family.' lamented Jimmy Melia while looking out of the passenger side window watching the green country road hedgerows flit past.

James Melia was prevented from saying how he too regretted being drawn in his father's lust for revenge, even if he was willing to gladly accept he and his family were to be the main benefactors from any ill-gotten gains, by the sound of his mobile ring tone.

The call from his distraught son, Brett, informed him through a broken dialogue peppered with sobs and loud sniffles, that his mother was on a life support machine and she didn't look good. He also said his gran and granddad looked worried too. The fact that he went on to mention two plain clothed police officers had arrived at the ward put an end to any ideas about seeing his wife.

Even if she makes a full recovery, the prospect of having to watch and feel his life decay behind bars for countless years, made him more determined he'd have to abandon his family to escape abroad. But to do this, he'd first have to make enough money to realise his plan, at the pit bull meeting the following night.

Chapter Fifty-One

'In my opinion I think it would be wise to insist Mansfield police take over the reins along with the expense that goes with carrying out such an operation. The station is already close to the red; this bloody government with all their austerity cuts have done us no favours at all.'

Richard Palfreyman had listened passively to his senior detective's update concerning the progress made in tracking down the main perpetrator responsible for the fraud and the fact that the same person was now wanted for the murder of an elderly woman. Palfreyman had tossed the plan of execution drawn up by Grey in the police canteen on to his uncluttered desk top after only giving it a cursory glance. His disdainful actions hadn't gone unnoticed by Starr.

'So that's it, then is it? Pass it on the Mansfield station. What if they turn round to say they too have no money to mount an operation? We might as well say to James Melia you're off the hook mate, and by the way you can keep the money and I'm sure Mrs Jackson's relatives will be pleased to learn the British police have shown such remarkable compassion to her killer when they finally arrive from Australia,' asserted Starr in a vexatious manner.

'Don't be so damn facetious, Dick.' answered Palfreyman sharply. 'I would expect one of my senior detectives to understand resources are stretched, and by the look of your plan a substantial amount of uniform and senior officer overtime will have to come out of the station's coffers.'

'Look,' said Starr impatiently, 'I have the phone number of the guy who sent a message to the driver of the car who'd by the way, tried his best to kill McCoy on the new by-pass. Should I see if he can alter his arrangements from a night time slot to a day time meet. Whether that will meet his approval, we'll just have to wait and see.'

The deliberate sarcastic offer was met by Palfreyman silently glaring back at him and Starr doing likewise in the opposite direction.

As usual when these two totally polar opposite personalities met, they always have to go through a period of locking horns, with Palfreyman being the one who usually gave way.

'I'll get on to the Chief Super at Mansfield so we can share the cost. By the way how is DS Cooper, his face looked nasty last time I saw him?' said Palfreyman trying to steer the discussion away from the main purpose of why Starr had needed to see him.

'He's fine, just the normal stuff most coppers have had to endure when coming up through the ranks. He'll get over it.' Starr found it necessary to include a barb in his reply to his superior concerning the young DS's welfare, which in turn, hadn't gone unnoticed by the increasingly fidgety figure sitting behind the desk.

'We have to take more care of our up and coming officers, DCI Starr. I'm sure with a different approach, the situation could have been avoided. The days when police operated in a gung ho fashion have thankfully been assigned to the past and I believe this is because the force has recruited and trained a more intelligent breed of senior officer and we are reaping the benefits of seeing fewer incidents where there is an exchange of violence between the police and criminals.' Starr had expected such a typical bigoted observation and therefore saw no good reason to rise to the bait. He instead elected to remain in his relaxed standing position with his attention drawn to looking at the photographs of past officers fixed on the wall behind the Super's head.

'I have also noted from your plan you intend for DS Cooper to have a prominent role in the operation. Whose decision was this? It seems to me it was made by someone who had no consideration at all for his well being. Hasn't this man already been through enough?' quizzed Palfreyman.

Starr switched his gaze from the framed images to refocus his attention on the seated questioner.

'It was DS Cooper's decision, Sir.'

'Well, I think it is your job to look for someone else to step in. I think this young man has already performed beyond the call of duty.'

'What about you stepping in Sir? If things kick off you will be able to demonstrate to us all how to deal with someone who is about to send their foot into your face or holding a gun to your head or knife at your gut.'

Palfreyman ignored the inference to then toss the flow diagram across the table in Starr's direction.

'I'll get on to Mansefield to commandeer a few of their officers. Just be mindful to keep me informed on any developments. That will be all DCI Starr.' Palfreyman signalled any further dialogue was finished by picking up his gold nib fountain pen to resume scribbling comments on letters needing his attention.

When Starr had gone from his office, Palfreyman cast his pen to one side, lent his head forward to then gently caress both of his temples with his fingertips. Five minutes or so later he was scan reading over a letter from a disgruntled member of the public having first consoled himself Starr didn't have too long before he was due to retire. That would be one big thorn he would be glad to have been removed from his side.

Chapter Fifty-Two

Grey and Cooper returned to the station to report on Becky Melia's situation.

'The doctor suspects Becky Melia's potentially fatal injuries are as a direct result of a serious physical assault. I wouldn't at all be surprised to learn that James Melia had something to do with this. If he can strangle old women with his bare hands and enjoy watching dogs tearing each other apart, then in my opinion, there is no telling what he and his ilk are capable of,' said Cooper.

'Quite,' agreed Starr.

Starr went on to report on the essential snippets of conversation he'd had with the station's chief superintendent and was now solely waiting on a response from him. Starr thought it expedient not mention the tension that had arisen between the two walruses when touching on the circumstances which had resulted in Cooper's injuries.

Until Palfreyman got back to them on the manning level request, Starr suggested they polished up the pencil drawn plan alongside familiarising themselves with the outer environs surrounding Croft Farm buildings from images provided by Google earth complimented by reminiscences from Cooper's teenage years when he was both a trespasser and a part-time garden nursery worker.

The two young DSs were pleased to be dismissed at a reasonable hour, Starr on the other hand, felt somewhat compelled to call in on Bruce McCoy to provide him with an update on their progress. He was as yet, undecided if he should quiz him on the visit McCoy had made to Jimmy Melia's home the very evening he was involved in the fatal car crash. Similarly, Jimmy Melia's strong accusation's he'd been assaulted by his old adversary was another issue which would need to be broached if there was to be a formal complaint. Starr thought this unlikely to happen when he considered Jimmy Melia had been prevented from being brought in for questioning by the baseball bat wielding intervention of his son.

Within the hour Starr had concluded his business with little of the deep probing he'd half expected from the retired DI. A shake of the hands allowed Starr to leave the McCoy's Victorian built home and on to his next destination, which was to be a pub carvery to enjoy a meal in his own company.

While he was wading through the piled high plate of three meats and veg, his mind had been fixed on the image he'd seen of Sally McCoy sitting at the kitchen table with her wide eyes transfixed on an imagined object in front of her. His welcome greeting to her had received no response, which McCoy too had not failed to notice as he ushered him through to the lounge to spare himself further embarrassment of his wife's continued slide into the abyss.

It was with great personal sadness for McCoy to admit the programme of medication and therapy Sally had agreed to undertake was having no effect. In fact, he later confided to his trusted pal, she had recently become worse, not better.

Chapter Fifty-Three

Seven thirty the following morning Starr opened up his email account to note a message from Palfreyman. Starr read that the super had gone to great lengths to secure the services of two senior detectives, whose names were familiar to him, and four uniformed constables to arrive at the station for twelve noon. A manned vehicle fitted with two covert HD cameras, as requested, was available to them due to there being no public event organised for that evening. The message finished with the usual caveat: 'Please keep me informed!' with no mention of hoped success in the operation.

Starr was not that stupid as to be totally ignorant of the station's superintendent's obvious agenda. If the operation went well Palfreyman would receive brownie points to support his ambition to become the County Commissioner. On the other hand, if it turned out to be a catastrophe, then he'd solely blame Starr for devising a weak strategic plan containing obvious operational shortcomings. His competence to lead effectively would then come into question, followed by an offer of early retirement, and if the stretched coffers allow, a sweetener in the form of an enhanced redundancy lump.

During the day Starr and his team of plain and uniformed officers met up with a similar contingent sent from Mansefield Station. Some might have argued the operation should have been led by the Bladdington's near neighbour police force in light of the fact the murder of Mrs Jackson happened in their jurisdiction. However, evidence of James Melia and possibly his father being involved in serious fraud coupled with the likelihood one or both of them were the architects behind the fatal car chase which failed to ram a potential witness into a concrete bridge, was enough for Mansefield's DI, Bob Stableford, not to become too precious about playing second fiddle.

Similarly, Bladdington police hadn't worked totally alone, they had been conscious to remain in constant contact with their senior leading officer throughout, and now faced with a detailed plan of attack, Bob Stableford and DI Geoff Fairhurst were happy to go along with what had been drawn up in their absence.

The late afternoon merged into early evening, this was the time for Starr to call together in the main incident room those who had been allocated some part to play at Croft Farm.

Superintendent Richard Palfreyman was in attendance having earlier accepted Starr's invitation to be part of the final briefing. The presentation was shared by the five senior detectives, very much like the breakfast news presenters where they take it in turns to read for the auto cue camera. An IT literate uniform officer was in charge of the hand held blipper to move on the individual PowerPoint slides when given a nod by that particular presenter for the content to be shown on the wall mounted large flat screen TV.

'Any questions?' asked Bob Stableford at the end of the slick presentation. Starr looked around searching the different facial expressions filling the makeshift seating area.

None gave him concern other than that of the superintendent.

Palfreyman really felt the need to ask the question: 'What if James Melia doesn't turn up? What will you do then? How will you explain the waste of finite police resources?' but thought better of it. He needed the operation to be successful but a little imp was prodding its hot trident into him hoping there would be some cock up he could blame Starr for.

'I wish you all every success this evening, I cannot help but be impressed with the effort and detail put into the forward planning of the operation. All we need now is a bit of luck and this time tomorrow we will have our suspects locked up.' Palfreyman then rose to his feet, gave departing nods around the room before disappearing to an area of the station where he felt less threatened and more comfortable.

The battered looking surveillance van was positioned in a dark lay-by close to the single track country lane leading to Croft Farm. Inside were two trained uniformed officers operating a vehicle registration reader which was connected to a secure internet connection to the DVLA in Swansea. The system linked into a data bank which would give access to the facial images shown on driving licence cards issued since replacing the old paper style, and of course, the car owner's insurance and MOT details.

The reader was kept fully occupied recording each of the wide range of cars, vans and 4x4s that took the turning into the lane. A full analysis of those dozens of people who had gladly taken up the invitation to both witness and take part in the barbaric blood sport event was planned for the following morning. A decision on whether this was to result in a wide sweep of arrests hadn't yet been made due to the strong correlation between those high and influential in society that are often drawn like moths to a flame to such an event.

Other vehicles essential to the operation were either placed on standby a short distance away from the event or had joined in the steady flow of traffic along the usually quiet lane.

Towards the end of the lane a queue had backed up due to each car being stopped in turn by a team of thuggish looking males, with two of them having Alsatian dogs chained to their tattooed hands to add a touch of fear to their already threatening presence. Satisfied the occupants of the vehicle were bona fide guests they were waved over to a dimly lit large concrete turning space used by reversing articulated trucks bringing in young plants mostly from Belgium and Holland, to take up an allocated parking space.

'I've not seen you three before,' queried a local accented shaven-headed male wearing diamond ear studs with a flowing blue sweep of a tattoo penned into the side of his bulging neck.

'It's our first time, we were asked if we wanted to come along by Davy O'Flynn, God bless his soul. My friends in the back are pals of James Melia and Damien Fox, grand lads they are as well. We hope to see a great spectacle tonight, too right, isn't that so boys?' DI Geoff Fairhurst's attempt at a Northern

Irish accent certainly seemed convincing to Cooper and Dale, who had togged themselves up in the style of gear as not to appear to be out of place from that worn by the majority seen getting out from their parked vehicles.

'Yep, too right, Martin. Hope it's up to what we see in Ireland,' replied Dale in a similar Irish brogue.

Cooper sat back in the murky shade of the rear passenger seat wearing dark glasses with a green waxed fisherman's cap pulled down close to his eyebrows. The bald man gave him a hard stare but any thoughts or intentions he had in mind at that time were curtailed with a couple of impatient hoots from a late registered Range Rover waiting behind. With a wave of his one free hand he directed the car over to the temporary parking area.

The sound of car doors being slammed closed joined in with the same mechanical noises made by the three covert police officers exiting their vehicle.

'Well, that's stage one done. I don't think he suspected anything untoward, and by the way, Geoff, that was a convincing impression you gave there.'

'Thanks,' said DI Fairhurst as the men walked in a huddle following the movement of other attendees.

'What about me? Didn't you think mine was good?' whispered Stephen Dale.

'Not bad,' replied Cooper.

A shadow cast pathway led the trio to a large airplane size hanger. The frenetic sounds of dogs barking accompanied by wild cheers became more pronounced as they neared a short excitable queue before being allowed to enter inside the building through a steel clad side door manned by two more bone headed looking characters.

Moving from the dark of the night and into the bright light being emitted from the ceiling mounted high wattage halogen lamps caused each of the visitors to readjust their focus before being able to take in their new surroundings.

'By Jesus,' whispered Geoff Fairhurst, 'there must be at least two hundred here all ready and there are still people coming in. Look over there,' he hissed before nodding his head in the direction he wanted his partners to look, 'there are even kids here, what kind of parents are these people?'

'Clearly the type who want their children to become anaesthetised to the public's reaction to blood sports. You know what they say, "start 'em young".' said Cooper as he took in the sight of three temporary arenas constructed from tightly packed rectangular straw bales. Trail lines of people were making their way to join in the ever expanding crowd surrounding each of the three straw perimeters.

'Can you see Melia, or Fox come to that?' asked Dale through the side of his mouth. The PC was not familiar with either of the two characters except when he'd tried to memorise their appearance from the mug shots pinned up in the incident room.

Being careful not to draw attention to them, each of the detectives scanned the faces of those from all different walks of society as they slowly strolled over to one of the arenas which had the fewest number of supporters gathered around its edge.

'Can't see either of them yet. They'll be here. I have no doubts about that,' Cooper said quietly.

Their appearance at the ring coincided with a "warm up" show before the actual combat later commenced between two heavily betted on demented animals.

Stood inside the ring was a "dog man" holding on to a struggling large white pet rabbit. A broad smile caused the dark deep wrinkled skin to stretch across his protruding sharp cheek bones as he brimmed in anticipation of the entertainment he was about to provide for the restless crowd.

The pit bull could be seen to be made excitable as the dog man teased the animal by jerking the paws of the firmly held petrified albino rabbit out of reach of the animal's snapping jaws each time it bounded up at his master. Soon the cruel baiting would come to an end to then signal the start of a short period of intense terror now awaiting the stolen and once much loved, family pet.

The grinning dog man kept a tight hold of the snapping, barking frothy jawed prized pit bull while he allowed the white rabbit to drop from his grasp to bound to freedom over the straw covered concreted surface arena to the farthest point away from danger. Some in the crowd laughed loudly as the petrified rabbit clawed desperately to scale the vertical straw walls. Alas, its efforts were doomed to fail and there was to be no escape. Amidst the urging cheers and animated gestures coming from the blood lust gathering the dog man required little encouragement to let loose the rabbit's nemesis.

A good display from his pit bull was useful in persuading punters to chance large bets on it when the bouts began. The dog man wasn't about to be disappointed.

The pent up animal bolted forward after being released from his master with the static rabbit fixed firmly in its sights. A swift dart to the right by the terrified rabbit saw the raging pit bull crash headlong into the straw bale to completely miss its target. The defecating albino scurried to the opposite side of the ring in a vain pursuit to find a safe haven. A mixture of laughter that had initially greeted the pit bull's failed charge was soon replaced by an increased tension by some in the baying crowd to eager to witness the chased animal being torn to shreds.

Before the pit bull was able to establish where the white creature had escaped to, it caught sight of a familiar horse crop held aloft by its master. His threatening stance provoked raw memories of the excruciating pain endured during the times the thrashing crop raised lines of angry weal marks across its already badly scarred body.

The increased level of noise coming from the tightly packed throng gathered round the makeshift ring of bailed straw, coupled with the twitching presence of the horse crop, the once gentle animal needed no more encouragement to deliver its master's wishes as he bolted at speed towards the trembling creature now fixed in its sights.

The wide jaws clamped on to the rabbit's spine causing the petrified animal to cry out in pain. A burst of cheers greeted the pit bull's success and continued unabated while the white fur object was savagely torn to bloodied pieces with specks of warm blood and fur baptising sections of the ecstatic crowd until there was little to discern from the gory lump being scooped up from off the arena floor by the proud dog man that this was once one of God's creatures.

The three undercover detectives turned away from the shocking spectacle unable to stomach the sight of the mean looking dog man avidly praising and roughly stroking the victorious animal who'd given a performance he hoped would make him a lot of money on the night.

This "warming up" of the dogs continued in the same bloodied arena with different dog men keen to put on their own special spectacle, and to the burgeoning crowds delight, this scene was replicated in the other two straw baled rings. The start of this part of the evening's entertainment signalled the end to the lives of many defenceless creatures, some of which would be old, infirm, or disabled pit bulls no longer able to earn their keep, but the majority of the cowering animals seen secured in wire mesh cages were those which had either been picked up off the street, stolen from garden hutches, trapped or snared in woods and hedgerows or just simply acquired from cruel people familiar to the dog men.

An announcement made over a loud hailer that bouts were to commence in thirty minutes and a reminder to place bets with the minimum stake set at £100 was met with an increase level of excitable chatter in the large open warehouse.

'This is absolutely mad; I've seen all I can stomach. Let's get all the units in and arrest the lot of them, the scummy bastards!' said Dale hardly being able to contain his temper.

Cooper and Fairhurst undoubtedly shared his disgust after witnessing the same depths of depravity many understood to have been left back in the Roman times.

'We don't have the manpower for one, and if we did arrest them all, the judges, who are most likely amongst this crazy crowd, would let them off with a slap on the wrist,' answered Fairhurst after being careful to check others around were not listening into their conversation.

'Look, let's not lose sight of our objective tonight, we need to have James Melia in police custody, or this whole operation will have been a waste of time. I suggest we split up and see if we can find his whereabouts. If necessary, we can keep in contact by our mobiles; if you look around there are loads of people on their phones so we shouldn't draw attention to ourselves.'

No more was said after Cooper's suggestion. The three officers went their different ways in search of the night's objective.

The brindle American pit bull terrier, which had been acquired at great expense from Damien Fox's brother, gave some indication of its value when it made short work of a limping adult male fox. Evidence from the kill dyed its scarred mean hard features which, to the handler's delight, served to add to its menace. Eager onlookers goaded the powerful animal to repeat the same level of savagery against a raft of other defenceless caged creatures when it became their turn to be forcibly tipped in to the inescapable arena.

Geoff Fairhurst observed Damien Fox apparently gainfully employed in his work behind the cover of a well-tailored male in the company of a similarly attired woman with two young teenage children seemingly enjoying the late night butchery.

It didn't take long for him to recognise from the photographs seen earlier in the day at Bladdington station, the man stood within the ring was James Melia. An adult black tom cat, still with its flea collar intact, was pitched on the straw covered floor. The animal braced itself in this alien environment unsure of what was to happen next.

Melia loosed the straining animal at the cowering wide eyed feline, the large domesticated pet instinctively darted to the right to chance its escape from the approaching terrifying snorting beast.

In normal circumstances, possessing the genetic prowess to scale walls and high fencing would be enough for the creature to evade capture when faced with the straw barrier stacked three bales high. Sharp, long claws dug deep into the tightly packed stalks for the heavy cat to haul itself up the vertical barrier until the route to freedom was blocked by a tight ring of humanity who were set against their enjoyment being spoiled.

The tom cat momentarily froze being unable to decide what course of action to take amid the high pitched sounds being made by the wall of frantic strange human faces. A sharp blow delivered by an onlooker's hand sent the cat flying back into the ring, and before it was able to recover from the shock of finding itself back in the blood splattered arena the animal suffered the same terrible death as those that went before it to the rapturous approval of the watching audience.

'This place is like Hades!' considered Fairhurst with the other two officers as he turned away from watching Melia, in celebratory fashion, holding aloft the animal's innards hanging and dripping from its shredded pelt such as a Roman gladiator would with the head of a slave. After the applause died down, Fox was ready with yet another wretched creature to slake the crowd's insatiable thirst for blood and gore.

'I'll fill Starr and Stableford in on what is happening here,' said Fairhurst. He was the most senior so he accepted it was his responsibility to call in with a report.

'Be careful, Geoff,' warned Cooper. They watched Fairhurst leave the building after he'd assured a dark eyed, ginger goateed security guard standing at the official entrance that he needed to go for a slash.

He retraced the dimly lit path that led to the makeshift car park looking for a suitable place to make the call. This he found to be was down a dark little used path laid between two of the original farm buildings.

'Geoff here, can't be long. Melia and Fox are here. Place teeming, even kids are here, can you believe it. Too risky to make arrest right now; need to leave it until most of the public have left. Some heavies about, you will need to be quick when we ask you to move in.'

'Okay Geoff, will do. We're ready at this end.' Starr was speaking in to his mobile while sitting with Stableford and Grey in an unmarked car hidden away from view behind a disused petrol station close to the single track lane.

'What the fuck do you think you are doing? I heard every word you said; you're the fucking filth aren't you.'

Fairhurst was just slipping his phone back into his inside pocket when he was forcibly grabbed by the shoulder and propelled round to take in the shadowy outlines of a thug like person who'd previously checked them over before being allowed to enter the main fight arena.

If there was ever a time to keep one's nerve, it was now. Though inwardly shaken by the man's unexpected appearance he was able to calmly respond to the accusations.

'No you must be mistaken my fine friend, I couldn't get a signal in the building, so I had to come outside. I was calling a friend to see if he wanted to put money on James Melia's dog My it does look a grand specimen. I t'ink he has a sure winner there, by Jesus I do.' Fairhurst explained in the Northern Irish accent he'd earlier used to fool the same person.

The shaven hulk maintained a tight grip on the shoulder material of his jacket.

'You're a fucking liar. You're no more Irish than my gran is the fucking Queen. You're coming with me mate.' No sooner had the man finished giving his orders and about to twist his bulked up body around with the intentions to drag his captive away for further interrogation, he was met by an almighty strike to the jaw. The force of the blow twisted and propelled his body to one side and the sound of a loud crack showed that his large head had struck hard against the unforgiving brickwork of the nineteenth century disused shippon.

Fairhurst felt the man's vice like grip on his clothing loosen, his unconscious state could not prevent his twenty stone frame from collapsing slowly to form a slumped heap on the cold moss covered path.

'Are you all right?' a concerned voice whispered from the dark silhouetted figure.

Fairhurst didn't immediately answer as he was trying to focus his sight to make out who the stranger and saviour might be.

'It's me Geoff, Bruce McCoy,' identified the dark figure wearing a long peaked baseball cap.

'Thank God it's you Bruce. What are you doing here?' he said in surprise.

'I'd thought at least you'd thank me for clocking that bastard,' McCoy said in half jest while looking down at the unconscious slow breathing weighty frame.

'Sorry, Bruce. Thanks. I didn't see him coming at all. He heard every word I said. The operation is over if he is able to tell his mates. How did you manage to get in here unnoticed?'

'I'll tell you in minute, Geoff, but first we have to make sure he isn't able to blab to anyone. Give me your scarf,' demanded McCoy with his hand proffered to take the scarf Fairhurst was busily unravelling from around his neck.

With the black scarf McCoy had himself removed, the combination of the two acrylic scarves and the addition of a long lace taken from one of Fairhust's walking boots, the tattooed thug was successfully bound and gagged and then dragged by his coat along the rutted surface without consideration of inflicting further injury to their prisoner, till eventually the men were grateful to roughly dump the heavy load in the dark depths of the old semi-derelict cow shippon. He was marked down to be one of the last to be slung into a police van at the end of the night.

Despite his earlier promises to Starr, Bruce McCoy had no intentions of not being present at the pit bull meeting. He wasn't about to deny his base instincts that justice should prevail, after all he had reasoned, he had sacrificed much of his life to the police service and wasn't about to allow a piece of low life scum to rob him of what was rightly his. He also considered his wife's rapidly deteriorating condition was directly attributable to the stress she suffered since being confronted with the financial loss.

McCoy badly needed to take in the sight of James Melia being finally led away shackled in tightly applied hand cuffs, his face creased and drawn at the prospect of spending years behind bars for murder, fraud and keeping illegal dangerous animals.

McCoy explained to Fairhurst he had crept in undetected by using the cover of the saplings planted in long rows in a large field backing up the site and he had only just hidden himself away in the shadow of one of the many buildings to evade detection by the patrolling security guard, when he saw him suddenly stop in his tracks and then disappear between two buildings and that is when I heard the raised voices. The rest you know.'

The two men quietly approached the hanger sized building and were relieved to find the two male security guards were no longer at the designated entrance door. On stepping into the brightly lit interior, it didn't take too long for Fairhurst to pick out the two bald security guards: one having an obligatory long greasy pony tail only growing from near his nape line and the other a plaited ginger goatee finished with a tassel of ethnically coloured beads woven in at the end. They had obviously decided to move closer to one of the packed fight arenas, each happily puffing away on freshly lit spliffs between joining in with their own shouts of encouragement.

McCoy was seen to yank the peak of his cap further down over his face as the two men split up to take up a position in the four deep crowd surrounding the straw walled killing arena Melia was to use for the loaned pit bull bouts.

Just beyond the brightly illuminated arenas a betting station had been set up, the chosen dress code of the five hard looking vocally animated males appeared to be a mishmash of authentic and cheap replica army wear. Their voices seemed to screech as they battled to be heard against the excited babble of the crowd to chant out the odds for each of the bouts now coming up in quick succession. Wads of banknotes could be seen handed over the rickety trestle tables in exchange for a handwritten chitty recording the dog's name scrawled by hand in black ink alongside the given odds. Gripping the piece of crudely printed paper, punters raced back to one of the straw rings keen to re-join the hedonistic squirming mob.

One punter in particular, who was seen to be betting heavily, was Damien Fox. After each of the frequent trips to the makeshift betting station, his grin appeared to grow wider each time as he stuffed his bountiful winnings into the large pockets sewn to the side of the army fatigue trousers.

Over the hour the number of pit bulls incapable of fighting grew exponentially. It was inevitable the early hard earned triumphs, won mostly at the expense of torn flesh, puncture wounds and a loss of blood, would lead to a weakening of both body and spirit. Defeat was lurking in the midst of victory for the majority of these creatures. What then waited for those been tagged a loser was either a callous beating, or if severely injured, a swift death to put an end to their misery and pain. A sharp pointed knife, thrust by the hand of a dog man into a walnut sized beating heart, was grateful relief for those whose faces had been near ripped off, or gaping gory holes left where an opponent had gripped and then torn away the creature's throat; it's agony prolonged by slow asphyxiation caused through the lungs filling with blood and frothy saliva.

Animals destined to appear in the arena again, either as a competitor or for the warm up sessions, would be those creatures that had suffered non-life threatening lacerations or relatively minor puncture wounds.

Due to the ferocious nature of the combat, only those legendary animals likely born from myth, had ever escaped the ring scot free of injury.

The time eventually arrived when those in attendance were left with one more bout to savour. Some rudely pushed and shoved each other to get a good viewing position around the straw built arena. Amongst the restless crowd were animated young children perched up on the shoulders of willing male parents pleased their little darlings had been successfully indoctrinated in the art of this particular blood sport.

This short respite in the contest presented the opportunity for the three detectives to stealthily come together without drawing any undue attention to themselves.

To any outsider the three men appeared to be no less interested than the others who'd gathered around to enjoy the final battle of power, strength and savagery. However, what those around the three covert officers didn't know was the iPhone each of them were holding and fooling around with weren't all being used for the same purpose of recording the hysteria leading up to the finale. It would be a call from Cooper's phone to DCI Starr that was to put into action the last and vital part of the plan which had been scrutinised time and time again for potential weaknesses. If they had missed or overlooked possible pitfalls, the time was fast approaching where they'd soon find out.

Uniformed police hurriedly set up a road block to prevent anyone in a vehicle leaving the site undetected. While this was happening, two riot specification police vans, each suitably equipped with three muscular tall males and a single female anyone in their right mind would never dream of messing with, quietly trundled down the pitch black country lane in front of one unmarked car.

Melia stood slightly leaning forward straining to hold back the powerful brindle pit bull. Facing opposite to him in the ring was a worried looking owner of a jet black cross breed staffie, which looked to have received a number of flesh wounds during the long tiring fights to get to this final stage. Above the din, on-lookers heard the owner encouraging the tired weak animal that it needed just one more victory to be crowned champion.

A whistle was blown by a person recognised to be some sort of referee to signal the beginning of the end for one of the dog's lives. After the owner's had excited the crowd with the sight of the dog's being goaded against each other, they were finally released to have the arena to themselves.

The smaller black staffie initially put up a good show; its motivation to do well probably due to its inhumane owner waving nylon rope which was purposely made to have large knots running throughout its length.

Melia needed to express no words of encouragement or make threatening gestures in order to motivate his animal. The American pit bull was an absolute killer. He understood why the animal had cost so much money to acquire. Someone must have spent a great deal of time building up the dog's mighty strength and high level of fitness alongside subjecting the animal through a long list of experiences designed first to corrupt its nature and then secondly to condition the mind to such an extent to have no qualms in ripping apart any animal when goaded to by its master.

A sickening yelp echoed around the hollow building signalled the end of the staffie's participation in the one sided fight. Excited onlookers then witnessed the brindle drag the limp animal by the throat in a victory parade around the ring until he eventually tried to release the staffie from its wide bloodied jaws. While momentarily catching its breath the victor stood motionless to peer at the weakening slow rise and fall in the chest of the still body lying on its side.

Without any warning and to the absolute delight of the invited crowd, the brindle resumed its deadly assault by reattaching its wide fang lined jaws to the prone staffie's heckle area to snap the beast's neck and spinal cord.

'Nearly time to move in. It won't take too long for the crowd to disperse.' commented Geoff Fairhurst while he watched the dead black dog being tossed out of the ring without a smidgen of feeling by its owner. His attention fell back on Melia, who he observed to be in conversation with Fox; both having a distinctly pleased look about themselves while ignoring the champion dog sniffing around the straw floor covering for more of its favourite juicy mince morsels Fox had tossed in the ring at the end of the one-sided contest.

'They're here. Let's move.' Cooper had spotted the reason for some of the event's attendees to be noisily scattering and hurriedly making their exit through the side door used to access the building was due to the unexpected appearance of a tall black figure clad in riot uniform joined by three other similarly attired officers.

The three detectives swiftly surrounded Melia and Fox. Before either were able to utter a word, PC Stephen Dale recited what they were being arrested for, followed by a reading of their rights.

In the background all hell was being let loose. Those gathered in earnest at the bookmaker's trestles soon dismissed any thoughts of collecting their winnings and instead focussed their concerned minds on escaping to preserve their precious reputations in the local and wider community. Dog men likewise rushed about to gather up their animals and other evidence that might be later used to incriminate them.

Dale and Fairhurst reached for their handcuffs while Cooper stood directly behind the two men to block of any chance of escape.

'Go!' called Melia. Both men turned their heavy frames to make light work of barging Cooper clear of their exit route. For a second or two the officers froze having been taken by total surprise.

'We can't let them escape. Come on!' McCoy called to then race after the fleeing pair down the long building.

Cooper got to his feet to join the pursuit some thirty yards behind the chasing pack's wake.

An open access door at the far end of the building, similar to the one used by the diminishing group of panicking spectators, bought Melia and Fox a bit more time to get free of the building.

'Our best chance of getting away is across the fields. There are likely to be cops swarming all over the place back there,' gasped Melia.

Fox was unable to answer; his lungs were bursting even after only running a couple hundred yards. As long as his legs and lungs held out, he was happy to follow Melia in the hopes he knew where he was taking them.

The chasing officers had initially been frustrated by Fox having slammed the damp swollen exit door tight shut in the frame. A couple of hard tugs from Dale got the door open again at the expense of wrenching the aluminium handle clean from its screwed fixing.

'There they are,' someone called out spotting two dark figures getting over a wooden turnstile some fifty yards ahead of them.

For all his years and legendary hatred about anything to do with fitness, it was McCoy who led the group by some margin. Maybe his motivation to see proper justice being done was the reason, or was it he was just simply fitter than the rest?

'Agh!' The chasing pack heard the distinctive shriek of pain come from the blackness ahead of them.

Melia instinctively reacted to the distressed call and turned to see his partner in a heap on the dew laden turf.

'What's up? Get up you stupid idiot,' he angrily hissed having reluctantly come to a halt.

It's me ankle, I've gone over on it. It's fucked man!' moaned Fox.

'Come on you stupid fool, you'll end up inside if the cops get you.' called Melia using encouraging hand gestures to join him.

'Can't, not only that, my lungs can't take any more. Here take my share of the money. Swear you will get it back to me when I get out?'

'Swear,' replied Melia having added the thick wad of notes in the opposite side pocket to where he'd stashed his own slice of the winnings.

Fox watched from his enforced sitting position, Melia disappear again into the dark to continue his desperate escape up the hillside. At the same time his attention was being drawn to the sounds of pounding feet mingled together with gasping breaths coming up fast behind him.

Thoughts raced through his mind whether he should he try to impede their progress to give Melia more time to avoid arrest. Or should he just tamely surrender himself to them?

Inside, Fox understood it was unlikely he would ever see Melia again, and even more, any sight of the money he'd moments before handed over to him. A rush of angry emotions then unexpectedly swept over him. Melia had so often used him for his own ends, not only on this occasion alone, but on many others in their joint crooked pasts.

Quite rightly, he understood he was in deep shit, but maybe not enough to go down. A sympathetic lawyer paid out of legal aid was all he needed to do the trick.

What he didn't yet know, no matter what lawyer he was able to get to represent him in Crown Court, he or she would fail to persuade the judge not to send their client down for fifteen years for the manslaughter of Rebecca Melia and other serious offences taken into consideration.

'There is one of them ahead,' called out McCoy.

'Wait for us, before you approach him,' warned Fairhurst running up the gently sloping hill about ten yards behind.

Fox remained in a sitting position while averting his gaze away from the heavy breathing men surrounding him.

'Where's Melia?' pressed McCoy as Cooper bent down to shackle Fox's wrists together.

'Don't know. He did a "u" turn and went back down the hill,' he answered cockily.

'Fucking liar, drag him to his feet DS Cooper.' The young DS needed no further encouragement to carry out Fairhurst's order and seemed to enjoy the further calls of pain from Fox as he danced around on his badly sprained ankle.

'Look, you can see footprints in the dew, he's up ahead somewhere,' called McCoy flashing his pocket torch along the grassy surface.

'You stay here Max with Mr Meatball and phone in for assistance to cut off Melia's escape at the bottom of the hill. Bruce, Stephen and I will go on ahead.'

Cooper was reading Fox his rights out loud to the receding sounds of fast falling feet disappearing into the dark.

Melia had reached the crest of the hill only to find he could go no further. Ahead of him lay a large expanse of tranquil water created by the on-going quarrying for silica sand. A rusting single strand of barbed wire nailed to the tops of rickety posts driven into the soft ground was all there was to protect trespassers from the near vertical drop eighty feet above the freezing cold water below.

'I know this area,' whispered Fairhurst. 'He can't go much farther because Bison's sand quarry lies ahead. I think we should split up and approach the crest in a line. The top of the hill juts out in a narrow strip into the water and he will have no other alternative but to get past us if he is to escape.'

Melia's heart beat markedly increased when he noticed three murky shapes approaching in his direction with one of the figures calling out, 'You're going nowhere, Melia we've got you trapped. Give up now.'

Melia ignored Fairhurst's advice. He fleetingly gave some thought about running past the officers and back down the hill. But rapidly dismissed the idea knowing how knackered he was and there were bound to be other coppers waiting for him even if he was lucky enough to succeed with his plan.

A bright beam of light from a torch held by McCoy caught Melia's desperate attempt to flee the approaching ring of police closing in on him. The escapee flew a hand up to cover his eyes from the blinding light.

'Give up Melia. You are surrounded. It's over. There is nowhere to run,' the same voice shouted out in the still night air.

A sense of panic hit him hard in the solar plexus, Melia realised he'd either have to meekly surrender or gamble to chance an escape along the crumbling path beyond the barbed wire barrier. A call from the dark, 'Let's get him,' was all the motivation he needed to leap over the protective taut barb wire.

The dry sandy textured earth where his feet had heavily landed suddenly moved to throw him off balance. Without having time to think what was happening, Melia found he was standing on top of a great section of the quarry side making a crashing decent to the cold dark waters waiting for him below. The three officers remained like statues having witnessed the slab of earth, along with Melia, disappear from the eroding quarry edge.

Desperate cries of, 'Help, help, please someone, help,' suddenly echoed from beyond the quarry's crumbling edge.

'That's Melia!' Without any exchange with the other two officers, McCoy dropped to lie flat on his stomach then to cautiously belly crawl to the dangerous quarry edge.

'Be careful, Bruce. You've seen what happened to Melia.' McCoy noted the warning while scanning the powerful torch beam against the rutted quarry side face.

'Hang on, we will get you out, try to stop thrashing your legs about, the wire will snap.' The torch beam picked out an animated figure dangling like a rag doll in mid-air. Melia could count himself lucky to have grabbed hold onto the barbed wire just as the mass of earth started to move. Otherwise, being a non-swimmer, his chances of survival after hitting the water were minimal.

'He's hanging on to the barbed wire fencing that once protected the edge, we have to act quick, it might go at any time.' McCoy scrambled to his feet to grasp hold of the taut barbed wire stapled to a wooden post which looked like it was about to be pulled out from the sandy soil to join the other rotten stumps that too had gone over the edge in the landslide.

They followed his lead without hesitation having not given a single thought about the damage they were about to inflict on their hands as each took tight hold of the highly tensed wire similarly attached to a weather bleached leaning post on the opposite side.

'Pull, pull pull,' encouraged McCoy in spite of the sharp metal barbs biting deep into the soft flesh of his and the other hauler's palms.

After a series of determined pulls, a pair of gripping bloodied hands appeared above the quarry edge.

'Get me out of here, please, get me out of here!' Melia wailed knowing how close he was to being saved.

'Geoff and I will hold tight onto the wire, while you go to the edge and give him a hand up.' Fairhurst allowed Dale to take up the cutting tension on the twined wire before relieving McCoy, to again crawl along the slippery dew covered surface to the unstable edge.

'Take my hand.' McCoy had his head thrust over the edge so he could catch sight of the would-be fugitive, with the hand reaching out to Melia's. Abject fear tearing through his swinging body was likely to be the cause of him not being able to immediately taking up the offer. A cacophony of splashing noises caused by chunks of the quarry face crashing into the water below resonated eerily into the night air only added to the tense drama.

'Take my hand man! I don't think the wire will hold much longer,' urged McCoy looking into the near same eyes he'd stared at from beneath the cold waters of the clear stream a life time ago.

By removing the grip from the barbed wire he had held with his left hand, his body suddenly jolted to the right causing greater panic to strike.

'I'm slipping, no, no, help me, please someone help me. I can't hold on much longer.' Melia's haunting cries could even be heard by Cooper and the cuffed Damien Fox standing farther down the hillside.

McCoy in the meantime had grasped hold of his right wrist.

'I've got you tight here, just grab the fucking wire!'

In one final act of desperation he shot his groping hand out into the dark.

'I've got it, God I've got it,' shouted Melia ecstatically having regained his hold on the stretching wire.

McCoy then disappeared from Melia's view.

'Where are you going? You can't leave me here. Come back!' Melia called out in desperation. McCoy ignored his cries to concentrate on what he intended to do next.

'Keep tight hold you two,' instructed McCoy turning his head to see his co-saviours wrestling with the dancing wire like deep sea fishermen holding fast against a thrashing Marin.

'Don't worry Bruce, we've got him but I don't know how long we can last,' said Dale.

McCoy looked back over the edge to read from the man's face he was weakening, and just like his, Melia's hands were made slippery with blood from the cutting tension of the wire and uniformly spaced barbs, thus making it even more difficult to maintain a good grip.

McCoy sprang to his feet and having re-joined his colleagues, he took up a pulling stance on the wire.

'What's the matter?' asked Fairhurst while straining against the effects of holding tight against the swinging dead weight of a fourteen stone frame.

'He is too scared and weak for me to haul him up from the edge. We have no other alternative than to pull with all we have got left and hope either the wire doesn't snap or he loses hold when his body is being drawn over against the quarry edge. Pull!'

Three big pulls and Melia's straining tattooed arms were on view, soon followed by his head and upper torso so tantalisingly close to the safety of the flat horizontal land.

'Hold on. You are nearly there,' encouraged McCoy.

Two final exhausting controlled yanks on the rust coated barbed wire had Melia back over the quarry edge and he continued to lay there still retaining a vice like grip on the barbed wire. The three exhausted men looked on the prone figure seemingly hiding his face in the dew laden long bladed grass.

'Is he crying?' asked Dale while dabbing his bleeding hands with a handkerchief.

'Looks like it to me,' answered Fairhurst noting too the uncontrollable sobs together with tell-tale random body jerks. 'Just leave him for a moment, then we will cuff him. Well done lads.'

Chapter Fifty-Four

Richard Palfreyman scan read the report DCI Starr placed before him, his straight features remained unaltered after handing the typed sheet back to the officer who was responsible for the outcome at Croft Farm the previous night.

'I expected to receive a call from you to give me an update. What happened Dick?'

Starr glared at the po-faced chief superintendent. He was justifiably irked to have to hear the station's top man be more concerned about a call to him than to share in the celebration and resounding successes of the Croft Farm operation.

'Please forgive me, Chief Superintendent Palfreyman, I just plain and simply forgot. If you don't mind, I'll move my seat a little closer because it's going to take a while to explain the reason why it so easily slipped my mind to give you a call.'

Palfreyman made a nervous cough as he watched Starr deliberately invade his personal space by repositioning the seat so that he was able to rest his arms with both hands clasped stretched casually across a corner of the highly polished mahogany desk surface.

'I'll explain,' said Starr.' You will have read from the report, we were successful in achieving our primary objective, that was to arrest James Melia for the murder of Mrs Jackson, serious fraud, which of course you will remember involved one of our own, Bruce McCoy and a charge of being in control of a banned dog breed as stated in the Dangerous Dogs Act 1991. A number of additional arrests were made of those individuals found to be in charge of banned breeds alongside those we suspected of being the main players behind the organisation of the event.

'Added to this number are those who took it upon themselves to assault police officers and the RSPCA. I and most of the others involved in the operation only left the station at six this morning. It was hardly worth going home,' said Starr looking at his wrist watch which now showed the time to be nine thirty.' Before Starr was able to continue further, Palfreyman had butted in.

'Dick, exactly how many have you brought into custody? I thought we had an understanding to keep costs under control. From what you tell me so far, it's going to cost a fortune in overtime to get them all processed.'

'What do you suggest, we tell them not to be naughty boys again and just let them go? These people are bloody criminals. You were not there to see the carcasses of dogs, cats, rabbits and even foxes which had been torn to shreds to satisfy a perverted, evil lust for pleasure,' reacted Starr angrily.

'You're just getting emotional now, DCI Starr. This sort of thing has always happened and we do not have the resources to stop it. Let's deal with Melia and let the others off with a caution,' calmly suggested Palfreyman.

Starr would have normally blown his top on hearing such a ridiculous crass statement, it was only because he'd got a trick hidden up his sleeve that prevented him from doing so.

Outwardly, Starr's demeanour appeared to have remained calm and unruffled which had given Palfreyman fresh hope his leading DCI was considering his excellent solution aimed at easing the station's financial pressures.

'So okay, let's think this one through. We let off with a caution all of those who have blatantly contravened the Dangerous Dogs Act,' said Starr being deliberately slow in the delivery of his words.

'Yes, that's right, Dick. I'm glad you have come to terms with my idea. It's the right thing to do in this situation,' beamed Palfreyman.

'So what do we do about the newly elected police commissioner we've got locked up in the cells?' casually enquired Starr.

'New police commissioner? What on earth are you talking about, Dick?' gasped the chief super, his self-congratulatory smirk suddenly evaporating only to be replaced with a stare of pure apprehension.

'Yes, the right honourable Broderick Gilles, I believe you two have met to discuss the new strategic plan for the policing of Bladdington and outer communities.' Starr stalled to enjoy seeing Palfreyman's pasty complexion turn to green.

'DS Grey caught him hurriedly shoving his pit bull into the back of his Range Rover,' he continued to taunt. 'When she challenged him, the silly man swung out at her with a horse crop and caught her across her cheek.' Palfreyman let out another gasp on hearing things had become even worse.

'He took another vicious swipe at her and by God's mercy alone, missed her head and struck the padded section on her shoulder. While the lunatic was preparing to lash out at her again, Miss Grey had managed to get to her truncheon and then gave him a couple of hard cracks across his knees which dropped him to the ground. Now, Chief Superintendent Palfreyman, when I let this man go free with a caution and the charged dropped for GBH on an officer, do you want me to remind him of the appointment time you both arranged to meet again to continue your discussion? Maybe while you are having tea and biscuits he might present a convincing reason why he was in possession of a banned breed, attended an illegal bloodsport event and grievously assaulted a police officer in the line of duty?'

Starr's revelation had deemed Palfreyman speechless. For a few short seconds both men had to show great resolve not to expose the varying degrees of suspicion, disrespect, and loathing each held against the other.

'Well, what should you have me do? You are the boss after all, Chief Superintendent Palfreyman,' pressed Starr in a deliberate subservient manner.

'Throw the damn book at the lot of them. We will have to absorb the costs with Mansefield station. And by the way Dick may I be the first to congratulate you and your team on doing such an excellent job.' Palfreyman thrust his hand out for Starr to grasp. Starr hadn't been taken by surprise at all at the sudden change in the man now warmly shaking his hand. From the darkness had emerge a flash of brilliant insight, Palfreyman had realised he'd been presented with a golden opportunity to get a head start on his contemporaries and he intended to exploit the situation as only he knew how.

No sooner had Starr left the office, Palfreyman was on the direct internal line to call the county commissioner to spout on about his station's latest success in apprehending and bringing to justice a dangerous murderer, who was also behind a despicable financial fraud of a well-known charity raiser, and the *pièce de la résistance*, the dramatic exposure of a closet blood sport enthusiast, recently voted in by the naïve public, to be no other than, Broderick Gillies OBE, awarded for services to improving farm stock welfare. Bladdington Bugle was the next contact on his mental list, with the chief super at Mansefield station being the very last to learn the full extent of his station's success. After all, he had considered, if his ultimate dream was to be realised he'd be foolish to allow others to have an equal share in his personal glory.

When Palfreyman finally replaced the receiver, he lent back in his chair with his hands clasped behind his head enjoying mental images of himself being measured up for a spanking new county commissioner's uniform.

'Come in Dick, thanks for calling round,' welcomed McCoy standing in the small entrance vestibule of his late Victorian house. Starr couldn't fail to notice that both of his hands were bandaged in a similar manner to that he'd seen on PC Stephen Dale earlier on in the day.

Throughout that early morning junior members of CID dealt with those criminals who were found to be owners of banned dog breeds and were later seen leaving the station clutching a summons which outlined all the charges and when they were to appear in court. While the near full interview rooms and cells were occupied, a single room was kept spare to allow Starr and his team to conduct a series of taped interviews with James Melia. Satisfied they'd got all the evidence needed for a solid conviction, Melia was then cuffed and taken by police escort over to Mansefield station to face murder charges.

'We'll go through to the kitchen Dick, tea or coffee?'

'Is that you, Mother?' a familiar voice called from the lounge.

'No, it isn't dear. It's Dick Starr.'

'Oh, I thought it might be mother, she did say she was going to come over to see me today.' Sally McCoy was sat in an armchair and continued to stare out into space after Bruce had disappointed her with the news.

'Take a seat, Dick.' Starr took the same chair he sat in the last time he had need to see his friend. He remained quiet as he watched Bruce fill the electric kettle.

'Which is it, tea or coffee, Dick?'

'Coffee please.'

The sounds of the cups being placed on the granite work surface seemed to resonate around the high ceilings of the empty house.

'How are your hands?' enquired Starr just before taking a sip from the coffee cup.

'A bit sore, luckily I needed only a few stitches, Geoff's hands were torn to pieces, so I guess he would have needed a lot more. I don't mind saying though, the tetanus injection in my backside was the most painful by a mile, it's still sore even now,' said McCoy fidgeting in his chair while trying to get more comfortable. 'I suppose you heard what Sally said,' he continued but with a lowering of the tone of his voice.

'Yes, I did. I'm sorry, Bruce.'

'The area manager had the awful task of telling Sally she was no longer capable of running the charity shop. The charity head office had received complaints from the volunteer staff and customers alike and I suppose they had to be seen to be taking action. I have no argument with her decision; I could plainly see what was happening here at home. Even for all the medication and group therapy prescribed by her doctor, it won't stop her from succumbing to the same problems her mother suffered. Anyway, Dick I'm sure you are not here to listen to my woes.' McCoy trained his attention on Starr holding a false smile in an attempt to disguise his broken heart.

'Right, I'll make a start. Melia has admitted to being behind the fraud, he says it was all his idea. He'd grown up being constantly reminded how much his father hated a certain copper and been repeatedly told this man had stitched him up and was the cause of his mother's early death.'

Before he was able to continue McCoy butted in, 'That's absolute rubbish. How does he think I got this scar?' he said pointing to the disfiguring line.

McCoy shook his head in disbelief while he waited for Starr to recommence.

'It was only after his dad, Jimmy, had pointed you out in a photograph in the *Bladdington Bugle* taken at the police federation function, he became determined to cook up an elaborate scam to get revenge on you for the sake of his father.'

'So, Jimmy Melia had nothing to do with this?' queried McCoy.

'James Melia is adamant his dad had no involvement whatsoever, if he did or if he didn't we will never know, I suppose he feels obliged to protect his old man from going down for another stint.'

'Max Cooper told me it's highly likely Melia and Sproston are half-brothers, is that right?'

'Melia did mention he and his dad bumped into Sproston at a fuel station a couple of days back. It must have been after he'd reported his arrival back from America to me. There was a bit of an altercation between the two of them with certain things being said with Jimmy Melia later admitting to his son that what Sproston had alleged he could not properly deny.'

'Where is Jimmy Melia now?'

'Holed out at Bladdington Golf Club. He's taken up temporary residence in the course steward's accommodation building,' answered Starr.

'At some stage someone is bound to ask questions about my attendance at the pit bull meet and the antecedents leading up to the final arrest of Melia,' said McCoy while patently understanding he was as culpable as the other amoral spectators in attendance that late evening, and moreover, being part of an arresting team especially when no longer a serving member of the police force could create problems for him.

'The simple matter is Bruce; you should not have been there. You know that better than anyone else.'

On hearing his friends blunt but true words, McCoy's appearance changed to take on a crestfallen look.

'But who is to say if I was in your position I wouldn't have done the same? After all, one could argue, without your assistance, Melia might have got away, or failing that, he would have been unable to be saved from falling from the barbed wire, with frogmen at this very moment, patiently searching the deep waters for his body.'

'So what will be your official line?' pressed McCoy.

'If you agree, this is what I intend to write in my final report. You were there purely because you are writing a book to expose the increasing prevalence of blood sports in the northern shire counties. I will argue you were totally unaware a police operation had been planned to infiltrate the event with the primary objective being to arrest a man wanted for murder and serious fraud. Circumstances later that evening made it impossible for you not to lend your assistance to the police when it looked likely their target was about to evade arrest. Does that sound okay?'

'That's great, Dick. How did you think that one up? The last thing I want is for someone up there to start making noises that I should lose my pension. Then I'd really be in a mess.'

Starr then rose to his feet to take a final slurp from his cup.

'Time for me to go. My next stop is to corner Jimmy Melia at the golf club. I have arranged for Max Cooper to meet me there at four and it's close to that now,' he said looking at the kitchen clock.

'What do you intend to say to him?' asked McCoy.

'I'll fill him in on all the charges his son will have to face in court and how you were party to saving his worthless life. He'll likely show little response when he learns I will not be after him to answer any charges. How he will react when I tell him his daughter-in-law is dead, I'm not sure. Especially when the initial forensic evidence suggests she was assaulted before receiving the fatal blow to the head. Maybe James did her too, we'll just have to wait for the results of the DNA test.'

'Does Melia know his missus is dead?' asked McCoy.

'No, Miss Grey called the hospital for an update and was told then. I know it sounds unchristian, but I didn't want the job of passing the news on to him myself. So when he was carted off to Mansefield station, I rang Bob Stableford and told him instead. He agreed he should have the task of being the bearer of bad tidings.'

Star said he would let himself out, McCoy listened to the door close gently too, before returning to tend to his wife.

Having been officially informed of James Melia's admission of guilt in executing the elaborate fraud, together with a doctor's letter and a threat to involve the banking services ombudsmen the bank reluctantly fully recompensed Bruce McCoy for his financial loss. The large sum of money deposited back in to the McCoy's account was once seen as a heaven sent opportunity for them both to realise their joint and individual dreams. Sadly, Sally's admittance into a nursing home dictated the account would be soon emptied solely on her care.

Two weeks after his arrest, James Melia, handcuffed to an unemotional prison officer, was seen standing motionless, clutching a small posy of freesias and staring down into the deep clay lined hole into which his wife's coffin had been lowered, On the opposite side stood the stooped figure of Jimmy Melia holding the hand of his sobbing grandson, Brett. After the vicar had finished saying a few words of condolence he stepped back to permit Rebecca Melia's parents to be the first to cast a hand full of soil onto the unblemished varnished surface of their daughter's coffin.

Those who'd gathered in a solemn group behind the covered mound of earth shuffled round to take part in the ritual. Once they'd done, James Melia stepped forward to have a final look at the discernible brass plate etched in his deceased wife's proper Christian name and not the one he once gave her. He lifted the dainty posy of highly perfumed flowers to press a gentle kiss against a petal. The posy fell from his grip to twist and turn in the air before it landed haphazardly on the oak veneer lid.

The burial ceremony petered out. Those in varying degrees of grief, slipped respectively from the new graveside with the vicar seen to be offering his condolences to Rebecca Melia's elderly parents.

No words of pity were spoken to James Melia as the two prison officers escorted him back to an awaiting car and then on to HMP Bigsbury Hall. He'd have plenty of time in his lonely cell to brood over the fact his best mate, Damien Fox, had been charged for the manslaughter of his wife.

In the same cemetery the following day, Jimmy Melia had positioned his presence well back from the main mourners at the private family funeral of the Sproston's only child.

He'd read in the local paper of the funeral arrangements for the tragic schoolboy who had fought so valiantly to defeat leukaemia but tragically lost his battle for life in a hospital in Miami. A church service to celebrate his short life was to be conducted at St Peters church, Moulton, followed by a private family interment at Bladdington cemetery. He'd folded the paper back in two, his heart feeling black and heavy and was about to place it back on the bar at the golf club when something from a news feature column in the bottom corner of the front page caused him to open up the paper again and then quickly thumb through the pages to find the news article.

He was unable to prevent his eyes from watering up as he read about the reasons for Sally McCoy's retirement from the 'Dreams Come True' charity shop alongside an extended emotionally charged report written by the paper's senior reporter, Eric Carter, who was clearly determined to make sure the local readership were made aware of this woman's massive fund raising exploits which had served to provide great comfort and support to numerous families over many years of devoted service.

Later, someone had taken the same paper from the bar having lost patience for the barman to show up to serve them. It would take a while yet before Jimmy Melia reappeared to take up his bar duties. Riddled with guilt, he had taken to hiding himself amongst the aluminium beer kegs where he could be found to be breaking his heart for what he felt responsible for.

How he wished he could turn the clock back and not to have wasted so much of his life plagued with constant raging thoughts about seeking some sort of irrational revenge. Images of his son, James, his most likely other son, Barry

Sproston flitted in his mind. Sproston's mother, the lovely Patricia, entered his thoughts to make his torment even harder to bear. His mother and father, along with recollections of McCoy's face from when he was a young man, joined in a long painful succession of memories which formed a major part of his unfulfilled and sad past life.

He eventually reappeared at the bar and was seen to be reassuring glum looking customers that two barrels had gone down and it took a little while to get them both changed over. Those same customers would never realise the man who was about to serve them, was now seriously considering he no longer wanted to be part of this world.

The interment ceremony was a typical book read affair as conducted in the same cemetery the day previous, but with subtle important differences. The people gathered around this particular grave possessed a certain togetherness and a subliminal feel of love that was patently absent from the funeral Jimmy Melia had attended the day before.

Melia had patiently waited in the background till he saw the bereaved family group moving slowly away from the open grave, which had been sensitively beautified by the laying of a carpet of bouquets and bunched flowers. Then, clutching a small bouquet in his gloved hand, Jimmy Melia stepped tentatively towards the floral display determined to add his own personal dedication to join with those of the other mourners surrounding the green astro turf edged grave opening.

Barry Sproston just happened to turn to glance back on his son's grave to notice a stooped figure placing flowers, which then gave him reason to stop and peer closer at the dark coated elderly male.

'What's up, Barry?' asked his wife Debbie.

'You know, I think that is Jimmy Melia. What's he doing here?' he answered not taking his eyes off the sorry looking bowed figure.

'Come on Barry, leave him.' Debbie was well aware of her husband's family upbringing and what his gran had told him before she died. The "sods law" meeting up at the fuel station only added to support what her husband now believed, that Jimmy Melia was indeed his father.

'No, you go on ahead, Debbie. I won't be too long.' Sproston let go of his wife's hand to retrace his steps back to the graveside.

Being deep in guilty dark thoughts, Melia did not hear the sounds of the approaching footsteps until a funereal dressed young man was upon him.

His unexpected appearance shocked Melia into a bit of a panic.

'Sorry sorry, I, I know I shouldn't be here. I have left some flowers. I'll be on my way. Sorry,' he pleaded, and then turned to leave the cemetery using the seldom used rear exit.

'No, don't go.' Sproston grabbed at the coarse cloth of the knee length winter coat to prevent him from moving away. Melia reluctantly turned to the man blocking his escape.

'I'm not going to harm you. I just want to say thank you for being here. DCI Starr told me you had nothing to do with my identity being stolen.'

Melia remained silent while averting his gaze from the man who bore an incredible likeness to James. However, the difference between the two of them was one had been blessed with a calm, kind and patient disposition, while the other was prone not only to being hot tempered and ruthless but possessed the capacity to be cruel and sadistic.

Remorsefully, it was not altogether true he was innocent of any wrong doing. Being responsible for feeding his own hatred of a particular police officer into the mind of his son, James, the consequences of which only ensured the increased heavy burden of guilt, remorse and self-loathing he now rightly endured would never leave his shoulders.

'Look, I understand you did not know I existed before I lost my son, Wilson,' explained Sproston. 'I would like for us both to get to know each other more. I have lost a son, but hopefully I have gained a father. What do you say?' beamed Sproston.

'I don't deserve to be part of your life, Barry. I think it best I should leave and forget you have ever seen me.' Melia mournfully stated before making shuffling gestures to extricate himself from this emotional situation.

'Debbie is pregnant, and I'd love you to be around when the baby is born. Maybe you will give to him or her what you weren't able to give to me.'

The suggestion caused Melia's chest to tighten, the sincerity in the man's sentiments left him with an even deeper sense of him being an unworthy human being, as throughout his life, he'd always been swayed to be mean spirited rather than compassionate or caring.

Through misty eyes Melia saw Debbie Sproston in the distance standing alone waiting for her husband to re-join her so they could gather with the other mourners at their son's celebration wake. Was it too late for Jimmy Melia to have a share in this loving family's future? He hoped not.

Details of addresses and phone numbers were exchanged followed by a stiff embrace to seal a bonding of lost family ties and the going of their separate ways on that seminal day.

They were destined never to meet face to face again. Two weeks later a short column on the obituary page of the *Bladdington Bugle* announced the death of Jimmy Melia, aged 59, after being found dead in his home with the cause of death being pancreatic cancer, a post mortem had revealed.

Barry Sproston read the stark notice out to his wife, Debbie. She stopped ironing for a moment to glance over to her husband mentally re-reading the notice. The iron emitted a hiss of steam which prompted Debbie to get on with demolishing the basket full of ironing waiting to be done.

'Will you go to the funeral?' she asked amid the sound of yet another hiss.

He didn't reply. His mind was occupied with reading a sympathy card he'd, for some reason, removed from a particular bouquet of flowers laid at his son's graveside.

It read:

'To my dear grandson, Wilson.

One day we will meet in heaven and I will tell you all about what a wonderful, loving and caring mum and dad you had. Until then, sleep tight.

All my love, granddad Jimmy xxx'

Tears filled his eyes as he touched each of the neat hand written words knowing these inanimate marks were the only physical link he had to remind him of his lost father. The one he'd always wondered about.

THE END